Praise for Kate Moretti

The Vanishing Year

"A woman's perilous past and her affluent present converge in Kate Moretti's latest jaw-dropping thriller. Replete with unsavory characters, buried secrets, and a bounty of unexpected twists and turns, *The Vanishing Year* is a stunner. A perfectly compulsive read that's impossible to put down."

—Mary Kubica, *New York Times* bestselling author of *Don't You Cry*

"*The Vanishing Year* is a chilling, powerful tale of nerve-shattering suspense. Kate Moretti pieces together a stunning, up-all-night thriller with a throat-gripping twist that will leave the reader reeling."

—Heather Gudenkauf, *New York Times* bestselling author of *Missing Pieces*

"Great pacing and true surprises make this an exciting read. Fans of twisted thrillers featuring complex female characters will devour Moretti's latest."

—*Kirkus Reviews* (starred review)

"Moretti maintains a fast pace . . . chillingly satisfying."

—*Publishers Weekly*

"Fans of S. J. Watson, Lisa Unger, and Sophie Hannah will enjoy this fast-paced psychological suspense novel."

—*Booklist*

"*The Vanishing Year* is dark, twisty, edge-of-your-seat suspense. I read it in a single sitting and enjoyed every word. I highly recommend it!"

—Karen Robards, *New York Times* bestselling author of
The Last Time I Saw Her

"The tantalizing plot twists layered atop the juxtaposition of the protagonist's troubled past and the opulence of her current life not only are intriguing but will keep you reading *The Vanishing Year* far into the night. Well done, Ms. Moretti, well done!"

—Lesley Kagen, *New York Times* bestselling author of
Whistling in the Dark and *The Resurrection of Tess Blessing*

"*The Vanishing Year* is more than an engaging tale of utter betrayal. It's an intricate dance of realities, full of twists and turns you won't see coming. Kate Moretti has outdone herself. You'll miss your bedtime, guaranteed."

—J. T. Ellison, *New York Times* bestselling author of *No One Knows*

The Blackbird Season

"Crime fiction adores girls in trouble. Moretti's latest nail-biter is no exception, but it is exceptional . . . Though Moretti's emotionally astute tale can be heartrending, readers won't be able to look away. As slow, creeping dread sets in, so does the inevitability of the terrible situation the town finds itself in, offering a deliciously sinister glimpse into the duplicity of small-town lives and the ease with which people turn on each other when tragedy comes calling. Moretti's tale of jealousy and obsession is nothing less than dark magic. Witchery indeed."

—*Kirkus Reviews* (starred review)

"Moretti spins a tale of suspicion, deceit, and dreams that die as suddenly as a flock of starlings falling from the sky. A thrilling morality tale of the highest order, *The Blackbird Season* will make you question the lines between right and wrong, victim and criminal, and the unknowable intentions that form our innocence and guilt."

—Mindy Mejia, author of *Everything You Want Me to Be*

"A skillful blend of family drama and domestic suspense . . . it kept me turning the pages and was resolved to my satisfaction at the end. Highly recommended."

—Eileen Goudge, *New York Times* bestselling author of *Garden of Lies*

"Moretti begins *The Blackbird Season* with a sinister premise—a cloud of birds falls from the sky on the same day a teenage girl people call 'the witch' goes missing. A spellbinding tale of long-held secrets and small-town scandal, *The Blackbird Season* is one of those stories that sneaks up on you, each chapter building steadily to an ending that will haunt you long after you turn the last page."

—Kimberly Belle, bestselling author of *The Marriage Lie*

In Her Bones

"Morbid . . . Moretti pulls some tricky tricks when she sends Edie on the run, where she slips in and out of some neat disguises and suffers just enough to satisfy the most judgmental reader."

—*New York Times* book review

"Heightened language takes *In Her Bones* to a higher level than the standard thriller. Readers will enjoy this book for the suspense and plot twists but love it for the skill and mastery Moretti has for her craft."

—New York Journal of Books

"Captivating . . . Fans of twisty psychological thrillers will find plenty to like."

—*Publishers Weekly*

"Kate Moretti is incredibly talented! *In Her Bones* is at once chilling and compelling, frightening and insightful—and truly, madly, deeply satisfying. You'll gasp at every twist, and you'll turn these hauntingly sinister pages as fast as you can."

—Hank Phillippi Ryan, nationally bestselling author of *Trust Me*

"Kate Moretti's *In Her Bones* is a suspenseful, whirling spiral of mysteries within mysteries, plot twists you won't see coming, and characters linked by deadly fates that stretch across the years. Moretti's prose is crisp and masterful, her people rich and real. Don't miss this haunting, wild thrill ride."

—David Bell, author of *Somebody's Daughter*

"Reading *In Her Bones* is like watching a true-crime documentary . . . And you seriously won't be able to put it down."

—HelloGiggles

"A masterfully crafted, multilayered novel . . . Kate Moretti manages to cover all the angles, making the story deep and dynamic . . . *In Her Bones* is complex, honest, and heartbreaking. It is much more than merely a mystery and is well worth reading."

—Bookreporter

THE
SPIRES

OTHER TITLES BY KATE MORETTI

THE SPIRES

KATE MORETTI

THOMAS & MERCER

Published by Thomas & Mercer, Seattle

www.apub.com

Amazon, the Amazon logo, and Thomas & Mercer are trademarks of Amazon.com, Inc., or its affiliates.

ISBN-13: 9781542021715
ISBN-10: 1542021715

Cover design by Christopher Lin

Printed in the United States of America

To Sarah and BethAnn: We shared the "pinnacle of our lives," had our own language, fought and laughed and cried and drank and still never managed to burn the whole place down. Also, I finally worked in the calendar thing, you fatalistic little weirdo.

CHAPTER ONE

The handwritten letter came in the summer, the dead heat of July (or maybe August—hard to remember after working to put it out of her mind), and made her head spin when she read it. It arrived in a post-marked plain white envelope without a return address. *Is this a joke?* Penelope had thought.

> *Darling Pip, Coming up on twenty years, dear girl. I miss you like crazy. I miss all of you. I hear they're finally tearing the old place down. What would you say to a Spires reunion? Get the band back together? Clear the air, bury all the hatchets. Could give us all some closure (you were always big on that). I'll be in touch soon, think about it. Think about me. Ha, I knew you'd like that. Love you madly, Jack.*

Right after she'd read it, she'd run to the bathroom and vomited. Then she buried it in her sock drawer and tried very hard to forget it had ever existed.

She very nearly had.

CHAPTER TWO

February 12, 2020

"Pip."

It was a single syllable, formed by lips painted red and stretched across a too-white smile. Penelope noticed her teeth first: the snaggle-tooth canine straightened, the sheen bright and unnatural. Then, faint creases in her skin, around her mouth and eyes, caked with makeup. The raised topography of her cheek, the furious pink scar screaming from her left ear to the sharp angle of her chin (this was also new; the Willa she knew had a gentle swell, a pad of fat under each cheek, the wholesome grin of a cheerleader). Then the bright blue of Willa's eyes, framed by spidery fake eyelashes, familiar and blinking. Happy to see her old friend Pip.

Penelope's knees buckled underneath her. Almost gave entirely away, and she gripped the doorjamb and, despite being a long-lapsed Catholic, mentally crossed herself in thanks that Brett was still at yoga, and Linc, their son, was at a friend's house, and Tara, their daughter, was at school late (for what, she couldn't remember). It was a miracle Penelope was home at all, seeing how it was barely four thirty on a Wednesday.

No one had called her Pip in twenty years.

The nickname had come about in a deliberate way, unlike most nicknames that were bestowed accidentally, haphazardly. They'd been sitting around the common room, Jack on Bree's beanbag, a joint pinched between his fingertips, the smoke sweetly curling. They all had short, perfunctory names: Bree, Jack, Flynn, Willa (sometimes just Will). Penelope had always been Penelope, a mouthful as a child, stiff and too proper for a college student. Too much to say when your tongue was thick with vodka and weed. Jack had a laptop—gray, space-age looking and clunky, and he'd googled "nicknames for Penelope," and the fledgling internet had churned out *Pippa*. Long before the Middletons made the name household common, Penelope was anointed Pippa, and they had all screamed with laughter. *A dog's name,* Bree had protested half-heartedly, which only made things worse, thereby cementing it as fact. Penelope, with her white oxford shirts and sensible flats, was as far from a Pip as possible, and she'd spent the whole year pretending to be annoyed by it, hating how everyone orbited around Jack and even hating herself a little when she felt her head dip coyly, her cheeks warm, and her mouth betray her in a smile when he said *Pip* singsong from the common room, always beckoning to all of them the way mermaids sang to sailors.

And now, here was a reminder of her old self back on her doorstep. Pip. A single word, uttered and dropped in front of her like a steaming pile of dog shit in a bag left on her porch in an adolescent joke. She swallowed back the sick in her throat, felt the sharp twitch of a muscle in her bicep, her fingertips curled that tightly against the wood. If she had asked Brett, her husband of eighteen years (let's not even get into the timeline, how quickly she had married after the fire), or her children who Pip was, they would have laughed and said, *Who?*

It felt like an eternity before she said, "Willa."

"I had nowhere else to go. I'm . . . sorry to drop in on you like this." Her voice had retained its youthfulness, soft and high, a slight southern twang betraying her Louisiana roots. She had shoots of gray at her temples now, blended expertly in with the blonde.

Penelope stood dumbfounded longer than was considered polite, her mind unable to remember basic manners, human decency. She studied her old friend-turned-stranger for signs of recognition, her memory handing her snapshots of a younger girl, fresh and too happy, too eager to please, a *yes, ma'am* slipping out when she got too drunk, her eyelids drooping shut, and Jack carrying her up to bed.

There was only a small trace of this girl in the woman before her. Then, instantly, this new version of Willa and the Willa in her memories snapped together to form a singular person.

An expensive black sweater, no coat, even though it was February. Dark fitted jeans tucked into black boots. A heavy gold chain around her neck.

And then: faint blue imprints, round like marbles, underneath foundation a shade too dark, dotted along her collarbone.

Penelope knew, instantly, how Willa came to be standing here. Some women, she thought ungenerously, gravitated toward a certain kind of man, seeking protection, and only realized later, when it was too late, when they'd already let themselves become property. Willa, with her easy smile, her puppy dog geniality, her long-gone father and alcoholic mother, aching to fill a hole, would have accepted a love like that in a way Penelope would never have.

Only then did Penelope step aside, hold the door open, and let her old friend in, a faint smell of woodsmoke trailing behind her. That might have been Penelope's imagination, and she fought back an intense nausea. She thought of it then: that creased letter hidden in her sock drawer. Why was it always twenty years later when the past came back? What was so special about that number—just enough time to make a full grown-up kind of life? To feel, with certainty, the moment your old decisions crept back.

Willa stood in the hall—gazing up at the chandelier (it hadn't been dusted in probably years, and stupidly, Penelope searched for something to say to distract her)—Willa's eyes then flicking to the expansive staircase, the formal sitting room to the right that they never used, the sofa as plump and firm as the day it was delivered, and finally settling on Penelope's face, the understanding dawning between the women as to why Willa had to come here, and only here. What happened to the others? Penelope had spent two whole decades avoiding the answer to this question. She'd always assumed they'd all kept in touch. At least, at first, they did try to reach out to her. After the fire.

Which was why it made a cosmic sort of sense: why Penelope's house was the perfect place to hide out (later Willa would plead *only for a few days, I promise*) and why no one would ever find her. Penelope had deliberately cut herself off from them.

No one in Willa's life had ever heard of Penelope Ritter Cox. Penelope would have given anything to have it stay that way.

CHAPTER THREE
Then: Future Plans

They were sitting on the grass at Hillside Park, a nondescript copse of trees in the middle of Philadelphia. They could hear the cars, a bright burst of laughter from half a block away. Jack had a joint pinched between his fingers and inhaled deeply before passing it to Penelope. Penelope passed it straight to Willa, who smoked it in silence, sunk into herself and moody.

"So listen, I have this cousin," Jack said. "He lives in a place in Deer Run. He just bought this old church that was converted into a house, but barely, you know? Like it might need some work. But he got some crazy-ass fellowship in Spain, so he's leaving. He asked me if I'd live there."

"Where the fuck is Deer Run?" Willa asked, her voice raspy and tight from the weed. Willa had been born and raised mostly in Louisiana, moving north to the Main Line when she was in high school. When she was high, or emotional, her twang thickened.

"I don't know. Like an hour away, I think? In the country some-where. I grew up in Brooklyn; I know nothing."

Graduation was coming at them like a thundering herd. Penelope felt numb to all of it—she was much too tired. If she were Willa, she would have said *so fucking tired*, but instead she closed her eyes and wished for a night without studying or working on her final projects. Exams were next week. And that was it—her whole undergraduate education was ending.

It was strange to think that five years ago she didn't know these people, and now her entire identity was wrapped up in everything about them. Their lives so entwined it was hard to tell where one started and the other began. They spoke in code; just a single word, like *watermelon*, could send them into fits of giggles, leaving anyone else in their orbit confused and shrugging. Rolling their eyes. Penelope had never known anything like it.

Her freshman year, Penelope had sprung for an on-campus apartment. A single. An extravagance, really. Reserved for the richest kids with the biggest trust funds. And yet, she took her parents' inheritance and spent it that quickly. She was accustomed to being alone at the time—the idea of sharing a space squeezed at her lungs. The room next to her blared music at all hours of the day and night, until finally Penelope marched down the hall, banged on the door, and Willa answered, wearing only a towel, wax strips stuck to her leg, smoking a cigarette. *You aren't supposed to smoke in here,* Penelope said idiotically. She cringed at the memory.

Willa—blonde, smoking, drinking, brash—was whip smart and calculating. Penelope—quiet, pretty in a Laura Ingalls–way, not as smart as Willa but studied much harder. The first thing Willa said to her was, "Thank God, can you pull this off?"—holding her muscular calf out, her toes painted red and gleaming. They shouldn't have become friends as quickly as they did.

A few months later, Willa showed up at Penelope's door with Jack. *I found us a third,* presenting him arms outstretched like Vanna White. Penelope hadn't known they were looking for a third, but they clicked so easily into place she often couldn't remember the time before.

By sophomore year, they were planning their classes to end around the same time and later would congregate at Willa's spacious off-campus apartment to watch *General Hospital*, which would lead to endless analysis about the love triangle of Sonny, Jason, Carly. Sometimes Bree and Flynn would show up, tagging along behind Jack.

There were times, like now, when Penelope felt utterly invisible. Watching Willa and Jack's verbal sparring, their sharp exchanges that when written down would have looked harsh, like fights. Penelope loved them, not just the jabs, but the role she played—their watcher. The one who laughed at them, cut them off when it got too sharp. She loved that she had a group, and a role in it.

—⁂—

Jack got high or drunk and mostly avoided talking about what was next. Just that he had to, at some point, go home to his father (*Shithead,* he called him), their hardware store in Brooklyn, and decide what life he was going to choose for himself. Manhattan, some finance position on Wall Street, most likely. Penelope could see him working a room, shaking hands, giving that big toothy smile to every woman in the boardroom, the bar, the bedroom. He was Jack; the kinks would work themselves out. The other seniors all seemed to have *plans*— Anne Hemsley from her Business Simulation group had a position at a start-up called Greenchain waiting for her, and it was all she ever talked about. *Blockchain technology, VC funding propositions, Greenchain partnership strategies.* Yes, they had their group project to put finishing touches on, but Penelope started declining her calls and listening to her frantic voice mails later. *Penelope! Do you understand we only have two weeks left? Where are you!* The incoming texts were mostly in capital letters.

The other thing was, everyone had a home to go to. Penelope, orphaned at nine, was raised by her mother's sister, Belinda, who lived alone in a little blue saltbox in Elkins Park. A solitary woman, living on her sister's hefty life insurance left to her after the accident to raise a girl she'd barely known. The house bordered an alley, the curtains were kept drawn most of the time, and the only light at night came from the oversize television alternating between network news and the Home Shopping Network.

"So what, you want us to just move there, and we will be college two-point-oh?" Willa snorted. "So typical. You're Peter Pan, as usual."

"Oh, fuck off. I mean, doesn't it sound like fun? At least a little bit?"

"Tell me about the house." Penelope finally spoke, and Willa gave her a sharp look—*You aren't considering this madness, are you?* Jack snatched the joint out of Willa's still fingers to take the last drag, and she kicked at him with her bare toe.

"I don't know anything about it. Just that it used to be a church. Freaky, right? We could have séances there or some shit."

"That's satanic." Willa stretched, her back arched, and Jack reached over, slapped at her breast, and she screamed, swatted at him. In the sunlight, you could see Willa's long red scar under her makeup. Penelope hardly ever noticed it. She'd been in a near-fatal car accident as a child, and now, the everlasting remnant: a thick, knotted rope of flesh from her left temple to her jawline.

"That's not what Satanism is," Penelope interjected and felt Willa's eyes roll; she didn't even have to see her.

"You're the most goddamn pedantic person."

"We could all live together. Just one more year. In the country. Get jobs at like a coffee shop. Something lame. Like a gap year, like those European kids take." Jack was pushing harder; Penelope knew him. Watched him through slitted eyes, pretending to be sleepy. He wanted this. He didn't want to go home to his dad. He wanted college two-point-oh. He wanted them to stay together. Suddenly, fervently, Penelope wanted it too. More than she'd ever wanted anything.

"What's the rent?" Penelope asked, lacing her fingers behind her head. Jack gave her a smile, big, brilliant.

"Cheap. Like a grand a month? We just have to cover Parker's mortgage. It has five bedrooms. If we could find two more people, it's almost free."

"Bree," Willa said immediately. "And Flynn."

"You want me to live with Bree?" Jack closed his eyes, laughed, and fell backward on the grass in a faint, legs spread eagle. Bree. Six feet tall, skin white and chilly, long deep-red waves down her back. Her high, floaty voice, never grounded in real life. Bright-blue eyes, narrowed and all-knowing. All-disapproving? Some thought so. Bree made Penelope mildly uncomfortable, like her own skin was the wrong size, and when Bree was around, Penelope never knew what to do with her hands.

Jack had always been a little in love with her. It was her inaccessibility. She was a virgin; she stated it plainly and proudly and seemed uninterested in changing that status. Maybe it was the way her face closed off and no one could read it. You had to rely on her words alone. Maybe it was the way she barely looked at him, wasn't impressed by him. He was just so unaccustomed to it. He always did a little song and dance for Bree, and he thought no one saw it. Penelope did, and maybe she should have been jealous, angry at his posturing. She never was—probably because it was never returned, not even a little bit.

"Oh, God. Can you imagine? You'll just moon after her all day." Willa giggled helplessly, falling back against Jack's chest. Penelope wondered, briefly, fleetingly, how it would feel to casually touch him, when she spent so much time avoiding it. To have it be that easy, the warmth and steady thrum of his heartbeat directly under her ear.

"I don't moon," Jack grumbled but grinned bashfully.

"I don't think you have to worry about Bree either way." Penelope felt the flush creep up her neck and stood, brushing invisible grass off her bare thighs and khaki shorts. She looked away, down the street, shielding her eyes, even though the sun was behind her. "She doesn't give you the time of day."

"God, you're such a wench." Jack had his arm slung over his eyes. "I feel like you *like* to hurt me."

"You just say that because I won't sleep with you," Penelope shot back, turning her head only slightly, and tugged her hair into a messy knot at the base of her neck. She started packing up the remains of their picnic, the wedge cheese soft and slick with condensation, the mushy grapes, the empty wine bottle. When she turned back, Willa's eyes were closed, her face relaxed in a doze.

Jack's hand reached out, grazed her ankle, his thumb fitting neatly into the lumpy curve of bone at the base of her calf, and Penelope swallowed thickly. His pressure increased until she could feel the pulse there, jumping under her skin.

He smiled as he whispered, "Won't you, now?"

CHAPTER FOUR

February 12, 2020

Brett found them on the back patio, wrapped in blankets, sipping a merlot that Penelope had unearthed from behind boxed macaroni and cheese in the pantry. He stood uncertainly in the doorway, the sliding glass door open enough for his thin frame, sweaty and pinked from a hot yoga session. They'd been laughing, but their amusement died off with the slide of the door. Like they'd been caught.

Penelope studied her husband, tried to see him through Willa's eyes: the squared jaw, the too-long honey hair, the ruddy cheeks. The newly formed dullness behind brown eyes that he covered up with an open, friendly smile. Brett always looked like a Boy Scout to her: innocent and wholesome. She'd spent much of her marriage loving that about him. Of course, she'd been under the impression that growing up was a given, that it would happen organically. That she wouldn't find herself, at forty-two, nudging him along into adulthood the way you cajole a child into a kindergarten classroom.

His eyes flicked to Penelope's: *I didn't know we had company. Why do you always surprise me?* Or maybe she just imagined it. She tried to send a message back, telepathically. *I didn't know.*

"Brett, this is Willa. My roommate in college." Technically not the truth. Roommate after college.

Brett crossed the patio in three easy steps, his hand extended. Willa stood, and they shook hands. Penelope reversed her gaze, tried to see her old friend through her husband's eyes and found she couldn't do it. He smiled wide, but Penelope knew it wasn't real. He'd always been good, though.

"How was yoga?" Penelope asked him, her voice careful. Would Willa wonder why her husband had been to yoga in the middle of the day? Why he wasn't wearing a suit, preoccupied by his phone, maybe carrying a briefcase? Why did it even matter?

"All good," he said blandly, then turned toward their guest. "Staying for dinner, Willa?"

Willa glanced at Penelope, then back to Brett, picking up on the tension. Penelope nodded, smiled brightly, and said, "If that's all right, darling?"

Penelope had never called Brett *darling* before in her life. Sometimes *babe*. Once, as a joke at a holiday party, she called him *sweetie*. They were mocking someone else, but Penelope couldn't remember who; she only remembered the gentle, insistent pressure of his knee against hers under the table, his lips pressed together to hold in the laughter.

"I'll run up to shower and join you then," Brett offered amiably before shutting the door, but Penelope could tell he was thrown. He'd gotten set in his day. Yoga, shower, dinner, one glass of wine, bed. A dinner guest had not been penciled in on the wall calendar that hung next to the refrigerator. Penelope held up her index finger in Willa's direction, set her wineglass on the wooden table between them. It was warm for February, almost fifty. But by five o'clock, the sun was low in the sky. Willa's cheeks were red, her lips mottled purple.

Penelope followed Brett inside, expecting him to still be in the kitchen, but he must have booked it. She took the steps two at a time and found him in their bathroom, shirtless in his underwear, the shower running.

"I didn't know she was coming, okay?"

"Okay." Brett could be irritatingly agreeable, but Penelope never had any idea if he was truly fine or if he was *irritated* fine or *angry* fine. Lately she was just guessing. She remembered being sure—that easy confidence that came when you were together, in tune. She remembered a time when she'd know just by the set of Brett's shoulders whether his day had been good or bad. When she'd think, *No, not chicken tonight, we had chicken last night* because Brett liked to mix up his dinners, and she didn't mind doing things that Brett liked.

"Okay, like really okay?"

"It's just dinner, Pen." He didn't look at her, his hand waving under the spray, testing the temperature. He shed his underwear, his ass white as he turned away from her, and stepped into the glass enclosure. His thighs were newly muscular, cut from all the yoga and weightlifting. Some men bought cars; some carried on with women twenty years their junior. Brett got laid off and took up yoga. And Reiki. And bought a cross-fit membership. And a monthly credit card bill for something called a sound bath. He was spending their money on wellness as fast as she could make it.

"Actually, she wants to stay for a few days." Penelope rushed on, "I think she's in trouble, but I don't know what yet. She seemed so scared when she came to the door."

"Is this Willa from the fire house?"

The fire house. How casually he threw it out there. Penelope swallowed. Penelope and Willa hadn't even touched on the subject of the house. It didn't *feel* like they were avoiding the topic, but Penelope was positive they both worked hard to make the avoidance seem effortless.

"Yes."

"I didn't know you kept in touch with her." His voice took on an edge. "With any of them."

"I haven't. Not really. I don't think . . ." Penelope inhaled, the steam filling her lungs. She sounded defensive, *felt* defensive, but without reason. She hadn't done anything wrong. She hadn't told him about the letter, from the summer. "I don't think she had anywhere else to go."

"Okay," Brett said after a pause.

"*Okay* okay? Or okay-you-want-to-kill-me-but-I'm-your-wife okay?"

He didn't answer right away, instead choosing to scrub at his scalp, suds spattering against the glass, biceps flexing with the effort. Everything about Brett's body was new; he was hardly recognizable as the man she'd married. Wait, was he . . . tanning? She squinted at a faint line across the pale of his thighs.

"I just don't know that I'm up for all this, that's all," he said finally. "But I feel like that doesn't matter. You just do your Penelope thing, and I'll go along."

"That's unfair. I didn't invite her. A friend showed up and asked for help. We can help. We have the space." Penelope flung her arms wide, as if to show him, *Look how lucky we are.* "She just needs a few days, she says."

She paused, studied her own reflection in the mirror: her hair dark and glossy, her makeup a little worn but still intact, her lips stained red with wine. They *were* lucky. One look at Willa's neck, the faint blue dots, the pinched lines around her mouth and eyes told her that. She could open her door for an old friend, right? They didn't have to talk about the past—she was sure they'd both happily pretend for the week. Besides, Penelope hadn't had a real girlfriend in a long time. Wine on the freezing-cold patio felt nicer than she'd ever admit.

Finally, she said, "Brett?" and he sighed.

"Yeah, okay."

15

Later, she straddled him in bed. He'd gotten shockingly, gleefully buzzed on vodka sodas. Willa brought a celebratory air to their dinner—a giddiness that hadn't existed before—even if the reasons she'd come weren't inherently joyful. There was something about the performance that was fun. They exchanged stories about traveling and vacations, wine, and discovered that both Willa and Brett played squash regularly. At one point, Willa picked up Penelope's phone on the side table and took a selfie of the three of them, faces pinked by the February evening wind.

Linc stayed for dinner at Zeke's, a kid he'd known since third grade. Tara texted at some point during the evening: be home around ten, going to dinner with everyone. On any other day, Penelope might have texted back, who's everyone? But that night, she simply said, have fun. Tara wrote back immediately, really? Where's my mom? And Penelope didn't even reply.

She'd worked hard, these past twenty years, to forget everything she had loved about all of them. She couldn't afford to miss them—it was simply too much of a risk. What might she have done in a moment of weakness? Reached out, extended an olive branch? And then what? Doors that were opened could often never be shut again. But here she was anyway, flinging open a door. Why?

Penelope had forgotten that Willa was so funny. Or maybe not forgotten, but she hadn't expected it. Even despite whatever circumstances she'd arrived under, she was quick witted. They fell back into clever sparring, and now, Willa roped in Brett. Teasing him about aligning energies.

"Look, it sounds nuts, I know." He'd laughed as he said it, his drink more vodka than soda, thin peels of lime accumulating at the bottom of the glass. Penelope looked up in surprise. He'd never, not once in the past year, admitted to his new diversions sounding "nuts." He never treated them with a tongue in cheek. Never hinted that it was *comical* that a man who until very recently was a senior vice president of finance at a major—now bankrupt—insurance group, who until lately found personal fulfillment in budgeting, databases, spreadsheets, numeric predictions of how their life was progressing (on or off track), now relied on things like "universal energies" and "life force" as a source of anything other than the butt of a joke. He'd traded in his dark suits for linen pants, the pockets of which routinely contained colorful, flat palm stones—deep reds and purples, blues and oranges—the size of a silver dollar that she'd have to fish out before she accidentally ran them through the laundry.

But no, Brett showed absolutely no self-awareness that any of this was a drastic change or he could be razzed about it, even gently or lovingly.

So when Willa had the audacity to tease him, and Penelope had not, not ever, she'd held her breath and waited and he'd actually thrown his head back and *laughed*, it was the first time she'd found him sexy in a year. Who was this laughing man on her patio with lime in his glass and wearing his old Duke sweatshirt, with his thick, floppy hair and three-day beard? Was he flirting with Willa? It was a wild turn-on. To see him anew, and in turn, them, through her friend's eyes: the big house, cute husband, two social, well-adjusted children, who returned home late and were not, for the first time, cocky or sassy or any of the things they'd become in the past year. They were sardonic and smart and beautiful and quick (if not slightly confused about finding their parents not in separate rooms on separate electronic devices but together—drinking, talking, *laughing* with a pretty stranger).

Then later, sweetly drunk, after they showed Willa to her room, Brett promising to make them all breakfast and coffee in the morning, now that he was a "man of leisure" (he'd never been self-deprecating before), Penelope climbed on top of him, desperately seeking to prolong the evening, the most fun they'd had in ages, keep that man from the patio around just a bit longer, and perhaps steal a tiny bit of him for herself. She was intent on exploring the new dips and valleys of his body with her hands; this man she'd known for almost twenty years now felt like a stranger but in the most wonderful way, and she wondered, through a boozy haze, if this would be a blossoming for them and then laughed into his mouth at her own flowery ridiculousness. But still, she was hopeful.

Later, when she thought about how much hope she'd held that first night, how she'd let herself believe, with her sweet, floundering husband between her thighs, that Willa's sudden arrival could somehow be a reset, a way to see something in each other that they couldn't seem to find alone, it would seem unbelievable how naive she'd been. Later, when she tried to remember this first evening with any clarity, tease apart the fantasy from the reality, to figure out where it all went terribly wrong, the only thing she could really pull from it was Brett's voice, pitched with irritation, when he'd said, "Willa from the fire house?"

CHAPTER FIVE

February 13, 2020

Penelope found Willa in the kitchen. It had been a whirlwind morning. Penelope spent at least fifteen minutes longer than she should have looking for her lucky shirt—the one she always wore in audits at work. White blouse, a small detailed ruffle at the shallow V-neck. Very professional. The shirt seemed to be gone. She'd have to scour Tara's room later.

Tara and Linc caught a ride to school with Tara's friend Ruby, a newly minted driver with her very own Audi Q3, a nicer car than Penelope had ever owned. But such was the way in Wexford, New Jersey. Penelope and Brett found themselves getting caught up in the game—and then made a valiant effort to not care. Keeping up had always seemed exhausting, a fool's errand. And yet, Penelope still noticed the car. What did that say about her?

Her children were gorgeous, Penelope knew that: Tara was tall and slender, willowy in a way that made her fifteen-year-old friends envious. Penelope knew this because she listened from the hallway as they mocked her for raiding the fridge *again*, and they'd *love to be able to eat anything we want, don't you care at all about the carbs?* Long, golden, soft waves down her back and a full mouth gave her sex appeal that no fifteen-year-old should have. Every nerve in Penelope's body rattled when she thought about the way men watched her, pretending they weren't. Linc, Tara's younger Irish twin, was just as beautiful, but his features were more delicate than his sister's. Blond curls, blue eyes, blush cheeks on porcelain skin, reminding her since birth of Hadrian's Antinous—too pretty, too soft, too careful for a boy. Two babies that, born back to back with no break between them, seemed to have shared a womb. Every look exchanged meant something several layers deep, every emotion carefully masked from Penelope but plainly evident to the two of them.

Penelope had been the audience to their little play for as long as she could remember. She recorded it once: two toddlers sitting on a blanket, a tower of blocks between them. They'd laughed so hard they both fell over, little feet kicking with glee, and on the video, over the giggling was Penelope's reedy voice: "What's so funny, you two? What are you laughing at? Show Mommy." Later, watching it, she was ashamed at the sound of her voice—thin, irritated, needy. She made them each a best friend and, in the process, made herself redundant.

Which was *fine*, she insisted, if only to herself. *You want your children to get along.* And yet, every once in a while, she'd feel a little pathetic about it. There had always been a tiny part of her that held herself back, out of the main circles. She thought of the time at the Church House—her role as observer. Repeated now, in her own home.

Still, Penelope worried incessantly. Tara was too brusque, Linc too sensitive. What would happen to both of them in the world? Brett thought she was crazy; the kids were fine. He never worried—not before, when his mind was preoccupied with international meetings and portfolio management, and not now, when he spent all his spare moments finding his own inner energies.

"Your kids are great." Willa sat cupping a steaming mug of coffee at the table. She wore an oversize men's blue shirt and a pair of heather-gray leggings.

"I know," Penelope said, pouring her own cup of coffee from the pot she assumed Brett had made before his morning run. She was supposed to say *thank you*, but instead found herself smiling.

"And Brett is great," Willa said earnestly. "You're just so lucky, Penelope. I'm so happy for you. I wish we'd kept in touch. I wish . . ." Her voice trailed off. "Well, anyway. Maybe if we'd stayed friends, I would have made better life choices." She laughed, but it was forced, loud.

How would they have stayed friends? Each of them carrying their own burden from that awful night. They'd been ripped apart, the seam irreparable. Penelope had too much at stake—more than Willa could ever know.

"We're so alike, Pip," Willa said, her thumb running over the nick in the wood table. "Do you have girlfriends? You haven't mentioned, texted anyone?"

Penelope startled for a moment. She felt a bit splayed open, examined. She *did* have girlfriends—or used to. Nora, for one. Now she had Jaime, who was like a girlfriend, in his own way. What had happened to the parents of Tara's and Linc's friends? They'd been stay-at-home moms—meeting each other for morning yoga and midday coffee. While Penelope worked five days a week. She used to be invited to the moms' nights out, but hadn't been in a while.

"I don't have many friends myself. I see you. It's hard to get along when you're an island." Her voice pitched low, a soft rumble, like she might cry.

Penelope sat across from her old friend and studied Willa's face. She'd changed so much: harder, thinner, more glamorous, less ingenue. The Willa she knew had been curvy, soft, bubbly, and while she'd been made up, she'd also retained a sense of effortlessness. This new Willa seemed full of effort. The scar, covered with makeup even at this early hour, gleamed but possibly (probably) only to Penelope. It was likely that anyone else would not have noticed it.

"Do you want to talk about it?" Penelope asked her softly. She didn't want to outright inquire how long Willa would stay, but she knew Brett would ask. Perhaps tonight. He always preferred to be mentally, if not physically, prepared for all eventualities. Or at least he used to.

"Not really, but I don't suppose I can stay here indefinitely without an explanation." Willa fiddled with her spoon, stirring distractedly. "You've always been generous, Pip, but that would be a stretch even for you."

"Well, I understand you are in hiding. Presumably from an abusive man—husband?" Penelope said. Willa simply nodded. Penelope continued, "I'm willing to listen whenever you want to talk, but you don't have to tell me anything you don't want to."

After a pause, Willa said, "We were married three years ago. It was a simple justice of the peace wedding. I'd been married, and widowed, before. I don't know if you knew that?"

Penelope shook her head. Should she have known? After the accident, they scattered so quickly, and the next thing she knew, Penelope was married, and then pregnant. No time for following up. She shoved everything about the Church House into a little box in the back of her mind, except for the mornings she'd wake up panicked and twisted in the sheets, with the smell of solvent and fire. Everything about the accident, her four roommates who had once been so close a classmate had called them "toxic." She should have followed up more. She should have reached out at some point, right? No. Absolutely not. How would any of them ever come back together? They'd been turned by their shared trauma, their magnetic poles shifted so now they had no choice but to repel each other. They each had their own secrets to protect—no one more than Penelope.

"Anyway, I met him—Trent—at a bar. He seemed like a good guy. I don't know, my compass has been off. My first husband died of heart failure in his sleep. I was single for years. Then Trent came along, and I was just so tired of being alone. Of missing someone. I think I was just in a hurry. Anyway, he hit me for the first time on our honeymoon. We were in Hawaii, and he said I'd been flirting with the waiter at dinner. It was so fast, I didn't even scream. After that, I wondered how many other people were in their honeymoon suite getting quietly hit." Willa sighed, a big exhale. "Then it became fairly regular. He had money, his own business. I had nothing. He said if I left, he'd find me and kill me. So here I am, lying low until I can figure out what I do next. He'll kill me. I've never been so sure of anything in my life. I have to move, probably across the country. Change my name."

Penelope felt a shiver of fear for the first time. Had Willa put them all in danger?

Willa seemed to sense the question. "He doesn't know you exist. I wouldn't have come if he did. I only brought cash with me, no credit cards. I have a car, but it's mine, not his, from before we met. I stole a license plate on the drive and ditched mine, so even if he tried to call the car in, it would send them around for a while. Plus, state lines and all."

"Where did you drive from?" Penelope finally thought to ask. "Where did you and Trent live?"

"Oh. I don't know why I thought you knew?" Willa sat back against her chair and swallowed, wiping her upper lip with her index finger. "I found you a long time ago. I found everyone. Just a simple Google search, really. Not being weird or anything. I mean, I just assumed we all did that."

"What are you talking about?"

Willa reached over and gripped Penelope's wrist, her french-manicured nails biting into the skin. "Pip, I never left Deer Run."

CHAPTER SIX

Willa

The first thing that struck her was that Pip looked exactly as she remembered. *How do twenty years go by—twenty years of hardship or stress or illness or struggle—without someone showing any signs of it?* Willa herself had to stick her forehead with needles for hundreds of dollars, pay for the loose skin beneath her chin to be tucked back into its proper place. Her hair dyed every few weeks to cover the wispy white flyaways. Not to mention all the other nips, cuts, smoothers, peels, just to keep her looking like . . . well, like Willa.

Unless, of course, there was no hardship. That was always possible, she supposed. Maybe Pip had finally gotten lucky.

Pip came from nothing. She had no one—no real family, no friends that anyone could have named. When she talked about her life before Penn, it was with a wry mix of self-deprecation and apology. She'd used her life insurance from her parents' death to pay her tuition.

Willa had come from money—a genetic lottery. Raised in the South, moved north, and then later, her whole family scattered to different parts of the globe. Willa had been left alone save for a sizable bank account that she blew on booze. She'd been set to plow through the full balance—talking about a luxury apartment in Center City to anyone who would listen. Inviting the world to join her.

The year at the Church House had been a respite—a pause for all of them. A reason to extend undergrad, stay in their little bubble. Maybe it had been a final Hail Mary to get Jack to fall in love with her.

Jack, Willa's single-minded obsession since freshman English—that first waft of hair gel and cigarettes and musty laundry and toothpaste as he sat in front of her, his legs stretched out to the desk to his left, conversation bouncing back and forth between Willa and the pretty raven-haired girl in front of him. He took the raven-haired girl home from a party the second week of school, kept Willa on the hook as his "best friend."

It was obvious they all wanted Jack. It was almost embarrassing.

Six months after they moved in, he brought Grace home and sent them all into a tailspin. Grace with her long blonde hair, shining in big ringlets down her back. Her bright-blue eyes, smart, calculating. Knowing instantly that Jack was the sun; the rest of them were simply orbiting.

They'd met at the coffee shop. Grace told her all about it. Grace told her everything—more than she'd ever wanted to know. How they met, what she thought of all of them. All the nitty-gritty—she wasn't one to demur on anything.

Despite all that had happened at the Church House, before, after, during that one pivotal year, Jack would never have left Grace. As quickly as he'd denounced marriage once upon a time, he embraced it at the Church House. Suddenly it was all he talked about—growing up, settling down, becoming an adult, as though the rest of them were children. He acted like he couldn't wait for the year to end, that he was getting over it. That living with four other people was for college kids.

It pissed them all off, especially Willa. You couldn't blame her, really. Willa knew more about Jack than anyone—how much of his posturing was real? If history was any indication, almost none of it.

But still, he would have married Grace. Everyone believed that, without question.

If only she'd lived.

CHAPTER SEVEN

February 14, 2020

Happy Valentine's Day.

No hearts. No exclamation points. Just a simple text, plain as fact. Penelope had no control over her heart, which raced almost instantly, or her mouth, which smiled without conscious thought.

What will you do today? You breathing?

Their private joke—*just breathe.* She hadn't replied yet.

The last time he texted her, she'd left him hanging. Instead googled *married people with a crush* and found out yes, it's natural and common and of course it happens, and as long as no one knows about it, it's fine. Of course, she'd never act on it. The crush itself wasn't unfaithful. She'd never been a cheater. Penelope's father was a cheater. Serial, compulsive. She'd found her mother crying at the kitchen table in the early morning light on more than one occasion.

Penelope pinched the bridge of her nose. From downstairs she heard the rustling, faint sounds of morning—the surreptitious pop of the toaster, the suction of the refrigerator opening and closing. Willa. Penelope had told Willa to make herself at home. She was surprised that she had done it so easily. She'd been an easy houseguest—pleasant, accommodating, grateful. She'd made dinner the night before—homemade chicken noodle soup. Quick but also delicious. She'd cleaned the house, left the kitchen spotless, counters gleaming in the soft evening light. Penelope only briefly wondered what Willa would do all day in their home and then snorted softly to herself. Let her snoop—they were incredibly boring. Not even a vibrator in her nightstand.

Still. It was unnerving to have her back in Penelope's life. After so much time actively working to push her old friendships aside. They had been a family then—the only kind some of them had had. Twenty years ago, it had taken everything she had—down to the very marrow of her bones—to move home, away from them all, ignore voice mail messages and calls. Start fresh and new. Would she be able to do that again? Not likely. That kind of strength came maybe once in a lifetime.

She thumbed the screen open again, pulling at her lower lip as she studied the text. Finally, she wrote back. I don't know. Brett is still sleeping. Maybe dinner? I have a college friend in from out of town.

Is she cute? Would I like her?

Jaime Heller, you like everyone.

It was true; he was a shameless flirt even when his wife had been alive. Jaime Heller lived a block east. He was the father of Tara's best friend, Sasha. They'd been in third grade when Sasha's mother and Penelope's closest friend, Kiera, was diagnosed with a brain tumor. Her death had been swift and brutal, leaving Jaime to his own devices as a single father. Sasha was his light, his whole life. He'd learned how to braid her hair, paint her nails; taught himself, then his daughter, how to apply a maxi pad (thanking YouTube the whole time); wrestled with those early tween friendship dramas. Brett and Penelope had taken him in, invited him for dinners, even once invited Jaime and Sasha on a family trip south, to Virginia Beach. Brett and Jaime used to golf on Sundays, go to ten-cent wings on Wednesdays at the pub on Trapp Street. When Brett got laid off, at first he cited money worries and begged off golf. Then later he told Penelope that wings were terrible for you, deep fried in chicken fat. She watched her husband's world shrink with his waistline as he ignored texts, calls from friends, previously standing dates.

At first Jaime's texts to her were all about Brett. They started out light. Don't you ever let your husband out of the dungeon? Then took on a more serious, concerned tone. Is he okay? What's going on? She found herself confiding in Jaime, convinced they both had Brett's best interests at heart. Slowly, somehow without realizing, she went from talking about Brett with a concerned friend to talking about *her* feelings about Brett. Jaime felt more like her friend than Brett's friend.

Then one night, back in September, right after school was back in, about six months after Brett was laid off, Penelope invited Jaime over for dinner. She clipped her hair up, dark and glossy with ringlets around her face. She wore a black tank top and jeans—casually sexy. She swiped on mascara, some bronzer, a light pink lip gloss. Brett came home from the gym, sweaty and spent, and took one look at her, the whole plump chicken browning in the oven and went ballistic, stomping up the steps to their bedroom like a child.

"I don't understand," Penelope protested, following him into their bedroom. "We used to do this all the time. Why can't we have a friend for dinner anymore? What has changed?"

"You just do whatever you want. No one asks me what I want, or what I think! I don't want company for dinner. I don't want to come home after a long day and have to entertain someone."

"A long day doing what?" Penelope shot back. "Getting a hot stone massage? Lifting weights? Maybe spending a few hours in a sauna? How is this a hardship?"

"That's what you think I do?" Brett's voice had been low, menacing. She'd never seen him so angry at her in their whole lives together.

"How would I know? You don't tell me. We don't talk. I talk at you. You nod, pretend to be interested, or grunt if you're in a bad mood."

"So you want me to talk? About how I applied for over two hundred positions in the past year, some of which would move me halfway across the country? I got phone calls back about half of them, but the bottom line is, I'm old. Technology changes quickly in finance—new programs to use that I'm unfamiliar with the longer I sit out. We don't have young kids. I can't even say I helped raise them. You did all that. While working. What, exactly, do you think that feels like?" Brett came close, his nose inches from hers. He jabbed a finger into her chest, hard. He'd never come close to touching her in anger before. "Why do you think I do all these things? Why do I lift weights?"

"I don't know!" Penelope finally burst out. "I have no fucking clue why you leave us home alone constantly, where you go, or who you're with!" And then, realizing, "Why would you apply to jobs that would move us out of state without talking to me?"

Brett's face registered all the things he couldn't say.

"Unless you didn't want us to go?" Penelope finished softly. Oh, God. She pressed her fingertips to her lips. His eyes looked dead, flat and emotionless, and Penelope backed up, felt the doorknob in her back. She reached behind her and opened the bedroom door. She ran down the hall and outside to the front porch.

Behind the potted plant in the corner, she had stashed a pack of Marlboro Lights. She fumbled with the lighter and took a deep inhale. She imagined Brett knew she'd been sneaking cigarettes, but they didn't talk about it. She used mints or brushed her teeth. With his newfound attitude toward health, he had to find it disgusting. Was he actually repulsed by her?

She was on her third cigarette in a row, her hands shaky, her lungs a dull ache, when Jaime came strolling up the walk. Sasha and Tara had gone to the mall together and would be back by dinner, so Jaime had come alone. He sat next to her on the step, picked up the pack, and instead of crumpling it in his fist, which is what she expected him to do (to admonish her, tell her that smoking was bad for her, or some other platitude), he extracted a cigarette and lit it, blowing the smoke away from her.

"Want to talk about it?" He asked her, holding her gaze. She thought it was strange that she hadn't cried yet. How did Jaime know she was upset? She'd barely said a word. Her makeup still intact, her mascara still fresh.

His eyes were a deep brown; his hair thick, black, and wavy with streaks of gray; his beard salt and pepper. She noticed his hands—long fingers, big knuckles. His forearms—the muscled ridge that disappeared under a rolled-up shirtsleeve, a smear of blue paint on his arm. She knew he painted sometimes. He'd told her once—when, she couldn't remember—that art was an outlet for him. That smear of paint went right through her, seemed sexier than anything she'd ever seen in her life. She noticed everything, seemingly for the first time. But then, maybe not. Who had the lip gloss been for?

God, no, she didn't want to talk.

She felt the zing right down her legs. Something she hadn't felt for Brett in months, maybe years. They stared at each other, and the toes inside her high-heeled boots curled, and his mouth parted slightly, like he was going to say something, and she knew right that instant that he felt it too. He wanted her. It was so instant and powerful and irresistible, with Brett upstairs stomping around like another angry teenager, unable or unwilling to explain any of it to her. With his thoughts of leaving them bouncing around his head and never even talking about it. Had things gotten that bad? She hadn't thought so.

But then there she was: concocting an elaborate fantasy where she pulled Jaime to her, right now, and kissed him. She could almost feel the rough denim of his jeans, the smooth leather of his belt beneath her palms. The silky, smoky taste of his lips. Did he paint shirtless, like in the movies? She imagined his bare torso, a tiny swell of belly brushed with orange, yellow, greens, and blues.

She stood up, stamped out the butt with the toe of her boot.

"I don't think tonight is going to work out," she finally said, her voice throaty and dry. He nodded and turned to leave. He was halfway down the steps before he turned back to her.

"Are you okay?" he asked her, and it was almost the thing that undid her. The sound of his voice, the concern for her well-being. The simple care. How Brett had not asked her if she was okay in as long as she could remember. How she was always asking him, the kids, *Are you okay? Is everything okay? Can I do anything to help you?* And she hadn't realized until that moment, with yes, a little self-pity, how wearing it was to spend all your time thinking about someone who never seemed to think of you. And here was Jaime, with his speckled beard and his hooded eyes, simply caring. It made her want to kiss him fiercely.

But she didn't. Instead, she said yes, as firmly as she could muster and left him on the steps. Instead, she let herself back inside her own home, with its familiar shoes in the entry and its smell of laundry and baking chicken, leaned her back against the front door, and finally, *finally*, she cried.

CHAPTER EIGHT
Then: Moving Day

The day they moved into the Church House was teeming with rain and fifty degrees. It was late May, three days after graduation. Jack had fled the city before graduation—to set up, he said. Set up what? Everyone asked, but he never answered. He was just gone, a week before everyone else. Ostensibly living in a big empty church alone.

"Don't you want to walk?" Penelope had asked about graduation, horrified that anyone would skip their own degree conferral, and Jack had snorted.

"For who? Myself? Nah. Shithead? No. No worries, Pen." Jack always said *no worries*, sounding faintly British or maybe Australian. It always calmed Penelope, the ease with which he'd let it slip out, as if trying to talk them all down from a cliff. A balm to her soul, which seemed overrun with worries on a regular basis.

They'd been in Jack's room—unusually alone. Jack on the floor, his feet kicked up on the side of the bed, Penelope stretched out above him, her hair falling around her face as she watched him toss a foam basketball in the air. Willa had an afternoon class, and Penelope had become dependent on these two hours every Tuesday and Thursday. But soon she'd be living with Jack.

Sharing a house.

A bathroom.

She could scarcely breathe if she thought about it, so she avoided the whole idea. Had she wasted her entire four years of college pining for a man who might or might not feel anything for her? Possibly, yes.

When Jack proposed the group gap year that day in the park (his handprint still pulsing on her ankle), nothing would have kept her from saying yes. Still, she dithered around, pretending to be unsure for at least a week before Jack cornered her, literally, his hands braced on either side of her head, against Willa's refrigerator, his breath warm on her neck, tickling her ear, his back arched into her. *Pen-elllll-ope, what are you waiting for?* Her back pressed against the metal door, the thin faux-wood handle digging into her spine, and the room spun around her.

"Interrupting something?" Willa had appeared from the bathroom, eyebrows arched.

"No. I mean yes. I'll do it. I'll do the gap year thing." Penelope ducked under his arm, into the open space of the kitchen. Her face had been on fire, burning with the desire to touch his cheek—so close to hers—run a fingertip down his sharp jawline, the stubble soft under her nails.

And now it was move-in day.

Willa and Jack. Bree and her best friend, Flynn.

Flynn was straitlaced, almost formal in his speech and mannerisms, in khaki pants and button-up shirts when they'd drink at Jack's apartment. The rest of them would be in Penn T-shirts and leggings, shorts, but Flynn would have on a dark oxford shirt, tucked into trousers like he was going to church. Handsome, Black, athletic. She remembered seeing him at the gym, his shoulders wide and muscly in ways she didn't know existed, a dewdrop of sweat trickling down his tricep.

With two closed cardboard boxes stacked in those thick arms, he smiled at her now, teeth white and cheeks dimpled.

"Penelope." He leaned forward and kissed her cheek, and he smelled like soap and cedar.

Bree stood on the steps, holding a brass floor lamp like a scepter, the sun shining behind her, haloing her flyaway red hair. She laughed wildly and called to them. "This place is crazy amazing!" she yelled. Bree had a tendency to shout excitedly about almost anything—*The co-op had shelled pistachios today!*—while waving her long white arms around like some kind of flame-haired Aphrodite.

The house was immense. White on the outside, paint chipped and peeling, the only shining thing was the bright-red door, newly glossed. A single reaching steeple graced the roof with a rusted bell housed inside. The cross on top seemed to go up forever, a pointed, piercing spire.

Penelope didn't dare say so, but her first impression was that the house was a dump. Not only was the paint peeling, but the concrete steps out front were crumbling, the wooden gables above the windows were splintered, even the stained glass was cracked along the lead came outline.

The inside smelled strongly of oiled wood and incense. Thankfully, the house had been half converted prior to Jack's cousin Parker's purchase. The kitchen sat at the back of the house, where Penelope assumed the altar used to be, raised up two steps. The appliances were high end, gleaming under the bright recessed lights. What had been the main worship room was now an empty space—on a television show, it might be called open concept. Waiting to be filled with their mismatched furniture, Ikea end tables, thrift store prints thumbtacked to the walls. To the right of the kitchen was a gorgeous wooden, carved spiral staircase, breathtaking but dangerous. The wood gleamed gold in the mote-filled sun. Penelope could imagine Willa, drunk and tumbling, her blonde hair caught in the spindles. Above them, an enormous balcony where she imagined the organ used to be, now a wide-open loft space. Jack leaned casually over the loft railing on his elbows, watching their reactions, grinning, his hands laced in front of him.

"Where are the bedrooms?" asked Willa from behind her, breathlessly.

"Four in the basement. I'll sleep up here. I'm the night owl anyway," said Jack.

"This is the craziest house!" Bree had dropped the lamp where she stood and threw her hands up, twirling in a circle, her white dress spinning around her, her flip-flops smacking the wood floor.

"Who wears a dress to move?" Flynn hip checked her, and she stumbled. She shoved him back, and he laughed, slid next to Penelope, still holding the boxes he'd walked in with. "See, Penelope, I knew I liked you. You're sensible." He nodded to her shorts and T-shirt, and Penelope thought maybe he just meant boring. She was routinely regarded as sensible. Logical. Down to earth. Categorically, unequivocally the world's most uninteresting compliments. And yet, Penelope felt herself flush, pleased anyway.

Willa flung her arm around Penelope's neck. "You can't have her, Flynnie—she's my best friend."

Flynn laughed and disappeared down the basement steps. Penelope ducked under Willa's arm, escaping the hug. Willa was always free with her affection, and Penelope couldn't help the way her shoulders tensed up when she hugged her. It just wasn't how she was raised. Willa never seemed to notice—or care. But perhaps subtle indications of others' comfort levels were beyond Willa's comprehension.

Penelope hugged her own duffel bag closer (it contained only her immediate needs—pajamas, face cleanser, toothbrush, and a book; the rest would come later on the moving truck), and her breath hitched as Jack caught her eye. He smiled broadly, a grin meant just for her, and she felt something pop in her chest—a spring of hope. She wondered if now, after all this time, now that they would be together all the time, might he realize? She could almost, if she let herself, imagine the story she might tell her children: *We were friends first. Always be friends first! Took us four years to become more than that. To fall in love.* Even when she knew she was being ridiculous, she couldn't stop.

Then later, after the moving truck had come and gone, their once-large open space was filled with plaids and beige and microfiber over-stuffed upholstery of all kinds, merging their styles and budgets into one hodgepodge of coziness, and they nearly all pissed themselves laughing that the only furniture Bree showed up with was a *beanbag chair*, which was just so quintessentially *college*, until Willa lay down on it, kicked off her sneakers, red-painted toenails stretched toward the ceiling, tan calves flexing, and declared it *fucking heavenly comfort, bitches*, and Jack appeared with two bottles of Veuve Clicquot, and Willa, who could get away with saying such things, asked how the hell the son of a Brooklyn handyman got his mitts on two five-hundred-dollar bottles of champagne, and Jack popped the cork at her, narrowly missing her eye, and she tackled him right there on the gleaming heart pine floor, and Flynn grabbed the bottle out of Jack's hand before it could spill *(five hundred dollars!)* and put the bottle straight to his lips, his eyes closed.

"Look, we're growing up," Jack said. "And you called me Peter Pan." He shot a pointed look at Willa, who stuck up her middle finger in response.

Penelope spent most of her life feeling like she watched life happen around her, a floating sense of detachment so common she hardly noticed it anymore. Except now, with the shouting echoing in her ears, the champagne bubbling on her lips, the fabric of Flynn's favorite recliner scratching against her thighs, the warmth of Willa's hand in her own, she felt blessedly, and unusually, present. She felt part of something huge and wild and different and unexpected, perched on the edge of a black chasm and unafraid for the first time in a long time and ready to jump. Penelope studied the faces around her, wondering who else was bursting with indescribable happiness.

Then, even later, as they all stumbled off to claim their rooms, Penelope remembered her own bag with her practical toiletries where she had dropped it above them in the common room, so she crept back upstairs to see Jack lying with his head on Bree's lap, casually playing with a lock of her hair, her face dispassionate, even bored—a stark contrast to Jack's rapture.

She looked up and noticed Flynn paused at the foot of the spiral staircase, Bree's lamp in one hand as he watched them silently. Jack whispered something to Bree, and she smiled, close mouthed and polite, and Penelope watched Flynn's whole face contort with pain, and he seemed to hunch over, like being physically punched. When Bree saw them, she stood suddenly, crossed the room to Penelope and linked their arms, leading Penelope to the basement stairs, away from the boys, and down to their new rooms.

Penelope glanced back once over her shoulder and watched Flynn with interest. His mouth opened briefly to speak, then he seemed to think better of it and clamped it shut. The sudden realization hit Penelope like the force of a thousand fists. It must be what she looked like all the time—flushed and moonfaced.

He was a man in unrequited love.

Except it wasn't Bree he watched, his eyebrows knitted and mouth twisted in pain.

It was Jack.

CHAPTER NINE

February 14, 2020

Save for the errant text that morning, Penelope would have forgotten it was Valentine's Day altogether. The moment she arrived at work, she was pummeled with information. The FDA was on site.

Penelope hadn't been late to work, but she'd been on time, and that was bad enough. She'd spent longer than she'd planned trying to find a gold bracelet that Brett had given her for Valentine's Day the year they got engaged. It was a simple chain link, clasped with a ruby heart. She'd worn it every Valentine's Day since, and he always noticed. He'd notice if it was missing. She looked everywhere: her jewelry boxes, under the bed, under the bureau, her nightstand. It had just vanished into thin air. She'd been forced to go without or risk being actually late.

Penelope worked for Rusker Pharmaceuticals, a small company whose single blockbuster drug, a cholinesterase inhibitor, lessened the symptoms of Alzheimer's by blocking the breakdown of acetylcholine, a chemical messenger for memory and connections between brain cells. Penelope graduated Penn with a biochemistry degree, intent on pursuing a medical career, but needing the break. Then the Church House, then the fire. Then Brett.

She fell in easily with a position at Rusker, which was a biotech start-up at the time. It hadn't felt like a consolation prize. She was helping people, she reasoned, even if not in the way she'd always dreamed. Fifteen years later, she'd worked her way up to a regulatory position. A good salary, order and structure to her days, a large private office, and enough stress to keep her heart moving at a healthy clip, even when the mundanity of child-rearing threatened to unwind all her own brain cells. If pressed, she couldn't have said she *loved* her job. But she could get lost in it. Wasn't that the same thing?

Health-authority audits were nerve-rattling events—they were long and grueling, and often the days were scattered with short tempers and sudden outbursts as she and her colleagues struggled to sift through research that took place ten, fifteen years ago and justify it as safe by today's rules and regulations. Penelope's boss, Nora, was a Swiss immigrant in every way possible: a striving perfectionist preferring simplicity and, while fair, could be blunt as hell. All this was in direct opposition to the upheaval in Penelope's recent life, which was now overscheduled and complicated.

When Brett had a full-time job, she'd been allowed to sink into her professional life. Brett had done half the running around, as much as he could. They'd have conversations over the island in the morning, each with coffee in hand, a full day ahead of them, as equals—who had to be where and when. The whole family shared a complicated set of iCalendars, one for each of them, all feeding into one master schedule on their phones. Every practice, meeting, rehearsal, equipment pickup, car-maintenance appointment, medical checkup, dental cleaning. Their whole lives, cross-linked.

Ever since he'd been laid off, he acted as though the calendar no longer existed. He'd long stopped updating it, and Penelope patiently reminded him to check the schedule, but after a few phone calls from Tara or Linc being left at school followed by sullen rides home, she stopped badgering him. It was easier to do it herself than to fight with Brett about it, followed by doing it herself anyway.

The loss of a partner, not by death or illness, which might garner her a card or at least sympathy in the name of definitive labels, left her making excuses at work. *Brett had an interview. She had a doctor's appointment.* And sometimes, she found herself sneaking out of work— on time, mind you, not early—to pick up Tara at rehearsal and trying not to get caught, like she was doing something wrong.

She liked Nora, had worked with her for over ten years. She thought she had a mutual understanding and respect with her boss. But lately, it seemed, Nora found every reason to needle her.

By the time the auditors had left for the day and Penelope found time to use the restroom, she found her hair had come out of the bun, wild around her face, and she had a slight smear of chocolate across her cheek from—she checked her watch—over three hours ago. As she fixed herself up, a stall door opened, and Nora appeared behind her.

"Debrief for an hour, you'll stay?" Nora took her place at the sink next to Penelope to wash her hands. It wasn't a question, although it was phrased to sound like one.

"Of course." Penelope watched Nora as she dried her hands, pat- ted the side of her head, and turned to leave the bathroom. "I think it went well today," she offered at her boss's back, hoping for some kind of exchange—the warmth they used to share. Penelope had a memory of enjoying coffee with Nora in the cafeteria upstairs. Of laughing eas- ily. She had no idea when that had changed, but she suspected it was related to Penelope's furtiveness. Her darting in and out of the office rather than explaining herself. Really, how could she? *Brett has a sensory deprivation chamber appointment today; I have to get the kids!*

Nora didn't turn around. "We'll see tomorrow." And she was gone.

Her chilliness was unsettling, but it was more than that. Penelope sat through the debrief, offering insight when she could but her thoughts fully drifting. She knew she did a good job—although not as much of it as she had in previous years. She didn't regularly work late or take the middle-of-the-night conference calls with China anymore. She found herself, with age, becoming less ambitious, not more.

"Tomorrow, Elias, will you run the room?"

Penelope's head snapped up. That was her job. She opened her mouth to speak, and Nora gave her a quick headshake. Elias was eight years younger than Penelope. A bachelor. She realized with sudden dread that he'd been in his office every time she'd left work the past few weeks. Had he been there when she came in? She couldn't remember.

On the drive home from work, she stopped at QuickShop, picked out a card each for Tara and Linc, and then, as an afterthought, grabbed a glossy, cellophane-wrapped *for my husband* card without even bothering to read it. She was bone tired. Not sure where her children were—all of her texts had gone unanswered. I'm stuck at work, catch a ride home from play, please. Her lone text to Brett—Can you handle dinner? Be home by 7, I hope—had been flagged only as delivered, not read.

At a stoplight, she thumbed through her phone, her finger landing neatly on Happy Valentine's Day from that morning, and she reread the exchange and knew without seeing her own face that she was smiling. This was what this small, harmless friendship did for her—could it be that bad? If she smiled amid a harrowing day simply by rereading their texts?

The inside of her house was dark, but the smell of something warm and garlicky hit her as soon as she opened the door.

"Brett?" she called, hanging up her coat, slipping off her pumps. In stocking feet, she padded to the kitchen, which was dark at first. A light switched on, a cacophony of "Surprise! Surprise!"

"Happy Valentine's Day!"

Tara, Linc, Brett stood around the kitchen table, Willa at the stove, Penelope's apron tied around her waist. They all grinned at her, waiting, expectant.

"Well," she said finally, her throat thick. "I wondered what happened to you all. I've been texting all day."

"Linc took my phone because he said I'd spoil it." Tara shot her brother a murderous look.

The table held enough plates for all of them and, in the center, two dozen red roses and a large, lacy heart-shaped box of chocolates. Penelope looked around. The kitchen was spotless, except for a decadent chocolate cake on a glass platter on the counter. She turned and looked at the living room—all the clutter was gone, the rugs freshly vacuumed. Underneath the scent of bubbling tomato sauce, Penelope whiffed a hint of Pledge.

"You all cleaned?"

"The whole house, even our rooms." Linc rolled his eyes in the direction of his sister. Linc's room, always neat as a pin, had likely required almost no attention.

"Did this take you all day?" Penelope asked, incredulous.

"We had a half day of school." Tara pressed her lips together, maybe in disapproval, Penelope couldn't tell.

"Oh my God, I forgot." Penelope's hand flew to her mouth. Oh God. She never forgot them. *Never.* It was always on the calendar. But the audit. Nora. Elias. Brett. *Jaime,* her inner voice whispered, cool as the devil on her shoulder.

Willa waved her away. "It's fine. It's all fine!" She smiled broadly. "Your kids are popular. They got rides home, and their friends are charming!" Willa gave Linc a little bump with her elbow. Penelope rolled her eyes in mock annoyance: Linc must have gotten a ride home with his buddy Jerry Tamish. Brett had called him a real-life Eddie Haskell—all *thank you, Mrs. Cox,* and *Did you get your hair cut, Mrs. Cox?*

Brett came up behind Penelope, his hands flanking her hips, and kissed the top of her head, lingering more than usual. She heard the sharp intake of breath as he smelled her scalp, that earthy part of hair where clean shampoo and the essence of skin met. "We do manage to somehow get along without you," he whispered. "Although not always very well." Penelope felt herself lean back into him, closed her eyes. The way he rubbed her arms when he was soothing her, comforting her, showing affection. It felt strange to have these flashes of intimacy, familiar and foreign at the same time.

Willa motioned for them all to sit as she served lasagna, fresh from the oven. She turned down the dimmer over the table and lit two taper candles on either side of the vase of roses.

Penelope looked around the table at the shining faces of her family, and then at her old-new friend. *Willa did this.* Willa was fixing them. Bringing them all back together, whether she knew it or not, meant to or not. She'd done something similar all those years ago, not with sweetness but laughter. She used to be licentious—delighting in making Penelope blush and Flynn shift uncomfortably. Still, she'd come bursting through the door at six a.m., filled with stories about the men she'd gone home with. Everything felt dramatic, larger than real life. Bad sex, dramatic fights. *He wore a T-shirt to bed. Not the T-shirt he wore on the date. As in he took off one shirt, put on another shirt. Then had sex. Why? WHY?* They'd be bleary eyed in the kitchen, laughing too hard to drink their coffee.

Willa had mellowed with age, but she was still doing it. Her manicured hands flying as she talked rapid fire, the kids laughing; even Brett watched her, eyes shining. There were fewer curse words, and the stories were about her childhood, her teenage years, not about sex and heavy sweating men, but there she was anyway, using story to bring them together. Penelope could forget their shared history if she focused on the Willa here and now.

Penelope was filled with a rush of gratitude so strong it almost knocked the wind out of her. She couldn't remember the last time she'd sat down to a meal with her whole family without the need to tend to something—the next thing, the pressing thing. Without picking her words carefully, trying to mentally check something off the list. (*Was the director still giving Tara a hard time? How did Linc's science test go?*) But right now, at this moment, it all felt easy. She had no mental checklist. Tara dripped sauce immediately down her blouse, and Linc snorted and called it typical, and she tossed her napkin—cloth! Penelope had forgotten she owned cloth napkins!—and she saw both Tara and Linc sneak a sip of wine from Brett's glass, and Brett's eyes met hers across the table, and once again, she saw her husband through Willa's eyes and found him undeniably attractive.

After dinner, they cut into the cake made by Linc—one of his closest-held secrets was that he was an incredibly talented baker—and gorged themselves on moist cake with rich chocolate buttercream, until they all felt sick and sleepy. Finally, at eleven, Willa announced she would clean up and wanted everyone to go to bed.

"You've all made this Valentine's Day—a day that could have been incredibly difficult for me—a happy and memorable one. I'm so grateful." She wiped her eyes with the (cloth!) napkin.

Penelope stood up and put her arms around Willa from behind, hugging her old friend. She regretted not thinking to buy her a card with the rest of the family. Not even picking up a foil-wrapped candy heart. Did she regret the twenty years she'd avoided her? No, that was necessity. But they could start again, maybe. Maybe. Depending on how much Willa was willing to let slide. They'd never let each other avoid the hard conversations before, though. So many times they'd barged into each other's rooms, shut the door behind them: *Spill it, what's going on?*

"We're happy you're here," Penelope whispered, because she felt like she couldn't say any more. Her throat felt tight with tears, and she wasn't quite sure why. She looked at the beaming smiles of her family and was overwhelmed with her own gratitude. Willa hugged her back, her hand patting Penelope's forearm, and Penelope heard the familiar soft, almost imperceptible tinkling of jewelry.

Sliding beneath Willa's rolled-up sleeve was a gold-link bracelet. Clasped with a ruby heart.

CHAPTER TEN

February 15, 2020

Dawn filtered in through the bedroom curtains, hazy and insistent. Brett curled behind her, his arm slung heavily over her waist, his thighs against her thighs, skin to skin.

They hadn't slept naked in at least five years. Since the kids started barging into their room at all hours, no spaces left in the house were safe and private. She remembered the night before, a little wine-drunk. The Valentine's dinner glowing in her mind. The cards creased and crinkled, forgotten, in her purse while Brett presented her with the small jewelry box. A pair of diamond earrings.

She had opened it carefully, the eyes of her children shining as they bore witness to their parents' reunion. She could feel it in the house—a new electricity. She'd always felt this way about marriage, often wondering if every marriage was like this. Days, months, even a year, where everything felt off—little snipes at each other, quietly nursing private wounds—and then, something would change. A quick crackle of energy, a look, a gift, an olive branch. And then, something in her heart would inexplicably shift—those tectonic plates of love and lust and anger and fear, sliding past each other in halting motions like little earthquakes of the soul.

They'd find each other in bed, saying with their hands what they couldn't with their voices.

Except. Penelope had waited this whole year for the shift. Instead, she'd only found Brett leaving early in the morning, coming home at dinner. Searching for jobs hundreds of miles away. Without even telling her! She worked hard to file that one away. He would have told her eventually, he had pleaded with her that night. He would never have taken a job five hundred miles away. *I just need to know that I can still get the job. It was an ego thing.* He swore up and down he wouldn't have left. A tiny piece of her didn't quite believe it. Ever since that night—the night with Jaime and the chicken dinner and the fight—she still sometimes wondered what it would feel like to live alone, with only Tara and Linc. What if, *just what if,* Brett moved without her? Would it have been so bad, really? Lots of people divorced.

They divorced husbands who were employed. Divorces were expensive—lawyers and court fees and filing costs. She and Brett were barely making ends meet as it was. Besides, maybe it was just his midlife crisis. Didn't everyone get at least one? She'd schedule hers later, she always thought to herself with a wry twist to her mouth.

Sometimes, she even thought about leaving him. Leaving her husband. Aside from the money, things hadn't been so bad up until a year ago. They'd been a little dry, a little routine. But Penelope wasn't naive. She'd watched other parents in the neighborhood divorce, pick up with partners twenty years younger, just to come crawling back when all the wild newness ebbed away to reveal the dreary everyday person underneath—someone who still texted about going to the grocery store or threw their socks on the floor next to the hamper. She knew all about greener grass. Couldn't she stick it out, at least for a while? You had to make the effort to fix your marriage before you threw in the towel. And right now, in the thick of things, she didn't have the bandwidth for fixing anything. The battery for the living room television remote had been dead for six months. They'd all started just using their phones instead. It felt a little like that—finding workarounds to keep on going.

So, she stayed. Part obligation, part exhaustion, part necessity.

But still. He'd been living entirely in his own head and heart. She tried not to focus on the money—so much money spent on finding himself—yoga and therapy and even art classes (art classes!) for her wholly left-brained husband.

It sounded like a made-for-TV movie to say *he'd come back to her.* But it had finally happened. She'd hardly allowed herself to think the words. But it was how she felt: like she'd been living with a shell of a person, and now he was here in full. Present in mind, body, spirit. Penelope felt the release of that, a tiny pop of hope in her heart.

She hadn't said, *Brett, how much were these?* Or, *What credit card did you use?* She hadn't even thought those words until now, the new day shining its bright light on what she'd refused to see in the romantic glow of a candle.

His hand reached up, cupped her breast, made some noise of contentment deep in the back of his throat. Penelope moved his hand aside and sat up. He tugged on her wrist.

"Come back," he mumbled, his fingers tickling the inside of her thigh, inching up. "Can't you go in a little late? It's Saturday."

"No." She didn't mean to be sharp. But she'd told him yesterday. "It's an audit. I have to go in and catch up. I think I'm being replaced. I don't know, something is going on. Nora is . . ." She let her voice trail off. She hadn't told Brett about Nora's chilliness, her distance, the small ways Penelope seemed to be losing her purchase. It seemed a lot of ground to cover now, especially because she didn't trust herself to not let her own resentment creep in. To not let it slip that at least some of her work issues *might* be his fault. She knew them both well enough to know that she'd mention the calendar and he'd blow up, and she'd get exasperated and leave. No, it was better to change the pattern. "I'll explain later." She planted a kiss on his forehead and padded to the bathroom to get dressed. He grumbled and turned over, his back to her.

On the dresser, her gold bracelet glinted in the sunlight.

She had asked Willa last night: *Where did you find that? I have one just like it!*

She laughed and slid it off her wrist easily. *It's yours! I found it under the sofa and put it on so I wouldn't lose it. Then I completely forgot about it!* Her eyes had held Penelope's, wide and innocent, and Penelope had slid it over her own cuffed shirt.

When Penelope emerged from the bathroom fifteen minutes later, Brett was half-asleep again. On the dresser, she slipped the bracelet onto her wrist. *A day late, but not short,* she thought.

"What will you do today?" She'd meant it as a simple question, but it came out heavy with implication, and he answered her flatly, without opening his eyes.

"I don't know yet, Pen."

"I didn't mean anything by it," she amended lamely, her hands spread, as though grasping for something. He didn't reply, and she kissed his forehead and smelled his soap fresh from his shower the night before and felt his breath on her neck and let her lips linger there, silently sorry. Then she left.

The office was quiet—only a few people catching up from the week—and Penelope opened her email to 622 new messages. Audits didn't leave a lot of time for standard business; she'd fallen woefully behind. She clicked and read and filed and categorized, made notes to herself, and tackled some of the smaller, quick questions. The day seemed to pass in a slow glaze of time. She felt someone quickly touch her shoulder, and she startled, turned around. Nora.

"Great job, we can always count on you," Nora said, distractedly, a thin, impersonal smile on her lips. Penelope almost called her back, asked her to run upstairs with her for a coffee, but felt the buzz of her phone in her pocket before she had the chance. She looked at the caller ID—Willa.

"Hey, I was wondering if you needed anything today." Willa's voice was distant, tinny.

Penelope almost said no, but then checked the time on her laptop. After three! "Would you want to pick Linc up from lacrosse practice this afternoon? I'm running a bit behind, and I can't get in touch with Brett," she lied.

Why didn't she call Brett? She thought of his deep sigh that morning, the grumble in his voice. The way he chilled when she asked him about his time, his day, an automatic defense to her. She'd spent so much time the past year grilling him: *What are you doing? Where are you going? What are you spending? What the fuck is EFT meditation?* She remembered the feel of his hands on her waist, his breath on her neck. If she called him, would he just tell her he couldn't come? Would he just disappoint her again? If he so much as gave her one sigh, she would snap at him, and she knew it. She could already feel her nerves strung tight from the day, raw and frayed. She was working on a Saturday, and he was . . . what? At spin class? Again, cycle breaking felt important.

"Of course!" Willa's voice was warm, even excited. "Anything you need, Pip, just ask! I'm so grateful for all you've done this past week. I'd love to help."

Penelope sagged against the back of her chair and closed her eyes. It was so easy, then. Such a relief to reach out, ask for help, and simply be given it. A luxury she hadn't known existed. Linc was taken care of. Brett was none the wiser.

Sasha. Jaime. She realized she'd never written him back.

She'd forgotten entirely about him for more than twenty-four hours.

Jaime had been her lifeline for months now. Had a bad day? Text Jaime. Frustrated with Nora? Text Jaime. He was the one who knew all about her boss, her work situation. She'd even, she remembered guiltily, talked to Jaime when she'd found a long cigarette bent in the bottom of Tara's duffel bag. Not Brett.

She would have told Brett, but he had gone on a retreat for two days. *No phones,* he'd said at the time. When was that? October? Just an overnight. A wellness retreat. He was burned out from job hunting and needed one night away. One night seemed harmless to Penelope. She'd cleaned the house, picking up the kid clutter, distracted the whole time by her pinging phone. Silly, off-handed, funny, distracting texts. Then she found the cigarette.

What do I do? Penelope took a quick picture of it, pinched between her thumb and index finger, and sent it off.

Jaime replied instantly. First one you've found?

Yes.

Let it go for now, I think? IDK. Keep your eyes open. Have you ever smelled smoke on her?

No.

Eh, maybe let it ride. Throw it away. She'll figure you've seen it on her own. But I have no idea what I'm doing either. Want me to ask Sash?

God no!!!!

Ok. It's fine. Just breathe—this is what I tell myself.

God, you sound like Brett.

Ha! We'll get through it.

And with those four words, Jaime felt more like her partner than Brett had in a year. Their texting became incessant. Every thought that popped into her head—no matter how ridiculous—she dashed off to Jaime. He responded with enthusiasm to each and every one.

It was a drug—to be known that well. *To be known is to be loved.* Who said that? She used to test him and say utterly inane things. *I've always felt self-conscious about the size of my hands. They're enormous.* Or, *Do you ever wonder if people in Paris daydream about America? Do our lives seem glamorous to someone? Are we destined to always want what we do not have?* His responses were witty and quick. It was the speed that really got to her: How did he know exactly what to say just that fast? The perfect thing to make her laugh, sometimes think about for hours later? *The only enormous thing on you is your brain. Stop thinking so much. Wanting what we can't have is the human condition.* And that one made her heart stop.

Then one day, maybe six weeks ago, a card to her office, in a thick cardstock envelope. In the bottom of the envelope was a thin silver chain that held a ring. The word *B R E A T H E* carved on the inside. It wasn't expensive jewelry—probably ordered from the internet for less than ten dollars. The card itself, a hand-printed watercolor. Jaime's hobby. He'd sent it through the mail, left it mostly unsigned, save for his artist mark, to give her an easy out. *If wanting what we can't have is the ultimate human experience, I've never been more human. I have no idea if you feel the same way. I think you do. What is the upper limit on lifetime heartbreak? I've had one and didn't think I'd make it. I don't want to do it again, but the bitch of it is, it seems inevitable. I'm breathing. Are you?*

She could bring it up, or not. Push it further, or not. She never brought it up, and neither did he. But sometimes late at night, with Brett sighing softly beside her, the words would float up through her subconscious: *I've never been more human,* and she'd wake unsettled.

Jaime was the one she turned to, not Brett.

Until now. Maybe all she had needed was another person—someone to be there and a way to return the favor. There was something humanizing about offering help and receiving help in return. Something she hadn't known she'd been missing so deeply.

Penelope pressed the heel of her hand into her closed eye. She opened her incoming texts and saw one unread.

Where've you been? You breathing? You didn't get yourself fired, did you? I'm kidding.

Then, hours later, one more. Miss you.

CHAPTER ELEVEN

February 17, 2020

"What's the plan, do you think?" Brett stood in the bedroom doorway, shirtless in his boxers, his face half covered in shaving cream, his hand clutching a razor. Penelope dropped her purse, laptop bag, keys, and cell phone onto the makeup vanity on her side of the room and began making the bed.

"The plan with what?" she asked absently. It had been yet another long, heavy day. Her feet ached; her back twinged if she shifted too far left or right. The audit felt never ending. The workdays were starting to blend together. She'd put in some more catch-up time on Sunday from her home office. She'd been coming home later, almost eight or nine o'clock. Some days she'd arrange rides home for the kids; once she had to ask Willa again. She felt guilty about that. She did ask Brett, but he had therapy at six thirty twice a week. He looked a little guilty when he said it.

"With your little friend?" Brett's voice held an edge.

Penelope hated that expression, as though Willa hadn't sat with all of them at dinner last night, laughing, talking, drinking wine. As if she hadn't offered them all, at worst, a pleasant distraction but at best a much-needed helping hand, a way to see themselves and each other through the eyes of an outsider only to discover they still liked what they saw. Tara and Linc tossed barbs across the dinner table while Willa poured them each a very small glass of wine. (*They do this in Europe, you know! Fewer instances of alcoholism there.*) Brett only raised his eyebrows, and Penelope suppressed a smile, and Tara and Linc must have thought, *Could our parents be . . . cool?*

And now she got *little friend*. Penelope blew her breath out through her nose and mentally counted to ten.

"I don't actually know the plan. I thought we were enjoying her company?" Penelope intoned it like a question, but it came with a side of attitude, and Brett knew it.

"We can enjoy her company and still ask her how long she plans on staying."

"You seemed to be enjoying her company last night."

Brett held still, his razor paused in midair. "What does that mean?"

Penelope had come in late, as she had the past four nights, to Willa stirring something over the stove, the air suffused with garlic and fresh basil and the rich aroma of a bubbling white-wine sauce. Penelope had hovered just beyond the doorway, in the living room, watching them with interest. Brett stood behind her, his face pinked from the steam, as she fed him off a wooden spoon. They were both laughing, and Brett's hand rested lightly between Willa's shoulder blades. A shifting sensation that Penelope was watching a typical married couple prepare dinner—that *she* was the interloper.

Penelope sighed. "Nothing. I'm sorry. I don't know what's gotten into me." She plumped the pillows on the bed and sank down into the comforter. She could still see Brett in the bathroom, a direct line from the bed to the sink. "I haven't asked her. She asked for a few days. Maybe a week. I can probably bring it up tomorrow. Is that okay?"

Brett went back to shaving, grunting in acquiescence.

Truthfully, she had started enjoying Willa immensely. It had begun to feel nice that she had a confidante again. She'd forgotten that—in the years she became a mom of toddlers, then young kids, then middle school, and now, she'd made friends and lost them. Transient and shallow, mom friendships seemed to shift with the wind.

But long ago, Willa had been a bedrock friend. Foundational and solid. Could Penelope forgive herself long enough to trust her? Maybe. If she didn't think about it too deeply. Could she forgive Willa for what little part she'd played in their shared tragedy? Possibly. If she just let herself enjoy the feeling of knowing and being known by another woman again. That spark of recognition—*I see you*—that only women shared.

They sipped a glass of wine at night, usually bundled on the back deck in the frigid winter air. They talked a little about their year at the Church House, more about their time together at Penn. Stories about Jack—light, funny stories. That only skated on the surface, both of them avoiding any depth.

They still did not talk about the fire. They didn't talk about Grace. They talked instead of jobs (Willa had been a librarian during the day and a waitress at night). Kids (Willa had none). Family and politics and friendships. Willa had a knack for asking questions, and it seemed like Penelope would retire at night, her mouth dry from talking, and realize Willa had barely said a word. So unlike the girl she used to know.

"Are you okay?" Penelope asked. Brett looked tired, pale, in the mirror; his hand shook just a bit as he scraped his cheek.

"I think so," he said. "I've felt a little off all day—a little dizzy. I thought maybe it was all the booze." He grinned ruefully. "We've been having fun with Willa, you're right. But I'm not used to it."

Now she was Willa, not her *little friend*. Penelope sat upright, a sudden thought. "Could you be anemic?"

Brett had a genetic enzyme disorder—certain medications and common infections could trigger acute anemia, but he'd been careful, and it had never been an issue in their life. It wasn't something Penelope frequently thought about; in fact, she'd often forgotten it entirely. Brett knew to avoid certain anti-inflammatories, to watch for anemia when he got a cold or respiratory infection, and exercise became vitally important. The increase in alcohol could certainly affect his blood sugar. A mild anemia was usually righted with a trip to the doctor, a blood test. Whether he would pursue it or not was a different matter—why see a doctor when you could see a holistic nutrition specialist? With that uncharitable thought, Penelope went downstairs in search of Willa.

In the kitchen, Willa hummed as she pulled ingredients out of the refrigerator for tonight's feast.

"Willa, you don't have to do this every day. We can order in." Penelope sat at the island and watched her, the sinewy curve of her calves, the round pink balls of her feet. She was more muscular, leaner than she used to be. The Willa she used to know was all soft curve and shine. She was still made up—black spiky lashes and red lipstick, liquid foundation smoothed over the dips and valleys of forty-two-year-old skin.

"I love this—are you kidding me?" She flipped her hair behind her shoulder, tied it in a loose knot to keep it out of her eyes. "I forgot how much I liked to cook. We used to eat out a lot. Trent, well . . ." She moved her wrist around in a circle, waved her hand a little as her voice trailed off.

"You didn't used to cook," Penelope said with a laugh. "You were the queen of pasta seventeen different ways."

Willa snapped a dish towel in Penelope's direction and shot her a playful glare. "I learned. Later. I mean, everyone has to grow up sometime."

We can't all be Peter Pan.

"What's on the menu for tonight, then?" Penelope asked, surveying the countertop: cornmeal and shallots, okra, tomatoes, and a block of cheddar cheese.

"Polenta and okra. My southern grammy's recipe."

"Oh yes. I forgot you were born in the South. Georgia?"

"Louisiana!" She was up on her toes, digging in a cupboard, her voice muffled. "Aha! I knew I'd find it in here. Lord knows how old it is." She shook the sweet paprika in Penelope's face.

Penelope could only shrug. They weren't gourmet cooks in the Cox household. Usually too many moving parts—meals had to be quick, effortless, yet still hit all the bases. Which basically meant including a frozen vegetable 90 percent of the time.

"Pen?"

Brett leaned heavily against the doorway, his eyelids drooping, the left side of his body weak and sagging. "I think you have to take me to the hospital. Something is definitely wrong."

"Oh my God!" Willa dropped the spice jar, her hands flying up to her mouth. "Is he having a heart attack?"

"I don't know." Penelope felt panicky. Was he? A stroke? She told Willa to call 911 while she quickly googled *stroke test* on her phone.

He passed the stroke test with flying colors: his hands never wavered—held evenly in front of him—his smile was even and straight. He didn't slur his words. "Brett, what have you been taking? Supplements? You know you have to be careful—that stuff is not regulated. Who knows what's in it!"

Once when they first got engaged, Brett went into hemolytic crisis, but they could never figure out the reason behind it. The best the doctors could figure was that he was drinking a soy protein shake every day. He didn't actively avoid soy in his current diet; he just didn't eat very much of it if he could help it.

Brett sank into the chair at the island and closed his eyes, his face ashen as he concentrated on breathing. Penelope took his pulse, trying to parse his rhythms from hers, which was nearly impossible. Her heart was hammering a mile a minute.

"Brett, talk to me, okay? Tell me what you did today?" She cursed herself—that innocuous question had become a marital trip wire for them.

"I had a doctor's appointment," he said slowly. "Then therapy. Then the gym."

Two EMTs made their way into the kitchen. Penelope looked around wildly, seeing no sign of Willa. She must have let them in. The small kitchen felt claustrophobic. They checked his heart, his lungs, strapped him down to a stretcher, asking him an endless line of questions that he seemingly couldn't answer, his eyes clouded and fogged. He kept looking up at Penelope, blinking and slow. This was not Brett.

"He has a G6PD deficiency." Penelope told them several times, not sure if they'd heard her or if they even knew what that meant. They shuffled around the stretcher, past each other, past Penelope, the room filling up with the smell of bodies and the plastic chemical smell of latex.

"What has he eaten the past few days?" asked the man as he examined Brett's eyes. "Some jaundice," he said over his shoulder, and a woman wrote it down. "Tachycardia."

"I . . . don't know," Penelope stammered.

"Fava beans?" the woman asked, her voice clipped. Penelope shook her head. Behind her, Willa made a small yelp.

"The ravioli!" Her voice shook. "It was a recipe I used to make years ago. Fava beans and pesto as ravioli filling. Is he allergic?"

"Favism," the female EMT said to her partner. "He has acute hemolytic anemia."

"Oh my God!" Willa said again, sinking down onto the tile floor. Penelope wanted to shake her. "Is he going to die?"

"Willa!" Penelope snapped. There was a flurry of activity—indiscriminate talk between the two technicians, words and phrases that Penelope couldn't decipher. They instructed Brett to breathe slowly and deeply, but his eyes remained unfocused. Did he even hear them? Penelope felt the panic in her throat. *Oh God.* How would the kids deal with it if something happened to Brett? How would she? She had never heard Brett talk about favism. What the hell was that? *Was he going to die?*

The EMTs moved out, Brett on a stretcher, instructing Penelope to follow in her car. Woodenly, Penelope found her purse, her car keys.

"What if I killed him?" Willa's fingernails bit into Penelope's arm, but Penelope shook her off.

"Stay home for the kids, okay? Please?" Penelope didn't know what time it was—it felt like hours had passed since she watched Brett shave in the bathroom.

Willa nodded, tears tracking down her cheeks. How odd, thought Penelope, that her own eyes stayed so dry. Why could Willa cry for her husband but Penelope could not?

Willa said again, "Oh God, what if I killed him?"

CHAPTER TWELVE

Willa, present

Sometimes she thought she was incapable of love. True, real love so deep it almost broke your heart just to be in it. If she hadn't seen it in real life, for a brief few months after college, she might not have believed it was real. If she hadn't seen the way Grace smiled at Jack when she thought no one was looking, the way she accepted him in ways the rest of them never could, her moony gaze when she talked about him. She knew his weaknesses, that all he wanted was to be loved, completely, by everyone he met. That he needed that approval the way other people needed air, food, water, and didn't hate him for it the way the rest of them sometimes did.

And they did sometimes hate him. That loud laugh echoing off the stone walls of the great room, the way Penelope would wince when he came into the room and filled it up so completely. The way Flynn watched Jack move out of the corner of his eye—like a handler tracked a tiger. There was a subtle, fine thread of animosity connecting them all, tying it all together: love, lust, dependence, anger, even hate. All five of them baked together in that hothouse of a church, each turning into something completely new and unknown, from wholesome to damaged.

It seemed to her that the ways they seemed to damage each other were endless. Until Grace, anyway.

She didn't see that kind of love between Penelope and Brett. She wondered if it would have gone away had Grace and Jack gotten married. Faded into the dry ash of a once fiery ember, dampened by years of *Can you pick up milk at the store?* and *Did you forget to pay the cable bill?* Was it inevitable that wild love turned to tolerance? Passion to obedience?

Penelope and Brett seemed barely tolerant. Oh, they put on a decent show most of the time. Penelope did a lot of talking through her teeth with a tight-lipped smile. But she saw his surprise when Pip called him sweetheart. No, that was a show.

She couldn't see them being wildly in love.

Penelope's car screeched out of the driveway, following the ambulance. The kids would be home soon. She'd been able to pick her way through Pip's bedroom and a little bit of the office in the previous days, but Brett was always around—coming and going with no schedule. It had become impossible. Well, not anymore. A two-day hospital stay would do them all good.

She started with the downstairs bookcase—a wedding album.

Pip's dress had been simple: a long ivory sheath dress, no veil. A courthouse marriage. Brett looked handsome in a dark-blue suit, no tux. An older couple stood behind Brett, a lone woman, about Penelope's age, resting her hand on Pip's shoulder.

In one picture, he cradled her hand as they danced and laughed into her shoulder. Her head was turned away, but even from the back, she looked to be smiling. So maybe love was a factor then.

The date: July 12, 2001. A little more than a year after the fire. Interesting. How had they met? She would have to remember to ask Pip later. Of course, after the medical crisis was over.

Brett wouldn't die. Hemolytic anemia was rarely, if ever, fatal. The worst he would need is a blood transfusion and a few days at the hospital for monitoring. She thought it was interesting that Penelope didn't know that. Some people could go their whole lives with G6PD and never go into hemolytic crisis. But still. You'd think she would know *something* about it. If she loved him.

Upstairs in the office, she started with the desk drawers. Bills, insurance paperwork, old tax filings. Semi-interesting. They used to make a lot of money—close to $500,000 a year. Now they were down to less than two fifty—all from Penelope, she figured. Quite a fall from grace. She wondered what they had to give up in losing over half their income. Lavish vacations? They were still able to make the mortgage payments, then. Where did the money they used to make go?

The bottom drawer, stuffed with papers, unorganized and overfilled. Receipts for auto repair, cell phone bills. A credit card bill. Owed close to $50,000. Ah, that made sense. She scanned the charges: health spas and therapy offices. Penelope was right, then—Brett was blowing through their money. At a quick glance, Penelope barely spent a dime.

The office had a small closet that contained wire shelving, held office supplies, a few plastic totes of keepsakes, labeled *Brett* and *Penelope*. She pulled out the tote labeled *Penelope* and sifted through the contents. More junk: school pictures, half-filled notebooks, an apology letter from Tara, a dried flower. At the bottom, buried, a small card, the front adorned with a simple black-and-white flower with a splash of red and green. A homemade watercolor, she realized. Unsigned. She turned it over. On the back, an artist's mark. *JBH2019.*

If wanting what we can't have is the ultimate human experience, I've never been more human. I have no idea if you feel the same way. I think you do. What is the upper limit on lifetime heartbreak? I've had one and didn't think I'd make it. I don't want to do it again, but the bitch of it is, it seems inevitable. I'm breathing. Are you?

Well, now. Things just got interesting.

CHAPTER THIRTEEN
Then: Locks on the Outside

Willa stumbled upstairs to the kitchen, her eyes bleary and mouth open in a pant. She plunked down heavily at the kitchen table, and Penelope poured coffee for her from the carafe that Penelope assumed was Flynn's, because anything bougie, luxury, or unnecessary must have come from Flynn. The rest of them lived like savages most of the time.

"How was your first night?" Penelope inquired politely, and Willa gave her a withering look.

"Good, except I'm hungover as hell. Do we have any food?"

Penelope motioned to the refrigerator and shrugged. "I haven't looked."

Willa crossed the room and opened the door and gasped. The fridge was stocked with fruits and vegetables, cream and milk and butter and eggs. More than anything they'd seen in four years of college, where a chunk of sliming cheese might sit on a refrigerator shelf for a month alone.

"Where did all that come from?" Flynn stood perched on the steps. He'd run, showered, and changed into black cotton shorts and a pink golf shirt.

"It came from me," Jack said from the winding staircase. "We aren't college students anymore—let's try to behave like responsible adults, what do you think?" He descended the rest of the way, whistling. Jack always whistled—usually something unknown, sometimes pop music from the radio; once she swore it was "How Will I Know," by Whitney Houston, and Willa was merciless about it. "We've never all lived together before—should we make a plan? Everyone gets a dinner day? Five days, five of us. Saturday and Sunday are for takeout?"

Flynn, Willa, and Penelope gawped at him, but he kept talking, pouring coffee. Jack was unusually dressed up, almost like Flynn—clean, pressed shorts, a knife-edge crease down the front. His computer messenger bag slung across his chest and tucked behind him. His hair slicked back with gel. He looked like a model. Penelope felt her face flame, caught Willa's eye above her mug, her sleepy countenance transforming momentarily into shock, then a flash of irritation.

"Where are you going?" Penelope asked dumbly. As far as she knew, none of them had jobs—at least not yet. She had googled the town of Deer Run and saw a used bookstore in town. She sniffed the air. "Is that . . . cologne?"

Jack turned quickly, gave her a level glare. "No." A lie.

"I'll take Tuesdays." Willa yawned, her blonde hair wild around her face. Her cheeks puffed pink with amusement. "I can't cook for shit, but I can make pasta about twenty different ways."

Flynn looked from Willa to Jack to Penelope, and his face cracked with laughter. "That's pathetic."

"What, the cologne or the pasta?" Jack asked, his back still turned to them.

"What?" Willa protested. "Look, my money is on Flynn or Bree to be our resident chef. Penelope probably has two, maybe three dishes that she calls a specialty, and y'all know I spent undergrad eating bagged noodles and raw carrots. And Jack . . . who knows? I bet he's a grill man. That's like a testosterone-laden way of cooking."

Jack turned to them, cradling a coffee mug he'd found in the cabinet, and grinned. "Cooking with testosterone? This is a thing?"

"So you never answered the question," Penelope persisted. "Where are you going?"

"I"—Jack took a sip of coffee quietly—"am writing a book. At the coffee shop in the square."

He paused for a group reaction. Flynn looked impressed, like he wanted to ask a question. Willa surreptitiously rolled her eyes. As the one closest to Jack, she was likely the one who was most familiar with his broad proclamations and infrequent follow-through.

Penelope kept her face neutral, not wanting to appear overeager. "You can take my car if you want; the keys are always in the center console."

"No worries. I'll walk—it's beautiful out." He gave her a bright smile. "Thanks, though."

The Church House was situated down a fairly isolated street, at the end of a long dirt driveway, about a mile from the center of town. Penelope stood up quickly. "Actually . . . mind if I walk with you? I wanted to check out the bookstore in town. I'm thinking . . . of applying for a job there."

Willa raised her eyebrows. "Since when?" she asked, and Penelope shrugged, trying to slide behind her chair. Willa reached out and pinched Penelope's arm, the soft pad of skin behind her elbow.

"What the hell?" Penelope rubbed at the spot, softly cursing, and glared at Willa. She'd always hated when Jack and Penelope ended up doing something alone, without her. "Do you want to come with us?" Penelope asked, with exaggerated obligation. Willa snorted and buried her nose in her coffee, abjectly not pursuing any job leads on day number one. Penelope felt her irritation pitch and fall. Willa was always unpredictable—quick to anger but just as quick to laugh. It kept them all on their toes. Or on edge, depending on how you looked at it. She slipped past her and headed downstairs to change.

The bedrooms were small, just enough room for a double bed, a dresser, and a nightstand, more like dormitory living than many of the apartments they'd left behind. The carpets were old, gray blue, and thin—the same in every room. Jack had grand ambitions of pulling up the carpeting and refinishing the hardwood while they were there. He suggested once that they consider sweat equity—helping his cousin repair and finish the house in exchange for living rent-free. Penelope changed, quickly, from the tubs of her things that had been delivered by the moving guys the day before. She wondered briefly what had happened to Bree.

The sky cleared, and the sun beat down, hot and suffocating on the dusty driveway. They walked in comfortable silence, but Penelope felt heavy. Something about Willa's face when she said she'd walk to town with Jack. And Bree was missing. The whole house felt off kilter. She took a deep shuddering breath, more dramatically than she'd intended.

"He is rich who owns the day, and no one owns the day who allows it to be invaded with fret and anxiety," Jack said, nudging her with his elbow.

Penelope couldn't help but laugh. "What?"

"It's an Emerson poem," Jack said, rubbing the end of his nose, turning it red. "I'll find you the whole thing. You would benefit from reading it."

"Why?" Penelope didn't know whether to be offended and jostled him back.

"Sometimes . . ." He stopped and started again. "It seems like you carry the weight of the world around, you know? You're always so *serious*. Or worried? I don't know. I think about that line a lot: *He is rich who owns the day*. I try not to analyze what happened yesterday or think about what might happen tomorrow; it's all a tad bit pointless, right?"

"Well, maybe," Penelope murmured noncommittally. It seemed to her that *some good* came out of self-reflection, even if it was just personal growth. Not that she expected much personal growth out of Jack either way. She didn't have nearly enough liquor in her system to tackle existentialism and decided to change the subject. "Why don't you tell me what your book is about?"

"I'm not telling anyone." He shrugged. "It's the beginning stages now. I've tried this before, you know. To write a novel."

"And?"

"A bunch of manuscripts at various word counts ranging from eight thousand to fifteen thousand in a dusty folder on my thumb drive." Jack ran a hand up through his thick black hair. If Penelope didn't know better she'd think he was self-conscious.

"Okay, then what genre?" Penelope was never one to give up easily. People were usually surprised at her persistence. She always thought she looked like the kind of girl who would relent immediately.

"Ummm . . . maybe YA? But literary. It's a coming of age."

Penelope tried not to roll her eyes, but Jack caught her look anyway and laughed. "Look, I'm not a navel gazer by nature, but . . . well, it's half a memoir."

"So it's about a boy growing up in Brooklyn?"

"Yeah, kind of. Growing up Hispanic." He slid a glance at her.

Penelope studied him. She'd never thought about his ethnicity before; he never seemed to attach any heritage to his own identity. Not like Bree, who seemed to live and breathe Ireland: culture, music, food, posters hung on the wall of her apartment at UPenn.

"Avila?" Penelope asked. Jack's last name.

"My mother died of ovarian cancer when I was five. I have one memory of her. My father—he's Cuban. Kind of a dick, most of the time." He shrugged. "Still, I wasn't white. I'm *not* white. People don't really know that, though. It's just a weird space to be—knowing I could check a box and not checking it because it feels like a sham or something. I *look* white."

"What's the memory?" The humid air enveloped them like a bubble, and Penelope felt like she filled her lungs deep with water.

He pointed up to the building they stood in front of. Penelope hardly realized they'd walked all the way to the bookstore. She reached out and touched Jack's sleeve. "What's the memory, Jack?"

He gave her a thin-lipped, watery smile, the moment broken, and chucked her under the chin. "Ah, I'll tell you another time. Go get your job, okay?"

Shaking off disappointment, Penelope asked, "Do you want me to come get you when I'm done?"

"Nah." He was already turning around to walk to the coffee shop on the opposite corner. "I'll be home around dinnertime." His voice was kind, but distant. He gave a half wave and jogged across the street. Penelope pushed open the bookstore door.

—⁓—

When Penelope let herself back in the Church House a few hours later, the place was quiet and cool. Everyone had gone off on their own—to explore Deer Run, or maybe to venture out to the backyard. Maybe hiding in their own private spaces. Penelope ended up back in her little room, making her bed neatly, unpacking throw pillows, a knitted afghan that was a gift from her aunt when she'd left for college. Penelope had few possessions of her own, having only rented a small room in an apartment off campus for her senior year. She didn't know her roommates well; she'd answered an ad at the end of her junior year. She had no couches, tables, chairs, end tables. Just a comforter set that she'd purchased years before at a chain store.

Her little basement windows were open to the balmy warmth—there was no central air-conditioning, but the shade of pines around the church cooled off the living space. The subterranean bedrooms were almost chilly.

She could hear Willa in the kitchen, singing. Willa always sang—her voice clear and strong. Mostly Joni Mitchell (*She's my range, exactly,*

Willa had said), sometimes Norah Jones. Deep, rich altos with a jazzy melody. Penelope leaned into the sound, trying to make out which song. "It's coming on Christmas." Ah, "River," then. God, she loved that song.

She gave a small yelp when Bree appeared in her doorway, silent as a mouse. Her pale face even whiter than usual, her eyes narrowed.

"Where have you been all day?" Penelope asked. "Everyone's been looking for you!"

"I've been exploring," Bree hissed and beckoned to Penelope. Penelope followed her out to the hallway, and Bree continued in a quiet voice. "Look, the bedroom doors all lock from the outside."

The locks were square, black, iron, the kind that used a skeleton key. Penelope swung open her own door and looked at the lock—the exact same from both sides. It was a double-keyed lock.

"They probably used to be storerooms, don't you think?"

Penelope shrugged. The key that would have fit the lock was old, probably long gone. The inside had a secondary slide latch above the door handle. Installed recently, it was new, likely to be able to keep out tenants or guests. Nothing about it felt sinister or worthy of Bree's suspicion.

"It's weird," Bree said, her voice cut with danger, but Penelope still didn't really understand the urgency.

Bree always unsettled Penelope for reasons she could never pinpoint. She was sort of dreamy and flighty, but underneath, Penelope got the sense that she was always planning something. She had a manipulative edge about her. Always looking for an angle somehow. Although Penelope had once tried to say something similar to Willa, who had just laughed. *Bree? Manipulative? She doesn't even know which end is sky and which is ground.*

"You can probably just take yours off," Penelope offered, but Bree clenched her jaw.

"Not the point." She started walking away, motioning again for Penelope to follow her. At the far end of the hall was a small door, about half the height of the bedroom doors, the doorway arched to a point. She pushed it open easily, and it swung inward. A storage closet. The one wall contained shelves with toilet paper, towels, presumably stocked by Parker or maybe even Jack. Penelope followed Bree all the way into the storage room, and Bree reached behind her, shut the door. The only light came from under the door, a thin lemon slice of fluorescence.

They stood in darkness for a second, Bree's minty breath on Penelope's cheek. Her hair smelled like fresh rain, her fingertips cool on Penelope's arm and then her waist as she slipped past her, and Penelope felt her heart hitch. What was she doing? In the back of the closet, Bree pushed against the back wall. It swung in to reveal a dark dirt hallway.

Penelope gasped.

"I know, right?" Bree's voice was thready in the dim light, and all Penelope could see was the bright sclera of her eyes. "It gets crazier—just wait."

"Do the others know about this?" Penelope followed Bree into the hallway, which widened to accommodate a set of stone stairs.

Bree shook her head. "Don't tell anyone. It's just for us."

Why? Penelope wanted to ask but did not. It was Bree; she might not even get an answer.

They crept silently up the stairs, and Bree counted thirty steps before the stairwell narrowed to a landing. The landing held nothing but an old wooden ladder. Effortlessly, Bree climbed the five ladder rungs and pushed up on the ceiling above their heads.

She disappeared up through the trapdoor, and Penelope followed her, her heart wild and aching with anticipation. She placed her feet carefully on each rung, which wiggled a little with age and lack of use.

When Penelope finally emerged through the ceiling, she found herself standing in a long, narrow bedroom, the open trapdoor barely noticeable in the floor. Bree jumped a little, clapping her hands together silently. "Look where we are!" Breathless with excitement.

"Do you think he even knows this exists?" Penelope asked.

Bree shook her head, her eyes wide. "Don't tell him, okay? Promise?"

Penelope looked around—the familiar dark-blue bedspread, an acoustic guitar in the corner, a standing closet, open and filled with men's shirts pressed neatly together. Before she could stop herself, Penelope reached out, ran her hand along the clothes, the hangers making a musical trill as they clinked together.

Jack's bedroom.

CHAPTER FOURTEEN

February 18, 2020

Penelope had always thought she'd be the kind of wife who never left her husband's hospital bed. Who brought him water and ice chips and red Jell-O when he wanted it. As it turned out, she was not that kind of wife.

The hospital stay ended up being rather uneventful—which was a good thing, Penelope stressed to herself as she commuted from the hospital to work. Brett needed a transfusion, which was a standard treatment for a moderate hemolytic crisis. "No dialysis!" said the hematologist proudly, and Penelope almost choked on her dry bagel. Dialysis! God, had they come that close?

Brett assured her that he was fine, and it was surprising to Penelope how little convincing it took for her to leave him.

She popped home after work on Tuesday to make sure Tara and Linc were okay. She took a half day, was home by three. She had told Nora that Brett was in the hospital, and surprisingly Nora waved her off impatiently: *Why are you even here?* As though calling out during an audit would have been remotely tolerated.

Linc was in the kitchen, leaning over the island looking at a magazine over Willa's shoulder, and they were laughing softly. Her baby boy, his blond hair curled prettily over his forehead, his red full lips pursed as he read, his index finger and thumb massaging the hollow of his throat, like he always did in deep thought.

Linc and Tara had taken to Willa—she was Mom's fun friend, the one with the expensive makeup and bawdy mouth. They watched her comfort Penelope and flirt with Brett, and the ease with which she'd made herself at home, her arms flinging around any of them for any reason—so different from Penelope, who had never been naturally physical—fascinated and thrilled them.

Willa watched Linc, not the magazine, her eyes narrowed with intensity, and Penelope felt all the hair on her arms rise. The way she was looking at him felt predatory.

Or maybe she was being ridiculous.

Linc was a beautiful child, she knew this. Everyone looked at him this way, like they wanted to take a bite out of him, like his cheek might taste like vanilla custard or lemon meringue. His arms were long and graceful, his skin bronzed, even in February, his hair always clipped precisely, his nails trimmed straight. Nothing about him was boyish. She often wondered if he would grow into his manhood, or would he always be so dainty?

Willa turned then and gave Penelope a big, easy smile, and all the hair on Penelope's arms settled back down to its rightful place. She *was* being ridiculous. Willa handed Penelope a steaming cup of tea—chamomile, with the perfect amount of sugar and just a dash of milk—and Penelope drank it gratefully.

"Look." Linc shoved the local Wexford magazine in her direction. Tara's big toothy smile grinned back from the stage, her arms flung around her costar, a long-legged girl with blonde curling ribbons of hair. It was from last year's play, *The Music Man*, and Tara had been Ulele McKechnie Shinn, while the other girl had landed the role of Marion, the librarian. Tara hadn't batted an eye, Penelope remembered.

The article was about the thriving theater community in Wexford, with interviews from the parents whose kids were regularly in the county plays as well as high school teachers. Tara's name was mentioned three times, but Penelope's was not. Many of the other theater moms did not work—they trailed in at the end of rehearsal, sometimes bringing pizzas for dinner. Penelope smiled and pushed the magazine back in Linc's direction.

"That's great!" Penelope said with forced enthusiasm. "Has Tara seen it?"

"I showed her last night," Willa offered. "I picked her up from play practice."

"Linc!" Penelope interrupted. "Don't you have lacrosse tonight?"

"It's our day off, Ma." He grinned at her helpfully, then added as a prompt. "Remember?"

And Penelope did not. In fact, she couldn't quite remember either of their schedules at the moment. Was Tara coming home tonight? Was she up in her room? She felt too uncertain to ask. She was used to being so in control. This wild feeling was new, unsettling, and made her feel as though she was failing. At what, she couldn't have pinpointed. With Brett in the hospital, she hadn't so much as glanced at the family calendar. All her organization, the combined schedules, churned somehow just the same—with or without her.

"Can you take me to the meeting tonight, though? Just the monthly," Linc asked hopefully.

"Of course," Penelope said automatically.

"I can, if you want to get back to the hospital," Willa offered.

Penelope had spent a lot of time wishing for freedom—freedom of movement, of thought, of love, of priorities—and for once, she had it. Willa allowed her that by taking care of the things in her life that Penelope had been confined by—the schedules and the structure. In her darker moments, she used to think that if she could break free from the shackles of family life, maybe she'd be free enough to love her family as much as she was supposed to. No, that wasn't true. She loved them entirely, wholly. She sometimes struggled to find it through the litany of daily tasks. Didn't every mother wonder if she was doing enough? If she loved enough?

"No, it's fine. I'll take you." Penelope gave Linc a bright smile.

Linc blinked at her, sweet and fresh. "Are you all right, Ma?"

He called her Ma when he really, *really* loved her. When she brought him soup loaded up with crumbled crackers when he was sick. When she showed up to lacrosse practice with his mouth guard, left at home by accident. When she came home late, dead tired, and he rubbed her shoulders.

"I'm fine, sweetheart." She almost never called him sweetheart.

Willa cocked her head, studied her friend. "You don't seem all right."

"I'm tired. I hardly slept last night."

"Worried about Brett?" She clucked sympathetically.

Penelope murmured noncommittally.

When the doorbell rang, Penelope went in a fog to answer it. The lack of sleep was really starting to get to her.

"Where have you been?" Jaime stood on the doorstep, his hair gorgeously messed, his jeans fitted to his hips in a way that made Penelope feel electric. She hadn't expected him, had barely thought about him in the past few days, but now that he was standing here in front of her, she felt herself, bit by bit, start to unspool.

"Brett is in the hospital, my friend from college showed up out of nowhere . . . oh God, things have gone haywire." She pressed her hand to her forehead, and before she knew it, she was finally crying. It seemed to be her default with Jaime, to just start indiscriminately sobbing. So humiliating, so wildly out of her control.

He pulled her to him, his shirt smelling like sweat and sawdust and musk, her nose pressed right against the warm skin of his neck. He was wider than Brett through the shoulders, bigger all around, his arms thicker; the length of him against her felt like a blanket, the dull thud of his heart against hers, the splay of his fingers hot against her spine, and for a moment, she let herself go to pieces for the plain fact that someone was there to pick them up.

She felt, then, his deep intake of breath, a soft rumble in his throat, a noise made from both comfort and desire, and she was unable to parse one from the other, and she briefly wondered how it was that comfort often became desire like the lighting of a match. She reached up and without thought, traced the line of his jaw with her fingertip, and he muttered, "Jesus Christ, Pen," and she was so close to lifting up on her tiptoes just to feel the heat of that tender spot on her lips, the rough stubble against her mouth, and she imagined how he would taste, her tongue curling against the salt of his skin.

"Jaime?" Willa said from behind them, and Penelope jumped back as though burned.

From behind her, Jaime cleared his throat.

"Willa, hi," he said, his face breaking out into a smile that Penelope couldn't read. If he was flustered by the moment, she couldn't tell. He must have been, at least a little, shaken. She could still feel the warmth of his skin under her index fingertip.

"You two know each other?" Penelope asked, keeping her voice even, amiable. "Jaime is my neighbor. I don't know why when I saw him, I just started crying. I . . . haven't slept much. I'm sorry," she half turned, apologized to Jaime, and he waved her away.

"We're old friends." He smoothed over it, his arm slipping around her shoulder as though they'd been caught in a simple comforting hug. Penelope could feel the heat blazing on her cheeks. "So, Willa . . . is your friend from college?"

"We were roommates," Penelope and Willa said together, then laughed.

"How do you and Willa know each other?" Penelope asked, pasting a bright smile on her face. Her heart raced to keep up. *Her Jaime?*

Was he hers? She was both mortified to be caught midembrace and unsettlingly jealous that they'd already met. She glanced up at him; his smile was still frozen, but there was something lurking beneath it. He was pleased to see Willa.

"Ah, we met at Beans a few days ago." The small coffee stand a few blocks over.

"I bumped into him and spilled his coffee, so I bought him a new cup," Willa finished, her voice coy. Penelope looked from Willa to Jaime, whose attention had shifted from Penelope to Willa. His arm slid neatly off her shoulder, and he hooked his thumbs in his jeans pockets, adopting a casual, flirty stance.

"We've met every day since." Willa laughed. "Accidentally— absolutely not on purpose." Her voice was teasing, and she leaned backward, her hips swaying.

"Not on purpose at all." Jaime laughed, then looked at Penelope and coughed again. The silence between them settled, and Jaime and Willa exchanged a glance. About her? Penelope had no idea, and she felt her eye begin to twitch. The look between them had felt intimate and personal. "I didn't see you today! I was surprised."

"Well, Pip came home, and with Brett in the hospital, I felt like I should . . ."

"No, absolutely, you should go! Get coffee. Your daily coffee. How cute." Penelope was babbling, and she knew it.

"Are you okay?" Jaime asked her, and Penelope felt her blood pressure spike.

"Why does everyone keep asking me that?" She laughed, but it was shrill, cutting through the thick embarrassment. That's what she was, an embarrassment. How close she had come to kissing Jaime! God. And he'd been meeting Willa every day. So what? She was married. She had no claim on him; she knew that. He should be able to date. And Willa was single! They both deserved some kind of happiness, right? That was only fair.

God, she was so damn tired.

"You don't mind?" Willa asked, and Penelope waved her away, opening the door and practically shooing them together for their daily coffee date; the whole time, her stomach churned, her mouth cottony, her head a swirling cloud of confusing emotions, the most pervasive of which was piercing, all-consuming jealousy.

Willa's hips swayed as she walked down their sidewalk, and Jaime's hands stayed in his jeans pockets, his head bent toward her as she talked and motioned with her hands, and then they both threw their heads back and laughed. Willa punched him on the arm, a high-pitched *Oh God, stop it right now,* as he ducked away from her. They were unsettlingly cozy.

Penelope had no right to Jaime. She touched a finger to her lips, still tingling with the radiant heat of his skin. She could still feel his arms, the warmth of his fingertips through her thin blouse, his strangled *Jesus Christ, Pen.*

She was starting to come undone. Her feelings for Jaime were bubbling over, and the guilt clenched her stomach. Brett was in the *hospital.* What kind of wife battled attraction to another man with her husband in the hospital? A terrible one.

Everything felt like it was starting to unspool. Or maybe she just needed to sleep.

She ascended the steps in a fog and fell into her bed, kicking her pumps off until she heard them thump to the floor. The sleep felt immediate and deep, her unconscious pulling her under into heavenly oblivion. She didn't wake up until almost six hours later, confused, in the darkness of her bedroom. She blinked at the digital clock that read 10:11 p.m.

CHAPTER FIFTEEN

February 19, 2020

All in all, Brett was in the hospital for two nights and came home on the third day.

They helped him up to the guest bedroom, made a big deal about him, which he pretended not to love. Tara ran between the kitchen and the bedroom, fetching water and chicken broth. Brett claimed he wasn't hungry, but ever since his health kick started, his eating had become sporadic anyway. Had he been taking in enough calories? Maybe that's how his body ended up in acute anemia. Then the beans tipped the whole thing over the edge.

"It's better in here," Willa insisted. "I'll sleep on the couch downstairs. This way Penelope can go to work and won't wake you up!" She clapped her hands, and everyone snapped to attention. "Don't worry, I did all the laundry, washed the sheets and blankets. It's like your own little haven here."

Penelope felt the shiver up her spine. It *did* seem like it was boundary pushing—having someone around who was so helpful. Like the horror movie live-in nanny. But still. She was so tired all the time lately—and trying to keep up with their life while having Brett at the hospital. She also appreciated it. Could you appreciate something, even while acknowledging that it probably wasn't *exactly right*? Yes, until you couldn't. Tomorrow. Tomorrow she'd talk to Willa—ask her about her future. Her plans. Brett had wanted her to do that—only a few days ago.

Linc busied himself setting up the TV and streaming device in the guest room—they didn't typically watch television in their own bedroom, much to their kids' incredulity. But with nothing for Brett to do but rest, he'd need the distraction, Linc insisted.

"I really think I could just hang in my own bedroom," Brett said. "The doctor said a day or two of rest should do it. This seems like overkill."

"Dad, you needed a *transfusion*, for God's sake." Linc was exasperated.

"That's not as big a deal as it seems." But Brett seemed happy to have his pillows fluffed and meals delivered, just the same. "This all seems silly—like we're setting up a triage here."

"This way, Mom can come and go. Shower for work, fold laundry, and not bother you if you're sleeping." Tara, pragmatic to a fault. "Mom, unless you want him in the bedroom?" She held the remote control in her hand and paused in her pillow-fluffing endeavors.

"Whatever your father wants," Penelope said, waving her hand in Brett's direction. He smiled at her, trying to hold her gaze, but she looked away, feeling oddly disconnected from the whole scene.

Willa clucked around him, apologizing over and over and over again, her voice breaking and thin until finally Brett took her hand and said, slowly and seriously, "Willa, please stop. You didn't know, I didn't know. It was an accident. You beating yourself up helps no one. I'm fine, we're all fine, here." And Willa burst into tears.

Penelope felt a stab of tenderness for Brett and his kind little speech, so unlike his typical utilitarianism. Willa perched herself on the edge of his bed, announcing, "I'll just have to be your servant twenty-four seven. Whatever you need. Okay?" She looked from Penelope to Brett and back again. "Penelope can go to work, do her thing. I'll be here making sure everyone keeps trucking. I owe y'all that much, I really do." Her Louisiana accent was coming through thick. Penelope remembered that from Deer Run—emotion made her twang come out. She swiped a thumb under both eyes. In the sunlight, the pink knot of scar shimmered. She looked older than her forty-two years, her eyes red rimmed, lines formed around her mouth.

Willa hadn't let go of Brett's hand. Penelope stared at their entwined fingers and began to feel cold all over.

"You'll want some chicken soup. Lots of chicken, lots of veggies, okay? No supplements," Penelope scolded her husband. "And rest. Lots of sleep for the next few days."

Brett grinned at her. "How do you know this?"

"I googled it, okay?" Penelope struck a pose, hip jutted out. "I'll go pick up some things at the store. Tara, Linc"—she pointed at Brett—"whatever your father needs."

She was in the car, her forehead against the steering wheel, breathing deeply—in and out—in minutes. What was wrong with her?

She angled the car down Pine Street and without thinking hooked the wheel right onto Middletree Lane. She parked in front of the soft yellow bungalow with the wide front porch, the house that she'd loved almost more than her own. She felt all the more guilty for that considering it had been Kiera who had decorated it over ten years ago before she died, swift and painful. Nothing had changed.

She hoped Sasha wasn't home.

She rang the bell, and Jaime answered the door, keeping the screen between them. They didn't speak at first.

"This is crazy, Pen," he said finally, rubbing a palm along his jaw. She could hear the rasp of a five-o'clock shadow.

"I know. Let me in, okay?"

He swung open the door, and she stood in the hallway, close enough to feel him, but she didn't touch him.

"We have to just stop this thing," he said softly, his hand brushing her cheek. It came away wet with tears.

"What thing? We haven't done anything." But Penelope knew it was a shit excuse. "We're friends."

"Which is why you're standing in my hallway crying. Why you looked like you were going to die when I left with Willa the other day."

"I know. I know." Penelope straightened her shoulders. "Everything feels so out of control. Not just you. My whole life. I don't know. Brett got sick and Willa is there, but something isn't right. She's taking over everything. My kids, my husband . . . you."

"She says she's helping you?" Jaime raised an eyebrow—skeptical of Penelope or Willa? She didn't know.

Penelope took a step toward Jamie, reached out, and ran a hand across his shoulders, her fingertips cupping the back of his neck.

Her lips pressed against his before he could stop her. His mouth opened to hers immediately, his hands running down her back to pull her against him, quick and hard, like he wasn't surprised by the kiss. Like he'd been waiting for it.

She thought maybe if she just kissed him, got it out of her system, she could forget him. God, what a ridiculous idea.

His mouth was soft and strong, and she felt dizzy with desire. Had she ever felt physically dizzy from kissing Brett? She couldn't remember.

"Pen," he whispered hoarsely into her mouth. He pulled away, rested his forehead against hers, breathing heavily. "This is not okay."

"You're the one who sent that note to *me*," Penelope whispered, her fingertips running along his neck, watching the trail of goose bumps in their wake. "Don't act like you don't want this."

"God, I want this more than I've wanted anything in recent memory. I've regretted that note every single day since I sent it. I even hoped—" He took a step back and slammed his hand against the wall, turning his back to her. "I even hoped you didn't actually get it. You never said anything."

Penelope leaned her cheek against his back. "I didn't know how to tell you. I didn't want to ruin our friendship. You were—are—the one constant in my life."

After a moment: "What about my life?"

"I know. You deserve more than a tortured half affair with your kid's best friend's mother." Penelope stepped back. "Brett is home from the hospital. I didn't plan to come here. But . . . you're right. This has to stop. You go out with Willa. I'll go to therapy." She laughed hollowly, longer than seemed acceptable, and hiccuped. "Maybe Brett can recommend someone."

"I don't want to go out with Willa." Jaime tried to grab her arm as she left, but she stepped out of his reach. Back in her car, she practiced deep breathing—like Brett always talked about, with her eyes closed, feeling the breath deep in her belly—before she pulled away from the curb. In the rearview mirror, she could see Jaime through the screen door.

He didn't wave goodbye.

CHAPTER SIXTEEN
Then: Every Day

To the left of the kitchen was a set of big double doors that opened into the courtyard. A garden took up the majority of the courtyard, but at the moment it was overrun by tall, spiky wildflowers. The patio held cracked and broken flagstone, uprooted by weeds and moss. Off against the house stood a round wooden table and four plastic chairs, chipped and splintered. The remodeling felt very haphazard, as though Parker had chosen bits and pieces to tackle on a furious whim.

She'd only been out in the courtyard once or twice—the outdoors, in general, made her itch. The mosquitoes tended to feast on her, and she sweated almost immediately in warm weather. Nothing about being outside in June felt comfortable. Flynn and Bree worked together in companionable silence, and both looked at ease in the blazing sun.

Flynn had set up a wooden easel, a thin stretched canvas resting on the lip. He had a full set of jars and water, a palette of white cardboard resting on his knee.

Penelope tiptoed behind him to take a look and gasped. "That's Bree!"

Bree looked up from the center of the courtyard, a white vision amid the tall greens, a wispy smile on her face, and closed her eyes, preening. "He always paints me."

"Do you?" Penelope turned to Flynn, open mouthed in surprise. "Why?"

Flynn gave her a puzzled stare and shook his head. "She's beautiful."

"Oil?" Penelope asked, knowing nothing of art, just that oils were painted on easels and canvas, but Flynn shook his head.

"Acrylic. I can do the same thing with acrylics, but I like the sharp edges. Oils tend to bleed. Plus they make a mess." Flynn did come across as someone who was predisposed to cleanliness. "And the cleanup stinks." He made a face.

The painting was striking, particularly for how quickly he must have done it. Bree, in the center of the courtyard, was surrounded by plants—mostly wildflowers—in her eyelet white dress, her red hair braided with tendrils curling around her face. She was wearing her old plastic flip-flops and pulling at the giant plants. The painting captured the exact image in broad, bold strokes, Bree's hair a mane of orange and red, wilder on the canvas than in real life, the gentle slope of her back, the delicate curve of her neck.

"How do you do that?" Penelope asked Flynn softly. "See all the colors instead of the light?"

"I don't know; I just do," said Flynn. "You don't?"

"No. Where the sunlight hits Bree's hair . . ." Penelope reached out, traced her finger along Bree's hairline on the canvas, careful to not touch the paint. "It just looks like her hair to me. I don't even realize that the sun actually makes it a different color. I mean, I do *now*. Because you painted it." She laughed self-consciously. "Does that make sense?"

"Yeah, it's called color constancy. Your brain adjusts the colors based on what you expect to see. If we saw everything exactly as it was, we'd never recognize basic shapes in different lighting." His voice was low, smooth. Penelope thought she could listen to him talk about painting all day.

"Tell me more." She sat on the ground next to him.

He laughed. "If you saw an apple at noon, and then saw it at dusk, it's actually two very different colors. But our brains still assimilate. We know it's an apple, no matter the color. We would even say it's red at dusk, if asked. But it probably isn't. It's probably gray, or dark green."

"So is being able to see the differentiation and process it a talent of art or science?" Penelope asked, intrigued.

"Well, arguably both. There was a German poet once, Johann Wolfgang von Goethe, who published a book called *Theory of Colours.* He challenged Newton's theories that white light is a limited spectrum of color. Goethe instead relied on the human perception of white light and all its infinite variations. Essentially, he said Newton's error was trusting science over art." Flynn put his paintbrush down and looked at Penelope self-consciously. "I sound like a pompous windbag."

"No!" Penelope was transfixed. By his graceful movements, the soothing sound of his voice, the surety with which he knew his subject. "So what do you think? Is color science or art?"

"Well, it's both. I think the science is fascinating. We can process color the way we *expect* to see it, not necessarily the way it is. This is why optical illusions work so well. The art is being able to pull that out of your consciousness and transmute it onto the page."

"That's not just art. That's talent," Penelope said.

He laughed then, a bit raw and possibly flushed, but she couldn't tell. "So what do I do with my talent when I've spent four years studying science—numbers and accounting and business?"

"Oh, that's easy." Penelope held up her hands, and he pulled her to her feet. "Business is just as much art as science, right? Being able to pull nebulous ideas out of your own consciousness and transmute them onto a page?" She smiled and impulsively kissed Flynn's cheek. "That's your creative talent."

Flynn cocked his head, stared at her. "How do you do that, Miss Penelope?"

Penelope flushed, ignored him, and called to Bree, who was wrestling with a giant thistle. "What exactly are you doing?"

"I'm going to make us a veggie garden," she declared in her wispy voice. "What should I plant?" The weed came out in a lurch, sending her down to her backside. She giggled helplessly and stood, her dress wrinkled and dirty.

"No beets," said Flynn and Penelope together.

"They taste like—"

"Dirt." They started laughing, bent at the waist, and Flynn put a hand on Penelope's arm.

"What's so funny, you two?" Willa struck a hip-pop pose in the doorway, a vision: a full face of makeup, round flushed cheeks, red heart-shaped lips, long dark eyelashes. Her blonde hair cascaded around her face like an embrace. She wore a thin black dress with a plunging neckline and a delicate silver chain around her neck.

Flynn let out a long, low whistle. "Where are you off to, all gorgeous and glowing?"

"Nunya, as my gram used to say." She childishly stuck her tongue out at him, but her neck flushed, and she dropped her purse. She bent to pick it up as Bree called over, "Ya got a date?"

"Something like that. Don't wait up." She blew a kiss toward them all, and Bree rested her forearm across her brow bone, fingertips waggling.

Penelope jumped up and followed her to the kitchen. "Who with?" she asked, her voice low.

Willa twirled, gave her a small private smile. "You don't know him."

"Well, someone should know. For safety's sake, at least. If you never came home, we wouldn't even have a name to give to the police!"

Willa reached out and touched her chin, held it between her thumb and forefinger. "Oh, sweetie, you're such a little mother hen." She said it softly, but her eyes narrowed, a smile playing at the corners of her mouth.

"I care about you, you idiot!" Penelope was indignant. Willa's moods had always been unpredictable, and yes, their friendship had always revolved around Willa. But she wasn't letting her go off with a stranger without even giving him a name. "Did you tell Jack?"

"I'm just kidding—you know I love you." She leaned over and kissed Penelope's cheek, leaving a lip-gloss residue. "His name is Hal."

"Hal what?" Penelope called after her, but she was met with the high tinkling of Willa's laugh and the slamming of the front door.

Later, Jack came home whistling, a soft secret smile on his face as he chopped garlic. (Bree had been wrong about Jack—he loved to cook. Tonight was chicken française.) Penelope hopped up on the counter, her legs swinging next to him. "Guess what—Willa had a date. His name is Hal."

His head snapped up, shocked. "Really!"

"Is she not allowed to date?" Penelope teased him, poking at his arm.

"She hasn't since we've been here." He rolled his eyes at her. "I didn't know she knew anyone, that's all."

"She's Willa. She probably already knows the mayor." Penelope shrugged, breaking off a piece of peeled carrot and popping it in her mouth.

"Hal, you said?" Jack laughed. "There once was a farmer named Hal, who never talked to a gal, too timid and shy, to even say hi, spent his time with the sheep in the corral."

"Oh my God," Penelope covered her mouth, tried not to choke. "Where the hell did you get that?"

"I made it up." Jack shrugged.

"That's mean!" Penelope was impressed. "Just now?"

Jack laughed and shook his head. He opened his mouth to answer her, but Bree swung into the house, hugging an armful of greens.

"Look! Wild onions. Also, possibly a lettuce that is either delicious or poisonous." She let out a shrill laugh. "I'm kidding! It's fine." She plopped the bounty on the counter, pulled a towel from the rack in the corner, and wiped her forehead and her neck, damp with sweat. "God, it's so hot. What were we talking about?"

"Limericks. Dirty ones." He grinned wickedly at her and poured her a glass of wine.

Bree held up her glass. "There once was a man from Nantucket . . ."

"Bah." Jack waved his hand at her. "You can do better than that."

She thought a moment, cleared her throat. "The thoughts of the rabbit on sex, are seldom, if ever, complex. For a rabbit in need, is a rabbit indeed, and does just as a person expects."

Jack threw his head back and laughed. "You did *not* make that up."

"Correct, I did not." Bree took a long drink from her glass, and Jack watched her interestedly.

"Willa's on a date." Jack went back to chopping carrots, his voice unreadable.

"We saw her leave, all done up," Bree said distractedly.

"I haven't seen you date," Jack offered casually. Penelope watched the way his face changed, a placid mask. He was always so good at the stone face. It could be infuriating. He'd been so infatuated with Bree—a simple crush, maybe. But it seemed to Penelope that he'd become a bit single minded about it. It bothered him that he couldn't figure Bree out. That she didn't fawn all over him.

"I think I went on a date freshman year," Bree said, pulling the lettuce and the turnips apart. She shrugged. "Although, I will say, it's not really any of your business." She gave Jack a pointed look, and he laughed uneasily.

"It's just curious, that's all. Have you ever had a boyfriend?" Jack had his back turned to Bree, but Penelope could see his utter stillness, the smile playing out on his face. She wanted to slap him—both for making Bree uncomfortable and for the hot knife in her own gut.

"No. Everyone asks me that; I don't know why. What does it matter? I don't have a boyfriend."

"Why?" Jack's question was innocuous, or could be construed that way. Plausible deniability was Jack's specialty.

"I just haven't been interested in anyone." Bree's voice took on a razor's edge, sharp and thin.

"In all four years of college?"

Bree straightened her spine and held Jack's gaze, challenging him. "In all four years of college. Men are babies."

"What about women?" Jack's voice lowered, and Penelope suddenly felt like she was eavesdropping on an intensely private conversation, and she tucked a flat palm under her thigh, shifting, leaning in to hear the answer, feeling her breath come short in her lungs.

"I don't understand why you care so much." Bree faltered then, finally her voice breaking at the end. "I just don't have feelings the way everyone else does. That's all it is. I can't explain it another way."

"What about Flynn?"

"What about Flynn?" Flynn's voice was quiet from the doorway, a paintbrush in one hand, a color-stained rag in the other.

Jack grinned, either oblivious to the crackle in the air or deliberately ignoring it. Penelope would have guessed the latter.

"Why haven't you two cats ever hooked up?" A quick flash of Jack's bright-white smile, his eyes imperceptibly narrowed. In periphery, he didn't look affable and fun; his mouth twitched with tension.

Flynn and Bree exchanged a look. Bree licked her lips. Penelope felt her throat close. She imagined Flynn telling Jack, *I'm gay*, right there in front of all of them. It wouldn't have mattered to any of them, she knew. But *I'm in love with you*. Well, that one would land like a bomb. Maybe. On second thought, Jack might have loved it.

Flynn looked back at Jack and plastered on a wide grin. "Why haven't you two?" He gestured to Penelope, and she felt her face flame.

And just like that, the energy broke. Jack laughed out loud, the glass of wine in his hand sloshing. "Who says we haven't?" He slung his right arm around Penelope's shoulders and pulled her against him.

She felt the thump of his chest against her cheek, the smell of him, the soft scratch of cotton against her skin. Then he let go, and the room seemed to right itself. Bree laughed, Flynn smiled, Jack teased, Penelope demurred. They all found their roles again, the earlier tension so easily glossed over that Penelope later wondered, sleepily, if she'd invented it.

Except. Bree watched Jack after that when she thought no one was looking. Eyes narrowed, mouth pursed like a lemon. Penelope saw it more than once, and not just that night but later too.

—⚡—

After dinner (which was delicious, Willa's loss!), they beached themselves on the various couches and chairs in the common room, drinking wine and chatting, the remnants of the strange moment earlier entirely forgotten.

"I figured it out," said Jack, as though they had been in midconversation. "You're the sisters of fate." He grinned broadly as he settled in the oversize armchair, his guitar under his arm. "Willa is Clotho; she brings the life to the party. She makes us all whole, brings us all together. Penelope here is Lachesis. Sees all, knows all. She'd be a fair and just determiner. And you," he said, raising his eyebrows at Bree, "are Atropos."

"Why me?" Bree asked, unsure if this was a compliment or an insult, but slightly insulted nonetheless.

"Well, you're pretty ruthless out there with your scissors." Flynn laughed sleepily, gesturing toward the garden.

"They're *weeds*," Bree said hotly, clapping her hands in his direction.

"It's not just that," Jack mused. "Atropos is the inflexible one. You are kind of like that."

"That's rude!" Penelope threw an errant crumpled napkin in his direction.

"No, it's not an insult. Look, Bree does whatever Bree wants. She has her garden. She works in it while Flynn paints her. Bree doesn't eat meat, so we all eat tofu. Look, no worries! I don't mind!" He turned and gave Bree a disarming smile. "I'm happy to be at your service."

"God, you're pretentious," Penelope said. "Why don't we have a television?"

Bree laughed. "I've never had a TV."

"Oh my God, never?" Penelope couldn't envision such a thing. As a child, television was her friend, confidante, babysitter. Her aunt had been on the young side but acted elderly and rarely left the house. They had a living room and a den, and when *Wheel of Fortune* and *Jeopardy* were playing, Penelope would find her way to the small den in the back of the house. No air-conditioning and overflowing with a desk and paperwork, a pile of books on every flat surface, a small square television perched on the end table where Penelope would find reruns of old black-and-white shows: *The Munsters* or *The Addams Family*, *Leave It to Beaver*.

They agreed that perhaps tomorrow they should seek out a television. *For sanity's sake*, stressed Bree.

"I can't just sit here and drink wine and talk to you people all night and day," Flynn said, his voice light, but Penelope suspected the sentiment was sincere. It felt decadent, the ease of their friendship. But it also felt pressurized. They had to be witty, funny, cheerful. Come up with on-the-spot limericks, know the ins and outs of Greek mythology. Sometimes, the dazzle of them all exhausted her.

The pauses between sentences had become longer and longer as the night grew later, until Penelope felt herself dozing. She woke with a start at the sound of the door. Willa let herself in, late. After midnight. Jack stood up to greet her, whispered, "Are you okay?"

Penelope wondered why she wouldn't be and only glanced at the mascara on her cheeks before Willa waved him away and hustled downstairs to her bedroom, her heels clicking on the wooden plank floor.

"Is she okay?" Penelope whispered, careful not to wake Bree, who had fallen asleep on Flynn's shoulder, her arm linked through his.

"She's fine. She's coming down from a high." Jack shrugged when he said it, and Penelope felt her stomach give an oily turn. She hadn't known Willa to do drugs other than weed. "She always cries. At the end." He gave her a sardonic smile. "It depletes your serotonin, you know?"

"High on what?" Penelope's voice was sharp.

"Ecstasy. She did it on dates sometimes. In college." Jack touched her arm, shook his head. "I hate that we don't know who she was with. She can't do that shit—we don't even know anyone here."

It was on the tip of her tongue to ask him, *Has she ever done it with you?* The furious jealous streak lighting up down her spine. She'd never done Ecstasy, but she knew what it did. She'd seen the same movies, heard the same music. She could envision Willa's strong thighs wrapped around Jack's narrow hips.

"See?" He whispered gently, his hand thrillingly resting on the small of Penelope's back, a whisper of warm breath against her ear as he stepped closer. He nodded in the direction of Bree and Flynn. "They make such a gorgeous couple."

Penelope nodded, only half agreeing with him in practicality. He wasn't wrong—they looked like a painting.

"That's all I was trying to say earlier," he continued. "That they're just both so beautiful."

CHAPTER SEVENTEEN

February 19, 2020

Penelope took the time at the store to compose herself. She did not want to mourn Jaime and take care of her husband at the same time. She was ashamed, angry with herself for kissing him. For being driven by passion. *The most passionate thing you've ever felt in years?* a little voice inside asked, and she pushed it down, buried it. It was all irrelevant. The taboo nature of their friendship created the passion. They weren't Romeo and Juliet, for God's sake. She was just a regular suburban housewife in a floundering marriage. She was a daytime talk show cliché, wrapped in an advice column letter.

If she and Brett decided in the future to not stay married, that would be one thing (she did not think about that even a little, would not allow herself to latch on to a shard of hope as dismal as that), but as long as she was with Brett, she was *with him.*

All up and down the frozen foods aisle, she thought about Brett. The way he fit between her thighs, how he knew exactly what to do to her in bed to make her cry out, white knuckled and panting. The way he used to stop at the store on the way home from work, pick up bread and cheese—memories of their honeymoon in Aruba—french bread and gruyere cheese, cut into soft wedges. The way he used to make sure her tires were rotated because her commute was longer. The way he'd sometimes lay out her clothes before they'd go out on a dinner date. Not a demand, just a gesture. If she didn't wear what he suggested, he'd kiss her, whisper, *This is better.* The way he meant that.

The thing was, all that had stopped the year before. With his job loss. Is that all Jaime was to her? A way to fill the void? What had she done to make their marriage better in the past year? What things did she "used to do" that she no longer did that Brett missed?

There was lingerie in her drawer, long buried. She definitely used to buy him mini cards—the kind you picked up at the impulse counter of grocery stores—and wrote little notes in them. Sometimes silly, sometimes functional. Sometimes just red hearts. If she was at the grocery store and saw a syrah on sale, she'd pick it up. It was his favorite wine, which he'd never admit to anyone.

By the time Penelope had gotten home with bags of groceries— fresh vegetables and fruits and broths and greens, lots of vitamin C: ways to boost the immune system, the hematologist had told them— she had worked herself into a state.

She stored everything away and made a quick tea—one of his herbal varieties with actual boiled water (*Who microwaves water?* he'd asked her once)—and carefully climbed the steps back up to their bedroom.

She could see them from the hallway: Willa perched on the edge of the bed, her hair splayed over his prostrate form, his arm extended as she inspected the bandage on his arm where his transfusion had taken place. They'd said it would be more tender than a simple IV, but nothing to worry about.

Willa's finger trailed down his forearm, seemingly to pull on the taped edge. Brett's other hand came across the bed and gripped her wrist. He whispered something inaudible to her. There was a small feminine sound. A cry? A coo?

Penelope took a step back, behind the hallway wall, meaning to get her bearings.

"I won't tell her if you won't." Brett's voice was barely above a whisper. Penelope's heart raced, and she felt the flush of rage creep up her cheeks. Tell her what? The conversation was strangely intimate. She wondered, fleetingly, *Are they sleeping together?*

Her heel kicked something that skittered backward down the hall, clattering against the hardwood. She turned to see what it was: one of Tara's claw hair clips. By the time Penelope looked up, Brett and Willa had put at least a foot of distance between them, and they smiled at the doorway, calm and expectant.

Penelope paused in her confusion, trying to find the vestiges of what she'd seen on their faces, and came up empty. What *had* she seen? Had it been innocent? If she'd let them continue, she thought almost academically, how far might it have gone? *Won't tell what, exactly?*

"We're so glad you're back!" Willa said mildly, but her voice to Penelope's ears sounded brittle.

Her hand remained on Brett's arm. She did not get off the bed.

—⁓—

Penelope left her family—and Willa—in the guest room watching a sitcom and found quiet in her bedroom. The laundry had been done, folded in a basket on her bed. Her sheets and duvet had been laundered; the lamp at her bedside glowed softly. A glass filled with cold water sat condensing on her nightstand. The book she'd been reading propped against her pillows. She felt both unsettled and grateful. The room *did* look peaceful, and she longed to crawl under the covers, read her book, fall blissfully asleep.

Instead, Penelope began to put away the folded laundry and opened her closet doors to hang one of her work sheaths. Her closet gleamed before her, entirely rearranged. Her clothes prior to this had been a haphazard array of color, texture, and design. To find anything, Penelope often had to sift through racks of dresses, only to find blouses and even slacks mixed in. She wasn't naturally organized, and lately she'd been so tired that even hanging things up had been a hurdle. She was embarrassed to admit that she'd slept in her work clothes more than once.

But this. This was beautiful.

Dresses, blouses, slacks. Grouped together, organized by color. Her shoes, matched and aligned on her shoe racks. Above her, bins had been added to store various bags, scarves, boots, winter gear. Clear, all matching. Her closet looked like it belonged in a magazine.

Penelope closed the door, pinched the bridge of her nose. She felt simultaneously grateful and outraged, an emotional combination she hadn't known possible.

This was *her house.*

When had she started to feel like a guest in her own home? Why did she feel more comfortable alone in her bedroom, listening through the wall to her family huddled in the guest room together with Willa, laughing uproariously at a sitcom family? When had she lost complete control of her life? Had she really lost control? At least she knew where her lucky shirt was now.

She looked around and realized that her bedroom had been *cleaned.* The dust that had collected on her bureau top had been removed, and the cherrywood gleamed from beneath her jewelry box.

When Brett was laid off last year, he convinced her to get rid of the cleaning service. *I can clean,* he insisted. His cleaning had been sporadic and often did not include dusting their bedrooms. Penelope had learned to live with a fine layer of dust on everything until she hit her limit and dusted the bedrooms herself, typically on Sundays.

She had to talk to Willa. They had to have a plan moving forward. She could not stay indefinitely. If she needed more time, that was fine.

"Willa!" She called down the hall. "Can you come here a sec?" She kept her voice light, casual.

Willa appeared in the doorway in seconds. "What's up?"

Penelope took a deep breath. She didn't thrive on confrontation, but she'd never been afraid of it. "Look, this is beautiful. I appreciate it." Penelope gestured toward the closet. "But this is my space. My house. I feel like this is . . . overstepping some boundaries."

Willa's face crumpled, her eyes filling immediately. "I'm sorry you feel that way, Pip. Truly. I was only trying to help, I promise you. You've been so stressed, and with Brett . . . I just felt horrible about the whole thing. Like it was *my fault*! I know you said you don't blame me, but *I blame me*! You were talking about how you couldn't find your shirt. I started just putting some laundry away and then . . . I like organizing. I've done it for friends." Her voice broke, faltered. "Back home. Before I left, I mean. I'm honestly really sorry. I didn't even think it would upset you so much!"

Penelope absorbed all this, the steady stream of Willa's words, her immediate apology, the look on her face, pleading and sorry, and felt terrible. Of course it was in good faith. Penelope and Willa had always had a fairly boundless relationship—at least twenty years ago. Bedroom doors open, no question off limits. Although, Penelope imagined that Willa had that relationship with almost everyone.

"No. I'm sorry," Penelope said quickly. "I'm just tired. I feel like . . . nothing about my life is my own right now. Brett needs me. The kids need me . . ." Her voice trailed off, and she looked around the room.

"Which is why I thought it might be nice to have something done *for you*!" Willa touched her arm. "When was the last time anyone did anything for you? Who was the last person to make you feel appreciated?"

Probably Linc. Linc always appreciated his mother. Tara, sometimes. Brett, rarely, but it had been known to happen. Penelope gave her a thin smile. Pacified, mostly convinced, but still. Something unsettled her.

She reached out and touched Willa's collarbone. A thin silver chain, a simple flat ring resting prettily above her dipping neckline. Without looking, she knew what it said.

"Oh! You like that? Jaime gave it to me. He said it was something he liked to say to himself. Said it reminded him of me." She pulled it away from her skin, ran a painted nail over the letters, wistful. "He's so sensitive, you know?"

Penelope did know. She put a hand to her forehead to steady herself. Remind herself to breathe. She almost laughed at that, she felt that on edge. He gave them both the same necklace?

"Are we okay?" Willa asked, still fiddling with the necklace, fingertip still sliding over the carved letters.

Penelope nodded, not trusting her voice. Willa turned then, back to her pseudo family, back to her sitcom. Penelope stood motionless in the center of the room, listening to her hum as she walked down the hallway. The distant rumble of a laugh track.

The television woke her—from what felt like a dream sequence. She crossed the room, lifted the lid of her jewelry box, and absently flicked through a small selection of earrings, necklaces, bracelets. She wasn't a big jewelry person—some pieces from her mother, some fun chunky costume pieces, a few antiques, a Bakelite bangle from her aunt.

And one missing piece: a silver necklace, a ring carved with the word *Breathe*.

CHAPTER EIGHTEEN
Willa, present

God, he was cute. If she were Penelope, she'd be in love with Jaime over Brett any day. He was broad, dark haired, blue eyed like her own little Dylan McDermott.

He smiled at her, wide and white, from the counter at Beans. "Willa." People who said her name like it was a greeting charmed her, always. He had gray flecked around the dark hair of his temples, and his dark stubble contained flecks of gray. She loved that—men always looked great as they aged. Nature was such a cunning little bitch.

"Hey, you." She grinned and took a paper cup from his outstretched hand. There were four outdoor tables on a concrete slab, topped with umbrellas and surrounded by a handful of potted ferns. The morning was cold, but not brittle, and it hadn't snowed more than a dusting all winter.

She took a big breath—a gulp of air, the chill hitting her lungs like a shot of caffeine. Jaime's nose was red, a skullcap pulled low over his ears.

"How's Pen?" It rankled her, only a little, that it was the first question he asked. She didn't show it and instead tried to think of the best strategy.

"She's . . . okay, I think. It's a lot, you know?" She cocked her head to the side, sympathetic and clucking, and Jaime's face was pure concern: deep eyebrows, a slight frown, a warm flush in his cheeks.

"She has definitely dealt with a lot, especially this past year, but she'll be okay. She's one of the strongest people I know."

"She is. But . . . do you think maybe . . . ?" she started to say and then stopped. Toyed with her coffee cup, picked up and then put down the spoon.

Jaime touched her hand. "What's going on?"

"I don't know. I feel like . . . she's definitely not the Pip I know. She's brittle and angry or something. She's been saying things that . . . don't make sense. Last night, she accused me of stealing her necklace, something about breathing? I don't know, it didn't make sense. But I didn't have it, I swear I didn't! Why would I steal from her? I did her laundry, and she flipped out—she said I overstepped a boundary. But I accidentally put her husband in the hospital! I've felt horrible. I'm just trying to make it up to her. Her laundry was piling up. I can tell she's not used to being disorganized."

Jaime leaned back in his chair, massaged his jaw, thinking. Then, softly, "No. I mean, she's not obsessive or type A, but she keeps lists and keeps herself on track. She's not usually messy."

"There's another thing. She's forgetting the kids. Like all the time. They call me now. The other night she was supposed to take Linc to a meeting for lacrosse and she went to her room, fell asleep for *hours*, and forgot about him entirely. I took him, but I could tell he was upset about it."

"She never forgets the kids," Jaime said, his brows pulling together. Then, "Well, you're there to help her, right?"

She didn't correct him. *Of course she was there to help.* Nothing a little chamomile tea and a Benadryl couldn't cure. She was so sleep deprived, you know? And while she slept, Willa could do things. For her old friend Pip.

"Yes, but it's just so *unlike* her, you know?"

Jaime nodded, and she could see he definitely *knew.*

"A necklace, you said?" He was frowning, and she nodded encouragingly.

"You're such a good friend to her," he said and reached out, covered her hand with his own. She kept her eyes down, studying the wooden picnic table between them.

Then, because why the hell not, "How long have you been in love with her?" Her voice was a whisper, but his head jerked up as though it had been a shout.

Jaime's face went slack, white. She covered his hand with hers and held tight, not letting him pull away. "It was a guess, don't panic. I'm just a perceptive person," she said.

"I didn't think it was that obvious. At least, I'd hoped not." Jaime ran his finger around the lip of his coffee cup, staring at the tabletop, avoiding her gaze. "I'm trying not to be. It's not a healthy friendship—for any of us. I can't imagine my life without Pen and Brett. Brett was my friend first, you know? Then he kinda went off the rails, and none of us knew what to do with him." He paused. "It's been a weird year."

"And your girls are friends," she prompted.

"God yeah. The closest. Like sisters. I don't even think they fight." Jaime grinned as he said it and then looked a little crestfallen. "If our families fought, or even stopped speaking, it would kill them both."

"Strong words." She raised her eyebrows flirtatiously and took a sip of coffee. Leaned back in her chair.

"It was a metaphor." His gaze flicked down to her décolletage and back up to her eyes again.

God, he was cute.

—∿—

When she returned, the house was empty, thank God. She could hear Brett's measured breathing—the deep in and out of sleep. If she walked along the inner edge of the stairs, they made no creak. She'd learned that early on.

She closed the guest room door, but not before taking a peek inside. Brett *was* asleep, soundly by all appearances. If she hugged the railing of the hallway, which overlooked the living room below, the floorboards would not give her away. She'd learned that early too.

In Penelope and Brett's bedroom, she shuffled through drawers and didn't unearth even a vibrator. God, they had to be the world's most boring people, with the most uninteresting sex life imaginable. She envisioned missionary-style sex weekly, lights off. Hell, he was still sleeping in the guest room for the time being. Penelope said it was because she'd been getting up so early she hadn't wanted to wake him, but come on.

Brett was built nicely—no doubt. Although she had the impression that Penelope thought he was too thin, especially after his year of running and yoga and barely eating. Penelope had retained her figure from college. But she was still mousy. Fade into the woodwork. An absolutely beautiful face that she paid zero attention to. She had a bottle of foundation in the cabinet that had expired three years ago. What a waste.

In the closet (now gorgeously organized, with barely a thank-you to show for it), the hamper was half-full. Brett's side was dark—mostly black and deep-blue suits, limned with fine dust. They'd all have to be cleaned when—or if—he started work again.

When she'd reorganized Pip's closet, she'd focused mainly on her side. Brett's was sparse, clean. Now she moved to his side, pulling out shoeboxes, peeking inside before carefully replacing them.

Oh, Brett, are you really this dry and boring?

She feared he was. The closet was completely devoid of interesting skeletons. There was a trunk at the foot of their bed—antique, scrolled, cherry—that contained nothing but extra blankets and a few heavy wool sweaters that hadn't been worn in years, by the smell.

Pip's nightstand: cough drops, a small pack of tissues, a vitamin D prescription from six months before with only two pills missing, an OTC sleep aid, barely used.

Please, Brett, she thought, *be more than this. Please.*

She found the answer to her wish in the back of his nightstand. A small black Android device, seemingly current. Both Brett and Penelope carried new-model iPhones.

She held down the power button, expecting nothing. It could be dead. Old. Broken.

The screen lit up. Jackpot. She turned the device over and studied the back.

Imagine Wireless. A pay-per-month phone service.

This was a burner phone.

"Oh, Brett," she said softly, with not just a little bit of glee. "What are you hiding?"

CHAPTER NINETEEN
Then: Independence Day

"You don't seem like a Fourth of July kind of person," Penelope observed as Jack ticked off a list in his hand.

"I don't care much either way, but it's an excuse to have a party, right? Hot dogs, burgers, beer. Like when we were kids."

"I never had a Fourth of July picnic as a kid," Penelope said, realizing too late, as she usually did, how pathetic her childhood sounded.

"Never?" Willa arched her eyebrows disbelievingly.

"I mean, it's a barbaric holiday." Jack shrugged like this was irrelevant.

"Barbaric how?" Penelope echoed.

Flynn appeared at the basement doorway and said, "It's not even nine in the morning—why are we talking about barbarism?"

"Celebrating Independence Day. I mean, it's not as shitty as, say, Columbus Day, but people don't actually celebrate that anyway. No one is proud of that douchebag."

"Do you know a lot of Black people don't celebrate the Fourth of July?" Flynn shrugged. "I was adopted by white people, so I didn't know until high school."

"What! Why?" Willa looked appalled.

Flynn spread his hands wide, at a loss for words, and seemed to opt for the simplest explanation. "It wasn't our freedom then. Why would we celebrate it now?"

"For the party," Willa stammered. "Fireworks, sparklers, swimming, boating."

"We have two Americas." Flynn added cream to his coffee, shaking his head, his speech slow and deliberate, at the same time as Bree said, "Boating!"

Penelope knew Willa grew up rich. Like southern plantation, lake house, beach house, BMWs, and Mercedes (not Jags, though—she was careful to underscore that for reasons Penelope would never understand) rich. She didn't know Flynn's background, except that he was raised in Philadelphia, adopted, and got into Penn on a scholarship he didn't much talk about.

"There are a lot of different Americas," Jack offered flippantly, waving his hand like it was immaterial. "I just think it would be fun to have a good old-fashioned picnic, like when we were all kids."

"When *you* were kids." Flynn's voice was louder now. Firmer and resolute.

"Will we invite other people?" Willa asked, her face unreadable.

"Like your date?" Bree teased, and Willa shot her a look.

"Should we?" Penelope asked, staring directly at Willa, looking for a signal. What had happened on that date a few weeks ago? Had Willa come home crying? The next morning, Willa had behaved like business as usual, but she never mentioned the date, the Ecstasy, that night again. Penelope had tried to ask her, went to her room the next night. She'd waved her away with an eye roll and just said, *Ugh no. Men suck.*

Willa gave Penelope a barely perceptible shake of her head, and Penelope followed quickly: "Let's just do us—a bonding thing." She couldn't have invited anyone else if she'd wanted to. She was starting her job at the bookstore the Monday after the picnic. She didn't know a soul.

"Can I have a veggie burger?" Bree asked, and Jack pretended to fall backward dramatically.

"Just for one day, can't you have red meat like a real American?"

"What happened to a lot of different Americas? Or is that only true when it's convenient for you?" Bree countered, but she was smiling. "To be a real American now, you have to eat cow?"

"Yes, and drink Miller Lite, and . . . I don't know, maybe drive a truck? Wear red, white, and blue. What else?" Jack threw up his hand, the other still clutching a coffee cup.

"Know all the words to 'The Star-Spangled Banner,'" Penelope offered, because she felt sure they could at least muster that.

"Listen, y'all, I grew up in Louisiana. Y'all don't even know *real America* up here," Willa declared. "First of all, ya gotta wear one of those tall net hats that says like Tide or something on it. I had an uncle that wore one. He was a *real American*. Nice guy—my favorite uncle."

"YES." Jack pointed at Willa emphatically. "See, this is what I'm talking about. This Saturday—two days from now—it's on. We'll have a real Independence Day. Everyone in? Get your trucker hats."

They all agreed, but Penelope looked around the kitchen, the smiling faces of Jack and Willa, Bree pensive but grinning, and couldn't help but notice that Flynn had gone.

—⁓—

Flynn worked the grill, which surprised Penelope for more than one reason. Willa had pegged Flynn and Jack wrong again, but also Penelope couldn't have been sure that Flynn would even show up to the party. The others had been insensitive, and it was doubtful they'd even been aware of it.

Jack hovered over Flynn's shoulder, the way men do around a barbecue, discussing the temperature, smoke, cooking, meat, color. *Flip it now; no, not yet; remember Willa said rare.*

Willa came upstairs dressed in a fire engine–red gauzy dress and an enormous white straw hat. She twirled on the patio, stumbling a little over the uneven flagstones. For a second, Penelope wondered if she was drunk already, but it was only two. Flynn laughed and emitted a low whistle. Jack grabbed her hand and spun her in a little pirouette.

"Willamena! Sing to us," Jack called, and she cringed at the *Willamena*. He sat in the big overstuffed chair, his legs slung over the side, his guitar on his lap. She demurred, a coy dip to her chin.

"What should I sing?" she asked. Two bright spots appeared on her cheeks, and she chewed her pinkie. Finally, she smoothed the front of her red dress down over her thighs.

Bree emerged outside holding a tray of drinks: some kind of berry-lemonade-vodka thing she'd found on the internet. Willa had been keeping the bar fully stocked—vodka, rum, bourbon, gin. *None of that bottom-shelf swill,* she'd said. Penelope took a sip. It was delicious—and strong. Willa drained half her glass in one go, and Jack watched her, shook his head a little, and caught Penelope's eye. He mouthed, *River.*

Willa started, her voice loud, delicate, and clear. "It's coming on Christmas."

Joni Mitchell. Penelope always thrilled at the depth of her sweet, resonant alto. She could hit the highs and the lows with the same signature vibrato. Her voice was a little breathier. A little sexier. Penelope looked over at Jack, who looked rapt.

Anyone who didn't know her wouldn't guess that Willa's snark and sarcasm covered over this gorgeous voice.

"Oh God," Bree breathed, a hand over her mouth. She turned to Jack. "I've heard her sing around the house sometimes, but not like *this.*"

"This one's the Willa Special." He grinned and watched her, like a proud parent. Or maybe boyfriend. Penelope had an unwelcome stab of jealousy. She hated feeling envious over Jack and Willa, but their friendship had always felt impenetrable. Even when they were in college, they were the main act; she was the foil. Was it so wrong to want the main act, just once, for herself?

"Willa, are you drunk?" Penelope asked, as Willa swayed with her eyes shut.

"Shhh!" Flynn said.

Earlier that day, Bree had turned the patio and courtyard into an oasis. In the center was her garden, edged with wildflowers. She strung Ikea lights diagonally from the corner of the house to a pole at the far east side of the courtyard. Someone had moved out the beanbag chair, two couches, and a recliner. Terra-cotta pots were staggered around on ledges and boxes, different heights of bright, bursting annuals.

They flopped onto the transported furniture, sipping their fizzy lemonades and breathing in the smell of charred meat until the conversation petered out, and Penelope felt a buzzy little thrill when Bree brought her a second drink.

Willa finished her a cappella number, and Jack picked his guitar up from beside one of the couches. He strummed a few notes, then inclined his head in Willa's direction. "You with the sad eyes."

Bree clapped her hands and squealed, "I loved Cyndi Lauper!"

Flynn, pouting and nursing his drink, said, "You know it's not a fake band if half of you have actual talent!"

Willa's voice was beautiful, and Jack hit the harmony. Penelope closed her eyes, leaned her head back, feeling pleasantly drunk, fuzzy around the edges, and not just a little giddy.

When the song ended, Jack stood as though making a speech. "We are gathered here today to celebrate the life of America."

Willa snorted. "Is this a speech or a fucking eulogy?" She drained her lemonade in one shot and poured another from the pitcher.

"What if it was a fucking eulogy?" Jack raised his glass, paused to rethink his speech. "To Willa. The craziest girl I know. I really wish she hadn't gone skydiving. Or at least I wish she had gotten a lesson first. Who forgets to open their own parachute? She had great tits and an incredible voice and a big giant brain that people didn't expect because of the tits. She squeezed out every last drop of fun, our Clotho, giver of life, probably drank too much, swore more than a construction worker, and could make a helluva baked ziti." His voice lowered, and he blew her a kiss. "She was my best friend, and she deserved so much better than me and whatever asshole she ends up with ten years from now. She's better than all of us."

Bree pretended to wipe her eyes. "Oh, that was lovely, Jack. You've got a way with words. You should be a writer."

Penelope snorted, and Jack swiveled around. "Oh, is that so funny, then? You think you can do better?"

Penelope stood and delicately cleared her throat. "To Jack." Flynn and Bree both let out a groan. "The life of every party. A goddamn bastard"—howls because Penelope rarely cursed—"who only wanted everyone to know who he really was—his hopes and fears, dreams and ambitions. He finally finished that novel, and we're all so appreciative. It's how we ended up spending every summer together at his mansion in East Hampton. Sadly, he should not have stolen that boat, considering he didn't know how to sail and he was a tiny bit tipsy, but after all, he was dared by his best friend, Willa, and everyone knows Jack can't walk away from a dare. Even when he's fifty years old. He'd always wanted a Viking funeral. To Jack!" Penelope raised her glass, and they chorused, "To Jack!"

"A mansion in East Hampton? Based on book royalties?" Flynn sounded skeptical.

"And a movie deal, natch. The movie wins an Oscar." Penelope sniffed.

Jack grinned, so genuine and happy, and Penelope felt her cheeks flame.

"Okay, okay. My turn!" Willa stood, her glass raised. "To Bree. Wild and beautiful and happy and innocent and free spirited. Bree, who brought peace and light with her gorgeous flowers and her art. Bree, surprisingly cunning, a little manipulative. Always knew what we all wanted and gave it to us. Truly, a lost art. I loved her with all my heart."

Willa was half sitting back down when Bree cupped her hand around her mouth, called from the recliner, "No mention of my tits?"

Willa stood up, looked around, raised her glass. "To Bree's nonexistent tits. The woman could run five miles without a bra." She sat back down.

"To nonexistent tits!" Jack and Flynn said in unison and clinked glasses.

By then, they were all quite drunk on Bree's lemony concoction, and Penelope squinted at the strung lights and bobbed her head to watch them blur together. She realized suddenly that if Willa didn't eulogize her, it was likely none of them would. She was closest to Willa, had known her the longest. Then she found that she didn't much care. She was content to sit back and listen.

"Okay, I'll go." Flynn stood, and Penelope found that her pulse was racing. "To Penelope. Still waters run deep." His voice was low and deep naturally, but that night it took all Penelope's concentration to even hear him. "Everyone thought Penelope was sensible and practical. But deep down inside, we knew she had a wild streak. We were all shocked when she left us to become a Vegas showgirl, but as it turns out she actually had fabulous tits—a fact none of us knew—"

"Oh, I knew that," interrupted Jack. Penelope shot him a faux dirty look.

Flynn glared but continued smoothly. "And was an incredible dancer. Penelope also had a way of reaching right into your soul, plucking out your very essence, holding it up to the sun to expose all the terrible things you thought you were: sad or awkward or scared or worried. Without even trying, she saw the raw, unformed parts of you and not only loved you for them but made you love them too."

Penelope sat, shocked, staring at Flynn and his gorgeous speech and wondering where the hell it had come from. *Science and art;* she recalled their conversation on the patio. He took his seat, looked away, pressed a palm to his ironed khaki pants, smoothing nonexistent wrinkles.

"I think Flynn wins the writer award," Jack said thoughtfully, looking truly touched. "Maybe I've had it wrong all this time. Is it . . . Penelope you're in love with? Not Bree, then?"

"Not everyone is in love with someone all the time," Bree said, disgusted.

"Well, life is certainly more fun with a little romance, right? Sexual tension makes the world go round, or something like that?" Jack waved his hand in a circle, laughing.

"I'm not in love with Bree or Penelope," Flynn said quietly and stood back up. He disappeared into the house and emerged a few moments later with the pitcher of lemonade and his own glass full. "Whose turn?"

Bree stood. "It's too easy for me to do Flynn, but it's also impossible. I can't say in ten seconds everything that Flynn means to me—"

"Meant to you. He's dead, Bree," Willa interjected. "Play the game. Close your eyes; be dead," Willa directed at Flynn, who complied. She was getting drunker by the second.

"*Meant* to me. Right. He's my brother from another mother, sister from another mister. He's been there for me through thick and thin, in the best and worst of times." Bree shot a warning glare at Jack, and he clamped his mouth shut. "He was gentle, creative, intuitive, emotionally available, and would have made someone very happy one day. He would have been a wonderful father to his own children, a fun, loving uncle to his nieces and nephews. If he'd only been able to—"

"Oh my GOD!" Willa shouted, rolling her eyes and flopping back against the back of the couch. When she was drunk like this, red faced, the scar on her left cheek seemed to pulse purple. "Blah blah blah blabbity blah. It was just supposed to be fun. This is awful. Now I'm depressed. Goddammit!"

"You didn't even let Bree finish!" Jack protested.

"She's done! That was awful." Willa stood, unsteadily, and Jack snorted, his eyes tracking her across the room.

"I mean, as long as you're bored, Willa," Jack said, his voice suddenly dipping down low.

"What the fuck does that mean?" Willa whirled back to him, her face instantly contorted.

"Just what I said! When you get bombed, you start directing us all. We have to do what you want, when you want. You're in charge." Jack shrugged. "We all know it. We all do it."

"Do what?"

"Cater to the resident queen." Jack shrugged again, maddeningly.

"Why are you such an ass?" Willa asked him, and he laughed.

"I'm an ass because I call you out? You always do this! You get bored with a game; you declare it over. You don't want to play Risk, so we all play backgammon even though you can only play two people at a time. You won't eat certain vegetables, sauces; vinegar is out. We plan our meals around you, and you're not even the vegetarian! You're exhausting." Jack splayed his hands out calmly. "I know I'm not the first one to tell you this."

"You son of a bitch," Willa said softly; then she threw her glass in the direction of Jack's chair. He ducked out of the way, and it shattered on the concrete patio. Willa took a final look at all of them before turning and marching into the house. She left the patio door wide open.

There was a pulse of silence before Penelope said softly, "Jack, you're kind of an ass."

"Look, am I wrong? I know her better than anyone. It's not the first time I've yelled at her for acting like a selfish prick, and it won't be the last," Jack said. He grinned at Penelope and reached out, took her hand, his thumb caressing the inside of her palm and sending her heart into her throat. "Besides, I *know* I'm an ass."

Penelope gently pulled her hand away, her thoughts muddled with vodka. He always did this. When Jack and Willa fought, Jack came to

Penelope. Touched her, made her quietly want, more than anything, to be on his team. To be Jack and Penelope, and Willa be the foil. She felt an impulse, dark and slippery, to encourage him. It would be easy. *Yeah, you're right. Willa is always catered to. She's always late, always subtly rearranging our schedules to suit her, wrinkling her nose at dinner, declaring our evening activities.* He wasn't wrong; it could be maddening.

But it was who she was.

Penelope stood, followed Willa's path into the house, downstairs, and knocked on her bedroom door. When she pushed the door open, Willa was sitting at her makeup vanity, fixing her hair.

"I came to see if you're okay?" Penelope asked her. She didn't look like she'd been crying.

"Why wouldn't I be? Because of Jack?" She laughed, shrill and thin. "He can fuck himself." She applied lipstick in a careful arc and pressed her lips together. Then she stood, looked at Penelope expectantly.

"Will, where are you going?" Penelope asked her softly.

"Out. I'm not staying here." Her voice was cold.

"Please don't do this."

"Why? I already called Hal. He'll be here in five minutes."

"The guy from the other night? When you came home crying?"

"Oh, that wasn't because of him. That was because some douche-bag at the bar threw a drink at me." Willa tossed her hair behind her shoulder and stood in front of Penelope, who was blocking the door.

"Please don't go. You're mad." Drama followed Willa—her fiery temper and quick mouth were both the things everyone loved and hated the most about her. If she went out tonight, who knew how it would go. Who she would anger, what would happen.

Finally, she sighed and met Penelope's eyes. "Of course I'm mad. He's a shithead. You know this, right?"

"You guys fight like brother and sister," Penelope offered, trying not to fall into the same trap Jack tried to lure her into earlier. *Pick a side.*

Willa reached out and hugged Penelope tight, held her breathless against her cheek, smelling like something candied. "I'll be careful, okay?" She slipped through the door and was gone.

—⁂—

Back outside, Bree quietly made up another pitcher of lemonade, which Flynn, Penelope, Jack, and Bree drank under the fireworks that started to explode all around them. Jack whistled "The Star-Spangled Banner" softly, and Penelope thought about Willa, out at a bar, angry and drinking. Maybe popping a pill or two.

"No worries," Jack whispered, patting Penelope's shoulder. "She'll be fine. She always is. You'll pick up the pieces. Or I will." He grinned. "I was too harsh. She's just so . . . frustrating sometimes." He disappeared inside the kitchen, and moments later, Penelope heard the distant strum of his guitar.

She wondered if he felt bad about Willa. She contemplated following him, but before she could, Bree stood, swaying, and wandered into the kitchen. She heard, dimly, the click of the basement door.

Flynn laughed softly. "She always pretends she'll come back, but when she's drunk, she just goes right to sleep."

"It's only ten o'clock!" Penelope said. She was starting to forget the earlier fight, enjoying the fizz of the lemonade, the sour tang at the back of her throat, the heady fuzz of her mind. She turned and studied Flynn, aware that she had him alone for the first time since his overly kind speech about her—God, what a stupid game that was! "Thank you for the kind things you said about me." Penelope's tongue felt thick and her words awkward. "I feel so dumb for making up that idiotic story about Jack. I just thought we were being silly and—"

"Yours was great," Flynn cut her off, mercifully. "I was buzzed and emotional. I don't get that way often."

"Anyway, thank you. I'll remember that probably forever. It was just so *nice*."

"It's true, though. You don't even know you do it. You're the only one who ever listens to anyone. I mean, Bree is great. She's my closest friend, but even she doesn't *really listen*." Flynn let out a sound of frustration and slapped a hand against his knee. "That sounds so pathetic. It's not what I mean. I just mean . . . you have a gift. You can see people for who they are."

"Is it true that Black people don't celebrate the Fourth of July?" Penelope asked. She felt bad that everyone had just talked over that fact—it had felt so alive to Penelope. Salient, even, baked into the person Flynn was. Or maybe who he had become later.

"Yeah, sometimes. I mean, I'm sure there are Black families who do. We did when I was a kid, but my parents were white. Later, when I could choose my own friends, I hung out with the Black kids more. Earlier, well, my parents were friends with the church people. Anyway, my high school friends didn't celebrate. My buddy's dad made us listen to that Frederick Douglass speech. You know the one?"

Penelope shook her head, embarrassed. She'd heard about it, maybe in a history class along the way. She'd never, that she could remember, listened to it.

"Well, yeah, I mean, why would you know." Flynn sighed then, heavy and sour. The last of the pops could be heard in the distance. He paused, picked his words carefully. "I mean, the fireworks were always fun, I guess. But most Black families don't do it up the same way. It wasn't our freedom, you know? Like the *point of it* is to celebrate these awe-inspiring national ideals that we've never seen or felt, you know?"

Penelope didn't know, which made her ashamed.

"You think I see you?" Penelope asked, her voice wobbling then, as she thought about that first night in the house, Flynn's face as he watched Jack and Bree together.

Flynn turned to her, his dark eyes wide, framed with black lashes. "Yes." He said simply. "And I . . . you."

"If I'm the only one who sees you, how can you be in love with someone who doesn't? What kind of love is that?" Penelope asked, her heart flipping wildly. She was on the cusp of discovery, the slipping darkness of a confessional all around her.

After all, they shared this, a long-kept secret. Could either of them admit it?

"It's the only kind I'll ever be able to have. Do you ever feel like the world just isn't ready for you? Or maybe that you're not ready for the world?" But Flynn just shook his head, closed his eyes, and half laughed. "I mean, I could be one or the other, but Christ, not both."

CHAPTER TWENTY

February 21, 2020

The audit was over. Thank goodness. Penelope could breathe again. She took Friday off, slept late. Thursday night, Brett had slept in their bedroom, each of them firmly on their own side of the bed. Not angry, but functional.

Penelope made breakfast in bed for Brett, but then he was up, showering.

"Just going for a walk, okay? Not a run."

"Nothing strenuous. No yoga. You just had a *blood transfusion*."

"Everyone keeps saying that like I'm steps from death. It's not a big deal. I've been on a message board. A lot of people with my condition go through this, and they're fine. I just have to be more careful."

My condition. She was reminded that her husband had a condition now. She quelled the rising dread—as tenuous as their connection had been lately, she very much wanted him to stay healthy. He was the father of her children. Despite her uncertainty about their future, all their struggles, she'd never want anything to happen to him.

She watched him get dressed, wondering if she still loved him.

He left for his walk, whistling. He'd never been a whistler before.

In Linc's bedroom, she gathered the laundry but didn't touch anything else. His bed was perpetually made, not a sock on the floor, not a crumb on the desk.

Tara's room, on the other hand, was a different kettle of fish. She left a trail of disaster in her wake, always. Penelope started to gather stray clothing: socks, bras, nightgowns, boxer shorts that she preferred to sleep in, a mitten from the floor. A thin slip of plastic flew from a pair of jeans and landed neatly on the unmade bed. From a distance it looked like a credit card, light blue and shining. She moved closer. In Penelope's mind, almost everything in a fifteen-year-old's bedroom was her mother's business. *Almost.* She reached out with one hand and clicked it open; the lid popped like a clamshell.

Birth control pills.

—๛—

"Mom. I was just trying to be responsible." Tara, despite her trail of debris, had usually behaved responsibly. Penelope tried to breathe through her wild thoughts. Who? Why? How? She couldn't even form questions—too afraid of scaring Tara away with an endless stream of inquisition. Too confused to figure out which to utter first.

She settled on one. "Who?"

Tara shifted on her bed, clicking the clamshell open and shut. "So. About six months ago—"

"Six months!"

"Mom!"

Penelope shut up.

"Six months ago, Matthew and I started hanging out. We were friends. Then we kissed. Now I think we're boyfriend and girlfriend. Everyone acts like we are. We've never really *talked* about it, but Matthew is just *nice*, you know?"

Penelope did know. Her heart thawed just a little. Matthew Yost was what most mothers would pick, if they could, for a daughter's first boyfriend. He was polite, in the theater program with Tara, tall and handsome but not overly so, that he would know it. He had the right amount of confidence—the insecure boys would try to keep her down; the cocky boys would play games. Sometimes the dissecting, exacting thoughts of her analytical parenting mind shocked her.

Penelope chose to stay quiet, and Tara rambled on, nervous, picking at the hem of her skirt.

"We haven't . . . you know. But I'm going to be sixteen soon. I thought, maybe? Anyway, I'd read on the internet that it can take months for pills to be effective. I thought, why not now?"

"I agree with you," Penelope said simply.

"You do?" Tara's head snapped up, astonished.

"I do. It can take a long time to figure out the dosage, the side effects, what drug is right for you. By the time you're ready for sex—"

"Mom!"

"If you can't talk about it, can't even say the word, you're not ready. So don't *Mom* me." Penelope gave her daughter a stern look and continued. "By the time you're ready, you want to make sure you're fully protected. You should still use condoms"—she held up a hand to stem the inevitable mortified *Mom!*—"to protect from diseases, what have you. But it's a good idea. However . . . I want to know how you got them. You should see a doctor, get a checkup anyway."

"I did see a doctor," Tara said, her face changing. She looked almost proud of herself. "Willa took me."

"Willa!" Penelope felt the breath leave her lungs, a punch right in her core. She put a hand on her forehead to steady herself. "Tara. You have to talk to *me*. I am your mother. I will be there for you, but you need to come to *me*. Do you understand?"

"Mom, don't freak out. She's your friend! She's cool; I like her a lot. I hope she sticks around town. Anyway, I wasn't sure how you'd react.

And besides, I knew she'd be cool with it. She gave Linc condoms, and he's a year younger."

Penelope stood, shaking out her fingertips, her hands numb, and felt like she was going to pass out. *What in the hell was Willa thinking?*

"Linc. Are you serious?" Her voice came out deadly calm, and Tara shrank back, away from her.

"Mom, it seems like you're freaking out. Are you freaking out?"

"I'm fine, Tara. You're not the one who needs to worry here."

—⁂—

Penelope stood in the kitchen. Waiting. Seething. A pack of foil condoms in one hand, a thin plastic clamshell of pills in the other. Good God, what would Brett say? She'd confiscated the condoms from Linc with zero protest. He reached into his bedside table and tossed them to her without fanfare. *I thought it was a little weird, anyway. I wasn't even going to use them.*

She snapped a pic of the condoms and pills and started a text, then stopped. She would normally send Jaime this kind of thing. He would be appalled, then panic about Sasha. But. What if Willa and Jaime were together? She deleted the photo. Probably for the best. If cutting ties was her goal anyway, why not start now? Anger and distrust seemed like appropriate scissors for the task.

Penelope had no earthly idea where Willa was, or when she'd be home. She didn't know who would come home first—Brett or Willa. She doubted she'd be able to keep herself under control either way. In the ten days since her old friend had come, Penelope's life had been turned upside down. Her husband was admitted to the hospital, her jewelry had gone missing (and been returned, causing Penelope to doubt herself over and over), her bedroom cleaned out, her closet organized, her closest ally, Jaime, newly untrustworthy. Penelope had no idea when Willa was planning to leave. But the entire situation was beginning to make her crazy.

Penelope was about to text Brett when she heard the front door open and shut and then a lofty, "Hey, y'all!"

Was it Penelope's imagination, or was the southern accent getting thicker every day?

Willa appeared in the kitchen doorway, a pink shiny shopping bag in one hand. Without speaking, Penelope held her hands out so that Willa could see the birth control.

She laughed. *She laughed.* Penelope sucked in a breath and felt the rage pulse in her neck.

"Oh, girl, don't be mad." She smiled, all sparkly teeth as she plopped the glittery bag on the countertop. "They were old enough, and frankly, Tara asked, so I thought, what the hell, might as well get it for the boy too. You are too pretty to be a grandma just yet, you know."

"Willa. I will not tolerate this. These are *my kids.*" Penelope slammed her palm on the countertop. "Willa, this is beyond the pale. Look, I'll admit, twenty years ago, you did whatever you wanted, and I went along with it. Willa was the star, Penelope was the shadow. I am *not* that person anymore. I will be the one to buy them birth control. I will be the one to talk about major life milestones with them. Me. Their *mother.*"

Penelope expected her to fall apart, beg forgiveness. A repeat of the scene the other night.

"Look, I don't have kids, okay? Maybe I don't know what's complete boundary pushing and what's helping out. I thought I've been *helping* you! Tara *asked me* to get her birth control. I thought I was doing the right thing! You've been coming home and going right to sleep! Between work and Brett in the hospital, I've been holding it all down here." Willa's tone took an edge, something unguarded and sugary, like panic seeping in. "I would have told you! When life settled down."

"When would that be? When does my life settle down?" Penelope laughed, her voice brittle, her anger palpable. She could feel it, like snakes under her skin. "You don't actually live here. You are not actually part of this family."

Willa looked like she'd been slapped. Her cheeks flushed, instant and furious pink. She whispered, "We were always family. Then."

Then. At the Church House. The words went unsaid but still set flame to Penelope's blood. She battled guilt and anger and couldn't come up with the words. Guilt for the way she'd let twenty years pass without even contacting anyone, without checking on Willa. Did they understand that she couldn't? That she couldn't turn and face what happened the night of the fire? That despite everyone playing a small role in the tragedies that followed, that Penelope was the guiltiest of all? That she had the most to hide? None of them could understand.

Guilt because she'd been subconsciously using Willa for over a week. With Willa here, dinners got made. The house got cleaned. The kids were picked up when Penelope was stuck at work. A free place to live felt like an even exchange. But now—with all the boundaries not just pushed but broken, her life splayed open and examined—was it actually fair? If Penelope invited boundary pushing when it suited her, did she have a right to anger when they were broken?

Penelope took a deep breath.

"That was then. This is now. I am not the same person. *We* are not the same people." Penelope felt dangerously close to their own edge of truth. But she didn't say it. Why not? Her stomach roiled, a slick flip, and she felt nauseated.

"Look," Willa said. She reached out, held Penelope's hand. "Pip. I love you. I've always loved you, always will. I'm sorry about all the ways I seem to be . . . pushing boundaries. I know you don't believe this, but I'm truly just trying to help, okay? Like the bills thing—"

"What bills thing?"

"He didn't tell you?" Willa blinked twice, her lashes long and eyes bright blue and shining. Pools you could get lost in. "Brett called me from the hospital one day. He tried to call you, but he said you were at work. You didn't always answer—couldn't always answer, I should say. Anyway, he asked me to log on and pay your credit card bill. It was due, the late fees would pile up. He gave me the info, said he would tell you about it. Anyway, I did it, and it's fine. Girl, that balance—you're lucky, that's all. That woulda been a whopper of a late fee."

Penelope pushed her fingertips into her eye sockets to stave off a headache.

Can you be furious and grateful at the same time? She was right that it would have been a ridiculous late fee. The balance was so high. She felt only mildly embarrassed that Willa had seen it.

"Look, I've been helpful, too, you know. Not just this awful violating, lurking person. I've been picking the kids up all week." Willa's voice took on an injured undertone. "The other night, when you fell asleep? I took Linc to his lacrosse meeting." She saw Penelope's face fall. "You just remembered it, didn't you?" She shook her head, clucking softly. "You think I don't see it? You're falling apart here, honey."

Penelope took a breath and handed Willa back the condoms. She kept the pills, knowing that Tara had already started them and it was better for her health to continue with something she'd started than to switch. Practical Penelope. "Thank you for taking Linc to his meeting. And picking him up from practice this week. I won't need you to do that anymore." Her voice was wooden. She felt awful about Linc. Why hadn't he said anything? Her sweet, pliable, happy son. Was he mad at her? When was the last time they'd really talked? Penelope pushed her hair off her forehead and tried to focus. "I'm not falling apart—"

"You are! But it's okay. Everyone does. I'll pick you up the way you picked me up. I needed you, and you've come through. Let me *help* you."

"Not by buying my kids birth control. Taking them to see a *doctor*, for God's sake. That's over the line." Penelope's voice was firm, but she felt the previous blinding rage seeping away anyway. Willa could always do this to her—Penelope would always cave, always defend her.

"You're right. I'm so sorry, I am." Willa stood up straighter, swiped a thumb under each eye, and gave Penelope a weepy smile. "I've been here over a week. It's long enough. I'm going to start looking for a new place to go, okay?"

Penelope felt a sudden surge of guilt. She was *her friend*, for God's sake. She was abused. She needed help. Not constant suspicion. She swallowed back the lump in her throat. "You can take your time. I mean, we should all have a plan moving forward, but you don't have to like . . . move out tomorrow or anything crazy."

Willa's shoulders sagged with relief. "I owe you so much, Pip. Truly." She reached out and hugged Penelope, her hair a soft cloud, her breath smelling like peppermints.

Penelope patted her back, and they pulled apart.

"Hey, what happened to your necklace?" Penelope asked, lightly touching Willa's collarbone. "You know, BREATHE?"

Willa tilted her head, her eyes narrowed in confusion. "What necklace?" she said.

CHAPTER
TWENTY-ONE

Then: The Spires

They called her Pip now. It started on Wednesday.

They had gotten drunk together, lazed on couches, drinking long island iced teas—which were just a mix of whatever liquor they had on hand with a touch of iced tea, so not at all long island iced teas, but Jack kept proclaiming they were, and pouring them into tall glass tumblers he found in the kitchen.

Jack declared that after a few stiff drinks, *Penelope* was too hard to say, so he looked up nicknames for her, and they all settled on *Pip*. Penelope didn't dislike it—but she doubted anyone outside the Church House would ever call her that.

So now they were Jack, Flynn, Bree, Will(a), Pip. They sounded like a band. Spent a little bit of time coming up with a band name: the Heretics, Sunday School Dropouts, Existential Dread, the Holy Rollers, the Apostates—this last one was Jack's and, they all agreed, the most clever.

"What about *the Spires*?" said Willa then. She was outside, the back french doors open to the patio. She was looking up, the milky swan of her neck exposed. "We live here. In a church, right? The church, technically, has a *spire*. Plus, it means to be at the pinnacle of something."

"So this is the pinnacle of our life?" Pip asked. She felt like this could be true for her alone. If this was the pinnacle of everyone else's life, she felt sorry for them. What was that saying? *Why would I want to be part of a club that would have me for a member?* An old Groucho Marx favorite (she used to watch Johnny Carson reruns at two in the morning).

Willa threw her hands in the air. "I mean, don't you feel like that? Look, we're done with school. That stress is behind us. We've got nothing but the great big world ahead of us. I mean, fuck, probably kids and jobs and spouses, and goddamn, that all sounds awful. Right now, though, it's just us. We get to live here. Together. Having a goddamn party every night."

Bree made a sound from the back of her throat—half in agreement, half mocking. Flynn grinned widely. "I'm definitely having the time of my life."

Jack laughed and said, "Okay. The Spires it is. That's us. Beautiful. The world at our feet. The top of our game, baby."

Willa had belted from the garden, in gorgeous, rich vibrato, *Standing on top of the world!*

By Friday, Pip had worked all week at the Deer Run Used Bookstore. Her manager was a fiftyish woman named Amelia with brown bobbed hair, small gray eyes set too far apart, who smelled like baby powder and the waxy odor of lipstick, although she didn't appear to wear any. She was kind and laughed too much at things Pip said that were only mildly funny, but the days flew by as they categorized, organized, discarded donated books whose covers were too ripped or falling off.

At the end of the day, Pip would wait for Jack at the corner by the coffee shop, and he'd come strolling out, his messenger bag flapping against his back, and he'd greet her with a wide happy grin.

"How much of your book did you get written?" she'd ask, and he'd tell her a word count—usually five hundred to seven hundred words, and they'd walk home together in the sweltering heat, and little by little she got a little bit out of him about his book. Writers, she found, couldn't resist the call to talk about their work, if asked.

The sun was behind them, Pip's back on fire, the crown of her head hot to the touch, but Pip barely noticed. Jack was explaining about his book, growing up in Brooklyn, half-Cuban, his mother dead. "In this book, which is fictional, there's a murder. But the protagonist is only seventeen, so it will still be young adult," Jack rambled on. "Wouldn't it be amazing if I could sell it? God, I can't tell you. I feel like I've spent four years studying computer science and finance to wake up and realize it was all wrong. Now I have a mountain of debt, and I want to pay it off by writing a novel? I mean, I guess it's possible. Some novelists are rich, right? Why not me?"

She let him go on, enjoying the rumble and cadence of his voice, the soft soothe of his excitement and the way he'd say, *And then I had an idea; listen to this!* And clutch her arm, his neck flushed and hands gesturing, and she thought to herself, *Why not me?*

Then Pip thought about Flynn's face, shining under the firework sky as he looked not at the bright bursts of color above him but at Jack, whose arm was slung around Willa's shoulders, her head resting prettily on his arm, and thought, *Why not him?*

Did you have any control over who you fell in love with? A year ago, Pip would have said of course. She'd had a form of love before—in high school. Ronald Baure, the son of the local grocer. Sneaking out in the middle of the night and into his bedroom, or he into hers. Her aunt slept so soundly she never heard a thing, the television in her room blaring. She wouldn't have suspected Pip of being the kind of girl who could sneak a boy in anyway.

Actually, Pip wasn't sure Aunt Belinda thought that much about her at all.

Ronald Baure was the first and only boy she'd slept with, in high school. College was stringent and difficult, and Pip had thrown herself into studying, only to come up for air on quarter-draft nights with Willa, where she met Jack and they started meeting every Thursday to play pool at Yawney's bar. That was the extent of her social life junior and senior year.

Every once in a while, she'd end up at someone's apartment party with Jack and Willa, and if she saw Flynn and Bree (always the twosome), they'd all collect in a corner, drawn together, laughing, teasing, talking, sharing a bottle of wine, or taking turns nipping at the keg. Had she realized then, about Flynn? She tried to think about the moment she realized Flynn was gay—whether he'd said it or not—and found that she couldn't. Just that she *knew*—and also knew that no one else really acknowledged it or talked about it. She hadn't known about the depth of Flynn's feelings for Jack until that first night at the house.

At the Church House, Jack let himself in, calling "'Ello!" in a cockney voice up to the loft and down to the basement, tossing his messenger bag onto the overstuffed leather couch. Pip followed behind him; it was Friday, typically the night for cocktail hours and Jack's night to cook. Pip pulled a carefully wrapped brown-paper package of shrimp out of the fridge and starting chopping onions to help him.

"You don't have to help," Jack said, biting into a celery stalk at the same time Pip said, "What are we making?"

His mouth twisted up in a lopsided grin. "Paella." Then, "Bree can pick the meat out."

"Jack! It's all meat! Chicken, sausage, shrimp!"

He laughed wickedly but agreed to make her dish separately. "She eats seafood," he amended. He leaned over and kissed Pip's cheek quickly as he slid past her for the wine on the counter. "I'll do it for you. You're a good friend to her."

"Who's a good friend to whom?" Willa took the steps two at a time and flung herself into the closest dining chair.

"Pip. She's everyone's BFF. Always looking out." He said the last part in a singsong, smart alecky.

Bree floated in from somewhere, because that's what Bree did. Pip wouldn't see her for hours, and suddenly, poof, she'd appear in the room as if by magic. Or a trapdoor. She barely heard her—only rarely saw her come and go from the house at all. Where did she spend her time? The garden, Pip assumed, her face always striped thinly with mud.

She wore that white dress again—still filthy.

"Bree, do you want me to wash that for you?" Pip offered, but Bree laughed.

"This is my gardening dress. It's just so damn hot out there. It's the lightest thing I own, that's all." She pulled it out to the side, inspected the smears of dirt on the hem. "Don't mind me—I'm a mess!" But she didn't change out of it, instead poured herself a vodka soda, bare toes tapping on the hardwood floor, heels limned with grime.

Even as they ate dinner—stuffed themselves on Jack's paella, Willa liberally pouring the wine—Pip kept thinking, *How can Bree not want to shower and clean up before eating?* It seemed—like Jack had called the Fourth of July—barbaric.

Flynn came through the front door halfway through dinner, carrying a stack of old board games—backgammon and go and Risk—their box edges crumpled and broken.

"I used to love Risk!" Bree exclaimed, clapping excitedly.

"I found them in the trash behind the library." Flynn dumped the stack on the coffee table and helped himself to Jack's concoction growing gluey in the pan. He took his plate to the living room and began setting up the Risk board. Pip loved Risk, the strategy, the long game, investing in something that might not pay out immediately.

"I haven't played this since high school." Willa got up from the table, leaving her plate. She always left a small trail of debris wherever she went. Likely Flynn would clean it up later—his tolerance for untidiness was well below the others', and he spent most of his time at the house cleaning up after Bree's mess.

They each took their colors (so predictable, and would become permanent, although they didn't know that at the time: Jack—red, Flynn—green, Willa—yellow, Bree—pink, Pip—black), dealt the cards, and placed their game pieces. Willa poured everyone gin and tonics with limes she had picked up at the farmers market by the basketful. Jack stationed his men around Africa, the whole time Flynn insisting that you couldn't hold Africa for any length of time, while Bree quietly amassed an army in Australia.

"The problem with Risk," declared Jack much later, drunk, the red on the board down to two strongholds—one in Egypt and one terminally stuck in Madagascar, "is that there are only two, maybe three, workable strategies. And the players have to fight for those. And everyone knows what they are. There's no real intelligence. It's only pretending to be a strategic game."

"You're just saying that because you're going to lose," Bree piped up, her soft voice steely as she coolly handed Jack the red die set, bright-blue eyes blinking like an owl. The board was largely pink, with Flynn holding Europe and Pip keeping her hold in North America, a tight cluster of black. A streak of pink cut across India and the Middle East. As though she'd come straight for Jack.

"They call this a religious war, you know," Jack bellowed, standing up, blowing on the die in his hand. Pip drank deeply from the tumbler, which was now more melted ice than gin, but felt the burn anyway, the lime acrid on her tongue. "There was no strategy, no logic. It's too emotional. You came straight for me? Why, my sweet Bree?"

"Maybe I'm not so sweet." She grinned wickedly, tossed her long tangle of hair, and laughed as Pip refilled her glass. On her knees, Bree leaned forward, and Pip could see her blackened heels, the thick streaks of mud up her calves.

"That's not your problem," Jack countered, rolling a four and five to Bree's five and six before he plucked two of his men from the board and placed them back in the game box. "Your problem is you pretend. Sweet. Even innocent. Rich. But all the while, your mind is working under there—conniving, even. With your pink little pieces on your purple territory. Even your game strategy screams pretty princess."

Flynn hooted, but Pip shifted uncomfortably. Jack's commentary held a new edge, something sharp and hidden; the only one sensitive to it was Pip. Willa clapped excitedly, a rock of ice pushed into her cheek as she bent forward over the board, whisper-chanting *fight, fight, fight,* a gleam in her eye, cheeks flushed. Flynn leaned back against the couch, his eyes closed, his mouth curved slightly into a soft smile.

"Princess?" Bree expelled a breath through her nose, and Pip could see the twitch there, something moving under the surface. She rolled two fours to Jack's three and one, and suddenly he was down to two men, Bree's pink cavalry looking comically ominous.

"You've been killed by the princess army." Bree cocked her head, a smile on her face, but something about it made the hair on Pip's arms stand up.

"See? You just pretend to be innocent." Jack sat back down, his eyes flashing, and this time Pip was sure of the undercurrent. Flynn caught it, too, his gaze flicking between Jack and Bree, his hand cupping Bree's elbow protectively. She sat up then. "Bree, the virgin. Helpless Bree. But that's not it, is it? You're so far from helpless. It's an act."

"Why are you such a fucking prick?" Her voice was low, cut with venom. Pip had never heard that out of Bree before—not like that.

Jack shrugged, leaned back, an easy grin on his face. "Did Bree tell you her dad was a Hollywood star? Got an Emmy or some shit like that? Like, twenty years ago?"

It wasn't clear who Jack was talking to, presumably one of them.

Then, softly, "I looked him up. Was it true, Bree?"

She said nothing, her jaw set.

"Jack, why are you being such a douchebag?" Willa called from the kitchen. She crossed the expanse of hardwood, licking her fingertips. "Seriously, why do you get drunk and do this sometimes?"

"Do what?" Jack finally broke his gaze and looked at Willa. "What do I do?"

"Get drunk and be an asshole," Willa said.

Pip couldn't help it, felt sorry later for rushing to Jack's defense. "Doesn't everyone do that?" Then, quieter as they all swiveled to look at her, "Sometimes?"

"Look, all I'm saying is, Bree acts like she's this ingenue here. We all do her bidding. But she tells some lies. She kind of acts a little better than the rest of us."

"Oh, fuck off, I do not," Bree finally spoke. "I don't act better than any of you. I don't lie. I'm not an ingenue or whatever you said earlier."

"You know another word for virgin?" Jack poured gin straight into his glass and gulped it down warm. "A tease."

"Why do you even care so much?" Bree said, her voice breaking and chilled. "You're a sexist pig. All the time. What does it matter to *you*?"

"It doesn't matter to me," Jack said evenly, a smirk on his face, his eyes slitted. "It's just *interesting*."

"I think it fucking sucks that the most interesting thing about any-one is whether or not they've had sex." Bree spat the words out, her voice low and teeth clenched.

"I don't think it's the most interesting thing about you. I just said it was interesting." Jack held his hands up, palms out.

"I think you just don't like it that I won't have sex with *you*," Bree said finally.

Even Willa had shut up by this point, tucked into the corner chair, her chin resting on the armrest, her eyes tracking the fight, hand clutching a warm brandy snifter of vodka.

"I didn't ask, darling." Jack laughed then, too loud. But even Pip could see the faint flush up his cheeks. Was that it, then? Had Bree rejected him? Or was he preemptively striking out? She saw his jaw tighten, working.

Nobody spoke for what felt like an hour but couldn't have been more than five minutes.

Finally, Jack smiled. Charm returned. "I was mostly joking, you know."

"You weren't, Jack," Bree said. She stood, raised her eyebrows to Flynn, who also stood. She threaded her arm through Flynn's, her head resting on his shoulder, her face wounded. He patted her back benignly, unsure what to do in the midst of this unprecedented argument. They'd never fought before. Willa and Jack sometimes. But never all of them, choosing sides. Bree led Flynn downstairs, but not before shooting one last look over her shoulder. Penelope thought that maybe she looked not hurt or upset, but satisfied.

—◌—

Willa followed Bree and Flynn downstairs after reading Jack the riot act. "We were playing a game, you shithead." Willa stood, brushed chip crumbs from her skirt onto the floor, and started packing up the box. "Does anyone ever finish this stupid game, or does it always just end in a fight?" she muttered under her breath. Pip followed her lead and stood, silently collecting glasses and plates and carting them to the kitchen sink.

Only Jack remained seated, unaffected, arms slung over his knees, legs bent and crossed at the ankle. "I mean, you're not off base. I am, certainly, a shithead. I just feel like we should all be able to be honest with each other. Bree does act like she's better than the rest of us. Above us. It's grating."

"The only thing grating around here tonight is you." Willa slammed the basement door and was gone, leaving them alone.

Penelope stayed upstairs with Jack. He rubbed blearily at his eyes. "Maybe I'm just drunk. Do you think I'm an asshole?"

"I think you want everyone to love you best. Bree doesn't. It eats away at you." The vodka made Penelope bold.

Jack's head snapped up at that, and his bright-blue eyes met hers, and the current went from her head straight to her toes. He stared at her so intently for far too long. Finally, he said, softly, "You're so unsettling sometimes, Pip."

It reminded her of what Flynn said the week before.

She stood up suddenly, her head spinning, and mumbled something about going to bed. Jack reached up from the floor, grabbed her hand. His skin was hot, his eyes unfocused as she looked down at him, and his thumb caressed the inside of her palm, sending a shiver up her arm.

"I'm jealous, you know. She doesn't need anyone. How do you go through life like that?" Jack's voice wobbled and slurred.

"That's ridiculous. She needs Flynn."

"No, she doesn't. She pretends to." He tugged her hand to bring her closer to him, until they were only inches apart. Penelope could barely breathe. "Everything with her is an act."

"You're very drunk. I think we should all just go to bed." Pip snatched her hand away, her vision blurring around the edges. She backed away from him, but he didn't make a move to stand. "Will you be okay?"

"You're a good friend, Pip." Then, more quietly, "Better to me than I am to you."

Pip paused, considering. Almost turned back, almost asked him more. Instead, she left him there, staring at the ceiling.

CHAPTER
TWENTY-TWO

February 22, 2020

"It's Willa's birthday!"

Penelope was in her bedroom folding laundry when Tara came bounding in. It was only ten in the morning, and Tara usually rolled out of bed on Saturdays sometime before noon, but not generally by ten.

"Is that so? How do you know that?" Penelope kept her voice even while matching socks. She wasn't mad anymore, but she still retained a certain level of uneasiness. The BREATHE necklace was back in her jewelry box. She had not imagined the conversation, the necklace resting against Willa's tanned chest. Had she tried to swipe it, gotten caught, and secretly returned it? Why would she act like it was hers, then later pretend she didn't know what Penelope was talking about? *What necklace?* she'd asked. What kind of person would play a game like that, and to what end? Penelope had a niggling doubt. Maybe, *maybe,* she had been wrong. Maybe the necklace *had* been in her jewelry box the whole time, and it was a duplicate necklace. *Maybe* the conversation had been so mundane to Willa that she'd forgotten about it entirely.

She started watching Willa, *really watching her*. Humming around the house, padding through the halls barefoot, a soft smile on her face. Penelope found *herself* sneaking around her own damn house, tiptoeing through the front door. Carefully hanging her coat, lingering in the living room, listening to the conversation in the kitchen. For what, exactly? She didn't know. An affair with her husband? A whispered phone call? Something untoward with either of the kids? None of it could be discounted. There had been too many missteps, too many boundaries crossed for Penelope to feel entirely comfortable with Willa in the house, in her life.

The sooner they all moved on, the better. From the beginning, she'd promised her two weeks. Well, fine. She'd get her two weeks. But in the meantime, Penelope started locking her bedroom door. It was a simple privacy knob, a pinhole on the outside that could be popped with any generic sharp object. The point was to let Willa know that she wasn't welcome. Maybe it would be enough; maybe it wouldn't.

Hopefully, this would only be a few more days.

She handed the basket to Tara, who sighed theatrically and flounced away. Penelope suspected she'd just dump it in Linc's room and pretend she never saw it.

In the kitchen, Tara and Linc and Brett were huddled together, conspiring. When they saw Penelope, they waved her in.

"We're planning a party for Willa. She's been so great while Daddy was sick and you were working. Wouldn't it be fun to throw her a surprise party?"

"Come on, Mom." Tara leaned in, whispered to her girl talk–style. "I can tell you're still kind of mad at her. About"—*the pills,* she mouthed. "But just for fun? Can you be nice for a night?"

Yes. Yes, she could have been nice had Willa just not bought her kids birth control and gone through all their finances and rearranged their closets. If she hadn't pushed every socially acceptable boundary there was.

But. Brett didn't know about the birth control. She hadn't confronted him about the credit card bill he'd asked Willa to pay. Why? Stress, maybe? Stress was a contributing factor to a hemolytic crisis. Not the major factor, and it was anecdotal, like most things related to G6PD. Soy was anecdotal, too; still, he avoided soy. Either way, she was giving him a little bit of time before she brought more stress, more conflict into their lives. Either that or she was just procrastinating an uncomfortable conversation.

It felt to Penelope as though they were living in limbo. Waiting for Willa to leave. Waiting to see how their marriage would either come back together or fall apart.

Penelope looked at Brett, who gave her a small *whatcha gonna do* shrug and waved his hand to the two hopeful, smiling faces in front of her.

So? What else was she supposed to do? Her problems with Willa—whatever they were—were not her children's problems. What the hell. At least there would be wine.

Penelope retrieved a notepad from the top drawer. "Okay, make me a list," she said, resigned. The kids whooped, and Linc kissed her cheek.

Today, apparently, there would be a birthday party.

—⁂—

Brett asked her to text Jaime and tell him to come at seven.

"Why?" Penelope startled, a grocery bag in each hand. She placed them, carefully and while avoiding eye contact, on the counter and started putting away hors d'oeuvres—cheese and crackers, pesto spread, and crusty french bread.

"I think they're kind of dating!" His eyes were bright, happy. Penelope felt the nausea roll over her, but it faded as quickly as it had come. She didn't want to see them together, of course not. But. Who knew what the future held—for any of them, really—but if by some miraculous turn of events she and Brett stayed together in Wexford, and Willa moved in somewhere nearby, and Jaime and Willa did start dating, or maybe even got married—

"Penelope?" Brett held a bottle of wine in each hand, interrupting her careening train of thought.

"What?" she snapped, too quickly and too loud.

"Red or white?" Brett asked.

—⟋⟍—

Willa came home at seven with Jaime, who'd been instructed to keep her out for the surprise. She cried, her hands over her mouth, as if the idea of a surprise party was just completely unbelievable. As though there were fifty people in attendance.

They had made dinner—roasted pork loin, orzo and mushrooms, blackened asparagus—on the indoor grill. Wine for all, seemingly never ending. Penelope remembered the dinner a week ago, with Brett, and how glittery and sparkling everything felt with Willa around. She brought a certain kind of undeniable energy to a room, and after an hour and two glasses of wine, Penelope started to forget about the birth control and the bills and the closet and the boundaries. Mostly.

Willa was funny, witty, and beautiful, in a pink gauzy dress with long draping sleeves and a glittering crystal necklace. Jaime, Penelope noted with not a little heartbreak, was mesmerized. This was the Willa Penelope always remembered: alight, sparkling, loud, bawdy, fun. The one prompting the interesting conversations. The one with the most outrageous commentary.

There were no toasts this time, just lively conversation, the kind that overlapped and turned without intention; the best kind, where everyone talked at once, and then everyone laughed, and Penelope at one point had her head on her hand, gasping, the kind of laughter that made no noise, which Tara once told her was the best kind. She tried not to be charmed—but as the night wore on and the wine flowed, she found that she couldn't remember her anger.

She could remember the reasons behind it; she could enumerate the infractions: the bracelet (maybe), the birth control, the credit card bill, the necklace, Jaime (was that an infraction—truly?), the cleaned bedroom and closet. But she couldn't hold the anger—it kept sliding away from her. With every joke Willa told, she found her anger ebbing away until it was gone completely and all that remained was the hazy room, the burbling of laughter, the feel of Willa's hand on her arm.

Linc had made a cake, some kind of chocolate bomb with a liquid center, oozing and gooey, and they took their cake and wine into the living room.

The only time Jaime touched Penelope was accidentally, when he followed her from the dining room to the living room and he ducked his head and whispered *sorry* with a smile, and she *knew* that the touch did to him what it did to her, though they both tried not to think about it.

"You lived together after college?" Jaime asked, before eating a forkful of cake. The room quieted, or maybe it was Penelope's imagination, but even Linc seemed to still, his hand halfway to his mouth. "Wow, this is good," he said, unaware of the edge to his question or how they all knew not to talk about the time before—even Brett—just calling it the fire house. Years of *hmmmmms* and *Oh, honey, I don't quite remember* when asked about her college years, or the years immediately following, gave everyone the impression that it wasn't an enjoyable topic of conversation.

But Jaime didn't know any of that.

"Pen," Willa suddenly exclaimed, her voice pitched and excited. "Go get the photos!"

Penelope blinked at her, blankly. "What photos?"

"When I . . . organized your closet . . ." Willa's voice halted but recovered, her cheeks flushed with the memory of the infraction, a tacit apology. "I saw the photo album of us. It says *The Spires* on the front?"

"I have no idea what you're talking about." Penelope swallowed, but then, instantly, she did. She could see it, in the bottom of her closet bin of memories (movie tickets and subway tickets and loose snapshots and Polaroids and brochures for museums), a small little flip-book. Ten photos at the most. Clipped together with a little round paper ring. A tiny weight, moved from house to house, rarely looked at, but never parted with. The things that went into the bin never seemed to come back out.

"Please?"

Penelope knew the photos were from the early months. Halcyon days—before they argued—when they felt flush with love, faces pinked with liquor and the feeling of being on top of the world. Before Grace. Before the fire. Before everything got complicated.

The Spires.

"I've never seen these photos," Brett said, his voice injured.

"Let's see young Penelope and young Willa!" Jaime urged.

"I don't even know exactly where they are," Penelope faltered, knowing already that going along would be easier than resisting, so the protest felt half-hearted. Her stomach knotted; the cake felt like a lead ball. She set her plate on the end table and scanned the room. Linc and Tara gave her a *look—you promised to be nice!*

"I know exactly where they are!" Willa exclaimed, standing, going up on her toes and holding her hand out to Penelope to help her up. Penelope waved her away and went upstairs to retrieve them.

She returned downstairs, the small five-by-seven photo book in hand all yellowed and faded with twenty years of exposure to the air, but still, all of them at their peak, or so they believed.

The Spires. Someone had cut letters from magazines, pasted them carefully on the cover, so it looked slightly kidnapper-chic, just badass enough. She ran her fingers over the lettering. She didn't remember doing it—seemed like something Bree might have done.

Willa paged through the book, her face unreadable as she flipped. In order: the group of them on the front porch on moving day, Jack's arm slung around both Willa and Penelope, Flynn watching the three of them with bright, stark hope; the perpetual game of Risk they had going that seemed to continue the next day like no one had tipped the board over in a rage the night before (except for that one weird night with Bree—they all tried to forget about that one); the Fourth of July party on the patio.

Linc and Tara peered over her shoulder. Brett and Jamie casually waited their turn but smiled at the commentary.

"You look exactly the same, Mom!" Linc said.

"Willa looks different," Tara said.

"Oh, well. I was fat then," Willa said, shaking her head.

"What! You were never fat," Penelope insisted.

"I think I was at least twenty-five pounds heavier." Willa's voice turned dismissive.

Penelope flipped back to the photo of the five of them outside the church, the bell tower behind them. Their album cover, Jack had said. Willa's face was rounder, her cheeks ruddy with cold. Her eyes wider.

"God, remember that Independence Day party?" Penelope asked.

Willa studied Penelope, her face unreadable. "I think so. We had a lot of parties, you know?"

"Okay, but with the eulogies?"

"Wait, Mom, did you say *eulogies*?" Linc asked, his eyebrows shooting up to his hairline.

Penelope snorted, holding the back of her hand against her mouth. "Yes! Oh, it was probably so dumb. I don't even know who started it. Probably Jack." She rolled her eyes and looked over at Willa, expecting her to meet her gaze with the same level of derision, but her face remained passive, blank. "We all eulogized each other. Someone said that I joined the Vegas showgirls, and I said that Jack died in a sailing accident. How did you die?"

"Oh God, Pip, that was ages ago. How do you remember all this?" Willa waved her hand around, dismissive. She'd been so anxious for

Penelope to retrieve the photos, and now she seemed almost irritated by it.

"No, seriously! We always talked about it after. Jokes about our invented deaths. I can't remember yours."

"Pip, I can't either! I can barely remember what you're talking about!"

In the next photo, Bree was filthy from head to toe, and the rest of them—were they singing? The five of them holding various instruments they didn't know how to play—that was the joke. See, Jack played a guitar, but for pictures, Flynn always held it; Bree came flying in the door one day with a little metal triangle, and Jack claimed it as his. Willa was the singer, the voice of an angel; she was the only one they took seriously—they couldn't bear to not hear her voice, even if the rest of the band was a sham. Flynn—the resident dumpster diver—found a ukulele in the trash, and Penelope ended up with it. She couldn't remember if she chose it.

"You should sing tonight!" Penelope said with sudden inspiration.

"I can't sing anymore. I haven't sung since . . ." Willa let her voice trail off and motioned toward her face. "The smoke." The room fell silent, and they waited. Even Penelope's kids knew they never talked about the fire, even if they had never known why.

Brett knew there had been a fire and someone died. He thought her unwillingness to talk about it stemmed from love.

"I didn't know that," Penelope said, dumbfounded. Willa's singing was as much a part of the Church House as, well, the church itself. A high lilting, echoing off the high ceilings of the church. "God, what was that song you always used to sing? It was this low, sexy thing. Something from the seventies, maybe? Jazzy, you know. I can't remember?"

"Oh, I don't know; it was so long ago, Pip." She ate a forkful of cake, her cheeks full and flushed.

"How can you not know? It was constant, and God, you were great at it. Like, it was beautiful. The acoustics in the church were amazing.

It had these really high notes and then this thrumming, sexy baseline," Penelope said, watching Willa's face carefully.

"I said I have no idea, Pip—let it go." Willa's voice took on an edge, and she stood, brushing a crumb from her dress. She disappeared into the downstairs powder room, and Jaime caught Penelope's eye. She gave him a small shrug. Linc forked a piece of Tara's cake off her plate, and she swatted at him.

By the time Willa returned, the mood in the room had smoothed over. Brett was telling a story about college—he'd gone to a liberal arts college outside Philadelphia, small and intimate—and a roommate bar fight that ended at the county jail. Jaime was laughing, but Penelope was distracted. Willa had composed herself and was listening to Brett, rapt, but Penelope couldn't shake her uneasiness. How could Willa not remember the song? Or the way she "died"? It seemed no different than not remembering who had blonde hair or that Bree was a virgin or Flynn was gay or Jack was . . . Jack. All the parts of them had fused together to make the Church House and their year together a fulcrum in their lives.

Jaime had left with kisses on both their cheeks, and Brett had helped a bit, doing the dishes before going to bed. Linc and Tara were long gone, up to their rooms, their phones, their friends.

Later, as they were cleaning up, Penelope said, "'Both Sides Now,' right? Joni Mitchell?" It was just the two of them. She didn't know why she said it but just felt like the answer would be important. A litmus test of some kind that she could ponder later.

Willa smiled, all teeth, and laughed. "Your memory! You've always had that gift. I'd forget my head, you know? Of course that was it. How could we forget?"

She hummed a little, the tune *I've looked at love this way*, her eyes closed and dreamy as she danced a little across the room. She waved good night and went upstairs, leaving Penelope alone in the living room.

CHAPTER
TWENTY-THREE

February 23, 2020

"Willa brought Linc condoms. And Tara birth control pills."

Penelope kept her voice low. The high ceilings in the ten-year-old house had a tendency to echo, and Willa's room was right next to the master bedroom. She sat on the bed and traced the bedspread pattern with her index finger. Brett had come home from the gym—his wicking-fabric T-shirt tight across his new abdominal muscles. God, who looked like he did at forty-two? She should have felt luckier than she did; her husband was actually hot. Like, magazine and movie hot—no beer belly for Brett. She didn't feel lucky. She felt precarious. Like living on a bobbing boat.

"Why?" He rubbed his floppy hair with a microfiber gym towel and didn't look furious enough for Penelope. She had been livid. Yes, she'd softened in the face of Willa's apologies, but it still weighed on her. Where was his rage?

"I don't know. Tara asked her, I guess?"

"Why didn't she ask you?"

"Isn't that the million-dollar question."

"Maybe she felt like you would blow her off? Or get mad?"

"Wait. This is *my* fault? Brett, she bought our kids birth control."

"I get that, Pen." He splayed his hands as though searching for a word. "But our kid asked her."

"So. You say no. You say, 'Talk to, I don't know, *your mother.*'"

"And then what if Tara didn't talk to you? What if she just decided 'I'll figure it out' and in a year, winds up pregnant. Isn't this better?"

He was too nonchalant.

"Did you know?"

"Did I know what?" He turned toward the bathroom and tossed the balled-up towel into the hamper.

"Brett. Don't be coy. Did you know that she got Tara birth control?"

Brett sighed. Looked at the ceiling, then his hands, the bright gold band around his finger flashing in the lamplight. "She told me the night I came home from the hospital. She said you were too stressed but felt obligated to tell a parent. She was trying to do the right thing. She wanted to tell you and said she would. I promised I'd give her a few days, that's all."

I won't tell her if you won't.

Was that all it had been? Wait, all? Penelope took about ten deep breaths, trying to find a focus, a center. Which was worse—Willa sleeping with her husband or buying her kids birth control? Obviously the adultery. Of course.

"I'm going to talk to her tomorrow. She has to come up with a plan. She can't stay here anymore." Penelope expected Brett to agree—wasn't it only ten days ago that he stood in that very same spot and asked her, *What's the plan with your little friend?*

"I feel like it's helping us right now," Brett said, shrugging, pulling off the T-shirt with a wet *thwack*—impossibly soaked with sweat.

"You think having Willa here—what, permanently?—is helpful?" Penelope felt her eyes narrow, her hand clutch the bedspread, white knuckled. *Breathe, dammit.*

"Look. Your job has been an issue lately—your boss is acting up. Linc and Tara have an impossible schedule. I'm job hunting every day.

Willa is like our . . . live-in housekeeper." He sighed and then shrugged. "Not permanently, no."

"That's awful!" Penelope insisted, her voice pitching, and Brett held his hands out, a *shh* gesture. Besides, was he actually *job hunting*? She had yet to know of him attending an interview or a meeting. She did, however, know when he went to his Himalayan salt sauna class.

"I'm just saying, if she had to stay longer, it's actually helping us. I feel more relaxed than I have in months."

"Oh, good, as long as you feel relaxed." Penelope unclenched her fists, stretched her fingers. "Brett, there is something not right. She stole a necklace out of my jewelry box."

"That doesn't make sense. Are you sure she just doesn't have a similar one?" His head cocked maddeningly to the side.

"No! It was on her neck. I asked her about it, and she acted like it was hers. Then the next day, it was back in my jewelry box."

"Wait, so is it missing or not?" Brett asked.

"It wasn't there. It was on her neck. The next day, it was there. When I asked her about it, she acted like she had no idea what I was talking about. Like our conversation had never even happened." Penelope could feel her nerves starting to fray. She also didn't want the necklace itself to become a focal point.

"Maybe she has the same necklace. Which one was it?" Brett asked.

"It doesn't matter! I'm not crazy. She organized my closet—"

"Which you love!"

"It's too much! Then you asked her to pay the credit card bill! I feel like she's getting her hooks into our lives or something."

Brett closed the distance between them, took her hand. "You have been trying to keep all these balls in the air—the house, the kids, your job. Then I got sick. And Linc and Tara were still going to lacrosse and theater, and she was looking out for us. Besides, I've changed the password now, so even if she did have any . . ." He rolled his wrist in a circle and smiled at her. "Nefarious plans . . . they've been thwarted. Okay?"

He was placating her. Nefarious plans, like a television villain. Thwarted!

"Stop! Just stop!" Penelope stood up. "I am not crazy. I am not stressed. I mean, I am stressed. But I'm not *delusional*. She is fucking with me, somehow."

"How?" Brett laughed. "By picking up your kids? Organizing and cleaning our house? Cooking us gourmet dinners? Paying a bill while I'm in the hospital so we don't get a late fee? How exactly is she fucking with you?" He shook his head. "I mean, what would have happened if she hadn't been here?"

The implication, of course, being that she couldn't manage their lives. Was that what he meant? Or was she projecting?

Penelope sat down, hard, on the bed and watched him shake his head as he turned and walked into the bathroom. She felt a wash of rage.

"Do you have a thing for her?" Penelope asked softly. He stood still as stone in the doorway between the bedroom and the bathroom.

"I'm not even going to dignify that with an answer," Brett said and looked away.

"She called you at the hospital. How many times?"

"Just the once." Brett shook his head. "Not that I have to justify any of that to you. I don't know how to convince you: *she was helping us.* She is doing what you can't."

"What can't I do? Do the laundry? Pick up the kids? Cook?" Penelope sucked in a breath, quick and punching. "Be your wife."

Brett was in front of her like lightning, his hands on her biceps, his fingertips biting into her skin, his face red. "That's a shitty thing to say."

He'd never touched her while angry before. Never. Penelope swallowed, thickly, her pulse pounding in her ears, her vision swimming with fury.

"Well, it's a shitty thing to feel." She shook herself loose and grabbed her purse.

"I'm sure you'll just leave, Pen. That's what you do. The end of every argument with you is just a slamming door." His words were cutting, sarcastic, but his voice was resigned. Almost defeated.

Before she knew what she was doing, she was sitting in the driver's seat of her car, her breath coming in quick, hot gasps. Her heart hammering a beat against her rib cage. Brett wasn't wrong—many of their fights ended with Penelope leaving the room. The house. Mostly just getting in her car and driving around to calm down.

I will not go to his house. I will not.

She didn't always go to Jaime's. But sometimes she did.

But it didn't matter what she told herself, her car seemed to drive itself there. Up the street, around the corner, three houses down.

This was insane. She didn't dare pull in the driveway. She drove past the house, intending to park a block away and walk up, like a true adulterer. She wasn't going to sleep with him—she never had. She just wanted his comfort. It was selfish for so many reasons, the way she showed up at his front door whenever she needed him. Lately it seemed like all the time. He was always just there, letting her be whatever and whomever she wanted that day.

Brett was right—she *was* a shitty wife. But she felt a deeper stab of guilt for how she was using Jaime. How she'd been unable to cope without him. How was that fair? It wasn't, of course. While she was juggling her husband and her—what, lover? No, that sounded like something from an Ingrid Bergman film—Jaime, he was stuck with *her*. Not dating other, emotionally available women. She was tying them all up with her need.

Penelope had the faint tang of vomit in her throat—she was literally making herself sick.

Her headlights caught on a figure on Jaime's front porch. No, two figures. Kissing. The woman's legs wrapped around a man's waist—a passionate dark-night-on-the-sidewalk kind of kiss.

The bright flash of blonde, the expanse of shoulders Penelope would know anywhere. Willa and Jaime.

CHAPTER TWENTY-FOUR

Willa, present

She wondered if he missed the phone yet. It was tucked in the bottom of her small black purse, blending into the lining, practically ticking like a bomb. It had died before she'd been able to look through it, and Willa scoured the house for a charger but came up empty. The whole house was powered by Apple, it seemed. How stupid and frustrating. She'd finally found it in Linc's room, under his bed—a micro USB charging an e-reader.

Brett moved back in with his wife. Too bad. Some fun could have gone down, if she'd felt like pushing it. A middle-of-the-night "sleep-walking" visit? She chewed her nail and thought about the juiciness of that. She kind of wanted to feel the differences in the men: Brett's lean, angled frame versus Jaime's broad, solid build. She had a good feel for the latter, felt his strong back beneath her hands, his flannel shirt soft and thin under her palms.

He'd kissed her yesterday. On the porch of his little house, right where he'd kissed Pip. The only difference was, she hadn't cried like Pip. He was confused, in love with Pip for no earthly reason that she could see, but he was still a man. She wore a little angora sweater and a pair of tight black jeans tucked into boots. Everything about it screamed *kiss me*, and then he had, with *breathless passion*. Like a little trashy paperback romance, she had wrapped her legs right around him.

She was not supposed to like it this much, but what the hell—a girl could have fun, right? He was a great kisser, soft and ripe as a plum, and he smelled good enough to eat. She tried to push it—*Wanna go inside to warm up?* What did she care how fast they moved? She wasn't going to love him. That didn't mean she couldn't fuck him.

Well, anyway. He hesitated, and she backtracked. *Definitely a bad idea.* She'd been the one to say it first, but she could tell the little moan into his mouth—like a desire held back, *she wanted him so bad*—almost did him in. She'd give him no more than two more dates before he caved. Middle of the day, no one home? Yes, please. Sign her up.

She waited for the phone to power up. These little burners took fucking forever. She saw Brett the other day digging through the kitchen drawers, the end table drawer in the living room. She'd asked him if he was looking for anything, did he need any help. He just waved her away, a big smile: *Nah, don't worry about it. Just misplaced my gym card.*

Ha. Gym card, my ass.

Anyway, Brett was out, sans phone—back to his early-morning ways, claiming to job hunt, but she followed him one day, just for fun. The gym, a smoothie shop, a therapist's office. Job hunting happened at home, on a computer. Applications and emails and LinkedIn. Pip swallowed it all—she had to know it was a lie, right? She was too smart.

With the whole house asleep, aside from Brett, she could take the time to really dig in, now that the phone was charged. The weekend after the "big fight" had flown by. She made amends. Acted the part. Apologized profusely. They threw her a fucking birthday party. It wasn't even really her birthday. Pip accepted her apology, but she could tell she wasn't over it. Good.

The phone *finally* buzzed to life in her hands. There were only two text strings in the phone—both phone numbers, no names. Both contained unread texts. She clicked on the first one.

Hey, babe. Where you been? Miss you.

Are you avoiding me?

Brett? What's going on. It's been days.

Holy shit, Landon just said you were in the hospital. Are you okay? God, I want to come see you. Fuck. Please call me.

I'm kinda going crazy here.

I need to see you. Please come by the office. I'll meet you outside.

The last one, this morning:

Look I know I said I wouldn't but I emailed you. You aren't even reading these okay? Don't be mad.

Well, now. Brett had a girlfriend. Maybe from his old office? This family was endlessly fascinating. She clicked the second string of messages and felt her heart speed up. As Penelope would say, it was a whole different kettle of fish.

—✕—

Later, she stood outside Brett's old office building and waited. It was a risky thing, cruising around his old office building that he'd been laid off from. She was starting to wonder if he was "laid off" . . . or was he fired?

Soon enough, his car rolled up. She ducked between two commercial buildings across the street and watched easily from the alley. Oh, this was idiotic.

A dark-haired woman, small boned and lithe, bounded down the steps, looking up and down Pillar Street. She couldn't have been more obvious about it if she'd tried. Brett waited in his car, his face impatient, for her to see him. She finally did, nodded once, obviously—no subtlety at all with this woman. She suddenly felt protective of Pip—at least Pip would have handled this whole thing with more aplomb. The little brunette ducked into the alleyway between buildings directly opposite where Willa stood. She sank back into the shadows of the buildings to watch.

Brett exited his car and followed the woman into the alley. A heavy make-out session started, but Brett stopped, held her wrists with two hands, and they talked. She pushed against him once, said something indistinguishable. He went in, tried to kiss her again, but she pushed against him, angrily, shouted something, and left him standing in the dark. She disappeared back inside the gray-metal high-rise, and Brett ran a hand through his shaggy hair. He was so fucked. Or not fucked, more like.

Men got desperate. No one knew that better than Willa.

She was counting on it.

CHAPTER
TWENTY-FIVE
Then: Alone. Together.

Willa had a date. A different man than last time, or so Penelope gathered. She was tight lipped about it, but Penelope thought maybe that was because of the drugs. Willa had always dabbled in drugs, and Pen had always quietly disapproved. In their years together, Willa had likely learned to keep it quiet, away from Penelope's judgmental eye.

Bree and Flynn drove into the city to go to a club—for what reason, Penelope couldn't fathom. Flynn had left in his khakis and button-up shirt, and she almost, *almost*, asked him if he knew Bree meant the nightclub not the golf club but bit her tongue at the last minute.

Jack stood at the stove, stirring a pot of chili, a loaf of bread browning in the dutch oven. On the kitchen island, a portable speaker played unplugged Clapton, and Penelope swirled her third glass of rosé around her glass and felt a little bubble of happiness pop in her chest. Silly, really, but they were almost never one on one with any other housemate. It was usually all five of them, but sometimes a smaller group. Almost never one on one.

"How's the book?" Penelope asked.

With his back to her, he rolled his shoulders inside his shirt. "It's . . . coming. You're not supposed to ask that, you know."

"Why not?" God, this rosé was good. She'd never even known she liked rosé—she'd always drunk white, but this was like a light, bubbly party on her tongue. She giggled at that and clamped a hand over her mouth.

Jack half turned and gazed inquisitively at her. "Are you . . . drunk?"

"No. NO!" Penelope rarely got drunk. She didn't like to lose control, the room tipping sideways, her thoughts careening. She drank a glass or two, let the edges of the room get a little soft focus, then happily drifted off to sleep. They teased her about it quite a bit. While the rest of them stumbled around after dinner, slurring and acting ridiculous, making grand plans for imaginary trips to Africa and Greece, Penelope snoozed in the easy chair until the last one standing nudged her off to bed.

"Why don't you ask a novelist about his book?"

"Because if it's going well, they don't shut up about it. If it's not— and that's more likely—they want to kill you for asking."

"Do you want to kill me for asking?"

"A little." He laughed and turned to face her, pouring his own glass of red. "It's just the murky middle. No idea what's going on. If I was a real writer, I'd have to finish it. Someone would want it. This is why first novels take ten years to write. No one cares if you finish it or not."

"I care." Penelope took another swallow of wine.

"Well, you don't count."

"Why not?" She asked hotly, her face flaming red.

"Because you always care."

"What does that matter?"

He hesitated, picked an olive, and popped it in his mouth. His blue eyes held hers, and he cocked his head sideways, intent. "It's not a bad thing. It's just like knowing someone is always in your corner . . . it's not very motivating."

"You're not making it better," Penelope teased him, but still felt the sting, deeper than she should have.

"Put it this way—if I put the book away tomorrow, would you think less of me?"

"Of course not!" Ridiculous question.

"There you go. That's exactly what I mean. You'll go on loving me despite what I do or don't do."

Penelope made an exaggerated face. "Oh, sure, you think we all just love you."

"All of you but Bree." Jack let out a laugh and turned back to the cabinet above the stove.

"Oh, stop, Bree loves you. She's just . . . Bree," Penelope said.

Jack retrieved bowls and filled them with chili and hot bread, sprinkled sharp cheddar on top, and set one in front of her. It smelled divine, rich and spicy.

They ate in silence for a while until Jack sighed. "Do you think I'm writing a book just to make my father proud?" He flushed and amended, "I mean, that sounds asinine. I'm twenty-two. My father doesn't even read—at least not frequently. He's the son of a Cuban immigrant. Owns a hardware store—that's his whole life. I'm not sure he's left his own block in fifteen years."

"Everyone tries to make their parents proud, no matter their age. It's not asinine; I think it's totally normal." Penelope took a bite of the chili and swooned—it tasted as good as it smelled, thick and cheesy.

"You don't." Jack aimed his spoon at her, grinning.

"I don't have parents. They died in a car accident when I was nine. I lived with my mom's sister, and I think she really just did the minimum. She kept me clothed and fed. She died a year ago, and I haven't been back to her house since, although it's still mine. I pay the taxes on it, at any rate." She took a breath, not meaning to have revealed quite so much. The wine had made her chatty.

"Why haven't you been back?" Jack asked.

"I just don't . . . want to deal with it all. My aunt was a stranger to me. She was kind enough. But that house isn't a happy memory or anything. It's easier to be here, for now. Until I'm ready."

"My point is, everyone who has a family builds a life with that family in mind, for good or bad."

Jack thought for a moment, tugged on his earlobe. "My mom worked the hardware store in the mornings. Before she died, I mean. I'm sitting behind the counter counting nails, lining them all up—you know, with the heads facing the same way? They're all different sizes. One is green, and I don't know why. She's handing me butterscotch hard candies, and she unwraps them first. Every ten minutes or so she gives me another one. *Don't chew it.* That's the only thing she said, and I can still hear her voice, but only those words. I don't remember anything else—not her laugh, her mannerisms. Nothing." He gave Penelope a crooked smile. "That's the memory of my mother. You asked me once, and I never answered you."

"You said you had only one memory, right?" Penelope asked. The whole room had started to close in on them; all she could see was Jack's face, his sad smile, his eyes, blue and deep. She reached out, touched his arm, the air around them so thick she could scarcely breathe.

"That's the whole thing. I'm not even sure how long after that she died. I do know that if I even smell butterscotch, I get completely overwhelmed. Like, I can't even talk, my throat closes up," Jack said. "You know, none of us have a *real* family."

Penelope was startled to realize he was right. Flynn had been adopted by a Christian evangelical family in Ohio. Once, while drinking, he told Penelope he never told them he was gay, but they knew. It was why they never, ever called. He found reasons to skip holidays; they found reasons to justify it. When he was a child, and even a teenager, they'd loved him. Their rejection of him as an adult stung all the more for it. Flynn acted like this was fine, but he knew deep down it wasn't.

Penelope knew it too. When she'd taken his hand, tears in her eyes, had tried to laugh it off, something got caught, and it came out strangled.

Bree's family lived entirely in Europe. She talked about them in a rush, the glitz and glamour of it all. Jack said once, *Bree, tell them how your family are billionaires, not just millionaires. You know the difference between a billion and a million? A million seconds is eleven days, while a billion seconds is thirty-one years.* But Bree had looked at him murderously and told him to fuck off. Penelope remembered later thinking, *God, they never call her either.*

Willa was raised by a mother who was actively dying of alcoholism. Willa's mother *definitely* called, but Willa would see her name pop up on the caller ID and walk away from it, rolling her eyes. *I'll pick up when it's the Pennsylvania state police,* she joked.

"We have each other." Penelope shrugged, like this was a small thing. It wasn't—to her. For better or worse, the Spires were all she had for a family. Sometimes she found herself daydreaming about them living in the house together indefinitely. Holidays, birthdays, summers. Sure, it seemed unconventional, but if none of them had anyone else, wasn't it better to go through life known and loved than adrift in a sea of strangers? When she thought about leaving them, her lungs squeezed tight. "It's healthy, you know. To make your own family."

"Ah, the resident therapist," Jack joked, but his voice broke at the end, and he gazed at her tenderly. Penelope knew then that Jack thought about the same things: the five of them staying together, the skipping panic at the thought of the ending year.

"Right, because I'm so mentally stable." Penelope laughed, thinking of her own self-doubt, the moments in the house when she'd felt like an outsider looking in, watching them all laugh and let loose, and feeling tied in knots.

"Why do you do that? Why do you self-deprecate?" Jack fixed his gaze on her with an intensity that made her squirm. "Is it an act? Or do you truly not know how much we all love you? Even Bree, who is barely aware of anything past her own face, loves you best. Even more than Flynn. You're our Lachesis."

"I never know what that even means," Penelope said, dismissive.

"She measured out your fate. Determined how you would live your life. What you might become. The house mother, testing our mettle."

"Are you drunk?"

"Not at all." He took her hand, ran his fingertips along hers, along the blue veins running under her white skin. Without thinking, she lifted it, turned it over, and kissed his palm.

God, she should have been embarrassed. Humiliated! But the fourth glass of rosé had done her all in. Penelope—predictable, dependable, reasonable, logical. Sometimes it was so exhausting being yourself.

Why shouldn't she throw it all in for love?

She felt the sharp intake of Jack's breath and knew instantly that it would be too easy. Besides being easily seduced in general, Jack was particularly vulnerable to anyone who plainly adored him as much as Penelope did.

She stood, deliberate and slow, and moved to the other side of the island. He watched her, a shocked little smile playing on his lips, but he didn't pull away when she held his hand again. When she kissed it again, this time leaning into him so they connected shoulder to hip, all she could think about was *I might never have this chance again.*

He closed his eyes and mouthed, *Fuck,* and then out loud said, "Pip, what are you doing?" and "This is a terrible idea." Until she kissed his neck, the soft pulsing spot beneath his collar, felt the stubble of his five-o'clock shadow on her lips, and then moved up and pressed her mouth to his. His lips were warm and soft and tasted like wine and spice, and everything was suddenly, intently, on fire. Her mouth, her hands, a hot pull in her belly, the pulse between her legs.

And his rigid form went boneless against her, his hands finding her back, her thighs, lifting her up onto the counter, their mouths biting, his hands running the length of her legs, between her thighs, and somehow her shirt was off and she was pulling at his clothes, the fly of his jeans. She'd never known a moment like this in her life—marked entirely by lust, all her senses misfiring; she could taste his cologne, feel the salt on his skin, smell the need wafting off him; and she knew they wanted the same things.

"Upstairs, now," Jack growled into her mouth, and she followed him closely as he took the steps two at a time, not even caring that she left her blouse in the kitchen for anyone to see. In his bedroom, they fell onto the bed, and the next thing Penelope knew, she was naked, their bodies bucking and writhing together until he slid inside her and she gasped, clawing at his backside, and he said *fuck* again, and it was the most passionate experience of Penelope's life.

The next morning, she remembered precious little of it—waking with a brutal headache pushing behind her eyes. Jack's arm was slung around her from behind, his thighs stuck to hers from the trapped heat of the blanket, and she peeled away, wrapping herself in a sheet before glancing at the clock.

7:52 a.m.

God, the others would be awake. She had no idea where her clothes had ended up, but she had to get to her room—Jack's room was wide open to the great room. In the kitchen she could hear quiet movement— someone making coffee, the opening and closing of the refrigerator. She eyed the trapdoor in his floor and looked back at him, snoring softly as he turned over in her absence, his back to her now.

She felt sick—from the wine, she thought. Maybe it was also the fact that she'd *slept with Jack*! Her mind was scrambled, unable to make sense of any of it. What would happen now? Jack was a playboy; they all knew that. But still, they'd grown closer. Their walks to and from town, he told her about his mother. Was it unreasonable to hope? She had to get back to her room. She had to *think*.

She lifted the trapdoor and shimmied inside, keeping the sheet around her. She eased the door shut above her head and climbed down the ladder to the landing, then crept along the wall, feeling for the thirty steps with her toes. When she finally made it to the storage closet, she edged open the door to the basement hallway—just a crack—and peered out. The hall was empty. She slid through the crack, pulling the sheet behind her, and then turned to close it quietly. When she turned back, she gasped.

Bree stood behind her, in a long black kimono, twirling a single hank of red hair. Her smile was wide, teasing; her eyes flashed, and Penelope saw something flicker under the surface. Or maybe she imagined it. She looked up at the ceiling, toward Jack's room and back to Penelope, still wrapped in the bedsheets, shoulders bare.

Bree said, "Where did you come from?"

CHAPTER TWENTY-SIX

February 24, 2020

Penelope woke up early Monday morning. Brett's side of the bed was cool and bare—he'd likely been up for hours. He often left before dawn, preferring to work out when the gym was empty.

He'd been asleep when she came home last night, and she'd slid into bed, lying in the dark until well after midnight, staring at the moonlight glinting off her bedroom ceiling fan. Wondering at what point had she stopped being a conscious participant in her own life? She'd become so reactive.

She thought back to a mere three weeks ago, before Willa knocked on her door. All she could remember was a whirlwind of taking kids to activities, work, trying to squeeze in her own exercise, make dinner, clean up, go to bed.

She'd tried to stay awake, waiting for the telltale creak of the hallway floor, the click of the guest room door, but fell asleep first.

She woke up with a thought: *I will take my life back.*

She found Willa in the kitchen quietly making coffee. Willa wore a white sleep shirt, barely covering the smooth sculpt of her backside, her legs completely free of cellulite, tan and muscular. Penelope thought of those legs wrapped around Jaime's waist a mere seven hours earlier, and felt a tang of bile in her throat.

Willa's face had changed in the twenty years since college: the scar zigzagging from ear to chin was pink and taut in the bluish light, but her body retained the musculature of a twenty-two-year-old. She'd been rounder then, baby fat in her cheeks and thighs. Age had given her a leaner, more brittle look.

Penelope tugged self-consciously at her knit pajamas, long sleeves and pants, and felt matronly.

"You startled me," Willa said with a soft laugh, not seeming startled at all.

"Been up long?" Penelope asked, pulling mugs down from the cabinet. If they were going to have this conversation, then it would be civil, over coffee.

"I have insomnia. I don't sleep much. It's gotten worse since college." Willa shrugged, her long hair falling into her face as she dipped her head. Penelope had forgotten how beautiful she was, especially when vulnerable.

The Willa standing in her kitchen, quietly tiptoeing around to keep from waking Penelope's family, seemed harmless. Which one was real—the woman from a few days ago, apologetic and sweet and slightly manipulative when Penelope confronted her about the birth control, or Willa now, quiet and contemplative in the early light? She'd kissed Penelope's cheek, her perfume the same from college—something off brand with distinct musk—and sent Penelope's head swirling. She'd taken care of everything—*everything*—for all of them. Saved them, really. Was Brett right? Did she owe her?

No, she didn't. But, it was complicated. Their friendship years ago had been based almost entirely around Willa and Jack. Willa and Jack were the "show"—Willa's fiery temper, Jack's affable charm. Penelope was the straight man, the Moe Howard, the Zeppo Marx, the Bud

Abbott. Penelope was the one to smooth them over when they fought, the one to talk them all off their own ledges. She laughed at their antics, even encouraged them, scolded them both when they made terrible choices—which they always did.

Until the choices they'd all made sealed their fate.

Yes. She owed Willa two weeks—a place to hide out, food, shelter, warmth, help. She gave her that. It was enough.

"I think we need to talk through a plan," Penelope said. Her palms felt slick. She was nervous, and she didn't know why. Confrontation was never comfortable, she supposed. Even if it was gentle.

"You want me to leave?" Willa asked, without looking up. She stirred a small dollop of milk into her coffee and took a sip before meeting Penelope's gaze.

"I just feel like we all need a path forward. We have to be working toward something." Penelope was and always had been goal oriented. She was a woman who must have a plan. She squared her shoulders and drank her black coffee and studied Willa, who smiled to herself and looked around the kitchen.

"God, you have such a beautiful house, Pip. Seriously. You've done so well for yourself." It didn't sound like a compliment. Willa's mouth was a glossy pucker, her eyes scanning the ceiling.

Penelope didn't say anything.

"I understand why you'd want me out. It's a lot to have someone . . . in your space. In your life. Taking care of your kids . . . your husband. You don't have to feel threatened, you know."

"I don't feel threatened. It's not that, Willa." Penelope heard the defensive note in her voice, helpless, and she hated it. She corrected it. "I know you've needed us. We've been here for you. But we need to find you a more permanent solution. A shelter, maybe. An apartment. Something to keep your life on track. For *you*."

"Well, maybe *threatened* is the wrong word. I don't mean it like that, of course not. I just mean . . . " Willa took a deep breath and put down her mug. She took one of Penelope's hands in both of hers and gazed earnestly into her eyes. She looked so sincere, so pleading that Penelope felt herself thaw, just a little. "You've done so much for me. I don't wish to make you uncomfortable at all. I will find another place to go, okay? I promise."

"I don't need you to leave today, Willa. I just need to know what your plan is." Penelope pulled her hand back a little, and Willa tightened her grip. "Obviously, this is not sustainable." Penelope hated how formal she became when nervous. How stiff, uptight. They used to mock her for that.

"I know. I know! God. I've been racking my brain trying to come up with an idea. I had a friend keeping an eye on Trent, and so far, he seems fine. I thought for sure he'd come right after me, hunt me down somehow. But this . . . friend. She says he's made no move, nothing. Goes to work at the garage every day like it's fine. He asked about me, though. My friend, I mean." She shook her head. "Trent always said he'd find me and kill me if I left him. I'll come up with a plan, okay? You can even help me. I was thinking. What if I got an apartment under my old name? Willamena Blaine. Go by Mena. I mean, I'm not invisible then; I'm sure he could find a way to find me. He knows my maiden name." She twisted her bottom lip with her manicured fingers. "I'll find something, okay? I promise."

Penelope suddenly doubted herself. Was she sending her friend out into open waters? Why did they not have enough room in their house? Five bedrooms. Plus an office. A finished basement. My God, strangers could move in here and live for weeks unnoticed. But they wouldn't buy her children birth control, steal her jewelry, pay her bills, go through her stuff.

Penelope had always considered the house more Brett's than hers. He'd pushed for it: new, cavernous, sterile. When the Realtor had shown it to them ten years ago, the kids still almost toddlers, drooly and thick legged, Penelope had felt a surge of repulsion. She'd wanted character, warmth. *Character and warmth of this size, with all the amenities, are an extra three hundred thousand dollars.* He'd been right—New Jersey was expensive real estate. It was either new, echoing, white, or real stone, filled with six-inch moldings and heart-pine variable-width flooring, but without air-conditioning. Same price. She balanced one child on her hip while she signed the closing paperwork—didn't even remember which child.

"Look, Willa, wait. I'm not saying you have to leave effective immediately. I just want you to think about it, and we can talk about some kind of transition, okay?" Penelope felt a tug then—should she be a better friend? More forgiving, somehow? She heard Willa in her head: *Do you have girlfriends, Pip?* Was she inherently bad at friendship? she wondered.

Linc and Tara clearly loved Willa. Brett wouldn't be thrilled at this conversation; he'd urged her to be more yielding somehow. *She's helping us,* he'd said. She'd run to Jaime, saw them kissing on his porch. *Legs wrapped around his waist, his hands in her hair.* It had seemed so *passionate.* When was the last time she'd felt that kind of reckless abandon? Even with Jaime, she had been restrained. The last reckless passion she'd felt had been with Jack. That one night. No, she could *not* think about that.

Lately all she could think about was the fire house. The Spires. Jack. All of them, flooding her in the middle of the night, her memories clamoring for attention. Even the smell of Willa's perfume, wafting through the house, same as it ever was, hurtled her right back in time. Against any conscious wish.

Willa was shaking her head. "No, Penelope, you're absolutely right. Two weeks is long enough. I will figure out a plan, okay? I promise. Give me a day or so." She picked up her coffee cup and kissed Penelope's cheek. "I'll be out of your hair in no time."

Penelope started to protest, and Willa held up her hand. She sashayed out of the kitchen, tiny T-shirt nightgown swinging about her hips seductively.

When she was gone, Penelope exhaled, oddly bereft.

CHAPTER
TWENTY-SEVEN

February 24, 2020

Penelope left work at noon. Nora was out of the office, and Penelope couldn't focus. Her mind was cluttered, handing her pictures, like a flip-book. Willa, her legs wrapped around Jaime's waist. The Church House: a visceral memory of Jack cooking, whistling at the stove, his black hair flopping into his eyes. Brett, in early autumn, standing at the summit of the Lehigh Gap on the Appalachian Trail, the brisk breeze lifting his thick hair, the tufts of orange and yellow treetops below him. Tara, arms spread on stage, her makeup garish, in a white ruffled dress. Linc, his lacrosse stick swiping lethally, his powerful legs propelling him forward. Her loved ones, then and now.

She clicked *out of office* on her calendar, submitted the time-off request, and ducked out before anyone—namely childless, partnerless, free-to-devote-all-their-time-to-work Elias—could see her.

First, she drove around aimlessly. Riverwood was less a city and more a large town. Bustling center, a small block of moderate high-rises, a main street with boutiques that sold bath soaps and lotions, all-natural cruelty-free makeup, high-end clothes from New York City designers, overpriced antiques. A small café that was also a used bookstore, but also, a larger bookstore that hosted celebrities, athletes, politicians. President Obama was photographed buying books there—it had been in the *Riverwood Gazette*.

Penelope hadn't loved her house, but she loved Riverwood. It had a liberal, hippie vibe. Diversity in business owners downtown and LOVE IS LOVE signs on most lawns. A functioning and booming LGBTQ community center right in the center of Main Street.

Brett had called it hippie central when they first moved there. He said it tongue in cheek, with a smile and kiss. Penelope had no idea how he felt now. Aside from that one Valentine's Day night, they'd barely touched. Every conversation seemed fraught with undercurrent from everything that was still unsaid. His defense of Willa ate at her, clawing at her subconscious.

She maneuvered her car into a paid spot outside a French café whose *seigle feuilleté* she and Brett had fallen in love with years ago. It was a rye bread flavor with a croissant flakiness. Penelope hadn't had one in months. It reminded of her of Brett, the way she'd meet him here for lunch and they'd talk and linger until finally, at the end of a long lunch hour, he'd kiss her on the lips, tasting of butter and salt, a kiss that would promise more later. He'd make his way across the street, back to his office building, his back a little straighter, his step a little lighter. She used to feel pleasure in knowing that she did that.

The outdoor patio was open, even in February, when it was warm enough. They'd had virtually no snow, so a few tables contained patrons. Penelope ordered her café americano, which was still better than her Starbucks coffee, and the *feuilleté*. On impulse, she snapped a photo of it and sent it to Brett with no caption. He could take it however he wanted; sometimes an olive branch was a french pastry. She was leaving the café with her coffee in one hand, a warm buttery bread in the other, and a mouthful of decadent flakiness when she spotted Willa, chatting animatedly with a small dark-haired woman at a table outside.

On instinct, Penelope stopped, stood with her back against the wall of tacked bulletins—apartments for rent, babysitters needed, lost dogs—and took another bite. Who was she talking to? Penelope could see the table through the slit in the curtains.

The woman tossed her hair and laughed, and Willa grabbed her arm, playful. It looked like they were friends. As far as she knew, Willa knew no one in the area, had no friends. That had been the appeal of Riverwood, right? So she'd said. *It's hard to get along when you're an island.*

The woman looked vaguely familiar, but Penelope couldn't place her. She was tiny, long dark hair with streaks of auburn, and a straight, pointed nose. Her teeth were white against the even tan of her skin, her fingernails shining a deep berry. She looked like every upper-class working woman in Riverwood. Highly maintained and Botoxed smooth.

Finally, Willa stood, paid the tab, and left. Penelope stayed still and watched the brunette stand, move out of her view from the narrow window opening. Penelope skirted outside and walked, head down as though distracted by her phone, toward Willa's table. She didn't know what she wanted, exactly, but felt compelled to at least look.

The woman turned quickly, aimed her phone in the direction of her old table, and framed a photo. She seemed oblivious to Penelope, who watched her snap a picture and then, presumably, text it to someone, a small half smile playing on her lips.

After the woman left, Penelope looked down at the table. Willa's plate was clean, but the woman's contained a half-eaten *seigle feuilleté*.

—⁓—

Willa's car was not parked outside the house. But the inside air smelled like her: that faint musk that always followed Willa everywhere. There was something else too. The flooring in the house was entirely hardwood, even the bedrooms, and now, in the bright afternoon light, they gleamed. The smell of the familiar floor polish gave her stomach a lurch. It smelled just like the Church House—that sweet chemical tang of solvent. She took a deep breath, trying to pin it down but failing. On second breath, it smelled like Murphy's Oil Soap. Willa had cleaned the floors, and perhaps her imagination was running away with her.

Penelope quietly ascended the stairs, sticking to the wall side so they wouldn't squeak, and checked the bedrooms—Linc's neat as a pin, Tara's a hurricane aftermath. Penelope and Brett's bed neatly made, the corners pulled tight. Brett was a stickler for hospital corners—when he actually made the bed. Willa's bedroom door was closed, and Penelope knocked a little beat on the doorjamb with her knuckle and received no answer. She pushed the door open a crack. The room was empty.

"Willa!" She called. No answer.

Penelope quickly looked around the room: the nightstand, the closet, the small dresser that had previously held spare towels and sheets that Penelope had emptied right after Willa came to stay. The drawers were still empty.

Penelope pulled open all the desk drawers and saw only what she had left in there—unused journals, a pack of pens, a small box of old photo books from when the kids were young.

Willa's duffel bag sat, zipped shut, on the floor next to her bed. It was all she'd ever brought with her. She hadn't hung her clothes, hadn't left a thing in the guest bathroom. Penelope lifted the duffel bag and set it on the white matelassé quilt.

She quickly stepped into the hall and listened. There was no noise aside from the periodic passing car. Anyone coming to the door would pop on Penelope's SafeZone front-door video camera. She quickly checked her phone—notifications on. Good.

She opened the duffel bag and gingerly pawed through the contents. A few blouses and jeans. A dress that looked familiar, two pairs of shoes, a pair of sneakers. A hooded sweatshirt.

A black cell phone—no brand. A burner phone.

And buried at the bottom, a kitchen knife. It was heavy, expensive, and Penelope picked it up, her heart pounding. She studied the Zwilling logo, the pair of men that looked like they were dancing, the edge straight and sharp, the handle almost warm in her hand. This was a very fine kitchen knife, professional even, not a weapon of any kind. She let her hand go slack, felt the heavy weight of it. A thin brown line smeared the handle, and Penelope took it to the window to see it in the daylight.

She couldn't be sure, but it looked an awful lot like dried blood.

CHAPTER TWENTY-EIGHT

Then: Someone New

He chose a day when Penelope hadn't had a shift at the bookstore and brought her home for dinner.

"This is Grace," Jack announced to the stunned kitchen. Stunned because while Jack, of all of them, was most likely to have outside friends (Penelope being the least likely), they had yet to bring anyone home. The church was their commune, insular, a fortress against the outside world. Whatever happened during the day—and for some of them it was precious little—the house was a little haven, a bunker. The five of them, used to solitude for various reasons, felt their hackles rise when confronted with someone new.

Willa had been chopping onions for a soup. It was her turn to cook, and Flynn had been bemoaning it for over twenty minutes because he knew it would contain some kind of tofu or "soy sponge," as he called any kind of meat alternative. He always ate everything—Willa was learning to cook more than pasta. They were all developing into budding chefs.

"I hope there's enough. A little notice?" Willa raised her eyebrows at Jack, her whole face pinched. He laughed and kissed her cheek and pulled the new girl in front of him.

"This," he said, "is Grace."

Penelope felt a sick rise and fall of her stomach with the way he said it: reverent and a little breathless, like he'd been waiting for this moment his whole life. Everyone murmured a hello, watching her with interest.

She was blonde—Jack had a type—with soft curls around her face. The cheerful, guileless face of a cheerleader and a straight white smile. Big round blue eyes, framed with long lashes. A hint of makeup but nothing like the stage face that Willa put on every day. Grace laughed nervously and glanced at Jack, who touched her shoulder lightly.

Penelope watched the interaction—Jack's expression could only be described as luminous—and saw, with sickening clarity, that no one else in the room existed for him.

They hadn't talked about their night together. Penelope felt awful about it every single day. She walked the Church House moony and lovesick, her stomach in a perpetual cramp. Since that night, she'd barely seen Jack. He came and went with a dogged determination, avoiding her.

When they did see each other, he was steadfastly the same as always. Joking, laughing. Even making it a point to sling his arm around her shoulders. *See, nothing's changed, right?* His body language said more than any words could: their night together didn't change anything between them. Penelope had begun skipping the after-dinner parties— the games and the drinking.

Flynn had built them a small fire pit in the garden, and they took their drinks outside at night—Bree stoking the embers with a stick, feeding wood to the licking flames, Jack strumming his guitar absently, Flynn taking his turn as bartender. Penelope sat with them the first night, hunched over and desolate, until she eventually mumbled something about *coming down with something* and found her way into her own dark bedroom.

Willa had followed her, opened her bedroom door without even knocking.

"What the hell has gotten into you?" she'd demanded. Penelope shook her head, mute. If she talked, she'd blurt it out, the whole story. Jack, her delusional belief that they'd be together. Her devastation that Jack seemed unwilling to change anything about their relationship. "Seriously. You walk around here all sallow faced. You barely speak. You look like you're going to cry over everything. Flynn dropped an egg in the kitchen the other day, and you screamed like he murdered a kitten."

Penelope opened her mouth to speak but instead cleared her throat. "I have no idea what you're talking about. I'm fine. I just don't feel great. I've had a migraine for days."

"You don't get migraines," Willa snapped.

"How do you know?" Penelope countered, a slow burning fury working its way up, squeezing her lungs.

"Because I know everything about you," Willa said. "You bite your pinkie nail when you're really nervous. You observe a hell of a lot more than you let on. You have a calendar that you mark off all your days on, just an *x* over each one right before you go to bed, like you're counting down the days to something, except you're not, it's just an *x*. And it doesn't mean anything, although I'll say it's pretty fucking weird. You won't eat peas cooked, but you love them raw from Bree's garden. You hate, *hate*, Christmas movies because you never had a Christmas like anyone in them. You would never admit it, but your favorite holiday is Valentine's Day, even though you say it's just a scam to buy cards and candy."

Penelope stared at Willa in shock.

Willa continued, "So I know. *I fucking know.* Don't give me any bullshit, Penelope Louise Ritter."

Penelope swallowed. She'd never had anyone in her whole life run through her litany of quirks, preferences, secrets the way Willa could. It gave her a full-body chill to know she'd let this much of herself out *to anyone*.

Willa waited patiently. In the dark room, Penelope could see her jaw working, the whites of her eyes flashing as she blinked, the brightness of her teeth as she opened and closed her mouth, waiting. When Penelope said nothing, Willa turned and left, closing the door softly behind her. That had been a mere two days ago.

Now, in the kitchen with them all staring at Grace, Jack's mystery date, Bree was the first to speak (even Flynn had been speechless, a rare occurrence). "Welcome, Grace. Hope you like mystery meat!" She said it gaily, her cheeks flushed and full while she laughed, and it broke the tension.

"No one likes mystery meat," said Flynn.

"You do," Bree said, and Penelope almost laughed through her misery. She couldn't stop staring at Jack, who couldn't stop staring at the new girl.

"Grace works at the coffee shop," he said, beaming as though he'd said *Grace won the Nobel Prize.*

Willa snorted and said meanly, "Where you write your novel?" But her mouth curled up, and Jack simply shot her a look. He reached over and plucked a grape from the charcuterie tray that Bree had assembled, then poured two glasses of white wine and handed one to his new friend. She took it, hesitating, as she curiously watched them rib each other. They spoke in riddles—half sentences, private jokes, exchanged looks. Whole conversations flowed beneath the surface of their actual words, and Penelope loved them like this. Where *Shut up before you wake up on a sailboat* could send them into peals of laughter.

She loved their private languages, the small, nuanced way a shoulder nudge could mean *Did you pick up bananas like I asked you to?*

A flat-mouthed grimace: *I forgot; I'm sorry.*

An exaggerated eye roll: *Of course you did.*

A blown kiss: *I'm sorry; I owe you one.*

A stuck-out tongue: *What else is new?*

Bree was talking about her garden: the fall lettuce was coming in thick, and they should be eating salad for weeks starting next week. Jack made a retching sound, and Willa said, "You won't see old age with as few greens as you eat, you know. Does Grace know that about you? That you're going to die young, probably of scurvy?"

The new girl shook her head, mute, watching them all bump, cajole, tease each other, and with each passing moment seemed to shrink farther back into her chair.

Good, Penelope thought, unkindly. She hoped Grace would tell Jack later, *I'm sorry, but this isn't going to work.* Or, even less dramatic, a slow withdrawal, texts coming with less frequency, until they became acquaintances at the coffee shop again. Why not? That's how most casual relationships ended, not with a bang but a wisp.

Was it casual? Jack barely looked elsewhere the entire dinner. Certainly not at Penelope, who could still feel his fingertip on her cheek, her thighs, the soft sensitive skin of her stomach, whirling circles around her belly button. She hadn't known then to imprint the feeling, that it wouldn't happen again and again. She'd thought, stupidly at the time, that it would be a beginning.

And now, with Willa's spicy, wonderful soup tasting like hot water in her mouth, the crusty bread she'd baked from scratch might as well have been made of chalk. Penelope watched Jack watch Grace and *knew,* down to her bones, that this was it for him. That while he liked the four of them just fine, loved them even, he was head over heels for the little blonde sitting quietly next to him, ripping a hunk of bread into pieces nervously.

Willa and Bree took turns ribbing Jack, asking, "Does Grace know this about you?" Exposing all his shortcomings and flaws, and all he did was grin widely, dimples showing, and laugh. He was a lady-killer, a bit of a man whore, irresponsible to a fault, couldn't trust him with a secret, never, ever remembered a birthday.

"It's all true," Jack said to Grace conspiratorially, and she'd laughed, her shoulders loosening. "BUT! I'm thoughtful, right? Willa, I always bring you a muffin from the coffee shop. Bree, just the other day, I brought you home a new pair of gardening gloves because yours were so awful."

"This is true!" Willa exclaimed. "He's thoughtful." She studied him. "And kind. And hilarious." Sigh. "And so much fun."

Penelope couldn't bring herself to say a word. *He's actually incredibly attentive in bed?* She wouldn't think that Grace would want that kind of stamp of approval.

Flynn, Penelope noticed, was just as circumspect, mostly focusing on his own meal, or Bree or Willa or some topic of conversation other than Jack and Grace.

After dinner, Flynn broke out the Risk board and poured them all vodka tonics; for himself he prepared two fingers of whiskey, something he almost never did. Flynn liked wine, sometimes beer. If he drank hard liquor, he mixed it. Penelope knocked back her drink, welcoming the heat behind her breastbone, the immediate rush to her head, and waved her hand toward the dry bar while Flynn grinned wickedly at her. *Oh! Gonna be that kind of night, eh?*

Jack remained standing, his hand clutching Grace's, and said, "You all have fun," with a little bow and then led her up the metal spiral staircase to his loft. They all heard the springs on his bed move under the weight of the two of them and a soft giggle (hers), followed by a low rumble (his). The four of them were quiet, trying to eavesdrop, but despite the echoing space of the great room, the words didn't carry, just the rumble and pitch of their voices. Jack's bed was pushed against the back wall, far enough back that no one could see them.

Flynn looked ill, his lips pale. Willa and Bree seemed not to notice as they set up the board in their regular colors. Penelope drained her second drink and stood, unsteadily. Willa looked up then, eyed Penelope, and rolled her eyes.

"I'm actually not feeling great," she murmured to the group. Willa murmured, "Shocker," and Penelope fumbled her way out of the room, down to her bedroom. Like a teenager, she threw herself facedown on the bed and cried, feeling stupid for it the whole time. She was twenty-two, for God's sake! Her body ached with heartsickness.

Penelope had no idea how long she let herself cry—a few minutes—but she was still facedown on the bed, her cheek pressed against the cool side of the pillow, when she heard a soft knock on the door.

She stood, straightening her hair, to answer it. In the hallway, Bree put a finger to her lips and motioned for Penelope to follow her. Inside the storage closet at the end of the hall, Bree pushed open the little secret door and, with a sly smile over her shoulder, pulled Penelope in after her. They climbed the narrow stone staircase to the top; they could hear the voices of the others through the wall as they passed the main floor. At the landing, they paused, and Penelope felt a spasm of guilt shoot through her. She tried to turn to leave and hissed, "We shouldn't be here!" But Bree held up her hand, exasperated.

Beyond the wall, Penelope could hear them. Their voices were low, but they were talking, thank God—she wouldn't have wanted to hear anything else.

Jack: "Don't worry. They'll love you. They're a tough crowd, that's all."

Grace: "God, the way she looked at me! Like I was a cockroach in her kitchen."

Bree mouthed *Willa* at Penelope and covered her mouth with her hand to keep from laughing.

Jack (with a snort): "That's how she looks at everyone."

Grace, with low murmuring that Penelope couldn't make out, and then: "Is she in love with you?"

Jack, a soft rumble in his voice: "Nah. We're not like that. We're close, like a family."

Silence then, and Penelope envisioned them kissing, Jack's hand cupped proprietarily on Grace's hip, her fingertips tracing the deep groove of his jaw, where his dark stubble started at night. Penelope closed her eyes and remembered, her lips tingling, kissing that very spot, her tongue licking the salt from his skin and the soft groan he gave into her hair when she did it.

Grace, quietly: "None of you ever slept together?"

A beat of silence before Jack said: "No, we never did."

CHAPTER
TWENTY-NINE

February 24, 2020

Willa had gone out. She wouldn't be home for dinner, she said. Kissed Penelope's cheek before she left and whispered, "Probably good to give you all space." She squeezed Brett's arm and was out the door.

"Any idea where Willa went?" Brett asked Penelope, standing in the door between the bathroom and the bedroom. The man took more showers than anyone she'd ever met. The steam from the warming water was starting to curl into their bedroom.

"No," Penelope said. Then, "Turn the water off; I want to show you something."

She led Brett down the hall to Willa's room and quietly pushed the door open. Tara was at Sasha's house, and Linc probably had headphones on, playing a video game. Still, she didn't want him to catch her.

"Pen, this probably isn't a great idea," Brett's said, his voice faltering. He followed her anyway.

At the side of Willa's bed, Penelope sat cross-legged on the floor next to Willa's simple black duffel bag. She unzipped it, carefully pushing past all the clothing she'd seen earlier in the day—blouses and jeans, a dress, a sweatshirt. In the bottom of the bag, she felt nothing. Just an empty expanse of fabric. She rustled her hand around a bit more, careful of the fact that she was rummaging for a sharp knife, and came up empty. *What the hell?*

"It's missing," she said to Brett. She pulled the sides of the bag apart, and delicately removed the clothing, shaking it out and refolding it. No knife.

"What's missing?" Brett was impatient and glanced nervously back toward the hallway.

"I found a knife in here earlier," Penelope said. She pushed all the clothing to one side of the bag and back again, her motions growing frantic, her heart galloping. *Dammit! It has to be here!*

"You went through her stuff?" Brett asked incredulously.

"Yes. That's not the point. There was a knife in here. I think it may have had blood on the handle." She replaced Willa's clothing in the bag, frustrated. She knew her husband thought she'd finally lost her mind. First the necklace—*what necklace?*—now this. She'd never had anything less than a near-perfect memory, and she'd certainly never *invented* actual events, conjured objects from her mind like knives and necklaces. This was absurd.

"But it's not there now?" Brett asked. He took a step backward, like he was ready to leave. Bored with this conversation. Did he really not believe her?

"No. And the cell phone's gone too." Penelope sat, dumbfounded for a moment, before slamming her hand down on the hardwood floor. She longed to throw something—a glass, a vase—and hear it shatter against the wall. She was so tired of feeling this way—helpless, a little confused, unsure if she'd seen or heard what she thought she saw and heard. She wasn't used to it.

She stood, dusting off the front of her jeans. Looked around at the pin-neat space. She pulled open the side table drawers, opened the drawers in the little guest room writing desk. All empty.

"What cell phone?" Brett suddenly looked interested.

"She had a kitchen knife and a burner phone in her bag. One of those phones you can buy at, like, CVS?"

"What did it look like?"

"I don't know! Just black. Like a small, cheap smartphone. Plain screen. No case." Penelope waved him out into the hall and back to their bedroom. In their room, she hissed between her teeth, "I don't think the important part here is the phone. She had a knife. Maybe with blood on it."

Brett let out a breath. "Look, Pen. She escaped an abuser. Of course she grabbed something to defend herself with. That makes sense to me. And I don't know about blood or not, but you said it was a small smear, so maybe she nicked herself putting it in the bag? Maybe she packed in a hurry? Maybe it's fucking ketchup, and she pulled it out of the dishwasher on her way out the door. There are so many possibilities that aren't *your friend from college is a mass murderer waiting to kill our family.*"

"You are ridiculous. I never said she was a mass murderer. Why is it always zero to sixty with you?" Penelope stomped around their bedroom and then stopped, spun, and glared at her husband. "Why do you always defend her, no matter what?"

"I don't! I just don't see how you can be constantly suspicious. All the things you've mentioned—every single one of them—have a reasonable explanation. She's *your* friend. If you're this uncomfortable with her, ask her to leave!" Brett ran a hand through his hair and lowered his voice. "Where do you think the knife is now? And the phone?"

Penelope felt her reality slip a little. The room felt too dark, too stuffy. "I don't know. I guess she could have taken it with her?"

"Could you have been mistaken?" Brett asked, a quiet hitch to his voice.

"Like I hallucinated a knife?" Penelope snapped, and he shrank back. "And a phone. And a necklace. And the smell of solvent on the floors. What else? Am I just making everything up?"

"No, Pen, I just . . . I don't know what to do here, that's all." He sounded defeated, almost hopeless. "I don't think it's entirely healthy to let her stay here and then watch every move she makes like a hawk. I get that you don't trust her, based on whatever happened with you guys years ago. And to be honest, I have no idea what that was. Neither of you seem happy to talk about it, but yet you both carry it around with you every minute of the day. It's a bit exhausting to be around you both." Brett ran a hand through his thick hair, scratched at the back of his neck. "But you need to decide what you can deal with and what you can't. Whatever you want to do, I'll support you."

"Oh, that's new." Penelope knew it was a nasty dig. She also knew it wasn't entirely true or fair. But it was a little true and maybe a little fair.

Brett paused in the doorway to the bathroom and stared at her for a long moment. "When Willa leaves, we should really talk." And he shut the door with a quiet click.

—◦◦◦—

Downstairs, she could hear Brett opening and closing the refrigerator. She imagined he was making himself dinner—sandwiches or something easy. She was in no mood to cook *(she's doing what you can't)*. Her phone pinged with a text from Tara.

Mom, do you have baby pictures of me? I need it for a school project.

Sure, when?

I just have to bring them in tomorrow.

With not a little resignation, she swung her legs over the side of the bed and padded her way to the walk-in closet. She had bins of baby pictures, back from when you printed photos at the pharmacy. She'd always delighted in taking her camera, and then later her phone, to the store, plugging in the little memory card. Holding her babies in little four-by-six images. She hadn't done it in years—everything was digital now. She pulled out the bin of pictures, and on top was an eight-by-ten black-and-white. She picked it up and studied it, positive she'd never seen it before.

It was an old photo, taken over ten years ago. In it, Penelope was holding a preschool-age Linc on her lap on their front porch. In their old house, on a rickety porch swing that she had loved but Brett had rightfully argued would not fit in in their *new* new home. Linc had been crying, the swelling evident in his face even in the black-and-white photo. She was midkiss to the crown of his head.

Her first thought was, *How sweet—Brett took and saved pictures of me?*

She'd never seen him take a photo in her life. Of anything, really. Zoo trips, family vacations, beach jaunts. All the photos were taken by her. Even once, at Home Depot, he showed her a fertilizer he'd wanted for the lawn but wanted to research the ingredients first. He'd pointed the back of the bottle in her direction—*Take a picture of this, please.*

The second realization hit her harder. The photo had been time-stamped: 1:32:19 p.m. She actually remembered this day. Linc had come home from preschool crying. A boy had tripped him on the playground.

Brett hadn't been home. How odd. She put it aside and dug through the bin of photos, old Polaroids, four-by-sixes, five-by-sevens, gap-tooth school pictures, chubby baby pictures, their edges worn. She probably should have put them all in an album by now, but life got in the way. Would a better mother have albums for her children? Maybe.

Penelope reached into the bin and pulled out a stack, spread them out on the floor, looking for Tara's signature Michelin Man legs. She'd always been such a chubby, happy baby. Always laughing.

Another black-and-white eight-by-ten nestled in the middle of the bin, among the other photographs. Penelope felt a chill slide up her spine. She hadn't taken that one either.

The four of them emerging from the theater after Tara's role in *The Addams Family*. She'd been Wednesday Addams, and the four of them had been laughing so hard, Penelope knew that if she could zoom in, there would be tears on her cheeks.

She put the two eight-by-tens together, haphazardly grabbed a few of Tara's baby pictures, and ran her hand through the rest of the photos, making sure there were no more surprises. There weren't.

She held them apart, one in each hand. They were each bordered in white, time-stamped with the time and date taken. They looked like they had been taken with either identical, or similar, cameras. The same font on the stamp. But (she did the math) eight years apart?

Quickly, Penelope snapped the lid back on the Rubbermaid tub and pushed it back into its place. She left the walk-in, her breath coming short. There had to be a reasonable explanation for them—but what?

Penelope sat on her bed to think. She looked around the room—not spotless, or entirely clutter-free, but very clean. Her bedroom was her sanctuary, her place to breathe. Lately, it had begun to feel suffocating.

There was something behind the mirror above her dresser, a white paper protruding between the wall and the glass. She stood, crossed the room. Penelope used her nails to extract it, to slide it neatly from between the brackets.

Another photo.

Penelope and Brett on a date, a year ago, right after he was laid off. At a table al fresco, Penelope gazed off into the distance; Brett looked at his watch. If the picture had been snapped a split second before or after, it might have caught her laughing—she remembered that date. She remembered it being melancholy, a little quiet, but not awful. They still laughed together, the wry, dark humor that typically came along with hard luck. This photo looked staged. If it had been at a gallery, it might have been called *Date Night Fight*.

Penelope closed her eyes, felt herself sway. She looked around her room. Where else?

On impulse, she got down on her hands and knees, checked under the bed: Penelope with Tara, walking to the bus stop in their old house, the giant blooming pear tree behind them, Tara talking a mile a minute and Penelope smiling down at her.

At the bottom of her underwear drawer, buried by old lingerie she hadn't worn in years: Linc, last year, on the lacrosse field midcradle, his bicep roped with newly thickened muscle.

Finally, under Brett's pillow, a photo that stole the breath from her lungs. Penelope, in Jaime's foyer, five days ago. The photo was taken from the street but zoomed. Her hand curled around the back of his neck, both of their mouths open, lips barely touching. Her eyes half-lidded. Their bodies pressed together, the desperation palpable. His hand gripping her hip—she could feel it just looking at the picture, the way he'd clung to her. Time- and date-stamped, but she didn't even have to look. The juxtaposition of the date night with Brett and the passion in her face, her eyes half-shut, when she was almost kissing Jaime made her feel sick.

She gathered all the black-and-whites into a small pile and fanned through them again. What the hell was she going to do with these? They were snapshots of her life—a full sixteen years of her life. Her life with Brett. Her almost-affair with Jaime.

Where had they come from? Did he have her followed their whole lives together? Nothing made sense. Could she ask Brett? Would he just think she was crazy somehow again? She remembered his tone when he said *we should talk*.

She looked around the bedroom, anxiously scanning for a place to keep them all. She needed time to think about what to do with them. Confront Brett?

The bookcase: high up on the top shelf sat a large false book underneath a vase of marbles. She stood precariously on the second shelf, retrieved the vase and the false book. After snapping it open, she slid the photos inside and returned the book and vase to their spot on the top shelf.

Downstairs the front door opened, and a happy voice called up "Hello!" with a burst of laughter. It sounded like Tara and Willa, arriving home together. She was just emerging from the closet when a soft rap came on her bedroom door. Penelope swung the door open, and Willa stood in the hallway, raspberry-red lips open in shock.

She peered past Penelope into the room beyond and smiled, white teeth gleaming. "I thought maybe you had a boyfriend in there," she said.

CHAPTER THIRTY

February 24, 2020

Later, she waited for Brett to come out of the bathroom. He'd shaved, his pajama pants hanging loosely around his hips. He rubbed a towel across his jaw and then hung it on the hook on the back of the door.

Penelope held the photo close to her chest, breathing, just waiting. He turned down the corner of the bed, picked up his cell phone. He'd set an alarm for the next morning. His nighttime routine was so ingrained in her she could have recited it, eyes closed.

Penelope laid the photo on the bed. She and a kindergarten Tara, walking hand in hand to the bus stop, oblivious. She made her voice light. "Look what I found today. Isn't that a beautiful photo?" She smiled then; it felt stiff and unnatural. Brett picked it up, his features softening.

"That's really nice," he said, a small smile on his face.

"Did you take that?" Penelope asked, rubbing lotion on her hands for something to do, something else to appear preoccupied by while she studied her husband.

"Take this picture? No, I missed Tara's first day of kindergarten, remember? We had a four a.m. call with China. Don't you remember? I was so mad."

She did remember. She cleared her throat, planned her next words delicately. "Would you have . . . hired someone to take this picture?" His face changed, and she continued quickly. "You know, so you wouldn't miss it."

"What? That would be pretty weird if I didn't tell you about it." He knitted his eyebrows and studied the photo again. "No, you know it was probably that neighbor friend in our old house. What was her name? Luna? Lila?"

"Leslie," Penelope said softly and tucked the photo into her nightstand drawer. She smiled at her husband. "You're probably right."

—⁂—

"Any idea of a plan yet?" Penelope asked casually.

She didn't plan to have this conversation again, but the events from yesterday swirled in her mind. Willa had stood in the kitchen, drinking coffee with Penelope (again) and promising that she'd know something soon—*not an actual plan yet, but as soon as I know, you'll know!*—and asked if she could bring a friend for dinner. Penelope had swallowed hard before agreeing. It was likely Jaime again. She thought of the black-and-white photos in her room, the kiss on the porch, and her hands trembled.

Willa clapped and kissed Penelope's cheek excitedly and bounced out of the kitchen on her toes like the dancer she always said she was, blonde ponytail swinging. The front door creaked open, slammed shut, and outside, Willa's car puttered out of the driveway.

Penelope was alone in the house. She waited an extra minute to make sure that Willa was actually gone and then texted Nora—Dr. Appt this afternoon. I'll be online this morning, but will be taking the afternoon off! Thx—and tucked the phone back into her pocket before heading back upstairs. The kids were at school; Brett had left early for the gym.

In the family office, Penelope sat in the plush wheeled chair, powered on the laptop that sat unused for days on end. With everything available on their phones—bills, banking . . . hell, even grocery delivery—she found they needed the laptop less and less.

She navigated to an incognito Google page and started searching: Willa Blaine. Willamena Blaine. Willa and Trent, Deer Run. Found a single Facebook profile for her, her picture fuzzy, like a filter over the camera, the edges of her cheek blurred, the scar rendered invisible. *Intro: Teacher. Dancer. Married to the love of my life. Workplaces: Accounting Teacher at Pellville High School. Married to Grey Hudson.* The rest of her profile was locked down for privacy.

Willa had said she was married to a man named Trent. Obviously, she could have given Penelope a fake name. Penelope clicked the link to Grey Hudson. *Intro: Loves to hike, bike, open mic. Macallan taste on a Bankers Club budget.* His profile picture was handsome—thick gray hair, a wide white smile. He wore a suit.

Not the garage dweller Willa made him out to be. He had no other photos available to the public.

All the nerves in Penelope's body were tingling, a steady thrum up and down her spine. She blew up the picture of Willa and studied it from all angles. It was definitely Willa—same narrow curve of her chin, same scar, same wide blue eyes, startled and watery. The same brilliant cheerleader smile.

She opened a new tab and in the white pages, typed *Grey Hudson, Deer Run*, and just that easily—snap of her fingers, really—a phone number and address were returned. She copied the address onto a folded piece of printer paper, and before she could think twice, she picked up her keys, grabbed her purse, and headed out to her car.

—⁓—

It was an hour and seventeen minutes from Wexford, New Jersey, to Deer Run, Pennsylvania, and Penelope didn't even think about the E-ZPass catching her tolls or what it would mean later when she had to explain herself. She didn't think to turn off her GPS, her phone location that the kids used incessantly to find out if she was on her way home from work yet and should they just pick up dinner without her.

As soon as the car rolled into town, the main street that Penelope hadn't seen in twenty years, her throat closed up and her hands rattled against the steering wheel. She was more anxious than she'd thought she'd be.

She rolled down the window, just to smell the brisk, honey-scented air of a town frozen in time. The bookstore she'd worked at—Amelia with her plain bowl haircut, her watery brown eyes, but her shocking loud, infectious laugh. The walks home after her shift with Jack while he talked animatedly, hands flying, about his book, his cheeks pinked with warmth, his smile and the way she felt it zing her whole body. Did he ever publish the book? Penelope had never looked. Whenever she'd thought about the Church House, the five of them, her stomach had twisted with something sick, and she'd swallowed it all back until she found something distracting to focus on. Linc. Tara. Brett. Dinner. Dishes. Nora. Anything.

She pressed fingertips to the bridge of her nose. All of this was too much. Too much, too fast. She pulled up in front of the address on the folded paper: a white ranch house, neatly decorated and landscaped, the lawn mowed green, even in the dead of winter, a row of boxwoods lining the paved driveway. In the back, a fence, a swing set, a small matching white doghouse. The whole property looked like something out of *Edward Scissorhands*.

Penelope rang the doorbell twice and waited. She heard footsteps, a high-pitched squeal, and the door opened to reveal what was very obviously Grey Hudson. He looked exactly like his profile picture.

"Hi, are you Grey Hudson?" Penelope asked, her voice shaking, and she cleared her throat to cover it up.

"Yes. What can I help you with?" He smiled at her, teeth and warmth and kindness, and Penelope hated that her first thought was,

This man could not have hit Willa, because honestly, how could you tell? This was why charming men got away with beating their wives—as long as they did it in places where the bruises didn't show.

"I'm actually looking for an old classmate of mine—Willa Blaine?" His face stayed frozen, and Penelope rushed on with a speech she had rehearsed in the car. "My name is Bree Haren. We lived together after college, and I was back in town for the first time in twenty years—I just thought I'd . . . you know, pop in to see her."

Grey's face had gone the shade of his hair. Penelope had a flash that the man could be having a stroke right in front of her, and she cautiously asked, "Are you all right? You look like you might faint."

Grey gripped the doorjamb, exhaled loudly. "I'm . . . fine. I'm okay." He shook his head. "It's just that . . ."

"If it's a bad time, I can come back," Penelope offered.

A tiny voice behind him piped up. "Daddy, what does that lady want with Mommy?"

Penelope caught herself as she gasped. A little miniature version of Willa stood behind Grey, all blonde pigtails and apple cheeks. She looked about four years old, with the squat, strong-thighed build of a budding cheerleader. Grey scooped her up and kissed the top of her head.

"This," he said to Penelope, "is Violet. She's four." Violet displayed five fingers, and Grey chuckled as he gently pushed down her thumb. Violet rolled her eyes at her father in a gesture so grown up, and so much like her mother, that Penelope almost said so.

"Hi, Violet," Penelope said to the child and felt instantly terrible for intruding on their life. This was the man who had hit Willa? This gentle gray-haired man with his little girl who seemed not at all afraid of her father? Although, surely it was true that some men would beat their wives, and their children were blissfully unaware? Penelope had no earthly idea. For all Brett's faults—and they were numerous—he'd never been violent.

In addition, Willa had fled to Penelope's, leaving Violet in the care of her father? Who would leave a child with a violent abuser? Not to mention, the entire time Willa had been staying with them, she'd never mentioned a child. She talked a bit about Trent (or Grey?) but nothing about a little blonde pigtailed four-year-old who looked exactly—*exactly*—like her mother. Did Willa plan to come back for her? When she talked of her plan—finding a life for herself—was Violet part of that? Did Jaime know Willa had a child? Penelope's mind was spinning, trying to make sense of the unexpected scene before her.

"I'm sorry," Grey said, stepping aside and waving her in. "Please come in. Sit down. I apologize for the mess. I'm trying to work from home, but Violet here makes it a bit difficult."

Still holding the child, he kicked newspapers out of the way with his foot. The inside of his house *was* a mess. Plates and coffee cups on the end tables, the pillows scattered on the floor, toys littering the hallway, children's books on the couches and chairs. He deposited Violet on the floor, and she immediately started to suck her thumb. He went about quickly clearing a spot for Penelope to sit.

Penelope feigned confusion (she was truly baffled, so this wasn't hard to do). "Is Willa home? Or I could come back another time?" She shook her head to drive the point home, and Grey sighed and sat in the chair across from her. She realized then that he was probably still in his pajamas—a flannel shirt and a pair of sweatpants. And it was the middle of a workday, which had been fairly terrible planning, if in fact Penelope had planned any of this.

"Look, I don't know how to tell you this." Grey leaned forward, elbows on knees, and tented his fingertips. "But about six months ago, Willa ran out to mail a package and never came home."

CHAPTER
THIRTY-ONE

February 25, 2020

Penelope had never had a poker face. At the Church House, they tried to actually play poker, and any good hand she had was immediately known. Jack would say, *What do you have, two pair? Full house? Can't be a straight.* He'd prattle through all the hands until he hit the one and then break into a full grin. *Yep, that's it; look at your face.*

Penelope must have shown some kind of shock because Grey immediately stood and retreated to the kitchen, returning only seconds later with a glass of water.

"I'm so sorry to just blurt it out like that. It's been a long few months."

Obviously there was nothing surprising about Willa going missing; after all, she was probably sitting in Penelope's kitchen. However, Penelope was utterly confounded by the fact that Willa had been gone for *six whole months*. Where had she been this whole time?

"What happened?" Penelope finally asked.

"Damned if I know." Grey sighed. Violet sat, staring at her father, her eyes a mirror of Willa's—bright blue and shining. He said to her,

"Violet, honey, can you please run to your room for a little while I talk to Mommy's old friend from college?"

She scampered away, but Penelope didn't hear the steps down the hallway and suspected the child was lurking right around the corner, listening intently, a cool, fat cheek pressed against the drywall.

"She seemed fine. I don't know. They found her car at the post office, no purse, no wallet, cell phone, keys inside. The camera outside the post office has her entering the building. A second camera inside has her exiting about ten minutes later, but it only captured to the vestibule. In the corner of the vestibule, there's a blind section. Between where the indoor camera cuts out and the outdoor camera clicks on. It's a few seconds, at the most. But *pfffft*." He made a waving motion with his hand. "She was gone."

"What did the police say?" Penelope was truly riveted, even though she could barely reconcile the cognitive dissonance. Willa, this sweet man's missing wife, a child's mother, was . . . what? Dancing barefoot around Penelope's kitchen? Kissing Penelope's neighbor?

"They looked for months. I still have a detective that shows up here once in a while. Nothing new to report." Grey shook his head. "They think maybe she just left of her own volition, but I know Willa. She might have left me. Might. We weren't perfect, but I thought we were doing all right. But if she left me, I could accept it. But she'd never leave that little girl." A fat tear escaped and rolled down Grey's cheek, and he made no move to wipe it. He didn't look embarrassed.

"What do you think happened?" Penelope asked.

"I've no earthly idea," Grey said, his voice hoarse. "One minute she was here, about to mail a package to her sister in Louisiana, and the next, nothing. We're just supposed to go on, then?"

"No cash missing from your bank account? No credit transactions?"

"Nope, nothing. We checked all that."

Penelope had a thought. "What kind of car did she drive?"

"A 2019 Honda CRV. Silver. It was at the post office, and they towed it here after it was processed by the police lab. It's in the garage now. I have no idea what to do with it. Sell it?" He ran a palm across his stubble, a soft scratching noise. "What if she comes back? She'll need a car, right?" His eyes grew unfocused, imagining a life where Willa would need to run to the grocery store, even the post office, again.

The car parked in front of Willa's house was a dark-blue beat-up Chevy. Probably an early 2000s model. It had a large dent in the passenger-side door.

"Do you mind if I look?" Penelope stood, indicated toward the living room wall—a mural of pictures. Grey waved her on with one hand but didn't stand.

The three of them at the beach, Willa with her head thrown back, her teeth white and exposed, the raw strip of neck pale where the sun didn't hit, her hair gleaming. In the photo, Grey and Violet watched her, rapt. In another frame, the ocean behind her, Willa smiled brilliantly into the camera, Violet perched on a hip. She wore the same clothes in both pictures.

Willa looked the same in the photo as she had that morning standing in Penelope's kitchen. The same cheerleader grin, a sparkling, mischievous glint in her eye, the same pink scar, faint with concealer. Penelope couldn't make sense of any of it—her mind swam with a thousand questions.

"It was a family photo shoot. We didn't usually do things like that, but Willa found a coupon on vacation. So . . . we did." He shrugged, helplessly, from the couch.

The air over by the fireplace held the smell of Willa—a distinct, light musk. The same scent that had been permeating Penelope's house for almost two weeks. It had seeped into her throw pillows, her couch, the chair she preferred to sit in, her legs tucked underneath her, reading a folded paperback. At first, Penelope thought it smelled lovely—and familiar. Now it was beginning to give her a headache.

She continued to study the family photos—older relatives she didn't know, a row of little kids holding hands. Likely nieces and nephews on

Grey's side, parents, and in one frame, a very elderly man in a wheel-chair. How could Willa just up and leave all this—this wasn't just leaving one man. This was leaving a whole *life*. This was grief for dozens of people who loved her, would miss her, cry for her, give small prayers at Thanksgiving in her honor or tiny memorial speeches at weddings.

Penelope felt the room spin slightly and sank down into the chair next to the fireplace, and the Willa scent grew stronger.

"That was her favorite chair," Grey said, a husk in his voice. "Hey, can I ask you a question?"

Penelope nodded, but she felt light headed. She studied the carpet pattern—a blue-and-white floral swirl—to regain her composure.

Grey cleared his throat. "It's actually kind of strange that you're here. She had gotten pretty quiet and secretive about a month before she disappeared. Taking phone calls in private, that kind of thing. I had asked her what was going on, but she said it was work. I guess I was an idiot, but I believed her. I told the police this, but only recently remembered something. I didn't think it was connected, but now that you're here, maybe I do?" His voice pitched up at the end with a slight wobble. Penelope nodded, and he continued, "She had a nightmare about two or three nights before she disappeared. She woke up crying, sweating, the whole nine yards. I got her water and helped her calm down. She was never really a nightmare kind of person, so it really felt off to me. But when I asked her what it was about, she just said it was about college."

Penelope made a valiant effort not to look startled and probably failed. She watched Grey smooth the sides of his hair back, fidgety and nervous. "See, she didn't talk much about college—or rather that year after college. We only met ten years ago; she just said that she had a 'bad year,' her house burned down, and that was that. I didn't ask too many questions. It never seemed . . . relevant. But I have to ask you now—" He stopped long enough to inhale deeply, his eyes deep and earnest and a sheen of sweat shining along his upper lip. "Did you live with someone named Grace?"

CHAPTER
THIRTY-TWO
Then: Widening circles

Grace had become a fixture at the house. In the kitchen, rooting through the refrigerator for a healthy snack *(You're all going to get scurvy, not just Jack)*; lounging in the great room, legs slung over the arm of Flynn's big chair, reading a book *(You guys really need to get a TV)*; leaning over the railing of Jack's loft bedroom while Flynn cooked dinner *(Remember, no mushrooms—I'm allergic to mushrooms!)*. The sound of her voice, the soft natural rasp that was actually, if Penelope weren't so anti-everything when it came to Grace, soothing and sexy. Penelope wasn't the kind of person to be easily driven crazy. But this was going to do it.

The night before, Grace had brought her sister to meet "all her new friends." She announced gaily, "This is Talia!" Talia was slightly smaller than Grace, dark haired, with huge glasses perched on the edge of a prominent nose. She'd barely said a word the entire time, and what she did say, she whispered to Grace, who repeated it for everyone else.

After she'd left, Flynn said, "Your sister seems nice. Super quiet."

Grace had sighed. "She's interesting, for sure."

Later, they'd see Grace duck out to the front hall, take a phone call in hushed tones: "It'll be fine; listen, you'll be okay. It's not a big deal, okay? Just calm down." She'd excuse herself after dinner, disappear into Jack's bedroom for an hour.

"Who is she talking to?" Willa asked Jack once, blunt in a way none of the others would dare.

"Her sister. She's . . . got issues, I think." He shook his head, shrugged. Then his face grew soft. "I think Grace takes care of her. Emotionally, I mean. Maybe financially? Not sure." Then he sighed. "She's just such a good person."

Penelope felt the sting of that, her cheeks flaming pink.

"Don't you think it's strange?" Bree asked one morning while Grace puttered around the kitchen. She had picked wildflowers from Bree's garden and was arranging them in a vase. Bree was lying flat on a yoga mat in the great room (no one actually ever did yoga on it, but it was always there), her red hair fanned out around her, her legs straight up in the air, feet flat like she was balancing an invisible book.

Penelope was irritated by all of them at the moment. Bree always started sentences vaguely: *Don't you think it's strange? Doesn't it make you wonder?* And made whomever she was speaking to ask, *What, Bree? What's so strange?* Usually Flynn complied, but Penelope felt herself stubbornly resisting, just to see if Bree would continue anyway.

"What's strange?" Flynn sank down into the thick leather couch, a cup of coffee in one hand. Grace had started to make them all coffee from a french press every day, and Penelope thought it tasted like charred toast, black and bitter. Everyone else seemed to adore it—Willa had started calling it Grace's special brew, so Penelope stubbornly switched to tea.

"Grace and Willa look more like sisters than Grace and Talia," Bree said, a soft smile on her face as she gazed out to the kitchen where the two were bent over the island, heads together, looking at something on Willa's phone and laughing.

Flynn swiveled around to get a better look and let out a short, quiet laugh. "Goddamn, you're right."

Both had girl-next-door features: blonde curling hair, apple cheeks, pert noses, long lashes, friendly white smiles. Grace was taller than Willa by almost a head, and broader, thought Penelope with some satisfaction. Her shoulders were wider, and she was muscular to Willa's soft curve. But something about Grace was more striking, magnetic. Simply put, Grace was gorgeous.

Jack appeared at the railing, shirtless and smiling, and they all looked up at him.

"Grace looks like Willa," Bree said conversationally, and from the kitchen Willa called, "Oh God, shut up."

"I never noticed that," Jack said, stretching his arms up, resting his fingertips lightly against the ceiling beam, and Penelope looked away, conscious of the mesh shorts that hung loosely from his hips. He called down to the kitchen, "I must have a type!" and Bree made a hocking noise from the back of her throat, in disgust. Jack grinned down at her and said, "Don't be jealous, Bree baby."

Penelope watched the whole exchange, her stomach rolling with nausea as she sipped her tea and focused on the book she'd brought up from her bedroom.

Grace's presence every day was starting to eat at Penelope. She found herself stomping around the house, angry at empty egg cartons and too-full trash. Finding fault with all of them—Bree was too messy, Flynn too particular, Willa too loud *(God, her laugh cut right through you)*, Jack too cocky. The running litany of faults in her mind was making her completely miserable, and she dreaded the after-dinner games she couldn't get out of.

They'd moved on from Risk to go, tournament style.

"You should get a pool table," Grace had suggested that night, and Penelope must have made an awful face because Willa burst out laughing. She shook her head slightly, and Penelope flushed at being caught. Grace looked at both of them, confused. "What?"

Penelope, feeling embarrassed and irritated, stood up and went to the kitchen under the guise of getting another drink but, once there, realized that the idea of any liquor made her feel sick and instead found herself just leaving them upstairs and going to bed. She hadn't meant to and paused to rethink it in the stairwell. She knew she was acting like a brat—she couldn't seem to help it. Her mood was so vile, and she felt heartsick every single day.

It seemed completely unfair. Jack had treated their tryst like a complete one-night stand, and the only time he brought it up was once, a few days later, in the kitchen. He crept up behind her, smacked her lightly on the butt, and she'd yelped, swatted at him.

"Ahh, no, you like that kind of thing. I should know." And he winked at her. When her face burned bright, he laughed again. "Pip, you're so sweetly uptight." And kissed her cheek before strolling into the great room with his coffee in hand.

And that was it. That was the only conversation they'd had about their one night together. No one mentioned the blouse left in the kitchen—Penelope had just found it folded nicely on her bed, with no idea who'd done it.

"Don't you think she seems on edge lately?" The voice was hushed but unmistakable. Definitely Bree.

Penelope stood, frozen on the second step, the door to the great room cracked just enough to hear the conversation clearly.

"Oh, who knows," Willa said. "Penelope is always a little bit of an enigma. Holds everything in and barely lets her hair down, that girl. We should spike her drink with Molly one night, just to see what she'd do."

Unexpectedly, Flynn cackled at that. "I'm not endorsing that, but it would be wild to see her unclench a little."

"You're all terrible people, you know." Jack.

"It's why you love us." Willa.

"Come on, Willa, quit yapping and take your stupid turn," Grace said, and they all laughed.

—⟶⟶—

Later, in the middle of the night, Penelope, wide awake, stared at the ceiling, a burning in her chest that felt like fire, bile in her throat. She padded to the little bathroom at the end of the downstairs hall, feet cold on the wood floor. She splashed water on her face, feeling cold, then hot, her T-shirt in a limp sweat.

Oh, God. She was cracking up. This is what it felt like to die of a broken heart. Your body didn't just quit, your heart stop, your lungs leaking out their final breath. It was gradual, almost unnoticeable, the sapping will to keep getting up, walking to the kitchen, eating a meal, getting dressed, walking to town to work. Walking, walking, walking. Living required so much movement, and movement felt so heavy.

She was thinking about the sheer heaviness of her legs—thick and unwieldy—when the nausea came on, so sudden and violent that she turned and vomited right into the toilet. A rush of bile and hot water, purging and purging and purging, and then there was Bree.

Opening the little window. Letting in the cool night air. Lifting her hair off her neck, blowing softly, until all the little hairs on Penelope's arms stood up straight.

Soothing sounds into Penelope's ear, clucks and coos and baby noises, and Penelope rested her forehead on the lid of the toilet and fumbled around for the handle, the swoosh of rushing water.

"Here, eat this," Bree said, a little coo into her ear. Penelope opened her mouth, a baby bird, and tasted the sharp sweetness of a ginger candy.

"This is awful—what is this?" asked Penelope, eyes closed, the chilled porcelain like heaven on her cheek. The candy had an acrid aftertaste and made her tongue tingle unpleasantly.

"Shhhh," said Bree, her hand deftly caressing Penelope's hair, her scalp. Penelope drowsily thought it was the most wonderful thing she'd ever felt in her whole life. "My sister ate them all the time when she was pregnant."

Penelope sat up, blinking, feeling as though she'd been doused with cold water.

Bree's face was placid, serene. "Oh, darling girl," she said. "You must have known. Didn't you?"

CHAPTER THIRTY-THREE

February 25, 2020

Penelope drove home on autopilot. Parked the car in the circular drive-way, stared up at the house—imposing and white, flat front with land-scaping that she used to think was minimalistic but now looked sterile and featureless. Square, sparse boxwoods; pea gravel and flagstone, all shades of gray and white. Before: easy, maintenance-free, clean. Now: completely and utterly devoid of personality. What had changed? The only answer: her perception.

Inside, she heard whistling from the kitchen. Willa.

Penelope pressed her thumbs against her eye sockets to stave off the oncoming headache.

Six months. Six months. Six months.

Did Willa leave Grey, with his earnest eyes, and have an affair with an abusive mechanic named Trent? That could explain the post office Houdini act. Trent's truck idling outside, a sweaty promise to *take care of you, baby*. But who could leave their child—a four-year-old, old enough to remember her mother, old enough to miss her? It seemed a particular brand of cruelty to leave a child who could remember your smile.

She'd fled the house quickly after Grey asked about Grace—making excuses about dinner—saying only that Grace was the *girlfriend of a housemate, you know how that goes.* She didn't know if her behavior seemed strange or not to the poor man, but she could barely think. She spent the entire ride back trying to come up with what she would do next, and failing miserably.

Could she tell Brett? Given how he'd reacted to the knife, maybe not. But this was different—there was Facebook evidence that could not be erased.

"Oh, good, you're back!" Willa called gaily before Penelope could decide what to do. Confront her? *Where did you go for six months? By the way, your husband and child are heartbroken. Where's the knife? Did you leave pictures in my room?*

Penelope wondered if she was truly starting to lose her grip on sanity.

"I'm back," Penelope said noncommittally. She watched Willa hum, sway around the kitchen, season chicken breast, chop a pepper, a carrot, celery and toss it all into a pan.

The table was set for six.

"Oh, right," Penelope said. "A guest."

Willa whipped around. "I hope that's still okay. I can cancel if it's not! I should have reminded you." Her big eyes were pleading.

"It's fine. I just forgot. No big deal." Penelope rubbed the bridge of her nose. "I just have an awful headache."

She waited for Willa to comment like she had all those years ago— *You never get headaches.* That had been her go-to excuse then. It felt right now too.

"Oh, go upstairs and rest. Relax!" Willa shooed her away. "Take a shower, and come down whenever you're ready. Do you need Excedrin?"

Penelope let herself be shooed, paused in the living room, listening to Willa's soft hum, the patter of bare feet, quick on the kitchen tile. *I've looked at love this way.*

Upstairs in the bedroom, Penelope heard the shower. So, Brett was home. She paused to listen and then quietly crept to her dresser. After pulling open the top drawer, she felt around underneath all the satin until she found what she'd been looking for. A single sheet of loose-leaf paper torn out of a spiral-bound notebook. Scrawled with a black pen. She stuck the note in the back pocket of her jeans, to look at later. Grey had said *six months*. She wanted to compare the dates. Call it an instinct—something felt wrong about the whole thing: the letter, Willa's disappearance. Later, if she and Brett went to bed at the same time, maybe she'd be able to sneak a few minutes of privacy in the bathroom. Either way, she had the note.

When she was done, she retrieved the false book from the top of the bookshelf. She pushed open the bathroom door, closed it behind her, and sat quietly on the toilet. When the water shut off, she said, "It's me; put the water back on, but come out here—I want to talk to you quick."

Brett poked his head out the glass shower door, alarmed. "What? Why?"

"Please, okay?"

He reached behind him, flicked the water back on, and emerged from the shower. He tied a towel around his waist and dried his arms and torso with a second towel. When he was done, he propped himself up on the bathroom counter, between the dual sinks, and gave her a pointed look. "Okay, what's up? What now?" He gave her a smart-ass kind of smile, but she didn't return it.

"I want to show you something," Penelope began, keeping her voice low, above a whisper, but barely. She remembered how badly this conversation had ended last time.

"Okay," Brett said, his voice edged with caution. This whole conversation was a repeat of the day before. From her nightstand, Penelope had retrieved the image of her and Tara walking to the bus stop and held it on top of the false book.

"Remember this picture of Tara and me that I showed you the other night? I found a bunch of them. Photos of our life together. Eight-by-tens. Taken with a long-range lens or something." She held the book in her lap, knowing that one particular image inside was likely to blow her marriage apart. Did she want to do this tonight?

Maybe it would have been better to show him the Facebook page. She didn't have time, not right now, to show him everything. But she was starting to feel a sense of urgency—like all the different pieces of the puzzle were adding up, filling in. Like maybe they were all in danger? From who, Willa? With her cheerleader smile? From Grey, with his sad eyes? No, that was silly. From Trent? Did Trent actually exist? She had no idea, but none of the events of the past few days felt coincidental. Not anymore.

"Okay. Do you think it's related to Willa?"

"I have no idea. But I'm freaked out. The necklace, the knife, the cell phone, now these pictures—" She omitted any mention of Grey, Violet. It was too much to tell him so fast, so quietly. She just had to focus on the facts—right in front of her. She lifted the lid off. She could hear Brett behind her, breathing. She could smell his shower soap.

She let out a small cry of shock and put a hand to her forehead. Penelope stared at the empty book in front of her, the dark-green felt interior. The whole room was starting to pitch, and Penelope sat, hard, on the edge of the tub, the box falling from her hands and clunking on the tiled bathroom floor.

"Again." Brett's voice was flat. He didn't move.

Penelope stood, left the bathroom, crossed the bedroom to the bookshelf. She ran her hand across the top. Dropped to her knees and scanned under the bed, the dresser. Neat as a pin—no pictures. *What the fuck?*

"She is trying to make a fool out of me. I know it. Unless you are?" She looked up at her husband, who studied her not with curiosity or concern, but pity. She curled her fist, wanting to punch him. Wanting to throw something very hard against the wall or possibly Brett's face. "Did you take pictures with a long-range camera for the entirety of our marriage and then place them strategically all over our bedroom recently?"

"What? Penelope, what are you *talking about*?"

"Don't you dare," Penelope seethed. "I am not losing my grip on reality here. I'm *not* crazy. There was a knife, a cell phone. Pictures. Now they're gone. Look." Penelope pulled her cell phone out of her pocket and snapped open the Facebook app. She navigated quickly to Willa's page. "See? This is Willa. But look, she's married to a man named Grey Hudson. Look." She opened the profile's photos. "See? There's a little girl." She clicked on the link to Grey Hudson's Facebook page to show him.

"What does this mean? Her husband wasn't named Trent—he was named Grey?" Brett shook his head, uncomprehending.

"And! She has a daughter. A little girl. Brett. I went there today. I met them."

"What! Penelope, have you lost your ever-loving mind? What the hell is wrong with you? Even if—and this is a *huge if*—she didn't give us her husband's real name, he could still have abused her. Are you so single minded that you could be blinded by someone who appears nice?" He pinched the bridge of his nose. "This has gotten completely out of hand."

"Brett! She has a daughter that she left!" Penelope insisted, touching the phone, the image of Willa with her daughter.

"For two weeks. Maybe she's trying to figure out a way to get them both out. What are you saying? What do you think is going on?"

"I don't know. But she's not who she says she is." Penelope put the phone back in her pocket. She was overloading him with information, conveying none of it clearly or rationally.

"How long have you been home?"

"Pen." Brett hawed around the question, his eyes not meeting hers.

"How long?" Penelope knew her voice might carry. She no longer cared.

"I don't know . . . an hour, maybe?"

"Was Willa here before you?"

"Yes."

"Were the kids?"

"No. They're still at Sasha's and Zeke's houses."

"So, Willa was in the house alone?" Penelope pressed, and Brett pinched the bridge of his nose again.

"Yes, but Pen, do you hear yourself?" Brett asked her, his tone soothing, kind. He was placating her. "Honestly, you're starting to worry me."

"Fuck you," Penelope spat and pushed past him out of the bathroom.

In her back pocket, her phone buzzed. She took it out and checked the screen. Willa.

When you guys are done doing . . . whatever (:D) . . . come downstairs. I want you to meet my new friend!

She had assumed it was Jaime coming for dinner. She'd been prepared for Jaime. Willa had made another friend? Penelope turned her phone to face Brett so he could read it.

He sighed and tilted his head up to the ceiling. Penelope left him in the bedroom and found her way downstairs, distracted. She could hear Willa talking animatedly from the living room. She could face Willa, smile pleasantly for the sake of whoever the *friend* was, beg a headache, and get back to her bedroom.

She envisioned an evening locked in her bedroom, scouring the internet for all the proof she would need. For Brett, for the police if it came down to that. By tomorrow, Willa would be gone. Penelope would have her house back. It sounded like heaven. Penelope took a deep breath, clenched and unclenched her fingers.

A woman sat on Brett's chair, small and dark, her hair brushed away from her face in a sweep of glossy brown and secured with a turquoise-and-silver comb. Penelope felt a prickle on the back of her neck at the sight of it.

The woman's delicate hands cupped a wineglass, overfilled with a pink rosé. It took Penelope a moment to realize that she was the same woman from the French café, eating lunch with Willa. She flashed on the memory: Willa's head thrown back in laughter, a light touch on her arm. They'd seemed to know each other well. But Willa had called her a *new* friend.

"Oh! I'm so happy you're here!" Willa stood up and hugged Penelope, giving off a faint whiff of cigarette smoke, her fingertips on Penelope's forearm like pointed icicles. "This is my new friend, Genevieve. We are talking about how I might rent one of her apartments in town."

Genevieve waved from the chair and gave Penelope a wide, bright smile. "I'm so excited to meet you! Willa talks about nothing but you! Pip this, Pip that. All good things!"

She still couldn't get used to *Pip* again. Penelope said, "Well, Willa exaggerates. I'm mediocre at best." She smiled blandly and sat on the opposite end of the couch. "Everyone but Willa calls me Penelope."

Genevieve's smile faltered, just a little, her eyes going to the hallway and back. "Such a pretty name." She stumbled a bit when she said it, and Penelope could have sworn she paled a bit. "You're a kind soul to take in an old friend after twenty years. After all she's been through. What would she have done without you?"

"I'd be dead in a ditch without Pip," Willa said, her hand reaching out and gripping Penelope's. Still freezing cold, her fingers prying. Penelope's face felt frozen in a smile, and she pulled her hand away sharply.

There was a silence then, heavy and slow, as everyone searched for something to land on. Penelope could scarcely focus on anything but

Willa. Willa, Grey, Violet. The pictures. The knife, a smear of blood. What did it all mean—all of it together? Why was Willa still in their house? What did she want from all of them? Why didn't she go home to her gray-haired husband and that little blonde girl?

Penelope smelled him before she saw him—that light, rainwater-scented body soap that her husband had worn for as long as she'd known him—and then suddenly he filled the doorway: a blue button-down shirt and a pair of dark jeans, slung low, his hair thick and still slightly damp, curled against his collar. Handsome and fresh. Penelope felt nothing.

He paled in the doorway, blurted, "Gen?" before trying to cover it up. The realization came in slow motion: the familiarity (he knew this woman), the shock (she was out of place, here in his home), the fear (his wife would put it all together).

And she did. Put it all together, that is. It was that fucking comb.

They'd taken a Siesta Key trip a few months after the layoff. Brett had been distracted and snappish. It ended up a mediocre weekend of long silences set against romantic sunsets where they both half faked it. It had been months ago, the previous October. When things were just starting to feel forced. The whole vacation was filled with halting conversation. They got drunk and made love once. Later, after they'd returned, she'd found this comb.

On the underside, Penelope would wager the whole house, was a small silver sea turtle, about the size of a pea. Penelope had been cleaning out their suitcase, unpacking, doing the laundry, when it fell out of Brett's shorts pocket. It was small—only about two inches wide—and light. Wrapped in tissue paper. She left it on his side of the bed and later that night asked him about it, her voice light. *Oh, for Tara! I found it in that beach shop under the hotel, and I don't know why—I just bought it on impulse. It seemed like something she'd like?* And Penelope remembered thinking, *What about Linc?* And then also, *It's not at all anything Tara would like.* It was delicate and pretty and much too small. Tara's thick, unruly hair was in a perpetual ponytail. But then the comb disappeared, Penelope forgot all about it. She could have sworn she saw it on Tara's dresser at some point, but couldn't remember when.

And now, here it was. In "Gen's" hair.

In slow motion, Penelope watched Genevieve watch Brett. Her mouth open and closing, wordless protest. Her husband and the quick, almost unnoticeable shake of his head, just for a second, before plastering on a big smile.

"Genevieve worked in my office," Brett said, smooth. He was always smooth. God, so fucking smooth. "Well, works. I was let go. She wasn't. One of the few left!" He laughed then, an *aw shucks* attempt that fell like an anvil. No one else laughed.

Genevieve's face had gone deathly white, her lips bloodless. She stood shakily. In shock, with some detachment, Penelope wondered how this would go down. Which one of them would scream and yell? Likely neither one. Brett didn't do screamers and yellers.

Genevieve was tiny, poised, her skin light and smooth. Next to her, Penelope felt giant, coarse, old—and furious.

"I didn't know this was your house. I knew the neighborhood . . ." Genevieve said, her voice trembling, her eyes downcast, her fingertips fumbling with her purse. "I think I should go."

Penelope felt an odd surge of power and, conversely, a heady sense of impatience. Finally, this was how her marriage would end. And before she could control it: *Oh, thank God.* She closed her eyes. When she opened them again, her gaze landed on Willa, who twisted her own wedding ring around her finger nervously, looking confused.

Later, Penelope would analyze the night for hours. Their words, the ugliness of it all, how it came out in a tumble, and wonder if she could have done anything differently, more elegantly, better than her blunt, utilitarian Penelope-ness. She'd close her eyes and remember their faces: Brett's shock and fear, Genevieve's grief, and somehow the most unsettling part of the whole night would be that moment when—before all hell broke loose, before Penelope pulled the plug on their little domestic fantasy—she'd remember Willa. Perched on the edge of the couch, twisting, turning that ring, watching them all, her face blank in horror.

And just once, so quick that Penelope couldn't be sure it happened at all, the gleam of excitement in her eyes and a small self-satisfied smile.

CHAPTER
THIRTY-FOUR

February 25, 2020

"No one is leaving," Penelope said. Inside, she felt a pulse of wild rage, her heart railing against her rib cage, her mind skipping from thought to thought. But this was what she did: at work, at home. She projected calm. Kept her voice even, kept everyone comfortable.

Well, fuck that.

"You." Penelope looked at Brett, really looked at him. The crow's feet around his eyes, the broad planes of his cheek, the bright, sad blue eyes.

"Pen. It's not what you think," he offered lamely, the refrain of cheating husbands everywhere.

"What do I think?" She folded her hands in front of her to keep them still. *You cheating bastard, you cheating bastard, you cheating bastard.* She couldn't stop thinking the words, like a refrain. She was tired of trying to do the right thing while it seemed like everyone around her gave in to their basest impulses. Penelope would hold it all together; Penelope would fix it. Penelope never lost her shit. She'd fought against a full-blown affair because it was *wrong*. For what?

"It just happened." He sounded tired, impatient. Where did he get off being impatient with her? She'd expect contrition. Even begging. But *impatience*? No. Absolutely fucking not.

"Do you have anything but platitudes and lines you've seen on soap operas?" It was a deep cut, and Brett winced. He *had* started watching daytime television. Not soap operas, per se. But reruns of television dramas on Netflix—shows he'd missed while he was working. *Grey's Anatomy, Brothers and Sisters*. Penelope had teased him more than once about it—*What's going on in your stories today, dear?* A subversive reminder that he now had time on his hands, although she hadn't thought of it like that at the time.

Genevieve was trembling, inching across the living room, toward the door.

"I said, no one is leaving," Penelope hissed at her, and Genevieve stood deathly still, her eyes darting between Penelope and Brett.

"Pen." Brett's voice—that placating, soothing tone he'd taken with her lately—was going to be the last proverbial straw. Penelope clenched her teeth together. "You can't keep her here," he said, infuriatingly reasonable.

"When did it start?" Penelope asked them both. She felt a pulsing need to make this whole conversation as unbearable as possible. She wanted them both to feel humiliated, embarrassed, regretful. She would not do her Penelope thing and go along to get along. She would *not*. When no one answered her, she stepped toward her husband. "When!" It was a demand, her voice inching up higher.

"September. Right before Siesta Key."

"After you were laid off."

"Yes."

Genevieve said, "I didn't know—"

"That's ridiculous, of course you knew. You knew he was married." Penelope waved her hand dismissively and for good measure said, "Shut up."

215

"He said you were separating," Genevieve whispered it, and Penelope felt the shock of it right in her breastbone. She took two steps to her left, reached out, plucked the comb from Genevieve's hair. She'd never put her hands on another person in anger in her life. She never even spanked her children.

In that moment, though, she was not careful. When a few strands of glossy hair tangled in her fingers and she yanked, she did not feel anything but rage and triumph when Genevieve cried out in pain.

"For Tara, you told me." Penelope held the comb inches from Brett's nose, and he sighed. Impatient with her! How dare he.

"Penelope, this is unlike you. This is . . . inappropriate," Brett said quietly. "Genevieve can leave, and we can talk about this like adults."

"Are you fucking serious?" Penelope took a step back, looked at all of them. She dropped the comb on the ground and then carefully stepped on it. She felt the satisfying crunch under her shoe, the snap of the cheap silver, the grinding of the turquoise sandstone. Genevieve looked away. Brett looked embarrassed, but not for himself. Penelope studied his face. He was embarrassed for her! First pity, now embarrassment? No.

He gently tugged her elbow, bringing her closer to him. He turned his back to Genevieve, spoke quietly. His blue eyes narrowed, and while his voice was gentle, cajoling, his expression was hard. She was crossing him in a new way. "You haven't been yourself for weeks, Pen. You're paranoid, delusional. You've been blaming poor Willa for everything that's happened around here. If you would just calm down, you would realize this was inevitable." His hands swept the room. What *this* was he referring to? The affair? Willa? The dissolution of their marriage?

That, at least, they could agree upon.

Penelope was so tired of making Brett's life comfortable. Of worrying about his mental health, his state of mind. The whole time he was . . . what? Fucking a coworker. How provincial. And truthfully, she realized, this was where her anger stemmed from. Not the affair.

No, she was furious—at herself. She'd been martyring herself for a *whole year*. Acting like she was being a good, dutiful wife. While lusting around after her daughter's friend's father. The whole time, trying to make accommodations for Brett—he was tired, he was stressed, she would get the kids, cook dinner, take care of the house while he went on a wellness retreat. Licking her own wounds in a dark bedroom while Brett . . . what? Fucked his coworker. God! She was a doormat.

Penelope even felt a slice of jealousy then. Not for Brett, the cheat. But for Jaime. She'd been wrestling with her own attraction for months. Keeping herself in check. For them, for their marriage. It was all a facade.

"How much of the past year was a lie?" Penelope turned her gaze to Genevieve, who had the good grace to look like she wanted the floor to swallow her. "The health retreat he went on? Was that with you?"

Genevieve's gaze bounced back to Brett. "At Pike Springs?" She seemed to be whispering everything. She closed her eyes.

"So, that's a yes, then." Penelope nodded, once. Stepped back. "Just so I know."

"Pip."

Penelope had forgotten Willa was there. She whirled around, stared at her friend. "You sit the fuck down."

Brett and Willa audibly gasped.

"Penelope, this is not you. Honey, please." Willa's eyes shone with tears. Penelope studied her. Big, fake crocodile tears.

"You're a liar too." Penelope was shouting now, her voice pitched up, sounding not like her own. She'd been sitting in the living room at Grey Hudson's house that morning, but it felt like weeks ago. She could barely remember it. Penelope could hear herself, feel herself coming unglued at the seams. Such an odd expression: she imagined her limbs being torn from her body, falling to the floor with a thump, all her stitching, her frantic attempts to keep herself together (keep them *all together?*), exposed and fraying. She was surrounded by people who claimed to love her but did not. By people who had been lying to her. Even Jaime's loyalties were suspect—*her legs wrapped around his waist, his hands on her ass.*

"Pen, I have no idea what you're talking about." Willa's voice took the same cadence as Brett's: soft and slow.

"Oh, you don't? Six months! Do you know where I went today? Your house. I've met your husband—not Trent but Grey. I even met your little girl—her name is Violet." Penelope inhaled a long shuddering breath. "And the knife! Why do you have a bloody knife in your bag? Why have you come back? What do you want with us?"

Willa looked at Brett, her eyes wide, and back to Penelope. "I don't have children, Pip. I have no idea what you're talking about. Who is Grey? Who is Violet?" She covered her mouth with a trembling hand. "What bloody knife? You are scaring the shit out of me."

Genevieve's head bobbed back and forth between them, sincerely afraid now, and she let out a small yelp.

Brett pressed the pads of his thumbs into his eye sockets before reaching out to grip Penelope's shoulders.

"What about the pictures? All those pictures? They were right on top of my bookcase, I found them all! And then they were gone. Photos of me with the kids, as babies! Who took all of them? I can't trust any of you!" Penelope screeched, her hands frantically clawing at Brett's as she tried to wrench away.

"Who were you with today?" Brett asked and turned to Willa. Willa held her hand over her mouth, tears streaming down her cheeks. "Do you know what pictures she's talking about?"

"Penelope, honey," was all Willa said, and the walls felt like they were closing in, the deep-red accent wall she'd chosen years ago because it was a "pop of color!" seemed to be closing in on her, and she wondered if she had realized at the time how close it was to the color of blood.

"Not the blood on the knife," she said and wasn't sure if she said it out loud, but Brett gripped her shoulder and shook it gently, but Penelope felt nothing but absolute blinding, all-consuming rage.

It was all connected; she was sure of it. Willa brought all this to her doorstep, somehow. Why would he try to silence her about Willa unless he knew something? Was Brett in on it too? And if *he* knew, what had he told Genevieve? Did they all have a good laugh at her expense before she got home? *Poor, dumb Penelope. Always so practical. Passionless.*

Brett had called her that once—years ago. In a fight. God, when was that? He said she was cold. Calculated. She couldn't just let herself go wild. Ha. What did he think now?

"Can you hear yourself? Seriously?" Brett shook her a little again, but harder this time, and her head snapped back.

Penelope saw red—like the color of the wall, and she always thought that expression was meaningless until that moment when she couldn't process anything but the swath of blood rage across her field of vision—and her palm connected with Brett's cheek in a shocking slap that reverberated up her arm.

Someone said, "Oh my God."

Her arm swung again. Harder this time.

She never did find out who called 911.

CHAPTER THIRTY-FIVE

Then—Changing Tides

Something had shifted in the house. It was subtle, and nothing could be done about it outright. They all just needed to try harder. But the cold fact was, it had been the five of them from the beginning, and while they welcomed Grace at first, it was a hard act to keep up. She just never got it. And even if they could explain it all to her, she'd have to duck out before the end of the explanation, take a phone call from her sister.

It wasn't just her physical presence; she wasn't as *invested*. How could you be? For the five of them, the only world that existed was within the confines of the house. Grace was a constant reminder that the world outside continued to turn. She went to work, came home with coffee shop stories that none of them cared about, talked about her own friends, a roommate. Sometimes whined that they spent too much time at the Church House.

"Don't you guys ever go out? Go to a bar? A restaurant?" Her voice held an unattractive pout, and she downed her drink.

"Sometimes. Grace, you should be an honorary Spire," Willa said, ice clinking in her glass, and Penelope wanted to throttle her.

"She's the Yoko Ono," Bree said, talking about her as though she wasn't sitting right there on Jack's lap.

"Didn't the Beatles hate Yoko?" Jack's voice was sharp, his hand running up and down Grace's side. "You guys love Grace."

"We do love Grace," Willa agreed, but her smile looked plastic. She rolled her eyes surreptitiously to Penelope, who tried not to laugh.

"See, Bree? You're so ruthless." Jack said it like a joke. "Atropos, for sure."

"What do you call them? The Fates?" Grace asked, wide eyed, a placid look on her face.

Jack grinned. "The Moirai. The three sisters of fate."

"I'm Clotho—the young pretty one. I create life." Willa unfurled her arms, wide into the air, and took a small bow. "Now it gets complicated. Depending on the day, we have Lachesis"—Willa pointed to Penelope—"or Atropos." Willa pointed to Bree.

"Atropos is the ugly one." Bree gave them all a wicked smile. "But she's also the most heartless."

"They're all ugly. He's such a dick." Willa got up to mix them more drinks. "Lachesis measures life; Atropos cuts the thread of life and ends it. I think that's Penelope. *Atropos* also means inevitable, and I've never met anyone who is more fatalistic than Penelope."

"I'm not fatalistic. I'm responsible. And restrained." Penelope snatched her drink away before Willa could pour more booze into it. Bree gave her a sharp look, and Penelope replied with a soft, one-shouldered shrug.

Jack coughed while laughing. "Bree is Atropos. She's got those pruning shears."

"Didn't Lachesis wear white all the time?" Penelope asked. She had looked it up on Jack's laptop.

He gave her a look. "Do you *want* to be Atropos?"

"I don't care. I'm just saying. It's not a perfect metaphor." Penelope pretended to look uninterested, examining her fingernails.

"So then, what am I?" Grace asked guilelessly, her cheeks pinked as she licked her lips.

There was a pause before Flynn said, "There's only three Fates."

"You're Aphrodite. The goddess of beauty and sexual pleasure." Jack leaned forward and kissed Grace, cupping her into him and swooning. Penelope turned her head, pretending to study the calendar that Flynn had hung on the wall behind the sofa. There was nothing written on it.

"The Fates aren't technically goddesses, you imp," Willa corrected, tipping back the last of her drink. She watched Jack kiss Grace again and rolled her eyes, this time more obviously. "They're like incarnations of destiny."

Later, she whispered to Penelope in the kitchen when they were alone, "Do you think she's actually dumb?" and when they turned around, Grace stood in the doorway, blinking like a doe.

—◊◊◊—

It could have been the days that Bree came breezing in with a tray of five coffees, only to look blankly at Grace and say, "Oh my gosh, I didn't know you were here, I'm so sorry!" Or maybe the fact that Willa kept buying vodka, even though Jack had told her, irritated, that Grace didn't drink vodka. She'd make vodka cranberries for everyone, putting a spoonful of pomegranate seeds in everyone's drink—*for fun, and pretty!*—and then Grace would sit on the end of the couch, sipping her rum and coke, which looked significantly less festive. Or maybe it was the weekends she'd missed when she had to drive to Maryland to stay with her sister, who was in college and *having issues*. She'd come back brittle and ill at ease and frustrated with their incessant clowning around.

"You all just don't get what the real world is like," she'd say, and even Jack would sometimes take a deep breath. Either they started excluding her because she'd turned a bit sour, or she turned sour because they excluded her—they could never tell. She wasn't wrong—they were avoiding the real world, on purpose. They'd started to resent her bringing it to them.

"Well, it's never on *purpose*!" insisted Bree when Jack would question them after Grace left. "We're just used to five!"

"Well, get used to six!" Jack said and stomped up the stairs. They dissolved into giggles then, until a pillow was launched over the rail of the loft, landing neatly on the Risk game, the colored pieces flying.

Flynn shrugged. "I was losing anyway."

And they all fell apart again.

Even Penelope had started to feel better. She could see the end coming. Jack was annoyed at them, but he laughed, too, sometimes. They weren't ever *mean* to Grace, but she knew he'd never stay tied to someone who didn't like his friends.

—✷—

Willa came home with a Polaroid camera and a box of costumes. She bought them at the thrift store in town. "Look at this! Groucho Marx, complete with hat!" She passed it to Flynn. Bree took a set of feather boas, a sequined tiara, and a pair of false teeth ("Ewwwwww, wash those first, oh my God!" Willa screeched). Penelope took a flapper costume; she was, after all, the go-go dancer, and in an uncharacteristic move, shimmied out of her jeans and socks and just wore the dress itself to dinner. It was gold and green, sequined, with a deep V-neck, and looked less like a costume than a stunning dress. Her body had changed shape, just a bit. Hardly noticeable to anyone but Penelope, but everything felt a little plumper, riper. Her cleavage deeper, a soft, subtle roundness to her belly. She smoothed the dress down over her new curvy hips, enjoying having an actual figure for the first time in her life.

Willa kept the pièce de résistance for herself: a lounge-singer costume, plunging red neckline, long cigarette holder that she insisted on smoking a real cigarette out of, making them all cough and ask her repeatedly, "Where did you get cigarettes?" She stuck a brown beauty mark on her cheek, lips painted bright red, and slid into a pair of black stilettos. On her head, she wore a black lace fascinator.

In the doorway, she struck a pose, and they all whistled. Flynn found a 1930s jazz CD, and when Jack came home, she tossed him a newsboy hat, a pair of suspenders, and a vest. "Saved the best for you, buddy!" She was at least three drinks in, and dinner hadn't even been served yet. Penelope poured him two fingers of whiskey, neat, and handed him the glass.

Bree was at the stove, giggling as she kept losing her teeth, trying to keep them from falling into the sauce.

Willa sang around the kitchen, "Put 'em in a box, tie 'em with a ribbon," while Jack in his Gatsby get-up twirled her around.

"Hi," said Grace, who had made it all the way into the kitchen without anyone noticing she'd arrived. Jack stopped twirling Willa, pausing for one still second before crossing the room and kissing her thoroughly, his whiskey sloshing in his glass. She pushed at him gently. "Didn't you just get home?" She tilted her head in the direction of his hand and his costume, and he laughed.

"Sure, but Penelope knows what I like," he said, winking at Penelope, and Grace did not reply.

Bree served dinner, by then a sloppy affair as they were all half in the bag. Someone had trailed sauce from the stove to the table, and Willa kept sliding in it in her stilettos. They all ate like wolves, ravenous and ridiculous, laughing at nothing, while Willa continued to sing Doris Day and Flynn tried to only speak in Groucho Marx lines. ("I don't want to be part of any club that would have me for a member!" To which Jack said, "Too late, you're stuck in it now!")

Flynn waggled his eyebrows at Grace, whose mood had turned more dour as the dinner wore on, and said, "Look, I'm not crazy about reality, but it's still the only place to get a decent meal."

"Bree, what is this? It's amazing!" Jack exclaimed.

"It's beef stroganoff!" Bree clapped her hands delightedly. They all stared at her, dumbfounded, and she giggled. "Made with tofu! Gotcha!"

Grace had barely eaten, only pushed her food around her plate, and was looking thoroughly miserable.

"Gracie-poo, what's wrong?" Willa teased her, poking at her shoulder.

"No, really. Something is definitely wrong," Penelope said, suddenly alarmed. Grace's face had expanded, her lips and cheeks were a bright shade of red, almost purple, and three times normal size.

"Were there mushrooms in here?" she asked thickly, through bloated lips.

"Yeah, it's stroganoff," Bree said.

"Grace is allergic to mushrooms," Jack snapped.

"Oh my God!" Penelope cried. "Do we have to go to the hospital?" She wondered immediately who around them was fit to drive. Maybe Flynn, if he stopped twirling his moustache. Only Penelope, who had been nursing the same drink for hours, periodically refreshing the ice to look new. Staying under the radar was becoming more difficult by the day.

"No," Grace said through her teeth. "It's just swelling and redness. It'll go away on its own. I didn't eat much."

"I told you all this!" Jack said, exasperated at them all, but not fully anymore, now that they knew it wouldn't be serious. "I swear, honey, I told them."

Penelope felt a little stab in her heart when he said *honey*.

They all watched her face seem to swell right under their eyes, a reverse metamorphosis from beautiful to hideous. In the background, Ella Fitzgerald crooned about "Taking a Chance on Love," and Willa couldn't help herself—she started singing in the awkward silence. Bree retrieved an ice pack from the freezer and brought it over to Grace, who took it gratefully. Penelope ran to get Benadryl and ibuprofen and presented both to Grace with a glass of water. She took it and drank it down and finally, blessedly, excusing herself, made her way to the stairs and up to Jack's room. Jack followed her.

After a moment, Flynn said, "Look, darling, if you're not having fun, you're doing something wrong."

And they all fell apart.

—⚭—

Later, Jack came back downstairs. Willa was passed out on the couch, her mouth open. Flynn had taken off the nose and moustache but said he rather liked the glasses and was playing a round of backgammon with Bree. Penelope was in the kitchen, cleaning up, barefoot.

"How's Grace?" Penelope asked. She was tired and anxious for her bed.

"She's fine. A bit embarrassed, I think." He shrugged sheepishly. "She's having a hard time. We're a hard club to break into."

Penelope grinned. "We're ridiculous." She was picking up the bits and pieces of costumes and putting them back in the boxes. Polaroids of all of them lay around the table. It looked like a wild party had happened, yet it was only a run-of-the mill Wednesday.

"We are," Jack said softly. He held two glasses of water and paused near the steps to the loft. He turned back to her, gave her a soft smile, almost unreadable, and leaned forward, kissed her cheek. He smelled like pine and citrus, something heady that made her head spin, and she felt herself grow weak kneed.

"You look amazing in that dress, Pip," he whispered.

And then he was gone.

CHAPTER THIRTY-SIX
Willa, present

Pip found the pictures. She met Gen. Things were moving along, although albeit a bit more dramatic than she planned. She didn't expect Pip to fly off the handle like that—she never used to have that kind of fire in her. *Ha! Fire.*

The comb was a stroke of luck. She hadn't planned that. So many things were just falling into place. Almost effortlessly.

She thought maybe it was time to start the final part.

CHAPTER THIRTY-SEVEN

February 26, 2020

Penelope's life had been a straight line for nearly eighteen years. She would not go back to the chaos of her life before. She'd made sure to live in a certain way, within the rigid confines of acceptance, to keep herself from falling back.

She'd met Brett leaving a ShopRite at the lowest point in her life. She'd never been lonelier, more bereft, and lost than she was in the time right before they started dating. She hadn't spoken to any of them from the Church House in months, not after the fire. All of them scattered, wrapped up in their own culpabilities, but none of them knew what she did.

That Penelope was the guiltiest of them all.

Brett didn't save her, exactly, because he never knew she needed saving. She'd kept that part of herself locked up in a box, shoved to a corner of her heart. She'd reinvented herself the only way she knew how: from the ground up. She went back to Penelope instead of Pip. She cut her hair and styled it straight, rather than simply brushed in waves. She began wearing dresses and sweaters—boho chic, instead of khaki pants. If she dressed the part, maybe eventually she'd *feel* the part too. While other couples talked of their lives before they'd met, Penelope spoke vaguely of college and only generally about the year before. She pretended with Brett, more than she'd ever pretended with anyone in her life.

She was funny. She spoke her mind, for the first time in her life. She was still practical, but she took pieces of them: Willa's sarcasm, Jack's charm, Bree's airiness, Flynn's quiet observance. She made them all part of her, used them all to make herself whole again. But it never worked. She'd *never felt* whole. She'd felt empty for a long, long time.

But with Brett, she could pretend. She could love him, just enough, to fill the void. To find purpose. He'd never question if she was whole. That's why he had been so safe. She saw that now. Had she loved him? As much as she was capable, maybe, at the time.

Instead, he pushed her to find a job she loved, take as long as she needed to do it. She took only three short months. It was easy to patch yourself up when you were only pretending. It was easy to pretend to be happy, and after a while, the act looked just like the real thing.

They married a year after that, had Tara a few years after that. Check, check, check. All the boxes ticked, and her life was back on track, like the Church House had never happened. Like the fire had never happened. Like no one had died.

Willa had been right about one thing—the gap year had galvanized them all, one way or the other.

But now, in the gray early morning of her small, surprisingly pleasant room at Wexford Health and Behavioral Science Center, she wondered maybe if it hadn't been a straight line, after all, but a circle.

How did she end up here?

Twenty-four-hour hold.

Just for observation, the nurse had told her. She had been kind, young, and pretty. Penelope's face was puffy; she could feel the plump of

229

her cheeks, her under-eyes fat with fluid and a thudding in her forehead that didn't seem to stop.

The police had given her a choice: twenty-four hours in observation or they'd book her for assault. The EMS driver was dabbing a fingernail gouge on Brett's cheek with peroxide and gauze at the time. She inspected her hands for blood and saw nothing.

"Assault? For a scratch?" Penelope had been furious, still. It seemed never abating, her fury. "I just found out my husband was having an affair with—" She looked around wildly, but Genevieve had slipped out. Penelope pinched the bridge of her nose and said to no one, "I am not actually crazy. She *was* just here."

Willa, hugging herself on the couch, said nothing.

"I understand, ma'am. It would be misdemeanor assault." The officer seemed apologetic, even kind, and the clarification meant nothing to Penelope, for she had no idea what degrees of assault existed, nor did she have prior knowledge of the punishment for them.

Everyone was being so kind. The room was positively heavy with kindness, and the weight of it was exhausting.

When they brought her *here*, in the back of the police car (no lights or sirens, no handcuffs), she'd been walked through the intake room by the same quiet police officer and brought to this little "hold" room, as it was called. The nurse had given her a Xanax and told her to sleep. That she'd be evaluated in a bit, but sometimes people under stress just needed a good night's sleep.

Now, she sat here, in this little room, at six a.m., with a bed and a nightstand and a small wooden desk with rounded edges (all the edges of everything were round, as if she was going to impale herself on a veneer corner) and used a toilet with no seat and felt, for the first time, completely and wildly out of her element. She'd spent her whole life, one foot in front of the other, walking firmly and resolutely away from the night of the fire, never once closely examining the past, just to end up here, twenty years later and nowhere to look *but* back.

Well, for starters, she *did* look back. Every morning, right before she opened her eyes. The name right on her lips, her heart beating in time to another.

At night, waking up sweating, the fire hot on her back. The dream fading away but the feeling of the heat and the sweat and the smell of burning wood and the cracking of the beams and the final click of the door, the one that sealed her fate.

She did look back, in one way or another, almost every single day. But one thing Practical Penelope had gotten very good at was flicking a switch inside herself. It was a talent to be able to turn your feelings off and on. And like she'd always told Tara, *success takes talent and hard work in equal measure.* Maybe she was born with the ability, or maybe she'd honed it during a childhood reared by *The Wonder Years*, and *Night Court*, and *Saturday Night Live*, and *The Price Is Right*.

But, she realized, she worked especially hard every day to keep the skill sharp. Brett, so lost, desperately looking for something to fill his void, and his wife staunchly unwilling to admit she had one.

Tara and Linc. They filled something in her, seemingly without her admission, almost violating in their need. This is what children did, she knew now. They violated any boundary you thought you'd set.

Where were they right now? Did they wonder what happened to their mother? Hopefully Brett had the sense to tell them to stay at their friends' houses. He didn't hate her enough to turn them against her, did he? God, she had really lost the plot there, back at the house. She felt not just a little foolish.

But also. She knew she had been right about a lot of it. The knife, the pictures, Grey, Violet, the burner phone, the necklace—missing, then present, then returned. Like a joke, somehow. Like Willa was *trying* to make her crazy. *Ha,* she thought. Look where she ended up.

Other things tugged at her memory. The wrong song—she sang the wrong song. It wasn't "Both Sides Now"; it was "The River." Always "The River." She tried to catalog all the missteps, all the violations since

Willa had come. Which ones were purposeful, and what was blind bad luck? And if they were purposeful, the bigger question was why. It was a lot of effort to insinuate yourself into someone's life, and to what end? To taunt them or play with them like a cat with a bird?

Upon intake, they had taken Penelope's cell phone and her clothes. She wore scrubs, green to the nurses' blues, and thought to herself, *If I wasn't crazy before, I would be by now.* The boredom was excruciating. She had nothing but her thoughts, pinging around, bouncing off each other, no rhyme or reason for any of it.

If she was being held for observation, she saw exactly zero evidence that she was being observed by anyone. No ceiling camera lens that she could see (and she looked between four and five o'clock, out of sheer boredom).

The far wall was painted with a bright swirling rainbow, the words *Be the sunshine in someone else's cloudy day!* painted in swirling white script underneath it, the whole mural shot through with yellow and orange sunbeams. She crossed the room, a little woozy still from the Xanax, and ran her fingertips along the wall. Her nail dragged on something in the dark-indigo stripe of the rainbow: a hole the size of a pencil eraser.

Ah, camera, there you are, she thought.

Penelope lay back on the bed and willed herself, finally, to sleep. She had no dreams.

—⁓—

"Good morning!"

A new nurse this time—plump and older. Penelope sighed with relief. She didn't trust her mental health to someone who looked like they might still get carded for cigarettes. What did someone that young know about life? Cheating husbands and friend betrayals and raising teenagers? She needed life advice, not a pedicure.

She felt calmer now. This was all a huge mistake—she just had to talk her way out of it. Surely anyone with a medical degree could see that, right?

"I'm Dr. Beck." She opened the blinds in the room and took a seat on the little (rounded) desk chair. Not a nurse, then. "We're going to talk for a bit. Just to get an idea of where you stand, what sort of out-patient help you might need, if any."

"Outpatient? So I get to leave?" Penelope felt both relieved and deflated at the prospect. Relieved because it was validation that she hadn't completely lost her mind. Deflated because where was she going to go? It was Thursday. Linc and Tara would be at school, hopefully. Brett, for all his faults, was generally a levelheaded and responsible father. He would have minimized her absence, certainly not told them she'd been admitted—*admitted, for God's sake*—until they knew what the outcome would be. Brett might be home waiting for her, and she wasn't ready to see him yet. And Willa? God knows.

"Yep. Fortunately, you don't meet the criteria for an involuntary hold. Just had a bit of a stressful night?" Dr. Beck smiled—more kindness. So much kindness. She had a clipboard on her lap and a laptop underneath it but made no move to open either one. She folded her hands and just waited.

Penelope closed her eyes and inhaled, and in a rush, all the events of the past few weeks came spewing out, without conscious thought. Brett's job. Willa. Brett's hospital stay. Willa's "help." The birth control pills and condoms. The affair. The disastrous dinner party. Then she rushed on and told Dr. Beck about the things only she knew to be true: the necklace, the photos that had been in her closet, the knife, Grey, Violet, maybe Brett's illness? It was all under a cloud of suspicion now.

"Well, first of all, we've done some research here. You should know that Grey and Violet Hudson exist—that is easily verifiable informa-tion. You are not having some elaborate delusion," Dr. Beck said sym-pathetically. What did Dr. Beck look up? How much did she believe about everything else? Penelope couldn't tell. "What do you think about Brett and Willa telling you that these things are not true?"

"I think that Willa is lying and Brett believes her. I mean, it's provable now. I could have showed him yesterday. But I didn't. I chose the pictures. I wanted some kind of *impact*. I wanted him to finally see what had been going on in the house. He's always so oblivious. And now he thinks I've genuinely had some kind of psychotic break. Because I was angry about the affair, or because we've been disconnected. Our marriage is complicated right now."

"All marriages are always complicated." Dr. Beck gave her a small smile and then wrote something on her notepad, tore off the top sheet. "I do want you to come back for cognitive therapy—I think that's just plain good for anyone. I see no indication that you're suffering under any delusions or hallucinations. I don't know what the story is with your friend, but it is likely not a result of your mental stability. For the time being, I think a mild antidepressant would aid some of the immediate anxiety." She paused. "I do know they could have booked you for assault, and you were a bit wild last night when they brought you in."

"I was angry. Furious, actually."

"Understandably so. But I'm simply trying to explain why we thought a night of rest would ease some of the emotional turmoil."

"Okay, so I'm just free to go?" Penelope glanced to the door, beyond the metal-mesh glass, and saw the officer who had transported her last night waiting in the hallway, hands resting on his belt. For how long?

"You are free to go."

Penelope's first thought was, *Oh, thank God.* Her second, *Free to go where?*

CHAPTER
THIRTY-EIGHT

February 26, 2020

The police officer dropped her in front of her house. The shades were drawn, and the house looked asleep, despite it being eleven in the morning. Brett, even when laid off, was up at dawn, stretching and meditating and drinking energy shakes, making Penelope nervous with all his jittery energy. He buzzed around the kitchen with his yogurt and his chia seeds, getting underfoot as Penelope marshaled the whole process of *getting the children to school*. Penelope was always proud of her lack of resentment for that—and that she never martyred herself. She didn't want anyone's *poor you*. She actually truly *liked* the mornings.

It was Wednesday. What had Brett told the kids about her? She checked her text messages, and there was nothing. Not even from Brett. At the *mental hospital*—God, that was such a foreign concept and completely disconnected with where she'd been the night before—they had taken everything. Her purse, keys, cell phone, clothes, even her shoes. They had given her hospital-issued socks, complete with rubber nonslip soles. This morning she had gotten it all back in a plastic bag before being discharged.

She wondered if Brett had gotten the kids off to school. Maybe Willa had? She felt a lurch of something sick in her gut. She had visions of them all resuming their morning routine—Tara eating cereal, something sugary and multicolored, while Linc housed down a banana and a hard-boiled egg. Tara with her coffee and Linc throwing back a large glass of milk in one guzzle, Adam's apple bobbing. She imagined Willa, pouring the cereal, washing the milk glass, humming at the sink. She imagined Brett, finding her in the kitchen in her sleep shirt. She imagined his hand sliding across her backside, his voice filled with grief and concern: *Have you heard from Pen?*

No. Just no.

She texted Tara: can you please go to Sasha's after school today?

A reply: Sure. Are you okay? You didn't come home. Where were you? Linc called and said it went to voicemail. Dad tried to downplay everything, but we've been worried! Dad said you guys had a fight.

Putting it mildly. Which was fine—she didn't want her kids to know any details about any of this until she could figure it all out. *Figure what out?*

She shot another text to Linc, asking the same questions, with much the same responses. She asked him to go to Zeke's, and he agreed. He also replied, I love you. Because he was Linc.

She turned and walked away from her house, down the street, made a right onto Middletree Lane to the little yellow bungalow with the brick-red shutters and wide wooden front porch.

He'd been sitting in a rocking chair—just sitting, which never failed to amaze her; Penelope had never, in her mind, sat and done nothing for one moment in her life—and he stood when he saw her, a cup of coffee in one hand.

Penelope closed her eyes. *Please, please, please believe me,* she thought fervently.

She stuck a hand in the air in a wave. Jaime waved back.

—〰—

It took her less time to tell Jaime everything—the affair, Willa's lies, the knife, the photographs, the dinner party, Grey, Violet—than it had Dr. Beck. When she was done spewing what had felt like word vomit, he sat back against the rocking chair and exhaled loudly. A gust of sweet coffee and peppermint.

"Do you believe me?" Penelope asked, her voice smaller than she wanted, her throat bone dry. She wanted self-assurance. *I am telling the truth and therefore must be believed.* Jaime paused for too long.

"Yeah, I do." Jaime said it softly, but resolute. "I knew something about Brett. I didn't know details, but I suspected." He stopped talking for a moment, picked at the paint on the white chair. Penelope had been with Kiera when she'd bought the rockers. An Amish roadside stand in the middle of Pennsylvania that sold nothing but rocking chairs, hand-made on site, a bearded man on a stool with a hand lathe and chisel carving her *real wood, none of that particleboard crap* furniture. Kiera was from California—everything glass and metal, shining in the bright seventy-six-degree sunshine. Pennsylvania had felt like another world, a quaint adventure. They shoved two white rocking chairs in the trunk of her Ford Explorer, ate streusel and *fasnachts*, and laughed all the way home at their sweet little *hallo* and jovial *mach's gut!* as they pulled away. For years later, they'd get together for after-dinner drinks, and when they parted, one or the other would say *mach's gut!*

Penelope had never sat in them before. As far as she could remember, she'd never seen Kiera sit in them either.

"You never said anything." It was a stupid thing to say, and Penelope knew it. If Jaime had said he thought Brett was cheating, Penelope would think it was driven by ulterior motive. She used to feel so confident of Jaime's attraction to her that she'd used it as fuel. Brushing her hair shiny before heading to the Stop N Shop, just in case she ran into him. Wearing the tighter jeans with the rip under the left cheek because he'd commented on it once, his voice a low, tortured rumble in her ear. The flirtation alone had been enough for her.

But not for Brett.

Penelope waited for the anger that never surged. All her rage had ebbed away. When she thought of Brett's affair, she thought *of course.* Like he'd fulfilled a predetermination.

She watched Jaime search for the right words—comfort or opportunism, which way would he go? What did he feel for Willa, especially now that he knew the truth? Penelope saw the broad flex of his shoulders as he rubbed the bristle on the back of his head, something he always did while thinking. She kept her eyes down, stared at his feet, at the soft-gray leather moccasins that Penelope had bought him for Christmas last year. She'd spent more money on Jaime than on Brett, she remembered. She watched the flex of tendon in his ankle travel up his leg, the muscle twitching under the soft, worn denim of her favorite jeans.

She would not touch his thigh, no matter how much she wanted to. Brett's affair was not a free pass.

She broke the silence. "I need your help."

"Anything, always, you know that." The smile he gave her was brief, sideways, a little sad.

"Do you believe me about Willa?" Penelope asked.

"Of course I believe you. You'd have to be crazy to lie about a husband. A child, for God's sake." Jaime caught his words then and, without thinking, reached out and took her hand. His hands were warm despite the cold morning. "You're *not* crazy. I'm sorry. I just meant . . . maybe there's another reasonable explanation."

"Like Willa is crazy?" Penelope challenged him. *Pick me,* she wanted to say. *I am the normal one.* Like sanity was a contest she deserved to win. She studied her hand in his and flashed on that night in the street, his hands across Willa's bottom, pulling her against him. Which one of them was the prize?

"No. Like there's a mistake somewhere. Could there be two Willa Blaines?"

Penelope gave him a hard, disappointed look. Men always looked for excuses.

He squeezed her hand and pulled her to standing. She followed him into the house. She didn't let go of his hand.

CHAPTER
THIRTY-NINE

February 26, 2020

"Willa Blaine, Bree Haren, Flynn Lockhart," Penelope said. Jaime typed them all into a Word document on his computer. "Jack Avila."

"We'll skip Willa—you've already looked into her." Jaime ran a simple Google search on *Bree Haren, Deer Run Pennsylvania*, and *Bree Haren, University of Pennsylvania Wharton*, which turned up a white pages listing. Penelope peered over his shoulder.

"She never married, which isn't surprising." Penelope smiled at first, thinking of the Bree she knew well—airy fairy and floating—and then wondered how much of it had been real. The night of the fire had exposed them all, their ugly interiors, ulterior motives, the darkness they brought out of each other.

Jaime raised his eyebrows in question.

"She had zero interest in men or women, sex, or romantic relationships in general." Penelope gave a one-shouldered shrug. "Marriage would have been a stretch for Bree, I think. I think now she'd be called asexual, maybe aromantic. But it wasn't a widely known thing back then."

"But she had you. The Spires." Jaime's voice hitched over the words.

"Oh, well, friendships are a different matter. But even that . . ." *We did it for the baby.* "And also, look at all of us. We've not fared so great, you know?" Penelope studied the long list of known addresses—all over the country. Utah, Missouri, Maine, Florida, and then inexplicably back in Pennsylvania, in Doylestown, about a half hour from Deer Run. Then, nothing past 2015. She reached over Jaime and clicked back to the search results. She typed in *Bree Haren Doylestown, Pennsylvania,* and her eyes were instantly drawn to the word *obituary.* She gasped out loud.

"Bree's dead." She took the laptop from Jaime and, heart racing, scanned the listing. No cause of death named, just a brief list of relatives—no husband or children—a mother and father living abroad, and a brother that she'd never spoken about. She remembered the eulogy they'd given her. *To her nonexistent tits,* Willa had said. Bree's eulogy had been the most impersonal. Well, of course, none of them truly knew her. Penelope felt a shiver down her spine.

Penelope returned to the search results and did a quick scroll, hitting upon an article in a local Doylestown newspaper. *Bree Haren, 36, was killed in a hit-and-run accident when witnesses say a blue truck slammed into her Toyota Camry on Thursday, August 6, 2015. The truck fled the scene, and authorities are asking anyone with any knowledge of the accident to please come forward.*

There was no follow-up article.

"I can't believe she's dead," Penelope repeated, feeling dazed. On one hand, she hadn't had contact with Bree since the night of the fire. On the other, she was still someone Penelope had cared for deeply during her life. She thought at one point that Bree cared for her.

She toggled over to Jaime's Word document and transcribed the article in broad strokes—*died at 36 in a car accident, hit and run. Not married.*

She repeated the Google search with Flynn Lockhart. Flynn had married and lived in Colorado from 2015 to 2018. In 2018, Flynn was arrested for masterminding a Ponzi scheme and stealing over $1.2 million. The Flynn she knew would *never* have done such a thing. It was unfathomable.

Oh my God. All of them.

Quickly she repeated the search with Jack Avila and felt a sweep of relief to not see yet another obituary or appalling news story. She did find an alumni article from UPenn. *UPenn Alum joins the Peace Corps.* Guyana. Then Botswana. Penelope ran a follow-up search on *Jack Avila, Botswana.* And hit nothing. She did a domestic search, and there was no information on a Jack Avila, roughly forty-two years old. No known US address.

She opened Facebook, Twitter, Instagram, but no Jack Avila in any of them.

"No one can be invisible in the digital age," Jaime observed wryly.

"If they live in Botswana they can. At least I'd guess." Penelope thought for a moment and then pulled up the Wharton Alumni page. She logged into her account and found a lone profile, a grainy image of the Jack she remembered, hair windswept and dark, eyes bright, against a backdrop of green jungle and muddy road, kneeling down to pose with a very large turtle. A big white smile. She could scarcely breathe.

The only thing listed was an email address: *javila@gmail.com.*

Penelope felt a stir in her gut at the memories, the feel of his arm across her shoulders, the pine smell of his shirt. Had she ever loved anyone as much as she loved him? At one point in time, she would have sworn that no one had known her like Jack had. Was that true? Had it just been an infatuation? She thought of their walks home from the bookshop: Jack's childhood, the story of his mother, their night together. Had it all been one sided? She hadn't let herself look back, to examine what she always believed to be the most influential relationship in her life. Now, she found herself wondering if it had been a love based not on rock, but on sand.

After the fire, she purposefully walled up her heart. But before? Maybe what she'd said about Bree applied to herself as well. Maybe none of them had known how to truly love someone. No. Not Flynn. Flynn loved openly, with his whole heart.

She quickly composed an email: Jack, it's Penelope. If you get this please give me a call. Something very strange is going on. I need your help. (973)-442-1876. Hope you're well. And hit send.

Jaime read over her shoulder. "So, Willa is technically missing, Flynn is in prison, Bree was killed in a hit-and-run, Jack is MIA. That's a lot of sudden deaths and tragedy for one group of friends. Almost statistically impossible."

Penelope had been thinking the same thing. "Do you think someone is killing us? Or trying to? If so, who?"

"Damned if I know, Pen."

Penelope chewed on her thumbnail, thinking. What would she do now? Where would she go? Jack might never email her back, or he might take days. "Can I stay here?" She couldn't go home, not yet.

"Of course. Always." He patted the cushion behind her head. "I'll sleep out here; you can have my room." She was grateful that he tackled logistics so smoothly.

What was going on at her house? Had Willa left? Was she there, waiting for them all to come home, to cook dinner again? Was she trying to take her place? She had a home, with a child. What would be the point? What was the connection between Willa and Bree's death and Flynn's bankruptcy? What had happened to Jack?

"Do you care if I bring Tara here after school? I don't know what is going on, but I don't want her in that house. With Willa." *Or Brett*, she thought but did not say. She didn't think Brett posed any kind of danger to her children, other than bad decision-making. If he was having an affair, letting Willa stay after everything they'd discovered, he wasn't making sound choices. "I sent Linc to Zeke's house."

"She's usually here anyway." Jaime smiled, rubbed a warm hand between her shoulder blades.

Penelope unlocked her phone and checked her messages. Nothing. Not from Jack, but not from Tara or Linc either. She didn't expect anything from Brett, although she did wonder what he was doing now. Had he chased after Genevieve last night? Or instead, were he and Willa staging a faux family dinner (her mind conjured up images of an elaborate roast, buttered vegetables, au gratin potatoes, prepared by Willa in a red-checkered apron)? Did they wonder where she was?

Dr. Beck at the behavioral health center assured her that she could not release information to anyone, not even if she was still a patient. In Penelope's mind, this indicated that she had at least a day or two to figure out her next steps.

Tara and Sasha came tumbling in the door after school, windblown and apple cheeked. Penelope hugged Tara fiercely, breathing in her hair, her scent. Trying not to scare her.

"What was your fight about?" she asked, her eyes filled with tears, the worry etched on her face. The kids hadn't been there when the police showed up.

"What did your father tell you?" Penelope asked her, holding her hands, trying to keep her face neutral.

"Just that you and Daddy had a fight and you left for the night to stay with a friend. Not here," she added hastily. "I knew that."

"Was there . . . anyone else at the house when you guys got home?" Penelope asked, swallowing thickly.

"Just Willa. She went to her room for the night. Daddy stayed in the living room watching TV all night."

"Anyone else?"

"Mom, no. Was there someone else there before?" Tara pulled her head back, studied her mother.

Penelope waved her hand around. "Just a friend of Willa's. I didn't know if she left."

Tara eyed her mother skeptically. "It was just Daddy and Willa. And it was weird and quiet and nobody talked and Willa kept crying."

Penelope sighed. "Well, it was weird, that was for sure." She smiled brightly, trying to move on. "Look, none of it concerns you. At all. I would just feel better if you were here. With me tonight."

She hugged Tara, breathed in her vanilla shower spray, her strawberry shampoo, her bubblegum lip gloss. A mishmash of teenager scents. "Everything is fine, okay? Seriously, don't worry," Penelope assured her. Moments later, Tara was bounding upstairs with Sasha, giggling, their fingers flying over their phones, Snapchat, texts, Instagram. Her mother appropriately forgotten. Penelope exhaled slowly. Gratefully.

Brett hadn't contacted her, but then again, she hadn't expected him to. He would text the kids; they'd likely tell him they were staying at Zeke's and Sasha's. Penelope knew Tara might tell him that she was there too. Which was fine with her. Let him wonder. Worry. Maybe Willa would comfort him.

What about at work? Had Elias taken over all her audit responses? She composed a quick email to Nora and dashed it off. Family emergency, I will be out the remainder of the week.

Penelope hadn't taken time off like this in years. She had accrued almost twelve weeks of paid time off.

With a few clicks of her thumb, she'd successfully given herself the gift of time. No work. No family. No Brett. No Willa.

Nothing to do but wait for Jack.

CHAPTER FORTY

February 27, 2020

Penelope had been sleeping lightly when the text came in. With nothing left to do but wait, she felt helpless. What would she do if he didn't write back? She fell asleep contemplating the possibilities.

But in her hand, her phone buzzed at 3:17 a.m.

I'm in Deer Run. Meet me? It's Jack.

The phone number was an 802 area code—she had no idea where that was based. She pressed the call button, and it rang twice and shunted to voice mail. A text came through.

I can't talk—long story. I'll explain when I see you.

She texted back, when and where?

The three dots appeared, then disappeared. The reply came a full ten minutes later.

The house, where else? As soon as you can.

—m—

She left a note for Tara on Jaime's kitchen table: *Had to do something, be back soon. Don't worry! I love you.* Her keys were in her purse, and it was a short walk from Jaime's house to hers. She didn't even go inside. The sky had just begun to lighten by the time she reached her driveway.

Penelope hesitated for a moment, staring up at her house with the large windows, shut like it was sleeping. She could smell the familiar tang of Brett's shower soap, even outside. The light floral of Tara's perfume. A hint of pot roast in the air. It smelled like home.

She almost called it all off. Marched back into her house. She could take back her life, get a divorce—people did it all the time.

Then she remembered the photos, Willa, the knife in the bag, her housemates missing or in jail or dead. She'd been changed in the past few weeks. By Willa's return, Brett's affair, the discovery of all the Spires and where they ended up in life. She couldn't go back to her old life, not as the same person, anyway. There was a reconciliation to be had, and part of it was with Willa, but the other part was with Jack. They were, perhaps, connected.

"Where will you go?" His voice cut through the quiet morning, and Penelope jumped. Brett stepped out of the shadow of the house, into the faint light from the front porch.

"I have to take care of something," Penelope offered vaguely, knowing it wasn't a real answer.

"Penelope, what are you doing?" He didn't mean right now; he meant in general. With her life, with their marriage. She didn't have the time or the inclination for this particular conversation.

"What am *I* doing? Have you forgotten who had an affair?" Her voice was sharper than she'd intended.

"Oh, really? Where'd you sleep last night?"

"You mean after I was released from the hospital, where you had me held for observation?"

She could hardly see him in the dim light of predawn, his outline limned in a gold glow from the front porch. He ran a hand over his hair—she recognized the gesture, as familiar to her as anything. Her eyes adjusted, and she could see him clearly. Brett, in running shorts and a sweatshirt.

"Have you been waiting for me?" He was always up early, running, hitting the gym. He wasn't sitting at the window waiting for her—he was going about his day, and she'd happened to be there. Even for him, four a.m. seemed unusually early.

"I thought if you came back, you might try to sneak in early morning or late at night," Brett said. "I couldn't sleep either way, so I was keeping an eye out."

"You're right that we have to talk, but . . . I can't do it now. I just have to take care of something." Penelope knew she was repeating herself. She knew that Brett, and probably Willa, thought she was having some kind of break with reality. A mental break. A psychotic break. It didn't matter—at least half of what she knew about Willa was provable. She couldn't tell Brett where she was going, could she?

Still, she hesitated. Even when things between them had been less than perfect, she'd relied on Brett as a sounding board. She'd ask him, over wine, *What do you think about painting the hallway green? What if we consolidated our credit cards? I'm thinking maybe Spain this year for vacation. Guess what Elias did today.* Even when their relationship felt fragmented, she'd navigated the pieces and found the place where they joined. She'd been angry, sure. Resentful. But she'd always *trusted* him.

And now, she couldn't. He'd tried to *commit* her, for God's sake.

"I know what you think of me," Penelope said, her voice loud, echoing against the black morning. "And you're wrong. I'll fix this, because I believe that what I've let into our lives is my fault. At least some of it. But I can't see a path forward, for us. Not now, anyway."

"Pen." Brett's voice was halting, disbelieving. She could see it in his posture: he wasn't surprised by her strength or even taken aback by her statement. He was *irritated*.

"I don't know the woman living in our house anymore," Penelope said. "I used to know her, but she's a stranger to me now. I don't know what she wants with us, but I can tell you that it's probably not as innocent as she's pretending it is. Do you know almost all our old roommates are dead or bankrupt or missing? Then she shows up here, I find a weapon, creepy old photos of our entire life together, she's missing from her real family and lying about it, you end up in the hospital, she brings your lover to dinner, she's trying to make me look absolutely crazy, and you commit me to a behavioral health center. If she came here to ruin us, she succeeded. If not . . . then, well, it's been a helluva bad streak of luck. And you know, if you were halfway intelligent, you'd find somewhere else to stay until I figure out what the hell is going on. Call Gen." The last part was probably unnecessary, but Penelope was past caring.

She unlocked her car door and climbed into the driver's seat, then backed out and rolled down the window. With the interior light flicked on, she could see her husband clearly. The deep lines in his cheeks etched seemingly overnight, his pallor almost green after her little speech.

"Oh . . . and, Brett?" Penelope said, and smiled sweetly. "Go fuck yourself."

CHAPTER
FORTY-ONE

February 27, 2020

By the time Penelope reached Deer Run, it was dawn. The narrow main street with the handful of stoplights looked exactly the same as it had twenty years before. Some of the shops had changed—the storefronts were different, more modern and updated—but everything about the town felt frozen in time. The same look—streetlights encircled with potted flowers, cobblestone alleyways strung with lights. Everything a little funky, a little artsy, dripping with old hippies who made new money.

The whole drive, she'd tried to sort through her thoughts, feelings, theories and still kept finding herself in circles. Was the letter she'd received in the summer—from Jack—somehow related to Willa's appearance in her life? When she did the math, she realized the letter would have been mailed around the time Willa disappeared from her old life in Deer Run. What did that mean? Maybe nothing. Still, she was drawn back to Deer Run, drawn back to *Jack* like a homing pigeon, and the possibility that he could give her information somehow. Had he been contacted by Willa in the past six months? Had he kept in touch with the others? Did he know what happened to Bree? Flynn?

Penelope passed the police station and circled the block, considering her options, before finally pulling into a parking spot out front. The parking lot was empty save for two vehicles, one marked, one not. Inside the police station, she told the woman working the window that she wanted to file a police report. She was led to a conference room and joined a few moments later by a large, sleepy-eyed officer carrying a Styrofoam cup of coffee.

"I have a tip on a missing person. I think she's staying at my house. Her name is Willa Blaine Hudson." Penelope felt the anxiety bubble in her chest, a *push* to get out of there as quickly as possible. The officer opened a small laptop and typed with two index fingers. She related the story: Willa came to stay with her two weeks prior, and she discovered in that time that she was officially a missing person.

"Are you holding her hostage?" the officer asked her, blinking seriously.

"Of course not," Penelope said, shaking her head, confused.

"So she's there of her own volition?"

"Yes. As far as I know. She showed up one day and asked to stay, and I said yes."

The officer typed it all out and then sighed, his belly pushing against the edge of the conference table. "There's no crime here."

"I'm sorry?" Penelope asked, not understanding. "I don't think there is a crime, but she's technically a missing person. I thought you might want to know that she's at *my house* in Wexford, New Jersey."

"I'll file your statement, but ma'am, she's staying there on her own. That's perfectly legal. I mean, it's a terrible thing to do to a husband and child but—" He heaved his shoulders up and released them, his rumbled voice paternal, but condescending. "People do terrible, but legal, things all the time."

"Okay, well, can you just go make sure she's still there? And at least tell her to go home to her husband?" Penelope was starting to feel ridiculous. And impatient.

The officer promised to relay the report to the detective in charge of Willa Blaine Hudson's case. Penelope paused. "She's not well, I don't think. She's stolen jewelry from me in the past two weeks, as well as turned my life upside down."

"Ma'am, stealing jewelry is illegal. I can include that in the report, and we can bring her in for questioning."

"Well, she returned it all," Penelope said haltingly. Nothing Willa had done had been strictly illegal. "Look, I don't think she's broken any laws, but she's a missing person and I don't think she's mentally well. Now, I have to go." She stood, and the officer nodded. He printed the report from his laptop and pushed it across the table with one finger for her to sign.

Moments later, Penelope was back in her car, heading back down Main Street toward the center of Deer Run. The whole detour had taken a mere twenty minutes. With any luck, the police would show up and question Willa this morning.

The used bookstore no longer existed, and in its place was a fitness center. Across the street, the café where Jack used to write had been replaced by a smoothie bar. As Penelope stared at it, trying to make sense of all the changes, the **OPEN** sign flickered on.

Her phone vibrated with an incoming text. Are you in town? Come to the house. I'm here now.

Now? She didn't feel prepared. The house? Oh, God no. The last place she ever wanted to go.

Can't you just come to the smoothie bar? It's the old café. I'll buy you a drink, for old time's sake.

The answer was swift and sure. The house, Pip. It's the only way.

The only way what?

Penelope sat in her car gulping down large breaths, her mind racing. She was going to see Jack—*her Jack*—after twenty years. She looked like utter hell, but it couldn't be helped. She did have the wherewithal to dig through her purse for some ChapStick and apply it with a quick glance in the rearview mirror.

And yet, still, in the back of her mind always was Grace. What they did to her. What she did to them. The tragedy that followed in their wake—and the very secret that Penelope had spent her whole life keeping locked away. What would become of it all now? She didn't know. With her marriage in shambles, her job probably in jeopardy, she didn't have anything left to lose.

Except for the one person she'd never had to begin with.

No, Jack was right. To go forward, she had to go back. All the way to the Church House.

She turned around and headed back down Main Street the way she'd come in, before taking the second right. At the end of the gravel road, she could see the burnt remains of the church. It had never been repaired. She slammed her foot on the brake, her hands trembling on the steering wheel. Her heart skittered to a halt, then started again, and she felt her breath come in a short burst, the air in the car suddenly too thick to breathe.

She pressed on the gas, easing into the driveway, and forced herself to breathe slowly, her heart to stop hammering.

The right side of the church looked collapsed—the area where the fire had started, from the fireplace in the great room. And in the back, behind all the char and the fallen stones, the piles of detritus, loomed a yellow bulldozer. Jack's letter wasn't lying. Someone was going to tear this place down. And soon. She bit back the taste of bile.

Above the whole wreckage the spire remained—whole and intact. A looming reminder of how far they'd all tried to come—only to come back to the beginning.

CHAPTER FORTY-TWO

Then: A Birthday Party

"It's Grace's birthday!" Willa announced, clapping her hands and going up on her tiptoes like a cheerleader about to toe-touch.

"How old are you?" Bree asked her, and she laughed.

"I'm twenty-five. An old lady! Call me a cougar."

They were sitting around the island eating breakfast. Penelope sipped her tea and listened to them all chatter around her.

"We should have a birthday party," Flynn said. He'd been loosening up, drinking more, wearing fewer button-down shirts. Maybe Flynn saw the writing on the wall when it came to Jack and decided not to brood over it anymore.

Penelope should have followed in his footsteps, she knew. She felt so tied up and sick with heartbreak and couldn't seem to shake any of it. She knew she walked around half-dazed, looking pale and furious. It wasn't healthy.

"Oooooh, a party!" Willa's eyes went bright, like a party would be any different than what they did every night. Pre-Grace, it was always drinks and games, Jack and Flynn would sometimes smoke weed, Bree and Flynn would have some dense philosophical discussion, Jack would strum his guitar, sometimes Willa would sing and eventually pass out on the sofa. Penelope was often a spectator in the whole affair—drinking just enough to loosen her joints, before going downstairs to bed, happy and sleepy and full.

Post-Grace, it seemed to be following a similar pattern, except as the evening wound down, Jack and Grace inched closer until she was sitting on his lap, softly kissing his neck, his hands running up and down her back like there was no one else in the room. Willa still sang softly, Bree and Flynn would debate politics *(God, would they ever stop talking about the election)*, and Penelope would go to bed as soon as they gave up on the board game.

She was embarrassed to admit how frequently she lay in bed, staring at the ceiling, hands low on her belly, trying not to seethe. This was *her* family. *Their* little cocoon away from the world. *Their* place to belong. And now, the anger raced around her veins; she could feel it pulsing under her skin. She'd been so close—what happened?

Her fantasy of staying in the Church House forever with Jack had been trampled. It was also humiliating how much time she'd spent imagining it—their quiet life. Jack would sell his book and use the proceeds to purchase the church from Parker. Make an office out of Bree's bedroom. A nursery out of Penelope's. She could work at the bookstore; Jack could write every day. He would be the stay-at-home dad when Pip (he'd still call her that, even when they were old and gray) had to walk in to work. Maybe—just maybe—if he sold enough books, they could buy the bookstore.

Deer Run would be their home.

Except Grace had ruined everything.

He *loved* her. Penelope could see it in his eyes, the way his face brightened when Grace walked into the room, casually unaware of her effect on him. But because Penelope had a *gift for seeing people*, as Flynn had told her, she saw it as clearly as if it was written in her own hand.

Bree saw it too. "Will you keep it?" She'd asked one day, her voice low in the kitchen when they were alone, and Penelope realized for the first time that she had a choice. She could just end everything. All the turmoil, the heartache, the vomiting. It would be so easy to just pretend it all never happened. She hadn't decided yet, but when she thought of severing that last tangible link to Jack, she felt a bit sick and not just a little relieved. "I'd go with you," Bree said, her voice a little whisper; then she was gone.

"Pip? Wanna have a party?" Now, Jack was standing behind Grace, his hand rubbing her neck, always, always touching her, kissing, whispering. His voice was jovial, oblivious.

"Sure! A birthday party! Fun!" Penelope got up, put her mug in the dishwasher, rinsed and dried her hands at the sink. She kept babbling, "I have to run out, I can grab anything from the store, just let me know!"

She was full of exclamation points. The rest of them looked at her strangely, which she ignored and headed down to her bedroom, where she leaned against the door, gulping big breaths.

She'd never been the kind of person to come unglued, but somehow since Grace had come—less than two months ago!—she was this awful, needy, clingy barnacle of a person.

No. She could be the kind of person who could throw a birthday party. Balloons, streamers, cake. She used to be. She remembered that day at the park, where Jack proposed the church house, Deer Run, his hand clasped around her forearm, thumb softly rubbing the inside of her wrist. *You're just saying that because I won't sleep with you.* And then, *Won't you, now?*

She remembered the lighthearted swoon at him, the way everything he said and did seemed charming and sweet, the future ripe as a summer peach.

Penelope left the house through the back door, the cross talk and laughter practically following her outside, then crossed the patio and over Bree's garden to the driveway. Her little beat-up Datsun. She puttered into town, collected all the party necessities.

She could be a different Penelope. She could be Pip, their quiet, introspective, but not uptight housemate. The one who thoughtfully threw parties for their loved ones. Who radiated love and acceptance and never petty jealousy or irrational, childish anger. She could be a completely different person.

She stepped out of the grocery store, into the midday sun, her hands filled with plastic shopping bags containing balloons, streamers, cake, matching paper plates, napkins, a fruit bowl, seltzer for mixers, of course. She stood still, swaying a little on her feet, before leaning over behind a line of planted arborvitaes and neatly vomiting up her breakfast.

CHAPTER
FORTY-THREE

February 27, 2020

With a shaking hand, she pushed through the front door. The first thing she smelled was the fire. Still. Twenty years later, and the wood still smelled like char. The second was the house—that combination of dust and linseed oil, wood and Willa's perfume, elaborate dinners and marijuana. Somewhere underneath all the rubble, pieces of them remained. All their blackened belongings—abandoned. They'd left town so quickly, scattered like ashes in the wind.

The smell alone brought the sick to the back of her throat, her stomach turning with such ferocity she thought she might vomit.

Penelope picked through the rubble to the back of the house, the place where the kitchen used to be. All that remained was the stainless steel stove, discolored. The refrigerator had been removed some time ago, judging by the ferns growing through the cracked floorboards.

Small saplings jutted up from the burned-out floor, ivy climbed the remaining walls. The loft upstairs looked unsteady at best, and the staircase to the bell tower appeared ready to collapse in on itself.

The roof remained largely intact, a hole open to the brisk morning air in the front of the house, above the fireplace where the fire had started.

She didn't think the fire had affected the basement much, but at the time Penelope hadn't cared. She drove home that night, blinded by guilt and grief and half in shock. She drove to her aunt's old house—a year after her aunt passed away—and slept in her childhood bed alone. She waited for the fire investigator, the police, and when they came, she told the truth. Or maybe what could have been the truth. When they closed the file—accidental fire, accidental death—she left that house, too, sold to the first bidder.

She moved to New Jersey, right outside the city. Got a job. Paid rent. Met a man. Married. Had a child. Climbed the corporate ladder. Had another child. Checked off some mental to-do list and called it a life. The whole time going through the motions, only to end up back here.

What did Jack know about the night of the fire? Sometimes she wondered if they'd all kept in touch, talked about her. Did they say it out loud? *Do you know what Penelope did?* Who knew what she had done? What *they* had done? Maybe they had all been blinded by their own culpabilities.

"Penelope," he said. He stood in the basement doorway—he must have been downstairs in their old rooms.

Jack looked the same. His voice, light and sweet. His beard, now gray. His eyes, still shockingly blue. His hair jet black and combed back away from his face in the way he'd worn it back then.

"I honestly didn't think you'd come," he said when she said nothing.

"Why are you here?" Her voice was low, sounding nothing like her own. She wanted to throw herself into his arms and sob, *I'm sorry.* She wanted to run out of the house and never come back. She wanted to slap him, rake her fingernails across his cheek for never coming back for her.

"Because you asked to meet," he said.

"No, why are you in Deer Run? I thought you were in the Peace Corps. I looked you up, tried to find you. It wasn't that easy." Penelope took a deep lungful of air, trying to control her emotions. She was getting ahead of herself. "Listen, have you talked to Willa? Has she been in touch with you?"

"No," Jack said slowly, stepping around a pile of timber. Stepping closer to her. "Have you?"

Penelope nodded. "She showed up at my doorstep one day. Said she needed help. Asked if she could stay with me. She's completely taken over my life. And do you know Bree is dead?"

"I know about Bree," Jack said. "I kept track of all of you. I don't know why. I lived all over the world—for the past three years in Botswana—but I still looked all of you up. Not all the time, but when I had reliable internet, I would google you."

"How did you end up back in Deer Run?" Penelope asked, confused.

"I came home about a year ago. I got an apartment in the city—just a one bedroom. My brother is married, with two kids I barely know. It was time to come home, grow up. Like Peter Pan, remember?"

She did remember. She didn't want to, but she remembered everything. All of it.

"But why are you in Deer Run?" Penelope asked again, her mind whirling.

"What do you mean? You sent me a letter." He reached into his back pocket and retrieved a handwritten letter on lined loose-leaf paper. Penelope felt her insides knot, recognizing the paper immediately. She saw the straight cursive, a swooping *s* and loopy *l*, all hallmarks of her penmanship.

"I never wrote this letter."

"Of course you did. It's your handwriting, I'd know it anywhere. You always wrote the grocery lists. B-a-n-a-n-a all one height—it would make me crazy sometimes, just looked like a bunch of circles." He smiled then and stepped toward her, tenderly, his hand out.

Penelope stepped back. "I did not write this letter. I wrote an email. Asked if we could meet." She turned the letter over and read the contents. It was short. And familiar in its cadence.

> *Dear Jack, It's been twenty years, this year. A kind of macabre anniversary. I would love it if we could all get together—a reunion of sorts. I feel as though the time has come for us to talk. There are truths to reveal and bygones to bygone. It will be healthy for all of us. I'll be in touch soon. Love you and miss you, Pip.*

"I would not have called myself Pip. I never have."

"That letter is one hundred percent you. I knew it was you. Bygones to bygone? That's how you talk—academic, dry. You love to be clever." Jack eyed her skeptically. "Healthy for all of us? You said that. That was your thing—always talking about healthy friendships, like a budding therapist. Then I got your email and text about meeting here."

Penelope reached into her back pocket and pulled out her own letter: white loose-leaf paper, black ballpoint pen. Written in Jack's maniacal scrawl.

> *Darling Pip, Coming up on twenty years, dear girl. I miss you like crazy. I miss all of you. I hear they're finally tearing the old place down. What would you say to a Spires reunion? Get the band back together? Clear the air, bury all the hatchets. Could give us all some closure (you were always big on that). I'll be in touch soon, think about it. Think about me. Ha, I knew you'd like that. Love you madly, Jack.*

Jack took the sheet of paper from her. "It does look a lot like my handwriting." He studied it, his brow furrowed. "God, did I really talk like this? What a pretentious asshole."

"This isn't from you?" Penelope felt her head spin, her vision blur. "Of course it is. *Darling, dear girl, love you madly, think about me?* This is all you. Plus, your handwriting was atrocious."

"Pip. Penelope." Jack corrected himself and took another step toward her. "I did not write this." He shook the paper in front of her, his voice reedy and a little shaky.

"Well, if I didn't write yours, and you didn't write mine, then who did?" Penelope asked, slowly. Her legs felt like water, and she was starting to feel faint. The sun had risen, and the heat of it beating on her head was making her sweat. She could feel the rivulets traveling down her rib cage under her downy winter coat. She knew—of course she knew who. She didn't entirely understand *why*.

"Hello, old friends. Welcome to the reunion."

Penelope recognized the voice at once and turned toward the loft. Willa was descending the spiral staircase, giving them both a white gleaming smile. Her lips red, a white angora sweater hugged her frame, her hair done in billowing curls around her face. The first thing Penelope noticed was that she looked beautiful.

The second thing she saw was the gun, in Willa's outstretched hands, aimed right at the two of them.

CHAPTER FORTY-FOUR

February 27, 2020

"Willa," Jack said, and then a wordless sound as he saw the gun.

"What are you doing?" Penelope asked, felt the sweat pop on her upper lip, her limbs go cold with shock. *Can your body be shocked while your mind is unsurprised?* Willa holding them at gunpoint did not feel wildly out of place. *Why?* Her mind raced, trying to put all the pieces together, missing something.

"I'm on what you'd call a fact-finding mission." Willa smiled, and her face seemed to light up from the inside. She looked luminous. "See. Twenty years ago, a tragedy occurred in this house, right here. And no one has ever been told the truth about that night. I want the truth. That's all I want."

Penelope closed her eyes, shook her head, dizzy with fear. "You've been told the truth, Willa. You were *there*. There was a fire. Grace died." That was the truth as she'd told it. *If you say something enough times, does that make it true?*

"We'll get to that. In the meantime, here's how this works. If one of you tries to get the gun, run away, fight back, I shoot the other one. How much do you trust each other?"

Penelope stole a glance at Jack, whose face beneath his gray beard had gone pale. Did Penelope trust Jack? After twenty years? She didn't know. She saw his eyes flick to her. Saw him wonder the same thing.

"Willa, this is out of control. Look, there was a fire. Grace got caught in it, and she died. We all felt responsible and heartsick over it. We all left town, went our separate ways. Including you." Jack kept his voice low, calm. The way Willa and Brett had talked to Penelope the night of the dinner party with Genevieve.

Willa closed her eyes, briefly, and shook her head, like clearing her mind. "I'm not included in any of this. We'll get to that. Who locked Grace in the stairwell?"

Penelope froze; her face felt numb with shock. Everything she hadn't thought about—deliberately avoided thinking about—for the last twenty years. Here it was being thrown out, spoken out loud. Just so *casual*. She felt sick with panic. What would happen to her if everyone knew the truth? What would happen to Tara and Linc? No. NO.

"It just *happened*. Maybe the door stuck. Maybe Grace got confused. It happens," Jack said. "I loved her. I would have saved her if . . . I'd known."

"Why didn't you know?" Willa asked, eyes down to slits.

"It was chaotic. It was an *accident*. It was no one's fault." Jack's voice took on a monotonous tone, repeating it all like a mantra. Was he going into shock?

"Unless it was yours," Penelope said softly, to Willa. They both swiveled to stare at Penelope. "You were high that night. You were drunk every night. I know you did some drugs too. What did you do, Willa? Percs? Oxy? We all know what you were doing. You spiked our drinks with Molly, for fuck's sake. It could have been you."

"I would never kill Grace!" Willa's voice was shrill, her head flicked to the side, like a nervous tic. Was she high now?

Penelope felt the panic rise, the frantic grasp at control. "We all had our roles in that night—just like our roles in the house.

Distinct. Maybe not equally responsible but at least partially culpable. All of us."

"Okay, look, if we confess that we did something here, what do you want with us? Do we just walk out of here and go on our merry way?" Jack held his hands up in a plea, his voice slow and measured. He was trying to charm her, talk her down, Penelope thought.

Willa laughed. "I mean, sure. Let's go with that."

"Okay. Flynn did it."

"See, that is a LIE." Willa stomped her foot. "I talked to Flynn. I know exactly what he did that night, and I know why. Do you know how much he loved you?" She stepped forward, her face a mask of fury, the gun pointed at Jack's chest only a few feet away.

Jack physically recoiled. Swallowed thickly before saying, "Yeah, I do. I loved him too. I was confused for a long time. I . . . didn't handle anything right. I hurt a lot of people. Probably all of you."

"Willa, when did you talk to Flynn?" Penelope asked quietly.

"You shut up. You don't ask questions, I do." The gun swung to Penelope and away from Jack. He shot her a glance.

Penelope couldn't slot it all together. They all told their versions of the truth that night, it was true. But why did Willa care? And why now, after twenty years? Willa never even liked Grace.

"Bree did it," Penelope said, finally, her voice a croak, her lips like chalk. She licked them, tried to clear her throat. It was a version of the truth. Her version. Isn't that all anyone has? Their own version of the truth? Isn't the truth more elastic than everyone would like to believe anyway? Twenty years ago, in a small dank hallway, filled with smoke and ash, the feel of Bree's breath hot in her ear. "Bree locked Grace in the secret hallway. Grace and I fought upstairs, she tried to . . . push me over the railing. Bree locked her in, to save me."

Jack closed his eyes. His face blank, his hand cupped around the back of his neck. A pose he'd had even twenty years prior, when he was thinking.

"See? This isn't so hard, is it? Now we're getting somewhere." Willa settled back into her stance, the gun still trained on Jack. "Except it's not the whole truth. Because Bree didn't actually lock her in, did she?"

Penelope pulled her coat around her shoulders. The February air was cold, whipping through the cracks and gaps in the church. She was shivering, violently, and trying to organize her thoughts. What did Willa want from them? "Bree is dead too."

"Yes, well, that one was no loss to the world. She existed in a solitary hell of her own making. Do you know what it must be like to go through life and never feel anything?" Willa laughed. "Because you know what? I do."

"You killed Bree. And ruined Flynn?" Penelope asked thickly. Willa meant to kill her and Jack, regardless of what they told her. She felt her hands go numb, the fear skittering up her spine and short-circuiting down her arms. Nothing about it made sense. Why would Willa kill Bree? Ruin Flynn? For revenge? For what? She'd had her own role in the night of the fire—she was far from innocent.

"What happened to Flynn?" Jack asked quietly.

"He's in prison," Penelope said, watching Willa, whose head swung wildly from Jack to Penelope and back again.

"Willa, why? Nothing about any of this makes sense!" Jack shouted, finally angry, his face growing red. "We were brother and sister, you and I. Yeah, it was crazy times, we were dumb and immature and tragedy struck and everything was awful for a long time and we were all fucked up from it, some of us for life. But I don't understand any of this. Why!"

The silver-pink scar down the side of her cheek. The forgotten Fourth of July party. Her singing voice, shot. The story about Trent. Grey, and Violet. Joni Mitchell, Willa singing *I've looked at love this way* in her kitchen in Wexford. It was the wrong song, always the wrong fucking song.

"Unless," Penelope said, breaking the thick silence, her heart a steady cadence in her ears, even her fingertips pulsing. "You're not actually Willa. Are you?"

CHAPTER
FORTY-FIVE

February 27, 2020

"See, you were always the smartest one." Willa smiled then. "At least that's what I heard."

Penelope saw it at once, the way her face was thinner. The athletic build of her body, so different from Willa's soft puff. Her hair, flaxen gold, when Willa's had been brassier, a hint of orange that she never bothered to get toned out. These were things that Penelope had automatically dismissed, things that came with age, money, or both.

Then, other things. The shape of her nose was narrower than Penelope remembered. The swell of her bottom lip fuller. Things that Penelope fitted to the Willa in her mind, a face she hadn't seen in twenty years, that she once knew as well as her own but knew how much a face could change in their forties. She dismissed the pull of skin tight at the bridge of her nose, the pinch around her eyes. *Botox,* she'd thought, with a private smugness that had felt uncharitable at the time.

She stared at Willa's face, the set of her shoulders, the curve of her backside, with her new thinness, and she gasped.

"You can't be Grace," Penelope stammered. Her heart caught and skipped on the word, and she felt like she might faint.

"Grace is dead," Jack said, flatly and quietly. He seemed to be in shock. Penelope held Willa's gaze until all that seemed to exist was the two of them, locked together.

"You're finally right about something. I'm not Grace." Willa laughed. "Do you remember me? Because I remember you."

Penelope gasped and reached out, clutched Jack's arm. He stared at Penelope, uncomprehending still.

All her features rearranged almost immediately, and Penelope could see it. Willa, who looked like Grace's doppelgänger, and Talia, Grace's younger, ugly duckling sister. Dark haired, mousy, quiet. The one quick visit to the house and no one thought a thing about her. Grace's comments, taking phone calls quietly in Jack's room. The needy cling of her troubled sister.

"Talia," Penelope whispered.

"See? The smartest one." Talia smiled. "If I had to bet, you'll also be the last one."

"Talia?" Jack said incredulously. "That's impossible."

"Family genetics are a miraculous thing. Underneath the hair and glasses, turns out Grace and I bore a strong resemblance. Plus a little plastic surgery, a fun afternoon with a straight-bladed hunting knife." She shrugged, turned her head to the side so the scar shimmered, then the other way. "You were all so easily fooled. Dumb little rich kids with ridiculous educations, and you can't spot a counterfeit *person*."

"Oh, God." Penelope felt her stomach lurch, the bile in her mouth. "What did you do with the real Willa?" She thought of Grey. The little Violet, her braids glossy and bouncing.

Talia waved the gun in a circle before training it back on Penelope. "Would you just shut the fuck up? Willa was a bored little housewife who got sick of her life and took off to have some fun."

Penelope shook her head, willing herself not to vomit. *She did not do that. She did not.* "You had to make her disappear if you wanted to become her. To lure us here. Why?"

"Having you both here was just a bonus. I only planned on one at a time. But then you went and emailed Jack, and you know, it wasn't too hard to make it work."

"How do you know that?" Penelope asked, buying time, her mind racing.

"Haven't you figured it out yet? I know everything. Everything there is to know about all of you. I know what you love, what you hate. I've read your diaries, your secret internet blogs, your emails, even some of your texts—you should really put a pass code on your phone," she admonished Penelope. To Jack, she said, "And you. Remember Ioana? Oh, my height but maybe twenty pounds heavier? Curvy, some would say. Dark-black hair. Romanian accent?"

Jack paled. "The night in Gaborone."

"I thought for sure the way to your secrets was through your dick, but as it turns out, you keep your closest secrets guarded *very* tightly. Either that or you have a lot of regrets."

"Jack, what is she talking about?" Penelope felt her whole body grow cold. She could barely think about it. She could hardly catch her breath. "Jack!" She felt the panic growing, a clawing thing.

"After all, the two of you have a few bombshell secrets, don't you?"

Penelope inhaled, too fast, the rush of February air paralyzing her lungs. *It couldn't be. NO.*

"Even if you are Talia, what do you want?" Jack asked, covering his fear. "You have what you know about me from the night in Gaborone. You know my sin the night of the fire." He turned to Penelope. "Right before the fire started, I was with Flynn. I left you upstairs and went to Flynn's bed. We're *all* a little guilty. Of something, okay?"

Penelope swallowed, her mind a fog. Jack and . . . Flynn? She recalled that night then, in fractured images: Jack and Flynn both appearing from nowhere in the great room, shirtless. She'd hardly given it a thought at the time.

"That's a lovely story, Jack, but that's not what I was talking about," Talia said, waving the gun impatiently back and forth between them.

Jack said loudly, "You have the truth. Bree locked Grace in the stairwell. But she's dead. You killed her after she told you her side of the story—which may or may not be true. What does it matter? We're all a little guilty of something. We were a toxic, fucked-up family in this house. I know that now. What do you want from us now, twenty years later?"

"Oh, so you think you just get to walk away? Start over? Grace was all I had in the whole world. I didn't have parents. We didn't have aunts or uncles or cousins or any other siblings. It was just us." Talia's mouth set in a firm line. "Do you know how that feels? To be utterly alone in the world?"

The truth was, they all did. Who among them had been the loneliest?

Somehow Jack had found Grace—a perfect sixth. So desperate to forge their own family, the six of them had fit their sharp edges together like a puzzle made of razors.

"Even if you didn't then, you will now," Talia said softly, a grim little smile on her lips. "But first, you will know what it feels like when there's no one left to care if you die."

Oh God. Tara. Linc. Brett.

She turned to Jack, whose face had grown pale. His fingertips found Penelope's in the dark, and he squeezed. He licked his lips before he croaked out, "What have you done to our son?"

CHAPTER FORTY-SIX

Then: The Fire

By the time Penelope returned home, dinner was sizzling on the grill, and Willa and Flynn were clamoring for party decor.

"What, no party favors?" Bree pouted from her perch on the island. Jack swatted at her to get off the counter and muttered something that sounded like *kids these days*, and Bree shot a raspberry in his direction.

"You're on your own." Penelope laughed gaily, trying out her new persona. The laugh came out loud and false, and internally she cringed. No one seemed to notice.

"It's fine! I have something for all of us!" Willa said, a sly twist to her lips, and Jack laughed.

Penelope began decorating the great room with the streamers and tossed the balloons in Jack's direction. "Here, you're full of hot air." And behind her Flynn hooted. In the corner Willa poured drinks for everyone—old-fashioneds, orange slice and all. She saw Penelope watching and grinned. "Grace said they're her favorite!" and Penelope shrugged, smiling. *I wasn't judging!* Willa delivered them on a tray, wearing a little red A-line, Betty Boop–style.

The final great room looked festive—red and blue and yellow and green everywhere, like a clown had spontaneously combusted. Penelope hadn't known Grace's favorite color, so she'd gotten the multipack of everything, and later Flynn grabbed her elbow, laughing. *Jesus Christ, Pip, it's a fucking Pride parade in here.*

Penelope sipped her drink very slowly, just to keep up appearances; her one to the others' three, then four; then, because they all got lazy, they switched to vodka tonics, and within a few hours, they were cranking up the music and dancing. Even Pip got into the act, arms swaying above her head, blissfully aware of the grace of the arc, and she felt flooded with happiness. God, she loved these people. Maybe she could get over Jack. Do the right thing, find a boyfriend. They could all stay friends. In ten years, she imagined barbecues together with their families, children running around.

The room had grown soft and blurred around the edges, and everyone looked so sparkly, their eyes and their teeth glowing white and happy. Willa came up and flung her arms around Pip and hugged her tight, and she smelled like gardenias—something fruity that had a memory attached to it for Pip; maybe her mother had worn it. She only had a handful of memories of her mother. She pulled Willa into her and smelled her neck, her hair, and Willa laughed and swatted at her hands—"What are you doing?"—and Pip said, "You smell like I remember my mother smelling! What is that perfume? It's beautiful!"

She'd only had one drink, though. Why did she feel like this—free floating and happy and dizzy and laughing? She couldn't stop laughing, laughing, laughing; across the room she saw Flynn and Bree slow dancing, and then kissing, Bree's leg hooking around Flynn's thigh, and she shook the confusion out of her head because . . . that wasn't possible, was it? Bree didn't kiss anyone, and Flynn, well . . . Penelope knew Flynn had slept with women before, so that one didn't seem so odd, but God, Jack had been right. Together they were extraordinarily beautiful, Bree's hair curled around Flynn's dark skin—it was like a painting or something from a museum. It seemed like a waste for the world that they couldn't be a couple; they could display their coupledom in public parks, and people could pay money to just come observe their perfection and donate the money to less-beautiful people . . . well, that didn't seem right. Maybe a charity—the one about fixing kids' smiles in underdeveloped countries, maybe? Penelope pushed her palm into her forehead and giggled.

"Party favorsssssssss," Willa hissed in her ear, and Penelope turned, feeling like her face would crack from smiling, eyes wide without under-standing, and she felt like she weighed ten pounds. Before Willa could explain, Jack grabbed her hands and twirled her around, and the air whipped past her face and her legs, bare and cold in her short dress, and she could hear the swish swish of the fabric—so soft against her legs, and between her legs with a gentle then insistent pulsing, and then Jack was kissing her, his tongue grazing her lips, hands moving up her waist, and nothing had ever felt more warm, and God, he smelled like cookies, and musk, and man, and vanilla, and pumpkin pie, and fresh laundry. *Jesus Christ, Jack, where's Grace?* The alarms sounded in her brain, but she couldn't make sense of anything, his palms hot on her skin, her nipples through thin silk, and her whole body felt taut with pleasure, every sensation on fire, like a full-body orgasm—was that even possible? Could she have an orgasm in her arm? Her pinkie finger? And then suddenly, somehow, she was in Jack's bed, hips rising and falling as she rode him, pounding and skin slapping and screaming words she didn't know existed, and he told her he loved her over and over, and somehow it didn't feel like a dream, but it had to be a dream, right?

Right?

—⚏—

When she woke, the house was silent, the bed cold and clammy, and she realized that she felt the breeze from an open window, but how?

There was no window in the basement. She felt along the bed and opened one eye and saw Jack's room. She pulled the sheets around her body and realized she was naked. It was still dark out, but she had no sense of time.

Oh God. Grace. What happened?

She must have said it out loud, because a voice from the corner said, "Willa gave everyone Molly."

Penelope felt the room tilt, but also couldn't place the voice—it didn't sound like Bree's—and she squinted into the darkness.

Grace sat on the chair in the corner, her hands folded in her lap, fully dressed. Penelope looked around, but Grace laughed, and it came out like a hoarse bark. "He's downstairs. You fell asleep; he didn't. I don't know whose bedroom he ended up in."

A pulsing headache behind Penelope's eyes made her groan. "Molly?"

"E, X, Ecstasy, MDMA . . . it has a lot of names."

Penelope doubled over, clutching at her stomach. Oh, no. No, no, no.

Grace moved across the room and sat down on the bed next to her, uncomfortably close. "I know you love him. But this night will fade away. He's not yours. He doesn't love you."

"Grace, I honestly thought I was in a dream. I don't know if it was the combination of alcohol or what, but I would never willingly do anything—"

"Oh, you would." She smiled then. "You all would. Wouldn't you?"

Penelope scrabbled to standing, and finding her dress with one swipe of her hand across the bed, she slipped it over her head.

Grace continued, stepping toward Penelope. "I'm not one of you. I'm not a *Spire* or whatever the fuck you call yourself, like you're the goddamn height of human existence—it's the most ridiculous bunch of drivel I've ever heard." With every step Penelope backed up, Grace came forward, closing in, her breath sour and hot on Penelope's face, her hair a tangled mess, until the loft railing was at Penelope's back, and without warning, Grace's hands were at Penelope's neck, choking, and she could only eke out the slightest breath. She wrenched herself away, flailing, and connected with the hard roundness of Grace's skull. Grace advanced again, and Penelope felt the fury surge inside her—she was being attacked! For a mistake. She reached her hand out; her fingers curved and carved four neat slices down Grace's cheek. She wailed, retreated for a moment, holding her face. Then screamed, "I hate all of you—your stupid games and jokes and the silent way you communicate and how Jack never, *ever* wants to hear a thing about any of you. Bree can cook me pasta with mushrooms in it—even though she knows I'm allergic—because none of you give a shit. And you're the worst one. He never has and never will *love you*. You sit around with your silent judgment and watch me, and you know what? I know your little secret now. I do. And no, none of it is going to happen, do you understand me?" Grace lunged at Penelope, her hands once again on Penelope's neck, whose back jammed against the railing of the loft, the cavernous dark below her. She writhed, tried to flip Grace around, without luck. Grace was taller, stronger. Penelope had always been a little mouse. Penelope was beginning to see little blinding pricks of light, unable to take a breath in or out. She kicked her legs out, connecting with Grace's stomach, and Grace doubled over, finally letting go of Penelope's windpipe, and she gulped air, desperate for it.

"Pip!" a voice from below shouted, and Flynn ran into the great room from the basement doorway, with Jack following close behind him, both bare chested. Flynn had a blanket wrapped around him like a cape, the air in the great room whooshing and cold. The fire had died down to cinders, but the blanket brushed along the hearth and dislodged a hot ember that skidded out along the wood floor. From the kitchen, Bree screamed.

Penelope didn't see it happen, but she heard, in the distance, Jack's voice. "Fucking hell." And later, when the police came, Flynn described it as an inferno. The ember skidded along the shining plank floors, thickly layered with years of linseed oil polish, and within seconds the fire had chased into a single straight line. It hit the pile of games with the loose and flowing cardboard, papers, and balsam boards and *whooshed* into a full-blown bonfire. The room was soon ablaze, and they watched, for what felt like minutes but couldn't have been more than seconds, as the line of fire chased across the room, sparking small spreading fires in its wake, hitting the wooden staircase, oiled and shining, exploding the pine like a bomb, splinters flying. The fire sped down the railing, Penelope and Grace crawled backward toward the bed as the inferno spread to the bedroom.

The house had filled with smoke, and Penelope felt her throat, sore from Grace's assault, close up. She coughed into her arm and pressed herself as low as possible to the ground. In front of her, the trapdoor opened a few inches, and Bree's white face appeared. She motioned *come on* to Penelope—who had forgotten entirely about the trapdoor!—and Penelope followed Bree down into the small enclosure.

They shimmied down the ladder onto the landing and came to the steps, when Penelope turned to Bree and said, "Do we just leave her up there? Grace?"

"She tried to fucking kill you. Yes, we leave her up there." Bree gripped Penelope's arm and pulled her around. They heard the creak of the trapdoor reopen above them and the soft thump of Grace hitting the landing.

"Go!" Bree hissed, and Penelope took off, her feet skidding down the steps and through the small crawl space. The smoke was starting to fill the tunnel; the room upstairs was likely consumed. Gone. The door loomed in front of them, and Penelope crashed into it, into the cool cement wall of the storage closet. The basement had not yet filled with smoke, and her lungs ached with every breath.

Bree fell against her, the door falling shut behind them as they both gasped for cleaner air.

Bree stood up and looked wild eyed at Penelope, who followed her. They stared at the door. Grace would come crashing through any second. Penelope lifted her hand and rested her fingertips on the dead bolt, the instinct to get away from her so deeply ingrained in such a short period of time, and then recoiled in horror.

"She won't do anything to me now. I can't do this," she whispered to Bree, who gently covered Penelope's hand with her own and, with no time to spare, gently clicked the dead bolt into place.

No. No! everything inside Penelope screamed.

Grace beat the door with a heavy fist. "Help!" she screamed.

"Bree. Please. This is awful—I can't do this." Penelope's voice was a rasp, a whimper, and Bree pulled her by the hand gently away from the door, from Grace, down the hallway, and up the stairs. Out the back door, and into the cool mist of early morning, the sky dark gray and beginning to lighten. Willa and Flynn huddled in the corner of the garden, and Penelope glanced back at the house for the first time: a complete and utter fireball. A crash as a window exploded out.

Oh God. They'd killed her. Penelope sank to her knees on the pavement. She was *killing* someone. *Someone who tried to kill me?* a small voice inside said.

Jack stood in the alley, between the garden and the street, and called to Bree and Penelope. "Where's Grace?"

Penelope felt dazed, unable to answer, her throat closed, her mouth filled with cotton, and she squawked out, "In the—" before Bree cut her off with, "I saw her run downstairs before the steps exploded! She has to be out here somewhere!" The lie came out so quick, so smooth. Penelope put her head in her hands and sobbed.

Bree ran her hands down Penelope's hair, *shushing* her. Lovely Bree. Always there. Always watching.

"I never had a father," she whispered. "We did it for the baby."

CHAPTER
FORTY-SEVEN

Penelope turned to Jack in astonishment.

Cole.

She thought about him every day—that tiny space between asleep and awake. He came to her, fully, at five, then ten, then fifteen, and now, almost nineteen.

By the time her feet touched the cool hardwood floors in her bedroom, her mind racing with the thoughts of the day, her boy would slip from her consciousness, only to return the next morning.

Her boy. Their boy.

She had no idea what he actually looked like. She imagined some cross between her and Jack—the black hair, the bright-blue eyes, with her quick wit and affinity for debate. Jack's easy charm. Her empathy.

After the fire, the short six months at her aunt's little blue saltbox. The looks exchanged between the nurses when she showed up at labor and delivery, alone. They'd asked her, over and over, who could they call? *I'm fine. There's no one to call. No, thank you, really, I'm fine.*

The private adoption, semiopen. She could find him; he could not find her. She could send him letters. And she did—every five years or so. She received two back, from his adoptive parents, sent through the agency, names redacted. He was healthy, happy, well adjusted. He knew he was adopted. Then, later, he played lacrosse (both her boys had picked the sport without any influence from her—genetics being a fickle, funny thing). He was accepted to Cornell. Wanted to be an engineer.

Why hadn't she terminated the pregnancy? That had been her quasi plan before the fire. Maybe because the month immediately after the fire passed in a fever dream, like moving underwater, and by then it was too late. Maybe it was that final severing—what had once felt like a relief started to feel unbearable. Maybe, just maybe, she'd hoped he'd come back to her. *We did it for the baby*, Bree had said. Had she intuited somehow that Penelope would never go through with it?

The letter she sent Jack, right before her wedding to Brett. Not knowing where he'd ended up, she sent it to the Church House, hoping at least his cousin—the homeowner—might intercept it and pass it along. Telling him about Cole, the adoption, the agency. All the information she knew. He could make his own choices.

It may or may not have been the best way to handle it. She'd only been twenty-two—no excuse, she knew. She tried to do right by Cole, by Jack. She truly did.

Jack turned to her then, and said quietly, his voice hoarse with regret and fear, "I've met him, Pip. About five years ago. I . . . I didn't know what to do, if I should tell you?"

In that moment, Penelope's world collapsed.

Talia said, "This is all very nice, but please shut the fuck up."

"Did you do something to him?" Penelope asked, her blood rushing, her throat closed.

Then she remembered: Tara. Linc. Brett. And now Cole.

"Did you do something to any of them?" Penelope asked again.

"I just told you. You'll know what it's like to not have anyone care if you live or die. Jack, you were a bit harder. You must have worked pretty hard to be that isolated in the world. No wife. No other kids. Not even a girlfriend. A one-night stand in Gaborone, where you confess all your life regrets. That's actually pathetic." Talia moved the gun between them as she talked. She looked at Penelope. "You know, new construction doesn't burn the way an old oiled church does, but it was easy enough to take a page out of the same book. It's taken a bit of time, but you have to admit the floors in your house have never looked more beautiful. I mean, everyone says so. Easy enough to leave a pile of rags, even give it a middle-of-the-night spark just to keep it all going according to plan." She gave Penelope a helpless smile. "You've been gone for a few days, you know? Do you even know what's happened to your family? I mean, do you even care? Everyone thinks you've checked out as a mother—the kids have practically been on their own. Except when your old friend Willa has been able to pick up the pieces."

Penelope felt sick, the room spinning a nauseous vertigo. Tara was probably okay, since she'd spent the night with Sasha, but what if Linc hadn't stayed at Zeke's like she'd asked?

From somewhere underneath them, deep in the belly of the church, they heard a thump. The floor seemed to vibrate just for a second, and Penelope had the sudden realization that they were not alone in the house.

"Who else is here, Talia?" Jack asked suddenly.

Talia swung the gun between them, a wild look sparking in her eyes that hadn't been there before, and Penelope looked from Jack to Talia and back to Jack, inclining her head, widening her eyes.

"Penelope." Jack's voice was low, almost slow motion. He did not look at her when he spoke and instead kept his gaze trained on Talia. "Listen to me. Remember the Moirai?" She did, faintly, something insistent, pushing in the back of her mind. The three sisters of fate. He looked at her then, a split second that felt interminable, and his mouth quirked up. An ironic half smile that seemed trademarked to Jack alone, his blue eyes wide and searching hers. The creases around them new and different, but she was suddenly thrust back in time, to their own private world, a language no one else knew.

Penelope closed her eyes, feeling the inevitability of what he was going to do. Knowing what would happen in the next few seconds.

He lunged at Talia, the gun's going off making Penelope's ears ring, her body going numb, her hands fumbling behind her and landing on the iron poker resting against the still-standing remnants of the stone fireplace, and she swung without thought or reason.

The iron rod connected with Talia's head, and she lost her grip, the gun skittering across the floor and stopping neatly next to Jack's prostrate form.

It was then that she noticed the bloom on his shirt, the crumpled way he'd fallen. Penelope lunged for the gun, dropped the iron rod. She could see the shallow rise and fall of his chest, the gurgled breathing.

She turned just in time to see Talia, the iron rod held in her fist like a scepter, swinging at Penelope's face. Talia's face, bright in the morning sunlight, merged back once again with the Willa that Penelope remembered, until she had the surreal sensation that she was pulling the trigger on her old friend, and she hesitated, almost couldn't do it.

And then she could. She felt the give of metal underneath her index finger, and a second shot rang out, echoing in the open air of the burned-out church.

With the recoil she stumbled back, tumbling against the wide stone mantel of the fireplace in stunned silence. Talia had fallen backward, a deep red pool forming beneath her, her eyes frozen wide. Penelope gulped lungsful of cold February air, her hands shaking, her fingers stiff.

She crawled to Jack, whimpering, her fingertips thrusting into his neck and finding no pulse. No gurgle of breath. Just a complete and utter stillness. *Oh God. God no.*

She heard the scream then. The far-off muffled keening that in her state of shock she thought might have been her own.

Who else is here, Talia? Jack had asked. He'd put the pieces together before Penelope did.

Penelope stood, with the gun held down by her side, and picked her way through the gutted great room and into the kitchen, toward the back of the house. A faint thumping on the wall grew louder. Woodenly, Penelope found the basement door and fumbled her way down to the stairs. Underground, the hallway was barely lit—only the dimness from two small ground-level windows to see with. She could hear it now, the screaming, a steady thump at the end of the hallway.

The secret staircase.

Penelope felt along the wall, letting the cool concrete of the basement walls hold her up. Their rooms had remained untouched, and in the faint light of morning she could see the outlines of dressers and beds, a wayward shoe.

Penelope held one hand over her mouth, fingers shaking, and paused at the storeroom door at the end of the hall.

Bree's hand over hers. The feeling of the dead bolt clicking into place. The cool touch of Bree's skin, always so chilled, even in the blazing heat of fire. "We did it for the baby."

The dead bolt in her hand, turning the other way. The door swinging open, not closed. A face, pale and streaked with dirt.

"Pip." A single word.

Talia. Still alive.

No, that wasn't right.

Willa.

CHAPTER FORTY-EIGHT

February 27, 2020

Penelope had fainted. When she came to, she fumbled in her pocket for a cell phone. She called 911, relayed her location and nature of the emergency, then leaned her head against the wall. She pressed the speed dial for Tara, and when she answered, felt herself immediately start to cry.

"I'm fine, Tara. But find Daddy and tell him to bring you and Linc to Deer Run, Pennsylvania. I'll tell him where to go. Probably the hospital, okay? Don't panic. I'm fine."

Tara was stoic, as Penelope had known she would be. If it had been Linc, he would have fallen to pieces.

"Mom," Tara said with just one quick sob. "The house burned down."

She'd known, of course. Talia had told her. *Your floors have never looked more beautiful.* Still, it felt like a blow. She was so tired. She rested her head back against the stone wall, reached out for Willa's hand.

Willa, next to her, rasped, "How did you know I was here?" Her voice was reedy and thin.

"I didn't." Penelope still felt the thick fog of shock. They held tightly to each other. As briefly as she could, Penelope told her the story of Talia. There would be time for talking later.

In the distance, she heard the sirens.

—␣—

Willa was taken to Deer Run Hospital and admitted for observation. She was dehydrated and hungry, but otherwise unharmed. Penelope was physically fine, but she felt brittle and disconnected, like she was floating above everyone. She was taken to the Deer Run police station to complete her statement. Answered the officers' questions, but on autopilot, rote and mechanical. They offered her coffee, and when they brought it to her, she gagged, vomited into the trash can. They brought her water instead.

Jack was dead. Penelope had known it the instant she saw the bright-red bloom on his chest. In the subsequent turmoil, Penelope hadn't heard him cry out or take his last breath. He was standing next to Penelope one minute, and the next, he was simply gone. She couldn't grieve for the man he was—she no longer knew him. She could grieve for the man she'd known twenty years before. She could grieve for the father of her firstborn son. She could grieve for her role in his death, which of course came back to Grace.

Talia was dead. When the officer told her that, Penelope tried to feel something but couldn't. The officers were kind and understanding, and they took her statement, asking many, many questions, and after three and a half hours, they let her go.

For the second time in as many days, she wondered where she'd go.

Brett showed up at the police station with the kids, and they hugged her and held her, and Linc and Tara cried, and Brett looked sufficiently stricken. He apologized softly into her hair, and she smelled his after-shave and felt his warm back, strong beneath her palms, and kissed his cheek, but still felt nothing.

"Where do you want to go?" he asked her, gentle, like she was made of glass and would shatter if he spoke too loudly.

"The hospital," Penelope said and ignored their glances at each other. "I want to talk to Willa."

Tara said, "Mom!"

"The *real* Willa," Penelope said.

—∞—

In the quiet of the hospital room, Penelope studied Willa's face. The pinked, zagging scar up and down her cheek. The soft pad of cheek under each eye. The youthful smile, now less bright than she remembered in her trauma, but still hers. The distinct sparkle in her eye. Her hair, thick and blonde with natural wave.

How could she have been so fooled?

"You hadn't seen me in twenty years," Willa said, reading her thoughts.

Penelope, unable to figure out where to start, simply asked, "How?"

Willa told her.

Willa had gone to the post office that day. Talia, in a baseball hat and glasses, had asked for help—a flat tire, just down the street, she pointed. Willa being Willa had followed the woman, chatting and bubbling; she didn't even realize she'd left her keys in her own car, her purse, her cell phone. *The spare tire was stuck in the trunk well, wedged all the way back— maybe the two of them together could get it out? She didn't want to approach a man alone* . . . The next thing she knew, she awoke in the trunk of a moving car. An hour later, the car parked, the engine running. She kicked at the trunk with bound feet, her hands tied with plastic handcuffs.

When the trunk opened, she saw her own face, or a close approximation of it, staring back at her. She tried to scream and realized she'd been gagged. The woman smiled, and that was the last thing Willa remembered.

When she woke up again, she was in the stairwell. Her bindings had been cut loose, but roughly, her wrists and ankles marred with shallow cuts.

"Jack showed me the secret stairwell," Willa said.

Penelope felt light headed. "I didn't know he knew about it. I thought only Bree and I knew."

Willa laughed, her voice hollow. "Oh, I think we all knew. Didn't you? That's how Flynn would get to Jack's room sometimes. At night?" Willa raised her eyebrows, waved her hand in a circle.

Light-headedness overcame Penelope, and she had to lean forward, waiting for the stars to clear. "I had no idea," she finally said.

"How long were you in the stairwell?" Penelope asked, her voice a whisper, already knowing the answer.

"Since August. She used to bring me food, sit outside the door, and talk to me. Tell me why. She had all these notions: We killed her sister. It was planned. We hated her." Willa took a deep, shuddering breath. Penelope could see the captivity on her: the deep sleepless bruising around her eyes, a missing canine tooth, the loose skinniness of malnutrition. "Some of it made sense. Remember when Bree made stroganoff and her face blew up and she almost had to go to the hospital? It was an accident. She spent a lot of time on that. She had this idea that she could bring us all back here. She started with Bree, but I guess Bree wouldn't cooperate. She tried to do the trunk-of-the-car thing to her, but she fought back. Kicked Talia in the face and escaped. It was reported as a random mugging, and when the police showed up, Talia was gone. A week later, Bree was hit by a car and killed. Flynn lived too far away to lure back here. I guess she tried? She was less angry at him. It was really more about the four of us."

"I let Bree turn the dead bolt that night. I didn't stop her. I was in shock, I was terrified. Grace and I had just gotten into a horrific fight." Penelope felt the tears sliding down her cheeks, the only time she'd ever said those words out loud. Until that moment she could have barely admitted it, even to herself. She'd felt removed, as though floating above them, watching the scene play out. She tried to feel *something*—fear, panic. Everything she'd worked so hard to keep secret. It was all coming out. All she felt was relief, a numbness through her body, into her extremities. Quietly, "I killed Grace. So why do this to you?"

Willa was crying, too, silently but steadily. "I gave everyone Molly. I drugged you all. I thought . . . I thought it was going to be fun." She covered her face with her hands, half sobbing.

"I'm so sorry," Penelope said. She'd never said it to anyone about that night. "Because of me, Jack is dead. Grace is dead. Bree is dead. Flynn is in financial ruin."

"But because of you, I'm alive." Willa touched Penelope's hand again. This time she did not let go. "My baby still has a mama. That must mean something."

Later, in the hallway, Grey found Penelope and hugged her close, little ponytailed Violet by his side. Penelope held him as his shoulders shook, a sob against her shoulder. She didn't know she was crying until she felt the cold wet spot on his shirtfront. She tried to apologize, but he waved her away.

"You saved her life," he said hoarsely. "You're a hero to us."

Penelope's stomach gave a slippery little flip at that. She shook her head no, and knew that he took it for modesty. When she finally extricated herself, she ran for the nearest restroom and vomited. Tara found her on the floor, crying.

—⁂—

Talia had kept Willa in the stairwell for five months and twenty-two days. She left her often with a loaf of bread and a jar of peanut butter that had traces of Restoril in it. For five months and twenty-two days, Willa was kept in a state of half consciousness. She was given gallons of water to drink and buckets to urinate in. The three weeks Talia lived with Penelope, she did not come back. Her intention, the police believed, was to simply let Willa die of dehydration.

When they raided Talia's apartment, and her computer, they discovered extensive tracking on all of them. Paid private investigators had followed them all for nearly a decade. An elaborate Ponzi scheme had taken Flynn's money and sent him to prison for five years. On Talia's computer, they found the details. The mastermind behind the scheme: Talia, operating as a venture capitalist, a man named Garrett Brooks—a beneficiary who worked on Flynn for years before Flynn trusted "him." Talia made Garrett Brooks disappear as easily as he appeared, and Flynn's defense merely looked like a pathetic attempt to cast blame. Had Flynn swindled innocent people out of their life savings? Or had he simply fallen for a line fed by Garrett Brooks? Penelope couldn't be sure, but she'd bet the latter. The Flynn she knew would *never* have done anything so immoral. Garrett Brooks was a mirage, and in the end all the accounting had Flynn's name on it.

You can do anything when you have money. You can kill people, you can invent people, you can appear and disappear with the snap of your fingers.

When Grace died, Talia spent five years stumbling around, looking for purpose. Taking a variety of lovers—some married, some not. Using plastic surgery to climb the social rungs of society until somehow landing, and marrying, a sixty-year-old communications company founder and CEO, Walton Jones. When Walton had a heart attack in his sleep at sixty-four, Talia inherited all $6.1 billion of his fortune.

With an endless bank account and nothing but free time, Talia disentangled herself from her late husband's life, sold and liquidated everything, and moved back to Pennsylvania.

Back to the one place she'd ever felt truly loved. And safe. With her sister, Grace. Ten years of study and eleven plastic surgery operations later, Talia looked like a passing doppelgänger to Willa Blaine Hudson.

The plan had been, quite simply, to lure them back to the Church House and kill them.

They found files on her computer titled *After*, filled with real estate listings on isolated South Pacific islands.

"It wasn't complicated," the officer told her on the phone a few months later, his voice oddly jovial. "It was all about revenge."

—⁓—

Penelope rented a townhouse for herself and the kids. She asked Brett, quietly and without fanfare, to get his own apartment. He didn't even protest, just nodded like she had said, *Can you please take out the trash?* She wished he would have objected, at least a little. Their life felt reduced to transactions, emotionless and rote. Whatever she asked for in the divorce, he'd give her.

She found him a condo on the other side of town where he could be close to his new office, a new job doing much the same thing as his old job, for slightly less pay.

A few months later, Willa called her. "Pen, the officer from Talia's case stopped by." Her voice shook a little at the end, and Penelope felt the gravity of it through the line. They hadn't spoken much—Penelope wanted to let Willa drive the friendship. Even though she thirsted for it. She'd had a taste of female friendship with Talia—those nights on the patio that had been all a ruse for Talia but had felt so rejuvenating for Penelope. She hungered for the real thing again, but would not push her. "He asked about the fire. 'Dotting the *t*'s,' he called it. I guess that's a joke?"

Penelope felt the air leave her lungs. She closed her eyes, leaned against the counter. "Whatever you said is fine," Penelope said but did not feel. She instead felt panic, a gripping vise on her throat. *Tara. Linc.*

"I said it was Bree." Willa's voice was a whisper. "I just thought you'd want to know."

There again, the crux of all the things she did not deserve and would not ask for.

CHAPTER FORTY-NINE

Then: After

She spent the next six months at her aunt's house. Alone. She spent two weeks in the house waiting for her imminent arrest, which never came.

The police showed up—twice, actually. Once within a day of the fire. The second time a week later. Both unannounced. She walked them through the night of the fire. She told them about the Ecstasy, the baby, everything. She did not tell them about the fight with Grace. Her throat had grown yellow with bruising, the weather still chilly enough for a turtleneck. If they wondered why she wore a turtleneck—the same black mock-neck—both times they came, they didn't let on. When the emergency room doctor had asked about the bruises, she'd simply said she didn't know. She wondered if that kindly doctor would relay the bruising to the police. She waited for it. But they never asked.

"How did you get out of the house?" The officer who asked was gray, older, and kind.

"We just ran outside. We were in the living room half-asleep when Flynn came in with a blanket, dragging it in the fireplace by accident. By the time I realized what was going on, the whole downstairs had gone up. I don't know why it just exploded like that."

"About a few decades of linseed oil," the officer said. "Used as floor polish but highly flammable. Usually not the first time it's spread, but with so many layers . . ." He opened his palms in a *know what I mean* gesture. "I want to let you know. A young woman passed away in the fire."

Penelope tried to arrange her features into something that would pass for surprise. Her heartbeat echoed in her ears, and she clasped her hands together to keep from shaking. "Who?" she whispered.

"A Grace Wilbur?" The officer referred to his notebook. "How did you know her?"

"She was my roommate's girlfriend." Penelope, no longer faking it, felt the tears flood her eyes. Could she cry for Grace? Maybe. Grace had been someone's daughter, sister, cousin. And she could cry for all of them. She could feel Bree's hand on hers. *We did it for the baby.* How were any of them supposed to be okay again?

"Do you know how she came to be stuck in the basement closet?" the officer asked her, tapping his pen on the table.

Penelope swallowed and shook her head. "The whole night was a mess. I was in the living room, and then the fire seemed to explode, then we were outside. I saw Jack and Flynn talking to firefighters. Bree, I heard, was taken by ambulance. I spent a night in the hospital but was discharged yesterday morning. I came straight here. I don't even have a cell phone." She gulped back a genuine sob. "I haven't even tried to call anyone. I don't have their numbers memorized anyway. Is everyone else okay?"

"Everyone else is recovering in stable condition," the quieter officer said and patted her shoulder before they left. When they came back a week later, they only asked her to recount how she escaped. Not how the fire started, what happened earlier that night, nothing. Just how she got out. She stuttered over her words, but she repeated the story she'd told the first time: she was in the living room, and they just ran out the back door. She and Bree.

If Bree hadn't told the same story, it would be their undoing.

The officers smiled and thanked her and left again. They never came back.

Weeks turned to months. She started getting out of bed, opening the curtains. She went to the doctor. Her belly swelled to twice, then three times its normal size. She made all the arrangements through an agency called Heart of Adoption, and her caseworker's name was Jeannette. She went for miles-long walks in the evening, alone, her mind a blank.

"We can't put a child up for adoption without the father's consent," she explained kindly. They agreed to mediation: they'd find Jack and be present when Penelope told him.

When Jeannette called her almost a full month later—Penelope's belly the size of a watermelon—and asked her to come in to the office, she sounded perplexed.

"It seems as though Jack Avila has left the country," she explained, and Penelope sat heavily against the chair back, the baby heaving inside her. "Apparently he joined the Peace Corps—an elite subgroup listed as *can leave immediately*. Often sent into more dangerous territory. I can't say I've ever had this happen. We can't even contact him."

"So what happens?" Penelope felt an emptiness, a yawning canyon, open up inside of her. Emptiness felt only mildly different from numbness, and Penelope prodded this as Jeanette talked, the way you'd poke at a missing tooth.

"Let's make sure you want to go down this path. Pennsylvania adoption laws are some of the least restrictive laws in the country, so we have some time yet."

Lying in bed that night, Penelope felt the tumble and turn of the baby inside her. Could she care for him? Love him?

She imagined raising Jack's child. Being a mother, tainted with the knowledge that she had killed someone. Not just anyone, but someone their father had deeply loved. She imagined him with dark hair and blue eyes, and every time she looked at him, she'd see Jack. What she did to

Grace. What she did to Jack. She'd see the inferno of that house; the only thing visible above the licking orange flames had been the spire.

She imagined that keeping the baby would ease the aching loneliness inside of her, but then what kind of burden was that to place on a child? She couldn't see a way out. She wouldn't ask her own child to save her. How could you love a child when you couldn't *feel*?

Penelope had no job, no prospects. Just a little house that smelled of mold and mildew and was filled with cat knickknacks and knitted blankets. She didn't even have health insurance until she applied for state insurance—which she was only eligible for because she was pregnant. So what happened when she wasn't pregnant?

Impossible to believe that mere months ago she'd been shopping for a birthday party. Her biggest problem had been an unplanned pregnancy.

She pursued the adoption. They followed the required number of contact attempts and filed "uncontested" in family court. Penelope sat down with a DVD and watched interviews with families. They all seemed fine. Good people from good families.

When she came across the Spencers, she sighed with relief. Alice and Jim. Jim had dark hair and blue eyes and a handsome, jovial smile. Alice taught kindergarten and spoke with a clear, firm voice. There was no giggling nervousness, just a calm sense of peace between them. They held hands. They finished each other's sentences and laughed together at jokes that only made sense to them. They talked about aunts and uncles and cousins. Joked that they had to rent a fire hall on Thanksgiving.

She signed the contract that day.

When Cole was born, she watched the pulse of his little soft head. She stripped him down to nothing and touched his little feet and his thin little legs. His long hands and his distended belly. She kissed him gently on each temple. Ran a finger up the delicate, impossibly small vertebrae in his tiny back, and he squawked a protest. She sobbed in her hospital bed, not knowing if she was making a mistake.

She wrapped him back up and gave him to the nurse. She went home, alone, her belly empty and aching.

Ten days later, she was leaving ShopRite, her arms laden with groceries bagged by an inexperienced clerk, and two of her bags containing glass jars broke, hitting the pavement with a dramatic crash. She began to cry, her belly still sore from a birth no one knew about.

A man rushed over to help her. He wore a suit and tie and had disarmingly kind brown eyes. He helped her load up her car and asked if he could maybe text her.

His name was Brett Cox.

She'd run from the night of the fire her whole life. She'd built up walls around it, told herself convenient excuses, even justifications. She'd avoided thinking about it entirely and instead let it eat her from the inside out. *Sometimes a piece of your soul can rot,* she thought. *If you can't get it out, it festers like an infection.*

That's what the fire had been: an infection of the soul. Everything that happened afterward—Cole, Willa, Talia, Brett, Penelope's new house, also burned—was all touched with poison from that first fire. Penelope owned her culpability in that; she thought about it every night before falling asleep and every morning upon waking and thought maybe she'd continue that pattern until the day she died.

There were many different kinds of prisons, she knew. And sometimes the ones you made yourself could be the most brutal of all.

CHAPTER FIFTY

March 7, 2020

Sometimes she still thought about Jack. She remembered the way she'd once loved him—in her memory they'd been wildly romantic, sepia toned, set to grand music climbing to a crescendo. If Penelope's defenses had been built of stone, Jack's were made of feathers. When life got too tough, Jack took flight.

I met him, Pip. The words he'd said at the Church House while Talia had held them at gunpoint.

She was not surprised, then, when a letter came in the mail.

To: Penelope Ritter Cox

From: Parker Avila, cousin to Jack Avila, executor of his will and estate
Penelope, Jack would have wanted you to have this.
Regards, Parker

Pip, I met our son. He's beautiful. He looks just like us—it's so strange. When he turns his head one way, I see you. The other, I see me. But he's so much better than us. God, he's perfect. You did the right thing—you gave him to a real family. He's happy, Pip. Really, really happy. You did good, kid.

I forgive you for everything, you know. All of it. You should work on forgiving yourself. His contact info is below. He said you can contact him anytime.

All my love, Jack

―⁓―

How did one go about forgiving themselves? If she couldn't forget the feeling of that hot metal lock turning in her fingertips—the soft *click*—and the roar as the fire bore down behind her, the feeling of the heat against her back and the flutter in her belly as Cole blissfully flipped in his pulsing cocoon.

Maybe redemption wasn't bestowed by others. When Jack turned to her, Talia's gun trained on him, right before he leaped to his death, he had said, with his ironic half smile, *Remember Moirai?* The three sisters of fate. Penelope had been Lachesis. The middle sister, Clotho's sidekick, measuring out the quality of their lives, what they'd all become. She was their mirror—Flynn had said it that night of the eulogies. Atropos, the ruthless one, the one to call the shots—that had always been Bree. It was just a game they'd played, Penelope knew that. One of their many jokes, another level to their private language. It was layered and complicated and deeply philosophical and self-important in the way only twentysomethings could be.

But maybe she could be all of them: Clotho, Lachesis, Atropos. She could make her own life, give it quality and weight and length and heart and love and all the things she'd always longed for, even if she hadn't admitted it. She alone could sever the parts that needed severing, cut out with Atropos-cruel scissors the guilt, the knee-jerk belief that she deserved less, that her life, half-lived, was enough.

Maybe he'd been trying to tell her that?

Which is how she came to be sitting at the coffee shop in Wexford at nine in the morning, the breakfast crowd thick, letting the March air whip around her at an outdoor table when he came loping up. Tall and lanky as his father, his flop of black hair, his blue eyes, but her smile. Her shy humor—she could see it in the dip of his head, the lopsided grin.

They hugged.

He told her about himself. He grew up middle class. The son of an electrician and a kindergarten teacher. Lived in a cul-de-sac where kids rode their bikes all year round, even in the snow. He'd always known he was adopted and didn't care. He never felt a hole in his heart—he'd read stories of other adoptees, and they had never resonated (Alice, being well adjusted, had put him in group therapy for adoptees, even offered to help him find Penelope, an offer he never cashed in). He never felt bereft, lost. He loved his parents. (Jim died of a heart attack only a year or so ago. Cole missed him every day.)

He had a brother, much younger. Turned out Alice and Jim could have kids—if only they didn't try so hard. He laughed when he said that part, and Penelope laughed too. He had a lot of cousins—Jim had a huge family. Aunts, uncles, first and second cousins, neighbors that he spent most of his life thinking were family. He'd never known loneliness. "I barely had a moment of peace and quiet," he said with another sideways smile.

This boy turned man—*her* boy-man—seemed so self-assured. So confident of his place in the world. It both warmed her and worried her. Would he find her lacking? She hadn't told Tara and Linc about him, not yet. They had enough to deal with, and she thought it best to wait until they'd met. Maybe he'd never want to see her again—then she could decide. Or she could ask him what he thought. Did he know he had half siblings?

He twisted a napkin around his finger like she'd seen Jack do a million times when he was thinking about something. *Genetics is a strange, rare bird,* she thought.

"What should I call you?" He laughed again, his father's good humor.

"Jack always called me Pip. I usually go by Penelope. It's your choice," Penelope said, suddenly shy. "Is this the strangest thing you've ever done?"

"To tell you the truth, Pip"—and the way he said her name brought tears to her eyes—"I thought it would be stranger."

"Because I didn't contact you for so long?" Penelope asked before she could stop herself. "Or because I left you?"

He looked up at her with astonishment and then shook his head. "I had the most incredible childhood. Better than any of my friends who grew up with alcoholics and dramatic familial arguments. I never had any of that. My whole life, I've always known that I wasn't just wanted. I was chosen." He reached across the table and took her hand. "I wasn't an accident, or something that just happened. I've always felt like that was something extraordinarily special."

The way he said it, clipped and soft, reminded her so much of Jack that she almost started to cry, right there at the coffee shop. He didn't let go of her hand.

"Would you want to . . . do this again? Meet, I mean? Just for coffee, dinner, whatever." Penelope felt her voice tremble. What if he said no?

"I'd love it." His face lit up instantly, genuine.

"Are you sure?" Penelope couldn't help it. When she was nervous, she fell back on old insecurities and wanted to kick herself for asking. "You seem to already have a lot of people in your life . . ."

"No worries," he said, his hand waving just like Jack's used to. He sounded just like his father, and Penelope's heart nearly stopped. He gave her a curious look, his head cocked sideways.

The day was brightening, the sun rising in the sky as morning turned to midday. The brisk air that had knifed through her sweater an hour ago had mellowed to a comfortable chill. At the other tables, people had begun to clear out, the breakfast crowd thinning, paying their bills, heading out to work, waving hello to neighbors and friends, reminding her that Jack had been right, all those years ago.

"He is rich who owns the day," Penelope murmured, and Cole looked up at her, surprised. She laughed. "It's an Emerson poem. Your father said it to me once. He also said *no worries* all the time."

"Really? I'll look up the poem," Cole said. He stood, and they hugged goodbye, with promises to call and stay in touch. Penelope watched his dark head move down the street among the people, dodging wayward children with good humor, melting into the crowd. She could have sworn he was whistling.

THE END

ACKNOWLEDGMENTS

Thank you to Jessica Tribble, Lauren Plude, and the whole Thomas & Mercer team, including Sarah Shaw, Jessica Preeg, Laura Barrett, and Gracie Doyle. I'm incredibly grateful for your investment in my career and commitment to finding a place in the world for my stories. Special thanks to Mark Gottlieb and Christine Hogrebe, who work tirelessly on my behalf, offer career advice, and answer my endless questions. Tiffany Yates-Martin, you've done it again. Forced me to dig deeper than I would have on my own and pulled this book straight from my heart. I truly love what you can get out of me and feel so lucky that I have our partnership!

To my readers, bloggers, Instagrammers, book clubs, Facebook reading groups, Bloomies, friends, family, sorority sisters: it's been a weird year! No in-person events means we've all had to improvise. And yet you all show up. Over and over again. I'm so grateful for your continued support and willingness to shout my books to the rooftops. It's truly kept me uplifted. Writing and releasing a book in a pandemic is a *whole thing, man*. I wouldn't have been able to type THE END without knowing that you're all cheering me on. Love you guys.

My author crew: The Tall Poppy Writers—my lady loves, my support system. The Calamity Dames: our group text is my reason for getting out of bed. I love when I wake up laughing at whatever text comes flying in: "What the shit is this?" It's like FUEL. We commiserate, we celebrate, we plan. I love us. To my beta readers: Kimberly Giarratano, Sonja Yoerg, Ann Garvin, Amy Impellizzeri, Heather Webb. You offer a special brand of no-frills, honest, and on-point advice that always has had a huge impact on my writing. You are the best.

My oldest friends and closest family—thank you for being there. With my eighth book just as much as my first. It truly never ceases to amaze me how you show up, tell your friends, share my social media, text me while reading. I am the single luckiest author I know to have so many people in my corner. I love you, Mom, Dad, Meg, Becky, Molly, Aunt Meej, Unk.

And now, my *family* family. Chip, the best husband everrrr. I can't keep telling you this with every book, can I? I'm just as thankful now as I was nine years ago when I first started on this crazy journey. I love our life. You provide exactly zero inspiration for any of the relationships in my stories because they're all terrible. Thanks for making me laugh every single day. I promise to try to do more laundry. To my girls, whom I love with all my heart: Thanks for always making yourselves breakfast and lunch. Thanks for crashing my Instagram live videos. Thanks for being patient with your forgetful mom who tries so hard. You guys are the best.

ABOUT THE AUTHOR

Photo © 2016 Pooja Dhar

Kate Moretti is the bestselling author of six novels and a novella. Her first novel, *Thought I Knew You*, was a *New York Times* bestseller. *The Vanishing Year* was a nominee in the Goodreads Choice Awards Mystery & Thriller category for 2016 and was called "chillingly satisfying" (*Publishers Weekly*) with "superb" closing twists (*New York Times Book Review*).

Moretti has worked in the pharmaceutical industry for twenty years as a scientist and enjoys traveling and cooking. She lives in Pennsylvania in an old farmhouse with her husband, two children, and no known ghosts. Her lifelong dream is to find a secret passageway.